Five interesting things about Susan Conley:

1. Covered in confusion as to whether to use a pseudonym or not, I flipped a coin in order to make the decision. Best two out of three, and my own name won.

2. I moved to Ireland for a year . . . ten years ago. I have dual citizenship and it seemed a shame to waste it.

3. I grew up in New Jersey, about which I always used to lie by omission. I began to admit to my roots when I found out – very late in life! Why didn't I learn this in school! – that the extraordinarily talented poet William Carlos Williams was from my home state. And then *The Sopranos* happened, and I'm considering lying again.

4. I could easily read a book a day, were I left to my own devices.

5. I have gone completely mental about horses and horse riding, and at this writing take lessons three times a week. I expect there's a horsey romantic comedy coming down the pike; until then, I blog my equine thoughts at www.flyingchanges.wordpress.com. I also blog about writing on www.susanconley.wordpress.com

By Susan Conley

Drama Queen
The Fidelity Project

The Fidelity Project

Susan Conley

little
black
dress

First published in 2009
by LITTLE BLACK DRESS
An imprint of HEADLINE PUBLISHING GROUP

A LITTLE BLACK DRESS paperback

1

Cataloguing in Publication Data is available from the British Library

ISBN 978 0 7553 4573 1

Typeset in Transit511BT by Avon DataSet Ltd,
Bidford-on-Avon, Warwickshire

Printed and bound in Great Britain by
Clays Ltd, St Ives plc

Headline's policy is to use papers that are natural, renewable and
recyclable products and made from wood grown in sustainable forests.
The logging and manufacturing processes are expected to conform to the
environmental regulations of the country of origin.

HEADLINE PUBLISHING GROUP
An Hachette UK Company
338 Euston Road
London NW1 3BH

www.littleblackdressbooks.com
www.headline.co.uk
www.hachette.co.uk

For the crowd chez Berlin
Paris, August 2008

Acknowledgements

Many, many thanks to Claire Baldwin for her excellent guidance, and her unflagging support for the story. Thanks to all at LBD, and to Sara Porter, not only for her enthusiasm, but also for not being appalled at the tweaky little tweaks that I tend to make on the proofs. The main part of the revision was done in five days in Paris, and I'd like to expand upon the dedication directed towards the chez Berlin gang: to Karen, Celine and Sean, for the seemingly numberless bottles of wine and fizzy water, the conversations into the wee hours, those barbequed sausages, and for being the perfect antidote to hours spent scowling and pecking away at my MacBook Air in cafés – which, in all honesty, is not the worst work in the world. *Merci*, lads!

Something's up, thought Maxine O'Malley.
Something's going on in here.

She paced the perimeter of her 'office' – a jumped-up cubicle, really, which happened to be closed off from the top of its flimsy wall to the ceiling with glass; glass which wasn't quite flush with the walls of the building, so that there was a gap between her office and that of her neighbour. They even shared a window, sort of, as their dividing wall cut it in half. Luckily, Max's next cubicle-neighbour was her creative partner, so it didn't matter that they could hear each other's phone conversations loud and clear.

Max inched open her door – at least the rotten little room had a door. In an advertising agency, days generally got off to a languid start, but even by her own torpid standards, things were ominously quiet for 11.30 a.m. on a Wednesday.

Her eyes darted around at her colleagues, who either seemed to be staring glumly off into space, or were whispering to one another frantically, their eyes darting all around the bullpen. It occurred to Max that she should just go out there and see what all the vibes were about, but she decided against it. Jax was the one who was best at the interpersonal office stuff – and knowing Jax, she already knew what was what.

Her foot slipped on a piece of paper that had been lurking near the door, and Max bent down fluidly, picked it up, and began folding it absent-mindedly.

Boy, the game's the same, no matter the geography, Max mused as she plunked herself down behind her desk. Since she'd transferred to Dublin from New York eight months ago, any cultural shocks she'd experienced were now little more than infinitesimal blips on her radar, which was finely tuned to all the frequencies necessary for survival in the ad game. And they were the same in Ireland as they were in America: who was flirting with whom, who'd taken that flirtation to the next level, who was suffering flirtation fallout, much more than the bits that actually had to do with business.

Where the hell was Jacinta? She wedged her head as best she could between the edge of the dividing wall and the window. She was in, but not 'in' in. Jax's handbag – a horrifying thing that looked like faux pleather, if that were possible – hung serenely from the hook beneath her desk, and that unbelievably dumpy tweed coat – it made Max's lungs seize up at the sight of it – was tidily folded up and sitting on the office's spare chair.

Max sat down again heavily, and, lacking anything better to do, still fiddling with the piece of paper, she started to spin herself around in circles.

Shouldn't she *know* what was going on? Wasn't she a senior executive writer thingamajig? Shouldn't she have been in whatever loop was currently looping? She dug the extremely pointy toe of her Carl Scarpa ankle boot into the threadbare carpet for better traction, and spun around faster. They'd gone to the trouble to headhunt her out of the agency's New York office – didn't they owe her the courtesy of letting her in on whatever was happening behind the scenes? Okay, so she and Jax hadn't exactly been made partners or anything, but they'd been making their mark steadily, and those ICAD awards hadn't hurt, either.

Max had already begun to spend her promotion bonus. She let herself spin down to a more leisurely tempo as she dropped her head back and went on a mental shopping spree: a trip to Italy for anything and everything they made out of leather; one of those teeny-weeny Mac laptops; a Morris Minor; a parking space; a decent sofa for her flat; those gorgeous—

Tap, tap, tap.

Max rolled her eyes at Jax's typically well-modulated knock.

'Don't knock!' she shouted as she threw the paper airplane she'd produced at Jax's cautiously entering head. 'You're my partner, you don't have to knock!'

'It's rude not to,' Jax replied calmly, as she started to smooth out the folds of the paper Max had pitched at her.

'So, what, I'm rude? Is that what you're implying?'

'I'm not *implying* anything.' Jax sat in the chair opposite Max's chaotic desk and held up the paper that Max had, in Max's own opinion, painstakingly coaxed into aerodynamic perfection.

'Did you read this?' Jax asked, averting her eyes from Max's disgusting desktop.

Max shrugged. 'That? What's that word you guys use – bumph? That bumph?'

'It's not bumph, it's a memo. An interoffice memo.'

'They wrote something down on paper and handed it out? That's adorable!'

'Sure, they knew no one'd read an email that wasn't a joke, and sent this round instead.'

'Oh, it's from "them".' Max started to spin around again. 'So what are "they" up to now – hey, is that why everybody's barely breathing?' She sent her chair for another spin.

'Read it yourself.' Jax handed it over, and sat back. Honestly, you'd think the girl was thirteen rather than thirty-three.

'Dear Team Players – ha! – blah, blah, economic climate – blah, political climate – blah, blah, *blah* . . .' Max sat forward, and Jax recrossed her arms. 'Unfortunately it has become necessary despite our best intentions – blah – exit packages.' She sighed. 'Blaaaaaah.'

'We were the last in,' Jax moaned, and struggled not to bite her thumbnail.

'We'll be the first out,' finished Max. 'Don't bite your nails.' She spun in a fast circle. 'Well, technically, yeah, we were the last in, kinda, we were the most recently promoted pairing of senior talent—'

'We'll be the first out!' Jax shouted, and they both craned their heads up to peek out of the window in Max's door. Every head in the bullpen turned towards the sound.

'Keep it calm, missus,' Max warned, and dug out the remote control for her stereo.

'Max, you can't swing a cat in here, why do you bother—' Jax was cut off by a blast of MGMT.

Max lowered the music. 'All senior executive advertising types use unnecessary gadgets. You need to get with the programme, Jax.'

'I'm running out of time to "get with the programme",' Jax grumbled.

'We don't know that we're going to get canned. We're

on a fucking brilliant run; they'd be stupid to give us the boot.' Max picked up an executive stress ball and started squeezing. 'Stop doing that.' Jax stopped picking at the dragging hem of her conservatively cut grey skirt. 'On second thoughts, if you fuss with it enough maybe it'll unravel and you'll finally have to throw it out.'

'This skirt is incredibly versatile!'

'That skirt is incredibly ugly. I don't understand how a senior executive creative director can have absolutely zero fashion sense—'

'I'll be having absolutely zero income soon enough! Senior executive yokie or not! And these jumped-up titles won't cover a tinker's arse when we're queueing for the bloody dole!' Jax kicked Max's desk and a pile of magazines, files and takeaway menus cascaded to the floor.

Max didn't even flinch, but she did lean forward towards her friend. 'Jeez, you're really freaked out about this.'

'I suppose you can feck off back to New York.' Jax bent down to tidy up the mess of papers.

'No. I'm not going back to New York.' Max spun ninety degrees and stared out her half of the window.

The CD player shuffled over to Sigur Rós. Jax sighed and got up to straighten the piles of newspapers that had shored up against the walls. 'I've a mortgage,' she began. 'I've car payments and insurance and my Mastercard is bouncing. I can't afford an "exit package". Jesus,'

'I know, "exit package" is so American. I apologise for my entire culture.' Max kicked at the window sill and a shower of plaster covered her boot. She shook her head and kicked the sill again, dislodging an avalanche of dust. 'This place! It's a – whatchacallit – a kip? A skip?'

'A tip.'

'It's a tip! We are senior creatives, we've been doing award-winning work, and they've got us stuck up here under the eaves of this crumbling Edwardian—'

'Georgian.'

'Georgian building, like – like we're the hired help—'

'Max, we *are* the hired help.'

'Jax, we deserve better than this! Don't you dare pull that face at me – we deserve better than this! So we get our books together and hit the streets. We'll start today! Now! Let's go! New job by the end of the week!' Max stood up and started tossing objects off her desk, exuberantly looking for, Jax assumed, her phone.

'G and C have already sacked – sorry, laid off – ten of theirs, and McMahon's is, I think, going under completely.'

'Shite.' They both sat down again, and the CDs shuffled over to Band of Horses.

'Look, we've been working together, what, a year and a half—'

Jax shook her head. 'Ten months, Max! Two when I was in New York, and eight since you've been here.'

'Huh.' Max spun around again. 'It seems longer. In a good way. Right, a year—'

'Ten months! Facts, please! Proper facts!'

'Facts, schmacts.' Max threw her executive stress ball into a corner and Jax flinched. 'The fact is, we're a solid unit, and it'll be easier for us to sell ourselves as a package than as lone rangers. Especially with that tourist board campaign about to come out . . .'

They grinned at each other. 'Jesus, that was a gas,' sighed Jax as she clutched an armful of discarded shopping bags to her chest.

'And it was a success, and it came in under budget, and we totally took over for the production company that bailed on us, *and* we ran it like a well-oiled machine. All five of those commercials, taken together – they're practically a sitcom.'

'Your script was brilliant, really, Max, really good, and yeah, they could hang together like a television show, or a mini-series. All those different characters, the way you made them real, like—'

'And your direction had more than a little to do with it. So here we are, a mutual admiration society looking for new members.' Max picked up two wooden paddles off the floor and tossed one to Jax. 'Okay, brainstorming time. Let's go.'

'Must we?' Jax ducked as Max lofted a small orange ball at her head.

'If we don't, they'll think we're not working.' Jax sighed and joined in. They were actually quite good at it, and kept the ball in the air.

'Okay. Idea: open our own advertising agency.' Max shot the ball into the air.

Jax caught it and returned it. 'No. Not enough business to support a new business, and you can't just do ads any more, you have to do websites and shite, *and* we're both a disaster with the accounts.'

'We hire an accountant!'

'No. We couldn't afford to have someone attached like that. Not in this "economic climate", remember?'

'We steal clients from here.' Max threw the ball at Jax.

Jax dropped the ball. 'Max!'

'You are so sincere.' Max gestured with her paddle, and Jax shot the ball at her head. 'How'd you get so far in this business?'

'Well, there's that talent you're always banging on about.'

Max caught the ball with her hand. 'My God, you are the first Irish person I've ever heard openly acknowledge one of their assets. Will you have to go to confession now, or what?'

'Fuck off, Max.' Jax threw the paddle on to the floor, then guiltily picked it up and put it on the edge of Max's desk.

'Okay, okay, out of order, I know, I'm a horrible blasphemer, boil me in oil. Next idea.'

Jax shrugged and pulled at her hem. 'Sometimes I want to quit altogether.'

'Quit advertising?' Max perked up. 'And do what?'

'I – don't slag me off – I haven't given it that much thought, now, like—'

'I'm intrigued – most of your best ideas are couched with hemming and hawing.'

A muffled bleating cut off Jax's reply. She started digging desperately around underneath Max's desk, trying to locate the phone. She came up blinded by dust as Max calmly reached under the pile of coat, scarf and hat next to her chair.

'O'Malley. Hmmm. Right now? We're in the middle of a brainstorm— Gotcha. Right. Cheers!' She quirked a brow at Jax. 'Meeting in the main ballroom. Everyone.'

Grabbing legal pads and pens for them both, Jax followed Max out of the little office.

If any of ACJ:Dublin's inwardly panicking employees had bothered to regard the pair of women sitting at the back of the conference room, they might once again have wondered at the apparent unlikely partnership of Max and Jax.

He or she would have been immediately struck by

their looks. Not so much by the fact that the women were extraordinarily good-looking – and both were very attractive – but by the fact that it was unlikely that there were two people who resembled each other less presently walking the planet.

The tall, angular one with the swingy, highlighted haircut was, basically, an advertisement for Grafton Street. Not a stitch on her was less than a week old, and she had, cleverly, mixed in 'good value' clothing from the local Dunnes Stores with pricier pieces from Pia Bang and BT2. In fact, if you asked her, she'd be delighted to recount the history of every bit on her back, with their relevant discounts, right down to her knickers (three for twelve euros at Next).

The smaller one would describe herself as 'roundy', but she had a clear shot at voluptuous, with a bit of Botticelli on the side, if not for *her* outfit, which seemed designed solely to make her blend into the background. Strong, curvy legs were sadly hacked in two by the unflattering cut of her skirt, its shade falling somewhere in the spectrum between cement and winter mud. She wore a blouse – and it could only be a blouse, never a 'shirt', much less a 'top' – made of what appeared to be a petroleum-based material, pulled around breasts which weren't being shown off to their best advantage, much less properly supported. The atrocity that was her cardigan cannot possibly be recounted. Her curly hair was stuffed into a scrunchy and straggled down her back, its dishwater blond crying out for a cut and colour.

Then there was the equally striking difference in personality. The tall one was American, and don't you forget it, buster. Her style was friendly yet brusque, playful yet demanding. She exuded the kind of confidence one imagined was injected into New York City's reservoir system, and yet she didn't seem completely out of place in the more laid-back environs of Dublin. She had a sharp sense of humour, a loud laugh, and a generous hand when it came to her round in the pub.

Her Irish colleague was soft-spoken and poised. Her nerves came out in various little tics, and her pitching persona was self-effacing at best, invisible at worst. And yet she had a handle on the kind of diplomacy that was vital in day-to-day business, an uncompromising aesthetic, and a stubborn streak a mile wide.

The women sat side by side, as far away from the droning suits currently trying to avert mass hysteria as possible. They seemed as absorbed in the palliative speeches as their colleagues, and yet . . .

'What was your idea?!?!' Max scribbled on her pad.

'Not now.' Jax shook her head for good measure.

'NOW!!!!! Or will we just die of boredom???'

Jax scowled. 'Must you always overdo the punctuation?' She dotted her question mark precisely.

'©#%$! THAT!!!!!!!' Max wrote, and smirked. 'IDEA, PLEASE.'

'And no more capital letters – Nosey Niamh has us in her sights.'

They both glanced over at Niamh Bourke – office admin and general nuisance – who was squinting at them beadily. Max stuck out her tongue.

'For fuck's SAKE!' Jax scrawled.

'Idea, please.' Max recrossed her legs, and pretended to listen to the latest suit. She suspected he was one of the consonants, but wasn't sure if he was A, C or J.

Jax hesitated, but then began to write, line by line. It was uncanny, but it was exactly the way she pitched in full voice. Max tuned into a question from the floor.

'What about our pensions?' A murmur broke out, and the suit raised a placatory hand.

'We can assure you all that your full pension will, of course, be part of the exit packages.' He laughed drily. 'And sure, it'd be illegal if it weren't.' Choked laughter all around. 'We do, of course, have continuing responsibilities to our clients, and, em, Noel, why not jump in here, if you would.'

Max barely suppressed a snort. Great. An account exec suit.

Max hated account executives.

With a passion.

An elbow in her ribs jerked her out of a detailed fantasy in which hundreds of glorified salesmen were hanging naked from the Brooklyn Bridge, by their pinky toes, in the midst of a freak snowstorm. She cast her eye over Jax's writing, which flowed legibly, and at length, and Max's face didn't give her away until she reached the end of the paragraph, at which point she raised her eyebrows, pursed her lips, and straightened her posture like a shot.

'Yes, Ms O'Malley?'

Niamh Bourke smirked, Jax swallowed uneasily, and Max didn't miss a beat.

'To be frank, I'm sure that our clients are the least of anyone's worries.' She sent a chilly smile towards the agency's chief vice-president in charge of accounts. 'What I'd like to know is why are we not discussing potential alternatives to lay-offs – sorry, redundancies. Like job-share, flexitime . . .' She let her voice trail off enticingly, challengingly.

'Em, right, well, Brian, that's your bailiwick . . .'

As A, C – or was it J? – scrambled to pass the buck, Max, with all outward appearance of attention, scrawled at the bottom of Jax's sheet:

LIQUID LUNCH. D&N's.

2

Late winter light streamed in the window of Doheny and Nesbitt's snug. The longtime local of the ACJ heads, it was the prototypical auld fellas pub, with walls covered in old-time metal Guinness-is-Good-For-You signs, shelves stuffed full of stone poteen jars, and the bar stools well broken-in, the lighting soothingly dim. What it lacked in spit and polish it more than made up for in its tolerance of its more exuberant patrons, chief among them Maxine O'Malley.

'Johnny!' Max called through the window of the snug that gave out on to the bar. 'Carlsberg and a G&T!'

'I'll just take a—' Jax fumbled with her coat.

'Nope, this is a serious idea, and we need to do some serious loosening of the imaginative muscles.' Max flopped down and wedged herself into the corner of the banquette. 'No Ballygowan for you, miss, until you tell me everything you're thinking.'

'I wrote out everything that I've got.' Jax hung up their coats on the hooks behind the door, and closed it.

'Good idea. There'll be a flood of ACJ heads in here in about thirty minutes. So.' Max dug into her purse to pay the barman, and the ensuing banter gave Jax a moment to look over her notes.

What in the world had possessed her? Having ideas was one thing, she had them every day, it was her job to have ideas every day, but a notion this big, this complicated, this guaranteed to get Max's antennae quivering – surely it had to be a huge mistake? She knew that look in Max's eye, and it wasn't so much that it boded ill as that it resembled the look of a bulldog eyeing a juicy bone which it wouldn't let out of its sight until it was safely between its jaws.

'Jax!' Max waved the glass of gin beneath her nose. 'There's no going back now. Tell me. Everything.'

Jax slowly poured the tonic out of the little bottle. 'Right, so. It was because of that shoot, that tourist board yoke –'

'Yes –'

'– And the way we, whether we wanted to or not, had to take over the full monty, all of it: the casting, negotiating with the agents, the crew, the locations, all of it – and they're all things that we do, separately, like, on different things we have to do. It wasn't so much that we hadn't done them before—'

'But that we had to do it all on our own, and all at once.'

'Right. And ... it seemed ... more ... it seemed a better use of what we're both good at. You hustled all those agents and caterers and that hair and make-up crowd, and you still kept the script on track, and you got the props people to go that extra bit further—'

'And you', Max interrupted, 'not only did an incredible job of casting in three days or less, of keeping the whole vision in hand, and of giving the whole thing a unifying look, but also managed to make friends with that dreadful cow from RTÉ, which made our lives so much easier.'

'She wasn't a cow, she was just under pressure. And I knew her from school, as well, which helps, as she might be a good contact for when we . . .' Jax trailed off again.

'When. We. *What?*' Max didn't bellow, but it was a near thing.

'Right. So. We both know how much that production crowd were getting paid, or had been contracted for, before they scarpered, and I just thought . . .'

Max grabbed Jax's notes. 'If I may quote, "that we ought to go out and start doing it for ourselves". Which I take to mean that we should become a two-woman production company.'

'It's daft.'

'So we don't start our own agency, but we do this instead?'

'I said it was daft!'

'This is called devil's advocacy, Jax. Come on. So? Why is this different?'

Jax blew out a breath. Stalled by taking a drink of her gin. She started to chew on a nail, then stopped at Max's warning glance.

Max took pity on her. 'I'll tell you why. Because it's something that we can start while ACJ goes through its slow, painful death throes – and it will be slow, I've been through this before; they come on all panicky and it'll take them at least until September to go completely belly up. So we can start building our business while clocking in nine to five, and be able to make the jump less dramatically.'

'Right.' Jax sat back and managed not to pick at her split ends for once.

'But. We're desperate with accounts, remember?' Max challenged.

'We'll hire somebody on a job-to-job basis, or get my father to do them, or take an accountancy course,' Jax answered. 'This is – it's different. If we get one good idea, and do it, just do it ourselves, we're made.'

'What'll we do for equipment?' Max rolled her pint glass back and forth between her hands.

'Em . . . well, I figured if we moved quickly enough, and if, as you say, we're not really out of a job until September, we could, er, use the stuff at the office.' Jax ducked her head a bit, but grinned when Max hooted with laughter.

'You'll go straight to the hot place, Jacinta Quirke. We could get some of the lads here in on it, just one or two – we could do a quality broadcast demo.'

'Exactly!' Jax bounced up and down on the banquette. 'We can do it practically on our own – I was looking on the RTÉ website, and they're looking for outside companies who can offer fully realised programmes. They've got a tender out for a prime-time slot, a one-off . . . it's due in seven weeks . . . I know it's tight, but I can talk to that girl, my schoolfriend, maybe get some hints . . . if we shoot on digital video and cut it ourselves—'

'I know how to shoot—'

'And I can get a copy of Final Cut Pro from the techies—'

Max nodded. 'I can knock out a script in between pitches—'

'And we've got the storyboarding software already up and running—'

'I'm *positive* one or two of the lads can be persuaded to give up a few evenings or weekends—'

'They owe us big time down in post production—'

'And we've got an inside connection at the station.' Max lifted her glass. 'This is desperately exciting.'

They clinked glasses and grinned.

'Now we just need a name,' said Jax.

'And an idea,' Max said.

The first big silence of their new venture spread throughout the snug.

And spread.

'Okay, just say anything,' Max prompted.

Silence.

'Reality TV!' Max shouted as Jax insisted, simultaneously, 'No Reality TV!'

'Why not?' Max demanded.

'It's over,' Jax shot back.

'I don't know . . .' Max mused into her pint glass. 'Maybe the idea just needs a tweak.'

'The idea itself was already a tweak of – of sitcoms and documentaries. It's a bloody demonstration of creative bankruptcy,' Jax said dismissively.

'I love it when you get righteously indignant,' Max laughed. 'And I'm not saying you're not right, but I will say that they are still getting produced at a blistering rate.'

'We need to come up with something else.' Jax finished off her drink and came over all lightheaded.

'We don't have time to be total trailblazers – but we can take the form and give it a twist.' Max nodded and looked at Jax. 'Yeah, we have to give it a twist.'

The second big silence of their new venture spread throughout the snug.

'Right,' sighed Jax eventually.

Max slammed down her jar. 'We've only just begun!'

They would, one day, Max was convinced, look back on this exact moment and laugh themselves sick. 'Remember when', she'd say, 'we were sitting there in our old office in

ACJ's Dublin headquarters – now a lapdancing club – and we were sitting in your half, Jax, and we couldn't come up with an idea? And we sat and sat, and I spun and spun in my chair until you threw your stapler at my head, and we sighed and stuttered, and then . . . ?'

Max figured if she projected them into coming up with a prize-winning idea, they'd actually come up with one.

Jax leaned forward and thumped her elbows down on to her desk. 'So at the very least we're both agreed that the reality thing is out—'

Jax's office door swung open and she clammed up as Max tipped her head backwards to clock the intruder.

'Not so much as a knock, Niamh,' she purred, and swung herself around to face her nemesis.

Jax rubbed her temples. The after-effects of a noonday G&T were exacerbated by their stuffy attic office (*atelier*, she could hear Max scolding, *atelier!*), and the last thing she needed was Max and Niamh doing their spiteful hammer-and-tongs routine.

Everyone else in the place went in fear of Niamh Bourke, even if they didn't know exactly what, if anything, she was in charge of. Max reckoned Niamh was employed to lurk and snitch, to eavesdrop and report to the big boys as to who was robbing the place of pens and Post-it notes and who was, innocently enough, making use of the office copier to make a few measly copies of a feature film script to send out to a couple of competitions. Max smirked, remembering Niamh's triumph when she'd shopped her on that one, and the grim disappointment on Niamh's slightly horsey face when Max had insisted on paying for the print-outs – in pennies. 'Just like a copy shop!' Max had laughed, leaving her to count it out for the rest of the day – as Max had insisted upon a receipt.

Niamh loomed in the doorway, running her eye over Jax's pristine space, and sneered at Max's obviously new boots. Won't be keeping herself in *those* for much longer, she thought, won't be running off to town in her lunch hour – a lunch hour that always stretched to a lunch hour and a half – to spend money she won't be making for much longer. She, Niamh, had no worries on that score: she had her pension sorted, and her savings organised, and someone like her, a useful . . . resourceful . . . person like herself, was never out of employment for long. But these *creatives* – there was not much room in the current economic climate for people who expected to be treated like gods simply because they spent the day time-wasting, pretending that what they did was *work*, acting as if they were better than everyone else simply because they sat around talking all day, staring ahead of themselves *thinking*, as if that was—

'Hate to interrupt your internal monologue, pet, but are you going to stand there thinking evil thoughts to yourself all day? We're trying to work here.' Max smiled into Niamh's narrow, pale eyes, her usually colourless and lifeless eyes – unless, of course, they were glittering with censure as they were now, since her nostrils – they'd put a sniffer dog's to shame – picked up on the lager and the gin.

'Work?' Niamh sneered predictably, and Max grinned. Jax dug for her paracetamol. 'Sure, you'll be lucky to find yourself another position after things shut up round here – not you, Jax, of course; you make a good fist of your duties, but this one, here, in her designer clothes and her expensive haircuts, it won't be long before she's back in New York City where she belongs –'

'Oh, Niamh, you're a period piece, so ya are.' Max laid

on her atrocious brogue, just for good measure.

Jax, ever the peacemaker, cut in. 'We *are* trying to get down to some work, despite the bad news of the morning, Niamh.' She ignored Max's glare and sent Niamh a placating smile.

Niamh sniffed. 'And so you should be. I'll have you know that things are fixed to finish up here by Christmas.' She jerked her chin triumphantly – she was a champion bearer of bad news.

'Christmas? I was sure we'd be washed up by September!' Max rose, and made a meal out of smoothing down her linen jacket. 'Excellent news, Niamh. Thanks a million. And what wonderful timing for you. Please think of us when you're organising your comp tickets.'

Jax sighed and covered her eyes with her hands.

Niamh stepped back, ever so slightly. 'Comp tickets?'

'For the Gaiety. Surely you're this year's pantomime witch?' And Max shut the door in her face.

'Ye've made a puir fist a yer dyooooties, Jacinta Quirke,' Max yawned. 'Four p.m. on a Friday in an advertising agency. Time to wrap things up.'

'That accent is atrocious, you do know that, don't you?' Jax slid the notepad they'd been decorating with half-baked notions and rude remarks into her shoulder bag.

'Practice, practice, practice,' Max murmured, and she got up to stretch. 'Hey, let's go for a stroll down to accounts, eavesdrop, you know, drift around the "real people". We're not getting anywhere by ourselves.'

Jax rose, pushing at a cuticle. 'It doesn't seem right, pouncing on our colleagues . . .'

'We are information gathering. We are looking for inspiration. They do it to us! How many Americans have they started casting in commercials since I got here? All's fair.' She opened the door and gestured Jax through.

The women strolled down two staircases that gradually became less grotty, and began to wander casually around the second floor. This was the agency's public space, and consequently the paint on the walls was fresh and clean, the carpet bright and new, the computer equipment top-of-the-line. And as this was where the crowd that dealt with the business end worked – and looked the part

– they were rewarded with the best of everything. Max didn't feel any envy – they also had to show up on time, leave late, and deal with those immortal eejits, the clients.

They were, as well, exactly the people who were deep into the reality TV phenomenon – and they would be the ones to point the way towards the next trend. Max knew the idea was floating around somewhere down here, among the secretaries, account execs and junior assistants. She could feel it in her bones.

'Hey, Keano, so, is reality TV dead, or what?' Max draped herself over Sean Keane's cubicle wall.

Keano smoothed down his designer faux-school tie self-importantly. He leaned back in his chair, his legs spread wide, in a move that Max liked to call 'leading with the tackle'. Jax muffled a laugh. He did it every time. Max grinned, and Keano felt, once again, that he was sure if he could get her in the pub, he'd get the leg over Maxine O'Malley.

Not in this lifetime, pal, thought Max, correctly reading his flickering eyelids. I'm only interested in you for your mind. 'So?'

'It's all but over, Maxie,' declared Keano, tipping back a little bit further, demonstrating his authority once again. Jax pretended to sneeze. '*Gesundheit*. How much further can it go? We've all but had live sex – it can only skew towards violence, and snuff films are going that bit too far.'

'Right, right . . .' Max moved off, and Jax hurried behind her.

'See you down the pub, Maxie?' Keano called, draping himself in the spot Max had left vacant.

'Don't call me "Maxie",' she called without turning around.

'Don't even think about snuff films, for God's sake,' Jax muttered.

'Jax! I've got one or two points on my moral compass, for crying out loud.'

'Hmmph.'

'Ouch!' Max stopped. 'I mean it. I may have a loose assortment of morals, but I have them all the same.'

'You do, you do,' Jax replied absently. 'What *is* it with those programmes? Why do people watch them?'

This seemed a better avenue of enquiry than one into her personal values, so Max leapt on it, and led Jax towards the back of the room. 'Voyeurism, watching people make eejits out of themselves, feeling better about *ourselves* because we're not such attention-seeking freaks. People just want to be famous.'

'But the thing that other people watch for, besides the failure, is the connection.'

Max paused, shook her head. 'I don't get you.'

'Connection. Who ends up with whom. Will they, won't they? Relationship.'

'Why', Max demanded, 'must it always be about sex?'

'Why', Jax countered, 'must you always make it about sex?'

'I don't.'

'You do! And sex is … it's … not the point, like; people are worried about more than just erections and orgasms – they want to connect. As people.'

'No, they don't. They want to continue to wrap it all up in romance and rubbish, and call it "relationship" when it's only about getting their hole!'

'You've done an extraordinary job of picking up the absolute worst of all our phrases and euphemisms,' huffed Jax.

'I'm right. You know I am.' Max shrugged off Jax's prudish reaction.

'You are not right. Underneath it all, we want a happy ending.'

'Keano does not want a happy ending. He just wants to keep tilting back in his chair until someone takes him up on it.'

Jax snorted, and Max felt the discomfort that had built up dissipate. Discomfort? Yeah, okay, so it had got a bit edgy, but it was brainstorming, not the meaning of life, for cryin' out loud.

'Anyway,' Max said, firmly changing the subject as they wandered further into the warren of cubicles that twisted around what had been a massive Georgian sitting room, 'The reality television notion is still alive and kicking. Because Keano never, ever knows what's what.'

'You'd think he would,' said Jax. 'He's certainly allowing enough air to circulate around his brains.'

And the thing about Jax that Max always forgot and loved to be reminded of, was her big, raucous, filthy laugh.

Especially when she was laughing at her own jokes.

'Max! Jax! We're planning Orla's hen!'

'Hen, schmen. I couldn't give a—' Max gurned.

'Information gathering!' chided Jax, and they turned in the direction of a deafening group squeal.

They both paused, momentarily overwhelmed by the cluster of blondes lounging near the bay window. Uniformly fakely tanned to a woman, their levels of successful grooming and slimming radiated outwards from Orla, a Dart Belt Debutante, a (very) late twenty-something passing for early(ish) twenty-something: tall, thin, pristine, aloof. She smiled, just about, in an effort to forestall future treatments of Botox, and allowed her minions to express her feelings for her.

Her gaze flicked down to Max's feet.

'Scarpa?' she drawled.

'Sure,' Max replied.

Orla had always wondered, idly, why she and the American hadn't bonded – after all, she herself used words like 'bonded', and had shopped the length and breadth of Manhattan for years. Her gaze flicked dismissively down the length and breadth of Jax, and Orla ever so slightly shifted her body to block her.

Which was exactly why Max had no time for Orla.

'Somehow, I'm not picturing you lurching around Temple Bar with your tits hanging out, Orla,' said Max, stuffing her hands into her trouser pockets.

Jax shifted uncomfortably – Max always came over all aggressive around these girls.

'We're doing a spa day at The Four Seasons!' trilled Sorcha, Orla's manic 'best office mate'. 'Em, numbers are strictly limited,' she added, after having picked up an infinitesimal cue from Orla.

'Bum*mer*,' breathed Max.

'Wedding plans going well?' asked Jax politely.

Sorcha's whole body shook, full as it was of information. 'The flowers are bespoke by Buds of May – they do all the European royal weddings – the dress is by Vera Wang – personally – the reception, preceded by drinks and hot and cold hors d'oeuvres, is for two hundred and fifty in Gleninaigh Castle, with a fleet of limousines hired to bring the guests down and back to town' – here Sorcha paused for a much-needed breath – 'and the cake is being flown in from the South of France.'

'First class, presumably,' muttered Max. 'Hey, Orla, I just don't see you settling down, even though what's-his-name – what *is* his name, you never mention him? – is apparently loaded.'

'They've been in love since second class,' Sorcha snapped.

'Death us do part and all that . . . ever give that any thought, chickens?' The blondes alternatively shuddered or glared at Max. 'Better or worse, richer or poorer. They're not just words, you know. Folks tend to think you mean them.'

What was *it with Max and marriage*, Jax thought, for the umpteenth time, as she slid into the increasingly antagonistic breach. 'I'm sure Kenneth is looking forward to the day,' she said, directing 'Kenneth' to Max.

'We're dying to know, Jacinta, have you set a date yourself . . . finally?' asked Orla, in her perfectly modulated tones.

Jax blushed faintly. 'We haven't, no.'

'Still in Dubai, is he? Finbar, is it?'

'Fergal,' Jax corrected.

'Have you seen the ring?' Max cut in, and watched six pairs of eyes swoop down like a flock of crows to land on Jax's left hand – which was unadorned.

'It's enormous – she won't wear it,' Max chirped, grinning into the glares.

Jax leaned into Orla's sightline. 'Orla, I'm delighted we've had this chat. Max and I are looking for subjects, blushing brides and all that craic, you know the way, modern marriage, for a concepting session. We'd love to speak to you personally, get you on tape. Video tape.'

Jax danced away from the sharp toe of Max's boot, as

Orla shook back her flowing locks. 'If it suits,' she said and shrugged, secretly thrilled.

'Grand,' was all Jax managed as Max yanked her towards the hall.

'Why in the world would we want to talk to that bitch?' Max stalked up the stairs.

'Did you not see her eyes light up?'

'I am not doing anything, not even a thirty-second spot, about marriage. I refuse to contribute to the pathetic conspiracy that is long-term monogamy, I *refuse*—'

'Would you ever get a hold of yourself, Max?' Jax moved up the stairs and headed for their offices. 'You were on to something there, in your rant about vows and promises. We could really make something out of this. I wonder what that relationship is really like. I wonder why she never, ever speaks of Kenneth. Why do people get married? What do they expect? We've only just got divorce in this country. What are those statistics? What do people really say to each other after twenty, thirty, forty years—'

'Try two or three,' Max snapped.

Jax paused on the landing. 'Someday, you'll tell me what goes on in your head every time someone mentions marriage.'

'Someday, you'll tell me all about Fergal and this ridiculous long-distance engagement.'

They trod the stairs in silence – a line had been crossed, and as peaceable as Jax was, and as confrontational as Max could be, it had to be backed away from, slowly.

'Look, we'll give it a rest, okay, and I'll see you at your folks' on Sunday?'

Jax nodded, her back to Max, her hand on her office doorknob. 'We'll leave it until then.'

'We've got seven whole weeks!' Max joked, and they smiled warily at one another.

'See you Sunday,' Jax said, and the door clicked quietly behind her.

There were times when Max opened her eyes of a morning and didn't know where she was. The disorientation shimmered through her body like a cold wave, and only through vigorous wiggling of her toes did she come back down to earth.

She squinted suspiciously around her bedroom, a light, bright, biggish room that overlooked the eastern part of the Liffey. Propped up in bed, and perched almost on her knees, she could muse out the window and watch the river flow by. It was positively exotic, after all those years of views of brick walls and other people's windows: the late winter sunshine glinting off the Liffey was as relaxing as a yoga class in New York Sports Club, or a brisk walk around the reservoir in Central Park. It was precisely what had driven her to Dublin. Tenuous Irish roots aside (a smattering of fourth cousins in Clare), Max had been drawn, right off the bat, on a handful of business trips, by the relaxed nature of this work-to-live, as opposed to live-to-work, society.

It was exactly what she needed at this point in her life: more time to herself, more time to just be.

Wasn't it?

Max shifted restlessly in the bed and kicked the duvet

on to the floor. The problem with working-to-live was the living part, and actually having to pay attention to quality of life, not quantity of hours worked. There were far too many mornings, therefore, in which one could wake up tense and disorientated, rigid with . . .

Fear? Max leapt from the bed and marched to her kitchenette and the coffee maker. Fear, schmear. While waiting for the burble and growl of the machine to do its job, she wandered around her living room, aimlessly kicking aside the newspapers, shoes, jackets, tops, handbags and loose change. Okay, so maybe she was a little shaken up by the carry-on at work. She'd been through it so many times before, it was pretty surprising that she'd get freaked out by ad-agency palaver. Back in New York, the little quiver of fear she was experiencing would have been so low down the food chain – superseded by office politics, money woes, aggro from the condo board, and the daily hassle of commuting on the subway – that her brain's synapses wouldn't have bothered firing over it.

Oh, they were firing away at the moment – and that must have been what woke her up at the ungodly hour of 10 a.m. on a Saturday. *Not cool, Maxine*, she thought to herself, and automatically went into what was, for her, coping mode: she started tidying up the flat.

I can just imagine Jax's stunned face, Max thought. Within minutes, cushions were plumped and straightened, laundry was divided into darks and whites, with a load already spinning away, windows were opened, newspapers piled up by the door, and clothes and shoes all put in their proper places. She reckoned that the sound of the Hoover firing up would have sent her friend into a swoon.

Max methodically, but without great finesse, pushed

the vacuum around the flat. The large living room, now set to rights, seemed a bit bare, and the bedroom, which had received the whirlwind treatment, now seemed a bit small. It certainly wasn't a patch on her last flat on the Upper West Side, with its spacious string of rooms, in one of the pre-war apartment buildings on Riverside Drive –

Could she turn up the volume on the Hoover? Because she really, really needed to drown out that train of thought. Maybe she should have moved to London, where it seemed that the lifestyle was pretty much the same as NYC, only with an accent. She hadn't reckoned on all this introspection – the whole point of moving overseas had been to dump great chunks of her life into the Atlantic, to forget a major upheaval or two, and get on with her life as a . . . single woman.

What she hadn't anticipated, Max thought as she banged the Hoover around the skirting boards, was the loss of the elaborate network of friends and distractions that kept her synapses firing away loudly, if superficially.

Nor had it occurred to her that it really wasn't possible to make friends and remain a blank slate.

She knew Jax was too smart not to start putting two and two together, and she'd already unwittingly winkled out the core of Max's secret, but she really didn't want to become the star of her own personal soap opera . . . again. Why couldn't she just *be*? Why did other people have to know things? What difference did her past make? Who cared what other people got up to?

But she knew this was ridiculous, because she was positively burning with curiosity when it came to Jax's love life. Who the hell was this Fergal guy? How in the world could they possibly be engaged to be married if he lived in flippin' Dubai? Why was Jax's entire family upholding this myth? Maybe she'd do a bit of digging at Sunday lunch.

Or maybe she wouldn't. Bit of a bad vibe there, yesterday, in the office. Jax, who in many ways made absolutely no sense to Max, was certainly her closest friend in her new life, and was the entire reason she chose Dublin over London. They had the kind of professional chemistry that couldn't be sneezed at, and that had to make up for the differences between them, as vast as they were. Jax, continuing that dubious commitment to a guy who wasn't even *there*, Jax who dutifully went home to Mother every Sunday, who morally couldn't miss a deadline. As she booted up her laptop, Max imagined getting underneath all that fidelity, teasing it apart, finding the weak spots – but knew, in the language of female friendships, that she'd have to reciprocate, and there was no room in Max's fresh, clean universe for the pesky past.

Speaking of the pesky past . . . Max sat down, propped her feet up on the coffee table, and started trawling through the archives on her computer. Maybe she had the big idea here, lying in wait in old pitches for clients that never flew, or in one of her several (many, if she was being honest) unfinished screenplays and teleplays. Scrolling down another document, Max shook her head at herself, at her own half-baked brilliance.

Maybe it was time to stick to one of these ideas and see if it had wings.

She cut and pasted a few notions together and emailed it to herself at work – she and Jax could go over them on Monday. Powering down her Mac, she drifted towards the window and stared out unseeingly at the river. Was this prospect a real goer? Or was it just another way for Max to wiggle out of something else before the going got tough?

'Why, look at the time!' Max said aloud suddenly, and dashed off to dress.

She bundled together a bag of clothes to donate to her local Oxfam, and feeling virtuous in advance, decided that she'd made enough room for something new in her closet, and her life. Shopping was, as far as she was concerned, the perfect way to live in the present moment and, dressing briskly, she left behind a clean flat, and the slightly more cluttered thoughts of the morning.

Jax stretched, hands rubbing the small of her back. Her garden was tiny, but it was hers, and she tended it as she did all things: with care, and with a quietness that masked a vision. Just because, she often thought to herself, she didn't make a huge drama out of everything, it didn't mean she hadn't made a mark.

She gathered up her hand tools and surveyed her little space. A north-facing back garden no more than ten feet square was certainly Jacinta's notion of a challenge, and one, if she said so herself, she'd met handily. The floral mosaic she'd laid in – a Celtic love knot adorned with bright red roses – made the perfect centrepiece on the curving flagstone patio, and she'd dug in and wired up the burbling water feature herself, a tier of glossy white marble that shone like a beacon over the mass of low, deep green ground cover. She'd been cutting that ground cover back, and even despite the relative gloominess of certain spots in the garden, pulling out weeds. Weeds, she was convinced, would grow in a cupboard in a basement. The ivy on the walls could do with a trim, but she'd leave that until next weekend.

It was the perfect use of a Saturday afternoon, even if it was mid-February and the light was fading fast. It was never too early to prepare for the spring ... and she recalled the perplexed and somewhat horrified look on Max's face when she'd waxed lyrical about winter gardening. You'd think Max was an African orchid, the way she took on about the cold. A *hothouse flower indeed*, thought Jax, wondering again what really made Max tick, wondering again about the secrets Max kept. What kind of secrets required the kind of cultivated silence that Max kept around the private pieces of her life?

Jax had been delighted when they'd been paired up during her stay in New York, and she'd been equally appalled by Max's work ethic, which seemed designed to ignore all prescribed notions of beginnings of days and ends of nights. She was convinced that Max had once spent an entire fortnight in the place – it could have been done, considering the mess Max always surrounded herself with. There were easily five changes of clothes draped over chairs and, God help her, piled up on the floor. Jax shuddered, but not from the brisk wind.

How Jax herself had managed to avoid getting sucked into such workplace insanity was one of her own secrets: bullheadedness, the least flamboyant of her mother's qualities that she'd managed to glean from her family's turbulent gene pool. It had taken her two weeks of grim determination, but she'd managed not only to keep to the proper eight-hour workday, but also to convince her ACJ:New York colleagues that she wasn't a malingerer. It was one of the crowning achievements of her career thus far.

Oh, bollocks, her career! What was to be done? She locked her back door behind her and ran her eyes lovingly over the Farrow & Ball paper she'd hung herself in the rear hallway. She thought about the career she'd edged into sideways: she'd trained in art college as a fine arts photographer, she'd fallen into graphic design, which she'd studied as a back-up moneymaker, then a freelance gig in ACJ's production studio had led to a concerted effort to get into the more creative side of things . . . where she was now. But for how long?

God, New York had been a gas, with the added bonus of having forged the most successful working partnership she'd ever had. But she'd been keen to come home, back to her little cottage in the Liberties, on the square where she'd run tame as a child, visiting her gran. Too bad Gran hadn't had the foresight to keep the place in the family – no one wanted to live in this little square in the seventies, and the family had been lucky to sell it off at all. Jax was lucky to get it back in the nineties, when things went mad and they were all chasing the Celtic Tiger's tail.

She scrubbed her hands in the kitchen sink and dried them on a tea towel, her back against the countertop. Her lovely little kitchen: she'd ripped out every last cupboard, replumbed the sink, painted, tiled, and then refitted it all, putting up those gorgeous glass-fronted Provençal cabinets herself. She peeked into her bedroom, an intimate affair that she'd draped with muslin from floor to ceiling, with fairy lights twined down the corners of the room. With the wardrobes painted white, and the duvet a blushing rose, the delicate femininity of the room was given an exotic flair by the grass matting on the floor; a bit of a desert seraglio vibe. Jax sighed, sat on the bed, and picked up the picture she'd uncharacteristically thrown on the floor last night.

Smiling faces stared out at her, one of them her own, the Alps looming in the background. She and Fergal had made a point of spending a holiday together two years ago in Chamonix, despite the fact that Jax was an indifferent skier at best. He'd had it up to his neck in sunshine, he'd said, and the travails on the mountainside during the day were more than made up for, in Jax's eyes, by the cosy nights spent in the chalet, with the comfort of the fire and the friendship. And the love! Love, too, of course; not so mad as it was in the beginning, but then they'd known each other for ages and it was logical that this far down the road they'd settle into a kind of groove, and, well, bugger it, they'd made a commitment to each other and stuck by it, hadn't they?

Maybe it was time to have a talk. She wandered out into her front room, the hearth sparkling clean after last night's peat fire, and picked up the other photographs that had taken the brunt of her frustration late last night. She and Fergal at university; at his older brother's wedding (at which he had proposed); at her own parents' fortieth wedding anniversary. In that one, her mother had playfully got Fergal in a headlock while her father, as usual, was dreaming into the distance. She herself had that face on her, that look of wincing indulgence that her mother – and if she was honest, Fergal – brought out in her.

Dusting down the frames, Jax rearranged them across her bookshelves, and decided that maybe it was time to move things along. A promise was a promise after all, and this one, the biggest promise of them all, was one that Jacinta Quirke was least likely to take lightly.

5

No matter how quietly Max shut the door of the taxi behind her, and despite the fact that the house was large and imposing and nestled in a leafy arbour, Jax always heard the car door shut. There were any number of buses that would bring Maxine O'Malley to the front door of her parents' home, but would Max take them?

Max rushed up the charmingly uneven walk, dashed up the steps, entered without knocking, and made her way, calling as she went, to the large, disordered kitchen at the back. It was like running a gauntlet of cosiness, and she had never been comfortable in Raymond and Angela Quirke's house until the day she'd been accepted as part of the attractively rumpled furniture and had been allowed to walk straight into the heart of the place without the formalities of reception rooms.

It wasn't that the place wasn't welcoming – far from it: the whole ground floor waited like a wide open embrace, ready to snatch Max to its breast and to smother her in its harum-scarum tangle of knick-knacks, art works, old hurleys, tattered volumes, various unfinished knitting projects, playscripts, wellies, scratchy wool throws – a hodgepodge of the belongings of everyone who had ever lived there; not abandoned, but left behind, like fingerprints, as proof that many had contributed to the life of the house.

Max found the constancy intimidating.

'Charging through like a *bull*! Are you a *Taurus*, by any chance?' Angela Quirke called from the pantry where Max heard the tinkle and splash of the cocktail pitcher. She accepted an absent-minded kiss on the cheek from Raymond Quirke, his hands full of thyme, and settled, sighing, into her chair at the family table.

As Max and Raymond comfortably engaged in their ongoing argument about home cooking – which Max always instigated with the latest news from the world of microwave cuisine – Jax wondered, again, what it must be like to see her father's kitchen through someone else's eyes. She'd always thought it looked like something out of a children's storybook, and throughout her youth she had been convinced that the cupboard to the left of the stove, the one that didn't open, led to Narnia. The majority of the cupboard doors hung slightly askew, and one was as likely to find reams of her father's spreadsheets behind a door as one would a salt cellar.

There was plenty of room in the place, as her father always insisted, even when the full complement of Quirkes had eaten, shouted, laughed, argued, cried and loitered within its four warm walls, loads of space for four boys, two girls, a mother and father and a variety of relations to move about in. The cathedral ceiling had a skylight that now filtered through the grey light of a Sunday mid-afternoon in late winter, and gently illuminated the two battered dressers that sat cheek by jowl against the wall.

The remaining walls were virtually invisible beneath Raymond's collection of calendars (begun in 1958, when he and Angela had bought the place for £5000), meticulously layered as though in advance of an archaeological investigation, and Angela's collection of posters of her past performances in Ireland, England and Australia – lately with the local music society, which were not discussed but, due to Angela's vigorous ego, were included.

Jax carefully shut the equally slightly askew door of the Aga after checking that it had fired up properly, and tried to straighten the tilting Edwardian clothes dryer. She cast her eye over the room once more; maybe it was less C.S. Lewis than Mother Goose, only around here, it was the old man who lived in the shoe.

'Well?' Angela's resonant tones emitted effortlessly, with yeoman-like help from her diaphragm. Said tones effectively cut short any other conversation that had ensued in her absence, and were accompanied by the thump of a glass jug of Bloody Mary hitting the oak refectory table. Draping herself across her chair, she alternately fixed Max and Jax with what they called her Lady Bracknell look and expelled a plume of smoke from her tiny brown cigar.

'Well what, Ange?' asked Max, tauntingly innocent, as she poured out the drinks. Raymond garnished them with celery. Jax could smell the vodka across the room.

Angela threw her tiny torso down on to the table, reaching an eloquent palm in Max's direction. 'Is there a part for *me*, darling?'

Max slid a brimming glass into Angela's open hand, and Jax winced, ever so slightly; even that minuscule, almost involuntary twitch was soothed in passing by her father as he passed from fridge to mixing bowl with the butter.

Her mother was an actress. A performer. If she hadn't got used to it by now, when would she?

It would never have occurred to Jax not to tell her father what was going on at ACJ, not to speak of her own and Max's nascent plans, and it would have been utterly pointless to try to keep them from her mother – her mother who could winkle out a plot at six hundred paces.

Which was, Angela liked to say, the only reason she'd been able to stick *that soap opera* in the early nineties.

After the endless phone calls yesterday – Jax had unplugged her phone after the eleventh – she was happy enough to leave Max to handle the interrogation and the blatant herding of the plan to incorporate the talents of a sixty-something leading lady.

'We're still working on the concept, Ange,' said Max, in reaction to which Angela changed posture again, this time perched on the edge of her chair like a robin.

A robin with the instincts of a vulture, Max thought, as she watched Angela's bright blue eyes flash – eyes that Jax had inherited, minus the predatory bent – and watched Angela fuss with the length of silk draped around her throat like plumage, silk of the scarlet red variety, dyed to match Angela's short spiky hair, or vice versa.

'Well, what's your genre, darlings? Modern? Post Modern? Isn't Classical the new Modern? When I did *Mother Courage* with the RSC –'

Max sat and thoroughly enjoyed Angela's performance, and, as ever, was totally amazed that Jacinta was the offspring of this showy and colourful and adorably mad woman. Jax never complained about her mother's eccentricities or her continual demand for the spotlight, or what were surely well-worn anecdotes – Jax never complained about either of her parents, which was really weird – and, as ever, Max came to the conclusion that, consciously or unconsciously, Jax's entire being clung desperately to the 180 degrees opposite her mother's every quality.

'– and *that*, me ducks, is what comes of brilliance without good solid *research* to back it *up*, so you've got to *back it up*, girls—'

'Angela.' Raymond breathed her name gently, and she threw herself into another pose, ramrod straight, chin raised; combative, but silent. 'Do let them speak up for themselves. And while they do, shall I give you this garlic to chop?'

'You most certainly will *not*,' she spat, and Raymond winked at Max, having already peeled the fragrant cloves himself.

Raymond Quirke was a dote, Max decided, as she did every time she spent any time in his company. Always dressed to a smart but casual standard, today he sported khaki trousers and a light-blue striped button-down shirt that he had surely ironed himself. She imagined that a tie had been worn to Mass, and that his weekday attire – in which he gently guided his accountancy firm through the ever-changing waters of Irish finance – was even more polished than this. He exuded a kind of quiet authority that Max admired: no milquetoast, by any means, he neither trampled his wife's spirit nor allowed her to run roughshod over his. As she watched him whisper in his daughter's ear, she thought about her own folks, almost the exact opposites of Jax's, with her mad dad and her ever unruffled mother, and remembered that when she'd first met Mike—

'I always forget that you're English, Ray—' Max cut off her own train of thought.

'By way of County Mayo,' Jax supplied.

'But didn't you and Angela meet in London, or what's the story?'

Angela threw off her sulk along with her silken wrap. 'The story! Never tell me you haven't been told *the story*!' Without waiting for a response she leapt to her feet and ran around the table to embrace her husband, who was a full foot taller than herself, from behind.

'Angela,' he breathed again, this time in surrender, his arms holding aloft the roast he'd been about to baste.

'Boy meets girl! Boy loses girl! Ah! Boy gives up all hope and leaves the country and girl pursues boy and convinces him to pursue her once more!'

'Oh, Mum,' Jax mumbled ineffectually. Angela released her husband and enveloped her daughter, who was only half a foot taller than herself.

' "Oh, Mum"! If it wasn't for me you wouldn't be standing here, gurning at me—'

'And if it wasn't for Dad, either, presumably—'

'And if it wasn't for your brothers and their marginally acceptable wives, and those lovely, gorgeous grand-children, where would I be, where would I *be*? Alone, alone, *alone*—'

'Boy meets girl?' prompted Max.

Angela returned to her chair, perching once more on the edge of her seat, and gazed off into the middle distance. 'I left Ireland when I was seventeen, travelling, Lord love us, with a panto. It was an, ahem, homage to *The Colleen Bawn*, *The Shaughraun*, and – good God – *John Bull's Other Island*.'

'Very highbrow,' cracked Max.

'Not at all. Good, clean, accessible, highly plagiar-istic fun.' Angela ran a hand down the side of her face, remembering. 'I was the ingénue. We went up the length and breadth of Britain, and then finally arrived in London.'

Max found herself breathing in tandem with the tale. Angela did have a way with it, after all. 'I had the clothes on my back and a tiny grip, and traded whatever I could with the other girls, but I was so tiny, you see . . .' She smirked, and winked at Max. 'God, we didn't need much in those days! In any event, we finally arrived in London.'

She paused for effect. 'It was nineteen sixty-two. I needn't tell you what that was like.' And then she proceeded to. 'Psychedelia, tuning in, turning out—'

'Dropping out, love,' Raymond corrected.

'—Carnaby Street, the *Beatles*—'

'The Beatles?' Max cut in, confused. 'But—'

'Parties – morning, noon, and night, before the show, after the show—'

'During the show – it was an improvement.' Raymond stopped spreading garlic butter on the baguettes and smiled at his wife.

'Every night, a different happening – and we girls picked up extra bits and pieces here and there on the side, nothing, well . . . *illegal* or *dirty*, just, you know, dancing around a bit in the background at a gig – I remember! Was it the Byrds—'

'But . . . it's too early for—' Max cut in again, even more confused, and Jax laughed, big and loud. 'Catching on yet, Max?' she snorted.

'Perhaps it was the Bees, love,' suggested Raymond.

'Byrds, Bees, there I was in the *middle* of *every*thing, in the West End in nineteen sixty-two—'

'Well, not the West End per se—' Raymond interjected.

'And then I jumped out of the cake and into Raymond's arms.' Angela paused for a healthy swig of vodka – they'd left off putting in the tomato juice ages ago.

'A cake?' Max shrieked. 'Naked?!'

Angela lifted her chin, regally. 'I have never done, nor will I ever do, nudity.'

'There were some strategically placed –' Raymond gestured with his drink.

'And they certainly weren't paying me enough to leap about in me pelt.'

'So what was the occasion?' Max leaned forward, enjoying the pair of them.

'It was himself's stag party.' Angela smirked into her drink.

'Ray, you dog,' Max joked, feeling inexplicably disappointed.

'Wait for it,' counselled Jax, reaching for the pitcher, now more a light rose colour than a tomato red.

'I must insist, dear, that I tell my side of the story,' said Raymond, as he slid the baguettes into the oven.

'Side? What side? There is only one story, only one side,' Angela said airily, lighting up another cigarillo.

Raymond opened a window. 'Max will think the absolute worst of me, and I can't have that.' He turned to her as he took down some plates from a cupboard. 'It was indeed a party for me, but there was never an engagement in the literal sense—'

'Ha!' Angela shouted triumphantly 'In the literal sense, my *foot*!'

'It was, at best, an understanding – one which, if truth be known, had in fact been less binding than it had been in years past, and the young lady in question—'

'The *young lady in question*! You should have been a *barrister*!'

'This, what is this?' Max murmured, and looked at Jax.

'This is familiar,' Jax agreed. They looked at each other blankly.

'It's on the tip of my brain—' Max began, only to be cut off by Angela's wildly flapping hands.

'Did you hear that, Max? The young lady in question pitched up at the stage door one day and *tossed* the contents of a glass jar into my *face*! I was certain it was acid, or – or arsenic, or—'

Raymond threw up his hands in response. 'It wasn't her at all, love, you never even met her.'

Max's brow furrowed again. 'Arsenic isn't liquid, is it?'

'Boy met girl, and how exactly did boy lose girl?' Jax tried to get the story back on track.

Angela took another deep breath, and Raymond, who so rarely did so, took over the telling. 'I pursued Angela relentlessly, until the day of my departure to Ireland, which was in fact the reason for the party and the cake. Angela then returned herself—'

'Abandoned! Heartbroken!' Angela wailed.

'—because the panto's run had ended. We reunited in Dublin, during which time Angela alienated my mother to such a degree that they have not spoken more than twenty words to one another in thirty years –'

Angela leaned fervently towards Max. 'Assumpta Quirke! The auld battleaxe!'

'– And then Angela very dramatically took leave of these shores, under the impression that I had treated her most discourteously –'

'You horrible, horrible man!' Angela took refuge in her glass.

'– And so it behooved me to follow her to Aberystwyth, where she was appearing in a Hiberno-Welsh co-production of *Othello* –'

'Desdemona,' Angela threw in with satisfaction. ' *"Some bloody passion shakes your very frame: there are portents; but yet I hope, I hope they do not point to me –"* '

'And I apologised and proposed, if I remember correctly, in the same breath.' Raymond expertly whipped the cream for the pudding.

'It's much better when I tell it,' Angela grumbled.

'And then you went off and got married?' Max shook her head as if the information would fall into all the right places in her head.

'Why, Max, you seem interested,' Jax purred smugly, and Max stuck her tongue out.

'It is a *deeply* interesting story,' Angela intoned, nostrils aflare.

'You see, Mum, Max doesn't think that people care about romance—'

'Romance sells, Jax, I was talking about the failure of the *result* of romance—'

'And I argued, you see, that the reason why people tune into reality television was because of relationship—'

Max turned to Angela. 'So what do you think of all that *Big Brother* carry on, Ange?'

Angela shivered. 'It is disgusting. I can't take my eyes off the stuff. Raymond' – and she gestured accusingly with her cigarillo – 'was secretly addicted to *Celebrity Farm*. I think he fancied that little fat thing, what was her name.' She brightened. 'Oh, do one of *those*, they're horribly fabulous!'

'No,' said Jax, shifting a pot of steamed carrots from the stove top.

Max shrugged and Angela arched a knowing brow. Jacinta could be so *stubborn* – she must have got that from the Quirkes. 'The concept is thirty seconds away from irrelevance,' Max conceded. 'But *why* do you find it impossible to look away?'

'It's the *suspense*,' Angela hissed, her eyes narrowing. 'Waiting to see who gets off with whom, who hates whom, who pretends they hate whom but who really pines for whom, who never thought they'd ever have a chance with whom but because they're trapped in the jungle and isolated they're thrown together and who knows!'

'Indeed,' said Raymond.

'Told you,' said Jax.

'Hmph,' grunted Max.

'Hmmm?' asked Angela.

'Okay, okay,' grumbled Max. 'It's just that Jax said the same thing.'

Angela clapped her hands. '*Darling!* We *never* agree!'

'But it's all crap!' Max rose and paced around the table, and Angela followed her avidly with her eyes. 'The result is pure fiction. Whatever the circumstances, the relationships, in inverted commas, that result from the proximity don't last, they can't last – what about the people who are partnered and, on *national television*, betray their marriage or whatever – the whole monogamy thing is a cod!' She looked at Angela and Raymond. 'Well, mostly.'

'Are your parents divorced, love?' asked Angela softly.

'God, no,' Max laughed.

Angela cocked her head. 'Are *you* divorced, love?' Jax's hands stilled on the potato masher

'No.' Max looked away, and Angela decided to mull that over later. Cupping her chin in her hands and leaning

48

on the table, Angela changed the subject. 'And Jacinta, naturally, begs to differ.'

'Not "naturally",' Jax protested.

'Oh, not *naturally*! Has she told you, Maxine, the story of the boy from up the road? They were all of three—'

'Angela.' Even Max bit her tongue at Raymond's severe tone, and she hadn't even been talking.

'We'll have lunch sometime,' Angela hissed in Max's ear.

'Given my experience of relationships, *I* believe that it's not impossible to remain faithful to one person your whole life.' Jax looked wistfully out the window.

'Fidelity is the new adultery!' Angela crowed.

'*That's* interesting,' said Max.

'That's – hmmm,' said Jax as she transferred the snap peas to a serving bowl.

'That'll do,' said Ray. 'Dinner is served.'

Later, Max turned it all over in her mind as she brushed her teeth.

Fidelity – the new adultery!

No.

Max finished moisturising haphazardly, distracted by the sound of RTÉ's Big Movie wafting in from the front room.

Unfaithful to faithlessness.

Faithful to unfaithfulness.

Huh?

As she washed her hands, she tipped her head to the side, focusing on the dialogue that was drifting through the door. What film *is* that? she wondered. And why am I listening to it? She spread paste on her toothbrush.

Monogamy – the new polygamy!

Ha! Please.

As if the film were tugging on her arm, Max finally paid it her full attention.

Slowly brushing, she walked towards the television.

As she watched, a shot of an older couple cut to Meg Ryan and the main action of the film. She dropped her toothbrush. Spitting into a houseplant, she grabbed the phone as another piece of the puzzle dropped into place.

Jax let her tea steep as she organised her fridge around the leftovers her father had pressed on her. She had her telly turned up high to ward off that late-Sunday-evening-lonely feeling. Adding honey and milk, she tuned into the film on RTÉ. It was *When Harry Met Sally*. They really had hit on something there, hadn't they? Almost twenty years later, and the ideas were still fresh and—

The mug hit the floor and shattered when the phone rang; Jax lifted it off the wall without pausing, and without greeting, shouted, 'That's what it was! That's what my parents were doing! They were doing the thing, the thing in the movie!'

'That's the hook,' Max crowed, and they both sat down, at opposite ends of town, to watch the film.

'But what do we do with the hook?' Jax whispered, as she and Max strolled towards ACJ's post-production department.

'We'll figure it out,' Max said confidently. She watched Niamh, who possessed about as much capacity for stealth as did a lame ostrich, attempt to melt into the shadows of the photocopying dock. 'Howaya, Niamh, nice weekend?' Max called, so loudly that the woman started and dropped four reams of A4 paper on to her toes.

'Nice weekend ringing the guards, shopping small children?' muttered Jax, who was rewarded with a cackle from Max.

'We'll figure it out,' Max continued as they both paused on the landing, 'by endlessly throwing ideas at it until something hangs off it. And we start now.'

She strode down the stairs, down to the foyer, and then down again, and Jax caught Max's literal and figurative drift.

'Max –' she began, as they stopped at the door that led to the building's lowest level. 'We can't—'

'Knock, knock, Your Holiness,' Max called out, and smiled up at the agency's production techie, he who was in charge of all things technical from the cables that got tangled up underneath your computer to the forty-five promotional DVDs you needed burned in half an hour.

'Fuck off, Max,' said John Paul O'Gorman. 'The man's dead, for God's sake.'

'Mea culpa, mea culpa,' she begged.

'You should know better than to get on the bad side of the production department,' he warned, personably.

'Leave him be, Max,' said Jax, smiling at John Paul, who, Max noticed, pinkened ever so slightly around the earlobes. *Hmmmm*.

'Production department? So you send memos to yourself, or what? All alone down here in the back of the basement . . .' She caught Jax's eye, an eye that was now regarding John Paul under a thoughtful brow.

He blushed fully under the scrutiny of the two sharpest females in the company. 'I don't know what you're inferring,' he said loftily, pushing aside the long, curly lock of hair that inevitably flopped in his eyes, 'But—'

'Free for lunch, JP?' Max cut across. 'My treat. I haven't abused my expense account in yonks.'

'L'Ecrivain?' He knew that when Max meant abuse, she meant *abuse*.

'Not on our first date,' Max laughed. 'But FXB is definitely on the cards. Cool?'

John Paul shrugged in agreement, a bit disconcerted by Jax's scrutiny. He hunched his shoulders and thought about fleeing back to the safety of the DVD burner.

What he wouldn't give for Jacinta Quirke to look at him like that, under different circumstances. Well, maybe not exactly like that, like she was trying to discern his species, or like she hadn't really looked at him before in her life, which he sort of knew she hadn't really, beyond the polite attention she showed everyone – she was one of the kindest people he'd ever met, and her eyes, those bright blue eyes . . .

But Max was another story entirely. 'What's up?' he queried, narrowing his own gaze at the American, eyes that Jax noticed were as big and brown as a doe's – not that JP was girly or anything, on the contrary . . .

Max grinned. 'We've got a project that we need to keep on the QT, and frankly, if we can't trust God's Representative On Earth to keep schtum—'

'Fuck *off*, Max,' said John Paul.

'—then who can we trust? In fairness.'

JP shoved his hands in the back pockets of his jeans. This sounded bad. It looked bad: the grin on Max's face was the very essence of foreboding. And Jax – well, Jax looked like she always did when Max was on a rampage: resigned, but with a flick of a flame of the same fire in her eye.

'Gotta keep this above board, Max,' he said, in what he hoped was an authoritative-yet-casual, detached-yet-with-the-promise-of-interest tone.

Auld softie, thought Jax, smiling at him.

Gotcha! thought Max, as she watched a fresh blush creep up JP's neck from the collar of his T-shirt.

She withdrew a wrinkled, crinkled, slightly torn, slightly smudged piece of paper from her pocket. 'No sweat. I've got the equipment request right here, signed and everything.' She stepped on Jax's foot lightly.

How long has she had that? Jax wondered anew at her colleague's ingenuity.

'Did this pass down to you from the Ark?' John Paul shook it out, once, twice, until it unfolded from folds it had held since the year dot.

'It's legit!' Max protested. 'Got everybody's signatures

and everything! I didn't take you for a cog in the wheel, Your Holiness—'

'So, em, what time for lunch?' Jax cut off another tirade, and smiled at John Paul.

He wished she wouldn't do that. No, he didn't. Yes, he did. Bugger!

'Max has been instrumental in helping me break the one o'clock national lunchtime rule – we usually go out at two,' Jax added.

'Deadly,' said John Paul, and the girls moved off. *Women*, he corrected himself: Max had nearly taken his head off the time he'd made the mistake of calling them girls. He edged back into what he liked to call the Bat Cave. Not that he'd *ever* tell anyone else that's what he called it, it *was* pretty lame, but he couldn't help it, he had to call his crappy little office something, and given its subterranean quality, the Bat Cave seemed the most likely—

'John Paul!' He turned and looked up at Jax, who was still smiling at him. 'I said I'll ring you when we're coming down.'

'Cool.' Exuding insouciance, he slouched backwards over the threshold, and almost tripped over the torn carpet.

Elbowing their way through the crowd on Baggot Street towards FXB, Max dropped back and let John Paul walk with Jax. Tall and lanky, he eschewed a coat, even in this bitter cold weather, but seemed to have layered what appeared to be every jumper he'd ever owned on to his torso. His jeans bagged at the bum, as per hetero male sartorial requirements. His hair tumbled around his head in disordered curls, which were cute, but which could use some pruning.

All in all, Max mused, despite the manky workboots

and the total obscuring of his true shape, not a bad specimen, and he already had the good taste to be mad about Jax.

Her eyes twinkled above her tightly wrapped scarf. Maybe the project had some reality TV meta-potential, she thought – it might not be a bad idea to keep the cameras rolling behind the scenes, as well . . .

John Paul gallantly held open the door. Jesus, Max was wrapped up as if she was trekking across the South Pole. Bit of a nip in the air all right, but nothing that warranted hat, scarf and woolly gloves. Surely they had winters in America?

Jax handed her coat to the girl at the door, and tensed a bit as she looked around the room. Her father, whom she wouldn't mind seeing at all, worked nearby, and her mother, whom she would prefer not to see today, often popped in here for a late lunch. Scanning the room, she breathed a sigh of relief – they had work to do, and couldn't spare the hour or so Angela would require in order to feel adequately tended to. Nor could Jax bear the scrutiny poor John Paul would find himself under – any man so much as breathing the same air as Jax was always taken for a potential replacement for the not-so-secretly loathed Fergal.

'Right, lads,' drawled Max, 'nothing too boozy, work to do, people to meet.'

'Niamh to avoid,' chipped in John Paul, and he and Max settled in to a lovely little bout of character assassination while Jax talked herself out of the grilled salmon, and then back into it again.

'And an appetiser, Jaxie,' said Max, without breaking the stride of her story about the time that she caught Niamh going through her handbag. 'I spent the rest of the day surfing the web, trying to figure out how to sue the bejesus out of her.'

'Any joy?' John Paul cast an eye over the menu and sighed with relief that ACJ was paying for this one.

'Nah.' Max sighed. 'Couldn't be arsed, really. I just put itching powder on her desk chair.'

Jax sighed, as Niamh-bashing stories took them through ordering, the first glass of wine, and the starter. Never comfortable with scurrilous gossiping, she decided to swerve the conversation closer towards the whole point of the exercise.

'Have you given any thought to what you'll do when ACJ closes up shop?' she asked John Paul as she forked up another bite of the lovely salmon.

'What a downer, huh?' Max offered, and John Paul shrugged disconsolately.

'I was the very last one in—'

'You'll be the first one out,' Max said cheerfully. 'Too bad, you're good at what you do.' She sipped at her wine. 'What is it you do, exactly?'

'See, that's the problem with advertising, nobody has any notion of what guys like me, stuck in the flippin' basement, do; how much we actually have to handle down there in the space no one else wants to work in.' John Paul stabbed at his sirloin. 'All those lovely, slick reels you people need? That's me. Reel-to-reel sound? Voice-overs? Do you know what people outside, in proper studios, charge per hour?' He didn't wait for a response, nor did he see the look that passed between the women. 'I just want a place to do my job, without having to worry about the whatchamacallits.'

'Peripherals?' Max sat back and signalled the waiter for another bottle of wine, despite Jax's mew of dissent.

John Paul went off on a rant, and Jax could sympathise with every word. His sleepy brown eyes lit up with passion and outrage as he gave out about the miserable conditions in ACJ and the paltry assignments.

'I am, if ya like, an entire production team all in one. I can do anything. I could production manage and technically execute a feature film shot on DVD – I did it at college! On my own! I'm just not much at the concept bit, not a writer or anything, that's not my scene –'

'That would be where Jax and I come in.'

'Come in to what?' John Paul realised that there was no such thing as a free lunch.

'We've got an idea,' said Max, and, topping up his glass, let him in on the scheme.

'We had better start saving these receipts.' Jax handed her menu to the waiter.

'This one is on the agency,' said Max. 'I can slip this one on to the account for that spa in Kerry, I'll file it under field work.'

'Some field.' Jax looked around at the loud and merry crowd that filled The Bank restaurant on College Green to bursting. Friday night in the city centre, and the place was hopping, as if no one in the world had to worry about losing their job in a struggling economy, as if none of them had any fears as to where their next pay cheque was going to come from.

'And I'll take care of it because I know you don't like spoofing,' Max concluded.

'I don't know that I'm cut out for this,' Jax blurted, clasping her wine glass in a death grip.

Max nodded. She'd seen this coming a mile away – or at least since Wednesday, as flurries of emails sent between themselves and JP, using addresses that were not logged on the company servers, seemed to solidify what had started out as a lark.

They had a project, and it was taking on a life of its own.

'Look, the whole point is to play to our strengths, right? That's what I came away with after our lunch with the pontiff. He wants to do what he does best, you want to do what you do best. Worry about the look of the thing, and the way we're going to have to trick – I mean, convince' – she grinned at Jax's wince – 'our subjects to give us what we need.'

'I'm not entirely sure I *know* what it is we need.' Jax reached into her shoulder bag for the binder she'd begun for the job.

'And that's why we're here, now,' Max said expansively. 'Let's get to work.'

'Right.' Neatly lining up the salt and pepper shakers alongside the table's vase at the edge of the table, Jax began to lay out their notes. Max helpfully cuddled the wine bucket on her lap.

Jax looked at the notes, a disordered mess of inspiration and nonsense. 'What exactly are we trying to get at?'

Max signalled the waiter. 'You ready to order? Let's get that out of the way and then we'll knock out a script.'

For the next thirty minutes or so the two women hunched over their notes, then their plates, then their notes again as they brainstormed, ate, discussed, argued and sat silent, stumped. Jax broke the points of two pencils and then proceeded to argue with Max about why she wasn't using a pen. They agreed to disagree on that, and also on the fact that another bottle of pinot noir was coming their way, despite Jax's audible groan.

'So don't drink any of it,' said Max.

'It's just that – and I'm still not sure how this came about – we're meeting Orla' – Jax consulted her watch – 'twenty minutes ago.'

'She's gagging to know what we've got up our sleeve,' said Max, 'and she was basically your idea anyway. She'll be a kind of test case. We can do a dry run of the script.'

Jax shook her head at the last sheet that remained on the tabletop. 'I don't know, it's still a bit rough –'

'Work in progress,' Max replied airily, as the waiter poured out from the new bottle. Jax gave in. She had a feeling she'd need a bit of a rosy glow to get through the next few hours.

'A toast.' Max leaned forward and raised her glass. 'To new enterprises.'

'New enterprises.' Jax sighed.

'Look, so it's a bit raggedy right now, but it's organic, like; we have to get out there with some cameras and see what we've got.'

'It needs a control, like an experiment.'

'Sure, sure, but let's see which way the collective wind is blowing before we get all set in stone. Loosen up, Jax.'

'I'm loose!' Jax burst out, nearly spilling her wine all over their notes. 'Fuck's sake!'

'Jeez, okay, okay.' What was going on here? 'Hey, so, his holiness is really working out, huh?'

Jax breathed in through her nose, out through her mouth. 'He's got potential.'

'Ummmm hmmm,' Max cooed. 'With a bit of refurbishing, I'd say he's got loads of potential.'

Jax felt her jaw lock. So Max had a *gra* for JP. So? What difference did that make? *It certainly wasn't any of her concern*, she thought, suddenly unable to maintain eye contact with her friend. Her fingers started to fuss with the hem of the tablecloth, pulling at some loose threads. She was, after all, engaged to be married, and if Max wanted to complicate her own life with someone they were working with, well, that was her problem, wasn't it? Wasn't it?

'. . . all those floppy curls, he's cute; he'd be a bit Hobbity if he wasn't so tall, so maybe he's like the off-spring of Frodo and Galadriel—' Max stopped and grabbed the tablecloth just in time as Jax had been inexorably pulling it off the table. 'Hey. Hello! C'mere, what's up?'

Smoothing the fabric back in place, Jax tried a deep-breathing technique to calm her suddenly racing heart.

'Nerves?' Max reached out and gave Jax's hand a squeeze.

'Nerves,' Jax agreed. 'Em. I don't "do" big impulsive risks very well.'

'We're doing this methodically, rationally, and on company time – a company that's going to be chucking us out sooner rather than later. It's not that big a jump, Jax. And you're not in this alone.'

Unlike certain other areas of my life, Jax thought bitterly. What? Where had that come from? She glanced around, panicked, as if she'd catch that stray thought running gleefully for the door.

'It's not just this, is it?' Max poured out the last of the wine and contemplated a third bottle.

'No more wine,' Jax ordered. 'Let's get the bill.'

'Let's have a proper chat,' Max returned. 'I know we've got this unspoken agreement about Himself, but is it Fergal?'

'I –' Jax fumbled, caught off guard. Max wasn't exactly afraid to ask a direct question, but this was the first time she'd breached the unspoken agreement the two seemed to have struck. She'd never asked directly about—

Saved by the bell! Jax grabbed up her phone, and all but shrieked her greeting. A terse and grating response, seeming to blare through Jax's head, alerted Max to Orla's displeasure at their lateness. She signed the tab, and saved her curiosity for another day – again.

'What's wrong with your handbag?' Jax hissed.

Max had been in the toilet for ages, thought Jax churlishly, chewing on the ice from her G&T. She was tired, it was brutally loud in Cocoon, and she wanted to go home. And now she was on the receiving end of a withering wince from Ms O'Malley, as if she'd said something dreadfully stupid.

For fuck's sake, Max had her bag hiked up right into her armpit! And was that a hole running down the side of it? What had she been doing in the loo?

'Bloody cheap tat from the sales! The strap is loose, I don't want to set it down anywhere.' Max winked at Orla and raised her glass. 'Designer rubbish!'

Orla smirked. Surely that bag wasn't a name. 'Haven't you discovered Costelloe & Costelloe? Sweet little place, loads of bargains.'

Jax decided that an unrelenting glare straight into Maxine's eyes was the only solution. They'd been perching on the slippery leatherette stools for thirty minutes. Thirty minutes of shouting inanities at people whom, she was finally allowing herself to admit, she utterly loathed.

Was this a social life? Let them have it. Jax reached blindly under the table for her shoulder bag and prepared to leave.

'I think Jax has a phone date, so I guess I'd better get to the point.' Max set her glass down, and tucked her handbag more securely under her oxter, 'I've got a bit of an ulterior motive for coming by tonight.'

Jax arched a brow in response to the curious looks of

Orla and her minions. 'It's top secret, if you like.' *Which is why we're sitting in the middle of a city-centre super pub shouting about it*, she thought wryly.

Sorcha, just back with yet another round she'd fronted, set the drinks down with a clatter. 'Hadn't Jax mentioned something about getting Orla to talk about Kenneth?'

Jax watched as Max stiffly turned in Sorcha's direction, swivelling like an android from *Star Wars*. 'Know him well, do you?'

Sorcha looked to Orla for the go ahead. 'Em, well, I've seen photos. In *Irish Tatler*, the society page. Emmmm . . . And then there was the time that I met them in Temple Bar, at the Market, and then we all went for a stroll down to—'

'Thanks, great, Sorcha.' Max ruthlessly cut off the waffle, and Jax couldn't fault her for it. 'So what we want to do is ask you a series of simple questions, designed to give us an idea of comfort levels, what's appropriate, what's not, if that's okay. Ideally, we'd like for Kenneth to have been here too—'

'I can answer for both of us,' Orla assured them, and Sorcha nodded vigorously.

'Right, so,' Max said brightly, shifting herself forward and bending herself slightly backwards simultaneously. 'You and Ken have known each other since . . . ?'

'Second class!' Sorcha chirped, only to wither under Orla's glare.

Orla shook back her hair (again! Jax thought; she must have been practising that move since she turned fourteen) and cleared her throat delicately. 'Kenneth's parents and my parents both bought into a boat – well, a yacht, actually – ages and ages ago, and we share a slip in the Dun Laoghaire marina – and we've known each other ever since.'

'And you immediately began, em, dating? Do eight-year-olds date?' Max grinned.

'Well, honestly, we were only children, but I'm sure our parents had notions, if you take my meaning. I mean, we already shared the boat—'

'And the slip!' Sorcha appeared unable to prevent herself from butting in.

'So, your first date . . . ?' Max prompted, and Orla went on and on, on and on some more, and Jax thought about fleeing to the loo, but knew she had to stay and take notes, even though the sum total of her notes thus far were comprised of 'silly bitch', 'get a life, Sorcha!!!' and 'yawwwwwwt'.

The tale of the first date threatened to bleed into the second and the third as Orla began to pick up steam; she was, after all, well used to talking about herself endlessly. Max cut her off at the pass.

'So how long have you been engaged?' *I am bored stupid*, thought Max, tossing a glare at Jax, who was randomly picking up glasses and draining them.

Jax delicately lifted her middle finger off the glass currently in her fist, and waved it at Max.

'. . . on the boat, well, actually, it's a yawwwwwwt, and anchored off the coast of Ireland's Eye. He had a bottle of Dom chilling, and, oh my God – so unexpected – from below deck came a string quartet, and he got down on one knee in the bow of the boat—'

'Yacht,' corrected Jax.

'And asked me to be the love of his life for ever.' Orla drained her martini and the lesser blondes applauded.

Booooooring! Max wiggled her butt on the little leather stool, her mind racing to think of a follow-up.

'Orla, I'm deeply interested in your story. The romance

of it. Breathtaking.' Jax leaned forward. 'But I'm desperately curious. Surely you've dated other people? As attractive and personable as you are? And surely Kenneth, as your mate, is as attractive as yourself . . . ?'

'Well. We haven't been in each other's back pockets . . .' Orla shook her hair back agitatedly.

Ah ha! Max leaned in. 'And I'm sure, with your family's connections, you've moved in some pretty interesting circles –'

'Politicians?' coaxed Jax.

'Ambassadors?' cooed Max.

'Royalty?' Jax purred.

'That Spanish prince, the one who just got married in *Hello!*, he once followed Orla home from a debs in Seville –'

Sorcha swallowed the rest of story under the most emotive glare that Max had ever seen Orla summon up.

'It's so deeply interesting, Orla,' crooned Jax. *This*, she thought, *was dead entertaining*. She flagged down a waitress and got ready to prime the pump.

'We both went away to university – Kenneth to Oxford and I to a finishing school in Switzerland – and, of course, we realised that people like us, well, we moved in circles in which, well, it seemed ridiculous to think that our, er –'

'Education?' Max offered.

'Education,' Orla agreed.

'Shouldn't entail, em, chasing foreign tail?' Jax paid for the drinks.

'Jacinta, it surely wasn't like that!' Max adopted a shocked tone. 'Are you suggesting promiscuity?'

Jax smiled thinly. Was Max working on her impression of her mother? 'Surely not,' she replied, 'but I am implying—'

'An open relationship, Orla?' Max asked.

'Open? You mean, like –' Orla looked swiftly at Sorcha.

'They dated other people, but it wasn't anything serious,' Sorcha asserted unconvincingly.

'Certainly, we were monogamous.' Orla gulped at her new martini, and Jax cut in with, 'So you did in fact date other people.'

'We *saw* other people.'

'*Saw* them? In the road? Out of the corner of your eye?'

'Socially, we saw others socially.'

'And you didn't shag anybody else.' Jax and Orla were knee to knee. Max kept subtly swinging back and forth in front of them.

'That's a very personal question,' Sorcha objected.

'It's only personal if she doesn't answer it,' snapped Jax.

'Em . . . what?' Sorcha bleated.

'I had a very busy social life,' Orla said, 'as did Kenneth, of course. Our families would have expected nothing less—'

'Did you have an affair in Switzerland, Orla?' This, thought Jax, was really, really entertaining.

'Neither Kenneth nor I ever intended to betray our relationship—'

'So you've discussed your views on playing away?'

The split second, the heartbeat, the breath of silence, bounced around Max's brain like the silver ball in a pinball machine hitting the bumper that flashed all those bells and whistles signalling 'JACKPOT!' A flick of the eyes towards Jax showed that she, too, realised that she'd finally asked the right question.

Max brusquely adjusted her handbag, and leaned

forward, as if she was trying to point it more directly at Orla, as if she was trying to focus the hole in the bag on Orla's scarlet face – Jax gasped, a delicate sound entirely lost in the relentless thump of Cocoon – had Max got a *camera* in there?

Orla, still at sea, went as far as to prod Sorcha. 'They're getting *married*!' Sorcha shrieked. 'They don't need to talk about that!'

'Hmmmm, you sure about that? Isn't that, like, about having similar values?' prodded Max.

'We have similar – our families – the yawwwwwt—'

'How would you feel if Kenneth betrayed your vows, Orla?' asked Jax.

'How would he feel if you betrayed yours?' asked Max.

Orla, very unlike herself, looked as if she were gasping for air, and she actually reached down to clutch Sorcha's hand.

'It doesn't matter when women do it,' said Sorcha, anxiously, thrilled beyond belief to have her idol reach out to her.

'Doesn't it?' asked Max, finally. 'That's very interesting, ladies. Very, very, interesting.'

Jax shot out the door of the bar and hurried after Max, who dove into a taxi that had barely come to a stop outside Cocoon.

'Max!' Jax shouted. 'What's in that bag?'

'Talk to you Monday,' Max called, and slammed the door.

J ohn Paul uncurled himself from his seated foetal
position, and wiped tears of laughter from his eyes.

'Fuck off, Your Holiness,' Max sniped, a bit put out.
She'd thought the old video-camera-in-the-handbag trick
had been pretty darn clever.

'I'll give you points for innovation, but that' – he
gestured weakly to the computer screen around which Jax
and Max had gathered – 'has got to be the worst footage
I've ever seen in my life.'

'It makes the CCTV from the Spar look like *Citizen
Kane*!' Jax snorted, and she and John Paul fell about in
gales of laughter. Maxine kicked the wall.

'I see where you're going, though,' mused John Paul as
he calmed himself down. 'It's starting to come together.'

'It wasn't a complete waste of time,' muttered Max.

'It was . . . a total gas,' said Jax, grinning.

'You were like thingie, that American one – Barbara
Walters.' John Paul swivelled around to smile up at Jax.

Had JP had a haircut? thought Jax. For some reason, his
eyes looked bigger and browner than they had last week –

'She was unstoppable,' laughed Max, her bad humour
over. 'I don't know, I think maybe I better stay behind the
camera.'

'Oh, no!' Jax blanched, and started to tug at the frayed edge of her jumper's sleeve. 'I couldn't – I didn't know – I mean, I suspected something – the way you were swinging around like R2D2 – but I couldn't, not for real—'

'Of course you could!' John Paul leaned forward, gazing up into Jax's flushed face. Her lovely, flushed face. 'It's not a bad idea, seeing as you're Irish; it might be less . . . em . . .'

'Pushy? Intimidating? American?' Max put on a fierce look, but was delighted when John Paul nodded in agreement.

'Exactly. Or, best idea of all, you double-team the way you did.'

They turned back to the monitor, which John Paul immediately switched off out of deference to his own sensibilities before turning up the soundtrack that, with a flick of this switch and a twist of that knob, he had managed to sweeten up enough as to be comprehensible.

He nodded again as they listened through to the end of the last bit. 'That's it there. The two of them discussed playing away, and then yer one saying "But they're getting *married*!"'

Max dropped down into John Paul's spare chair. 'That impression of Sorcha was just that bit too true to life, Your Holiness.'

'Max,' said John Paul, 'fuck off.'

'But what about the *When Harry Met Sally* idea?' Jax leaned her hip against John Paul's console, quite near to his elbow. Max could see the pulse jump in his throat. She shrugged with glee.

'This is the way it'll work. We basically set it up like, oh, twenty years on, as in *When Harry Met Sally*, talk about your relationship, how you met, blah blah, and then

– and it may suck, I don't know how we're going to screen anybody, we're going to have to talk to a lot of people – and then we drop that bomb of a question, and we say, hey, so, fidelity, monogamy, how does it really work, blah blah.'

'You insist upon assuming that we won't find actual people who actually love each other, and actually don't find it a terrible chore to keep their hands to themselves,' said Jax.

'Yeah, really,' muttered JP.

Max threw up her arms. 'We'll see what happens. You may, although I seriously, *seriously* doubt it, prove me wrong.'

'You've got to keep catching them on the hop, you know,' said John Paul.

'What do you mean?' Max picked up one of JP's remotes and started pushing buttons.

He started to explain. 'Catch on the hop means—'

'I know what *that* means, what do *you* mean?' Max threw down the remote, and Jax picked it up and put it on the console.

'You have to keep them off balance, or else create a way that shows them acting the way they always act, and not for the camera.'

'Wha'?' Max started kicking the leg of a table.

'When she starts thinking, she starts doing all these twitchy things,' Jax explained, handing Max a yo-yo she found on John Paul's desk. 'He means that we have to be even sneakier than you were with the camera in your bag.'

'Oooh, I like that!' Max exuberantly threw the yo-yo into Around the World. Jax and John Paul ducked in unison.

'But how?' she asked as she Walked the Dog.

'I've got a friend who used to work in a museum –' JP said.

'In the Holy See?' Max cracked herself up.

'— who can advise us about, I don't know, hidden cameras and whatnot.'

'This has got to be illegal,' worried Jax.

'It won't matter a damn if we get the right kind of people who want to be exposed on national television at all costs.' Max rolled up the string and tossed the yo-yo to JP.

'I'll talk to Lorcan, see if he wants to come on board. He's a bit of a case, but he's got loads of gear.'

'We love it when you talk dirty, JP,' Max snickered. 'Let's all meet later? Can you get him on the horn now? We can grab a few jars—'

Jax groaned. 'No more jars, Max,' she said, rubbing the back of her neck.

'Right, then we'll have a lunch at l'Ecrivain, we owe His Holiness, and it couldn't hurt to impress this Lorcan character.'

'No,' said Jax, as she twisted her head to one side, then the other.

'Breakfast at the Kylemore, is that casual enough for you, missus?'

'For fuck's *sake*, Maxine! Must you negotiate everything to death?'

If there was one thing Jax wasn't expecting, it was for Max to look like she'd been slapped.

'Forget it.' She spun on her heel and wrenched open the door.

'Max!' Jax moved forward and felt every muscle in her neck sing with tension and stress.

'Forget it!' Max answered tersely. 'We'll do it your way.'

Jax set her jaw, and JP melted further into the background. No way was he getting in between the two of them. 'Dinner. At mine. Saturday.'

'Fine.' Max slammed the door behind her and pounded up the stairs.

'Fine.' Jax slumped into Max's vacated chair and scowled.

'Here.' Without thinking – well, without thinking about it too much – John Paul got up and stood behind Jax's chair and gently squeezed her right shoulder. 'Looks like you're a bit tense . . .'

'Yeeeeeowwwwwessssss. Yeow. Yes.' Jax tensed, then relaxed, as John Paul's strong fingers kneaded her sore muscles.

His other hand settled on her left shoulder. 'Can't have you going around all lopsided.'

'God forbid.' Jax sighed, and closed her eyes.

The room filled with the hum of the company's server as JP rubbed Jax's shoulders in silence. Keep it shut, John Paul, he thought to himself. Don't say anything stupid, don't say anything at all, but especially don't say anything like, *heard from that fella you're meant to marry and are you really going to marry this bloke and wouldn't you rather go to the pictures with me instead, maybe, sometime?*

'Yeah,' Jax sighed.

'You would?'

'What?'

'Nothing.' *Eejit.*

'Would I what?' Jax sighed again, and rolled her head around on her neck. 'Would I murder you if you stopped? Yes.'

'Right. Okay.'

Jax dropped her chin to her chest, and John Paul thought that the sight of the nape of her neck would absolutely do him in. Had he ever even seen the nape of a woman's neck? Had he ever noticed before, ever, how delicate it could be, how fragrant it could smell, how soft it was to the touch? He ran his thumbs up and down the nape of Jax's neck, stroking back and forth, up and down the softness of it, teasing her hairline, massaging the knot at the top of her shoulders, but always returning to that soft place . . . he bent a little closer and smelled the freshness of her skin, and leaned yet closer, wishing he could simply lay his lips there, as though it were expected, and welcomed, and wished for—

The clatter of heels on the stairs had Jax's head snapping up smartly against JP's nose, and the door banging open had them both leaping up and away in different directions.

Oops, thought Max; she really ought to start knocking on doors.

Jax went scarlet and immediately bent down to her handbag for no good reason. John Paul tried to soothe his stinging nose in such a way as to make it look casual, as if it were quite normal to stand in the middle of his office with tears in his eyes.

'Hey, listen, just wanted to say sorry about before, and all . . .' Trying not to grin like a mental patient, Max edged up the stairs, backwards.

'Wait up, should get back – work to – well, such as it is – um, okay, bye.' Jax pushed up the stairs past Max.

John Paul continued looking casual.

Hee hee! thought Max, as she took one last look at the holy pontiff squirming in his boots. *Here we go!*

That Saturday morning, Jacinta decided to paint her sitting room.

Well, she'd had the tins sitting around for ages, and she still loved the deep burgundy she'd got on sale at Homebase, and it wouldn't take any time at all, would it, seeing as she was up and at it, already almost done taping the ceiling and the skirting boards, and it was only 6 a.m.?

If it was an ambitious, possibly unnecessary, even a totally foolish and pointless exercise when she was expecting guests in, oh, twelve or thirteen hours, well, who was there but herself to be bothered by it? After all, she was a dab hand at every kind of DIY affair, and she'd have everything back in order by the time her company arrived.

And if she didn't, if the books weren't back on the shelves, who was to mind? And if all her little knick-knacks and objects d'art weren't set about as she liked, it was only herself who'd be missing them. Who was to notice?

And if the photographs that were usually set about the place, photographs that Maxine had certainly seen when she'd last been round two weeks ago – if those photographs were put aside somewhere, out of the way, out of sight, where they wouldn't get messed by the paint, whose business was it?

No one's but her own.

And she had her reasons. Of course she did. It was, after all, her home to do with what she liked. It was hers, and she had a *responsibility* to keep it nice, to keep its value increasing, and to make it as true a reflection of her life and intentions as she could . . .

'That's no argument, considering,' she said aloud to herself. 'Considering the fact that your *intentions* are exactly the problem.' She trotted nimbly down the step-ladder and turned up her stereo as if to silence that inner voice – the one that could separate reality from fiction.

'Right,' she murmured, stepping around all the furniture she had pushed to the centre of the room, making her way to the nest of newspapers on which she'd laid out her supplies. Prying open the lid of the first litre of paint, she felt her whole body relax.

Peace.

Quiet.

A bit of home improvement.

It couldn't be lovelier.

The sound of the Mozart quietly building throughout the house – she and her father had wired the place up like professionals – soothed her soul, and was the perfect antidote to the noise she felt had been crashing around her for the past two weeks. As the strains of the *Requiem* began to soar, Jax felt herself take her first true, deep, relaxed and contented breath in what felt like ages. As she stirred the paint and poured it into the tray, she felt her heart sing and lift along with the 'Kyrie', so much so that she was tempted to lift her own voice along with that exquisite chorus of—

'Good *God*, how *morbid*.' Angela swept into the house and slammed the door behind her.

'Mum!' Jax splashed paint all over herself.

'Is that Mozart's *Requiem*? On such a lovely morning? Darling, you're making a mess.' Angela swept her gaze around the disarray and headed for the kitchen.

'I don't suppose knocking ever entered your mind. What is it with people and not knocking? What is wrong with observing common courtesies? And what are you doing, up at the crack of dawn?' Jacinta scrubbed angrily at her ruined jeans. 'Dammit.'

Angela swept back out of the kitchen, an empty mug in her hand. 'Jacinta Vivien Bernadette Quirke!' she gasped, clutching a fist to her breast.

'Don't take that tone with me,' Jax countered. 'And don't toss my names in my face.'

Angela *knew* she'd been right to drop in like this. 'I'm sure I don't know what you mean.'

Jax threw down a paint rag and stormed up the stepladder, splashing more paint down her front. She slapped the roller into the tray and began to lash the burgundy on to the wall, where it splattered like blood. 'You hate my confirmation name, and only trot it out whenever—' Jax stopped dead.

Hmmph. Angela assumed a frosty and aloof air. 'Whenever?' She sipped casually from the mug, forgetting that she hadn't had the chance to fill it with anything.

Jax looked down at her miniature mother. 'Whenever I dare question you.' She returned to her painting, this time with the care she would normally bring to the job in hand.

'Hmmph.' Angela leaned casually on the door jamb, belying her inner unease.

'In the future, please knock before entering,' Jax began.

'Yes, love.' Angela decided not to point out that she had a set of keys.

'In fact, in the future, before you even get to the stage at which it would be necessary to knock on my door, please ring ahead to ensure that your visit is convenient.'

She sounds more like me every day. Angela beamed. *Finally.* 'Of course, pet. Wouldn't want to walk in on something I . . . shouldn't.'

She could see her daughter's blushing cheek from across the room. *Hurrah! Jacinta had a new fella!*

I knew it, I knew it, I knew it!

Raymond owed her fifty quid.

'Forgive me, chicken,' Angela drifted over to the foot of the ladder, not an easy task given the state of things, but she was nothing if not graceful. 'We haven't seen you in weeks, and you know I hate those mobile phone things, I can never remember how to use them, and I rang and rang your landline, but you're never *here*, and then I thought to ring you at the agency, but I imagine things are rather *tense* these days, and –'

Jax stroked the paint on the wall in time to her mother's singsong litany of events that, if she paid too much mind, all seemed to be her fault.

It would be best if she didn't pay it any mind at all.

'It's awfully early for DIY, isn't it?' Angela had the feeling that Jacinta wasn't listening.

'I've got company for tea,' Jax answered, inwardly resigned to the ensuing barrage of queries and comments that were sure to follow.

'Isn't that lovely! And who are your esteemed guests?' Angela perched on the edge of the mass of furniture. 'Maxine, I'm sure – she's such a feisty thing, but I must say, I'm dying of curiosity. What's her *history*, you know what I mean, her *histoire des affaires du coeur*? She went all *funny* the other day when we were hashing out your project – your exciting project! I'm sure that's what's been keeping you so busy, isn't it?' That's what Raymond reckoned, anyway, but Angela was sure that her little lamb had a man.

'And who else? For your soirée? Friends from work? Colleagues?'

'Friends and colleagues.' Jax took up the edger and slowly worked the paint up to meet the ceiling.

Hmmmm. The last time Jacinta got her back up like this, Angela realised, was when she was trying to hide Fergal from the family. Angela squinted at her daughter's body language. Did that mean that he was in touch, that they were still an item? *Or* . . . did that mean there was a new man in her life and, knowing Jacinta, she wanted to keep the news to herself, like the secretive little mouse she was? And was she withholding things because she *still* felt absurd loyalty to that *tosser* who hadn't even the grace to *take* her beautiful, loving, lovely daughter off to the ends of the earth with him?

'Please don't kick the tarp,' Jax asked serenely, 'I don't want to get paint on the sofa.'

Angela stilled the heels she hadn't even realised had been battering away.

'If I'd known, I would have brought over a few bottles of that lovely wine your father and I picked up France,' Angela reflected. 'How many, do you think? Bottles, I mean? I can always call round with them later . . .'

Oh, Mum, thought Jax, *you are desperate*. 'I've plenty from my trip last October.'

'Good lord, you've wine left over since October? Where did I go wrong?' Angela popped off the back of what she now saw was the couch, and began to sigh and pace the room.

'Something on your mind?' Jax decided to bow to the inevitable.

'You tell me nothing! *Nothing!* My only daughter—'

'Theresa wouldn't be too happy if she could hear that.'

'My only daughter in Dublin!' Angela waved her arms around, dislodging one of the lengths of silk swathed around her neck. 'Darling, I am so worried about you!'

Generally this would be Jax's cue to drop everything she was doing and start bathing her mother in attention. Digging into reserves she'd never plumbed, Jax calmly poured more paint into her tray, and started on another wall.

'I've never given you a day's worry in your life,' Jax said, lovingly stroking the gorgeous burgundy over the wall.

'*That's* exactly what I'm worried about!' Angela crawled on to the top of something else, she thought it might be the sideboard, and peered up at Jax. 'I'm terrified you'll wake up one day and realise you've been holding out for a marriage that's never going to happen, and that you're just going to explode, or implode, or run off to the States!'

'I might like to *ex*plode,' Jax mused. 'I'm sure I must do more than my share of imploding. And I've already lived in the States.' She continued her deft stroking. 'If I was going to run off anywhere, I think it'd be Greece, maybe, or—'

'Oh, fine. Laugh. Laugh at your dear, loving mother, your concerned old mum, your beloved mammy—'

'Oh, mum.' Jax sighed, but still didn't turn around.

'When I think of what poor Mrs O'Malley must go through, wondering what her daughter is getting up to –

oh, the *poor* woman, the worry that must be on her, with her daughter all those miles away ... how many miles away is Maxine's family, pet?'

Jax got down off the ladder and Angela sat up, like a trained seal about to receive its treat, and wilted as Jax merely shifted the stepladder and continued on with her work.

Jax finally took pity on her mother. 'Her family are in Florida, the father retired early, or some such. I never met them.'

'What'd you mean, you never met them?'

'We never met.'

'Never?'

'Mum.'

'But you two are best mates—'

'Mum.'

Angela sputtered a bit, for form's sake, and moved on to the next item on her current burning agenda. 'Surely you met her boyfriend!'

'What boyfriend?'

'Surely she *had* a boyfriend?'

Jax stirred the next can of paint. This was a bad idea, and she knew better, but ... 'She was married to the job, as far as I could tell. She never – we used to go out, and she'd, er, meet someone, and then maybe, um, meet them again, and that would be it, I guess. I mean, we'd go out again and she'd, em—'

'Pick someone else up. Yes, yes, I get the picture, prissy madam.' Angela tapped her fingers on her knees. 'Very interesting.'

'She's – she's – well, focused on the job, I guess, and exuberant, and friendly—'

'I'm not judging, love, I won't be casting any stones,

but I wonder why our lovely Maxine doesn't want a relationship?'

Jacinta Quirke, stop this now, she scolded herself, *before you get sucked in to a false sense of security and believe that you can idly gossip with Angela* Hello!-*and*-OK!-*magazine-rolled-into-one Quirke*.

'This project' – *On your head be it, Jacinta* – 'she's determined to expose everybody as closet adulterers. It's as if she has to force everyone into taking her point of view. She refuses to allow for anything else.'

'Which is *why* I wanted to *know* whether or not you had met her parents,' mumbled Angela.

'Well, I didn't. She'd speak about them, in passing, like. Make jokes about how they were a tough act to follow, that they were perfect in this entirely undramatic, no-nonsense, mellow, easygoing way—'

'Surely Max was switched at birth!' Angela snorted.

'Which is exactly what she'd go on to say before she changed the subject. That's as much as I've ever got out of her. She tends not to talk about anything . . .' Jax trailed off.

'Personal?' Angela prodded.

'Personal, yes, maybe. More like – I feel like I hit up against these invisible walls, and she won't explain what's there, or what's behind them, not even to me, and I'm her best friend. I think.'

'It must be frustrating, especially when you're being honest with her. About your life, and such.'

There you go, miss – you asked for it. Jax kept her arm movements smooth and steady, and her gaze fixed on the wall before her. 'What exactly are you doing up at this hour?' she asked coolly.

Angela knew when to surrender the field. She'd

certainly coaxed enough out for one session, anyway; it might be a good idea to shanghai – invite Maxine out to lunch. Sighing gustily, she replied, 'Casting, darling. Some loathsome cattle call. A *low budget* movie.' She swept up several of her scarves as Jax turned to look down at her. 'Must get there bright and early, don't want to squander the entire day, queueing.'

Jax made her way down the ladder, and knew better than to let the sympathy she felt show in her eyes. How her mother hated the anonymity of a general casting call; she tamped down the surge of anger she felt at the heartless industry that tossed aside women of a certain age. She fussed with Angela's jacket and kissed her mother on the forehead. 'From my side of the table, there's nothing like being given the chance to make the right decision early, and to send the rest of the chancers packing.'

Angela ran her hand down her daughter's face and kissed her cheek lightly. 'That's the idea, chicken,' she chirped brightly, and turned in the doorway to regard the room before she left. 'Lovely colour, but you always had taste in spades. Generally.' She arched a brow at the empty walls. 'Nice to see all those photos put away. They really do bring down the tone, don't they, love?'

John Paul woke up at around the same time Jax was painting away and sat on the edge of his bed. It was the crack of dawn, but he reckoned that now would be a good time to figure out what he was going to wear.

Not that it was that complicated; he'd only recently realised that baggy jeans and ancient T-shirts weren't the way into, er, a woman's heart, and so had few threads that really merited contemplation. Should he iron his jeans?

Was that a stupid thing to do? He was sure Max would pass some sort of comment if it transpired that it *was* a stupid thing to do, and he could take it, particularly as Jax always seemed to jump to his defence whenever Max's teasing got too fierce.

He leapt up from the bed and headed for the kitchen. He couldn't seem to stop his thoughts relentlessly turning to Jacinta Quirke, and could only hope that short bursts of movement would delay them.

He shared accommodation with two IFSC lads in Smithfield – two lads who, luckily, worked like eejits; he often had the gaff to himself. The three-bedroom penthouse apartment – *Penthouse, me arse*, John Paul thought; it was only at the top of the building – looked out west, over what had been the large main square, and was now still the square, but with the addition of a massive apartment complex which scuppered their sunsets. JP once again considered moving, now that he had – or *had* had – gainful, steady employment. Bugger. He yawned, and did a few of the stretches he did on a good day, the kind that got him loose for his martial arts practice. Gently kicking his legs out, one after the other, he thought about the project they had going. He, too, was getting impatient, getting ready to get stuck in to something with more shape and focus, and he looked forward to dinner at Jax's to start hashing out the day-to-day practicalities of—

'Cop on to yerself, man,' he muttered as he slopped some instant coffee into a mug.

Taking his coffee out on to the terrace, he leaned against the railing and looked south to the river. Work was one thing, but he had a different gig on in his mind.

The best thing he could do would be to scope out Jax's place for clues. Mementos, what kind of art she had, especially photographs ... JP took another restorative gulp of caffeine and nodded to himself. He'd make the best of this invitation, and hope it wasn't his last.

The conveyor belt lay silent, and in some strange sort of reflection, Fergal Delaney exuded a similar cool, calm collectedness, helped along by his impassive face. It was impassive, as the faces of those waiting in an airport to retrieve their luggage often are, but there was an added repose to his features above and beyond the circumstance. Mrs Delaney claimed it was a combination of good genes and excellent mothering, resulting in a confident handsomeness that imbued his aura with an unflappability in the face of the vagaries of life.

Mrs Quirke claimed it was an utter lack of brains and personality, the combination of which resulted in an aura that spoke less to sophisticated inscrutability than to frontal lobotomy.

In any event, Fergal Delaney *looked* cool, calm and collected, but inside – well, inside he was as agitated as he ever got, which wasn't much, but it was significant that he was even aware there was call for agitation.

In his relatively privileged and pampered life, anxiety was something he'd had little experience of. An only child, an only son, his world-view was coloured by indulgence, its soundtrack comprised of an endless murmur of approval. Not especially athletic, and truth be told, not especially *bright* when it came to book learning, he had an instinct for security, having known nothing but security his entire life.

It was an instinct that proved itself useful in his choice of career, in the delicate handling of bonds, in the capriciousness of the stock market – what better person to judge the rise and potential fall of a commodity, of an investment, than one who'd never doubted himself for a moment throughout the course of his existence.

It was a gift, and such was Fergal Delaney's utter lack of awareness that he didn't even know he had it.

It was good to be back, he thought. He tugged at the knot of his tie and fiddled with a cufflink. Mother was so pleased, Father gruffly delighted. And that penthouse he'd bought in Dundrum in 1998 was yet another of his prescient personal investments – what with the LUAS and all.

He unbuttoned his jacket then buttoned it again. Starting up the Dublin branch of the Saudi firm he'd been working for, for the past five years, was assuredly the next correct step in a flawless direction, and he looked forward to reacquainting himself with extended family and neighbours and friends and . . .

He cleared his throat and thrust a hand in his trouser pocket. He removed the hand, flexed his fingers, and returned the hand to the pocket.

And Jacinta. Of course. He'd ring her soon, wouldn't he? Let her fix a time and place to meet – surely that was chivalrous, wasn't it? Leave it up to her, when she wanted to see him. And should she choose not to see him, well . . .

Not that Jacinta would ever choose not to see him. Of course not. She was a stalwart, was Jacinta. Steadfast. Resolute. Constant.

And that was exactly what Fergal Delaney was afraid of.

'**D**id you paint in here, or something?' Max sniffed around the sitting room and then went and tossed her coat on to Jax's bed.

The colour's only gone from one end of the spectrum to the other, Jax groused to herself as she filled another ice tray and slid it into the tiny freezer of her tiny fridge.

'Those look gorgeous!' Max grabbed up a squat tumbler of clear liquid and crushed mint. 'What are these things called? Capoerieas?'

Jax laughed. 'Remember when we were in that snooty bar in the Hamptons?'

They both howled, and Jax marvelled at the healing qualities of a good, sentimental hoot. Max sat down at Jax's kitchen table – a table, she noted, that had as lovely a vibe as did the one in Jax's family house – and crossed legs that seemed impossibly long in her new moleskin trousers. 'Who was it, Thingie from the house next door, the one who kept asking you about your hometown – London.'

'Where she got off, cringing every time we opened our mouths, and she without a notion of geography.'

'You've got a gift for a grudge, Jacinta Quirke! Remind me not to get on your bad side.'

Jax mixed another pitcher of – now, what were they

called? Max had her completely mixed up. 'She had the nerve, looking down on us, when she didn't even have a basic grasp of races outside her own pampered, Upper East Side crowd. It was the least we could do, torturing her with our apparent gaucheness—'

'Oh, forget about her. What are these things *called*?'

The door knocker went. 'Saved by the brass! I'll get it.' Max drained her glass, passed it to Jax, and headed for the door.

Wiping her hands on a tea towel, Jax kept her breathing steady, and only briefly entertained the notion of changing outfits. Max looked her usual impeccable self, and for the first time, perhaps ever, Jax was lamenting her wardrobe's total lack of flippy tops and sexy bottoms. She fussed a bit with her button-down shirt, and decided that tucking it in her jeans might make enough of a statement.

Max pulled open the door, and leaned a hip against the jamb. 'Howaya, lads,' she purred. 'And don't you look likely.'

'That's us, all right,' one of the lads replied, grinning. 'And hoping the lasses are just so, as well.'

Max smirked, and focused on JP. 'New shirt?' she asked, tilting her head to the side.

John Paul stuffed his hands self-consciously into his new khakis. Was he a khaki man? He wasn't sure, but they were comfortable enough. His subtly patterned shirt was kind of silky, but not in a girly way, and he thought it looked okay tucked in his trousers the belt was new, what was the point of covering it up, like?

'Uh, yeah. New shirt. This is Lorcan. Lorcan, Maxine.' He took his hands out of his pockets, then put them back in again.

'Maxine, have you stranded my dinner party on the

doorstep?' Jax came out with a tray of drinks, and smiled at the assembly in the doorway.

'Howaya, Jax,' John Paul called over the threshold.

'Well, come in,' Jax chided, smiling.

Now that was a picture, John Paul thought. A smiling Jacinta welcoming him into her home, her *warm* home, not that it was roasting or anything, she had a few briquettes on the fire, sure, but there was something about it, maybe it was the colour of the walls, and the deepness of the rug, but walking into her home was, he imagined, like walking into her arms.

'I'm Lorcan.' His friend buzzed by him and raised Jax's hand to his lips.

Wanker! thought John Paul.

'Hmmph, I didn't get such a chivalrous greeting,' Max grumbled, eyeing Lorcan brightly.

'I'll have to make up for it at our parting,' Lorcan drawled, and Max blinked at him, once, slowly, and then ignored him.

'Jax made these lovely Brazilian things, only we can't remember what they're called.' Max handed Lorcan a glass, still not looking at him, but feeling very, very aware of his gaze.

'They're called – oh, no, that's the exercise caper,' John Paul offered.

'We said the same thing,' Jax laughed, and gestured everyone into seats.

There was a beat of awkward, pre-dinner-party silence, made worse by the fact that there was a stranger in the mix. Both Jax and Max, in that slight but measurable beat of discomfited hush, appraised Lorcan in superficial but fairly accurate readings.

Bit smooth, thought Jax.

Ooh, Mr Silky, eh? thought Max.

Max is going to flirt like an eejit with this guy, Jax sighed.

Jax is going to totally hate his guts. Max giggled into her drink.

'Been working on those already?' Lorcan asked, eyeing Max.

'Might be some of the hangover from last night,' Max sighed. 'It was epic.'

As Max regaled Lorcan with last night's doings – which only served to underscore Jax's firm conviction that Max was going to play him mercilessly – Jax got up to fiddle with the stereo, and started sorting through her CDs.

'Need a hand?' JP left Lorcan to do his worst – and he'd seen his worst, and it was pretty bad – and shifted over to the musical part of the room.

'I should have had this sorted out beforehand, but the day just got away from me,' Jax explained. 'I did the walls this morning—'

'These walls? This morning?' John Paul nodded in approval. 'Must get you over to my place.'

'Dead smooth, Johnny,' Lorcan called. 'You're a real operator.'

'Takes one to know one.' Max smirked, and they continued on as Lorcan shared *his* Friday night escapades.

'He's a bit of a prat,' John Paul began, 'but he knows his stuff.'

'Well, we're not marrying him,' Jax said, and they both blushed.

She fumbled through the jazz section of her CD collection and pulled out some Ernesto Badim. 'Is this too obvious? He being Brazilian and all?'

'Not at all, he's grand. I saw him in Vicar Street two years ago—'

'I was at that gig—'

'Unbelievable show—'

'Amazing vibe in the place—'

And the party got off to its proper start.

Around the dinner table, the Brazilian theme came to its delectable apotheosis. Following on from a moqueta – a spicy fish stew – and several more rounds of *caipirinhas* – John Paul extracted the word from his memory banks, to a rousing roar of approbation – Jax trumped herself with a sticky toffee pudding à la Rio de Janeiro.

Max licked her spoon, somewhat more theatrically than the circumstance warranted, simply because Lorcan was tragically flirtatious. 'You are a domestic goddess, Jacinta Quirke,' she sighed.

A goddess all round, thought John Paul, gratefully accepting thirds.

'I'm delighted you liked it. It's the first time out for those recipes,' Jax replied modestly.

Lorcan made a business of gagging, and pretending to choke, which was greeted with disdain from Max and disgust from John Paul.

Right, thought Lorcan. *Not a sense of humour between them.*

'Right,' he said. 'Just joking, Jax. Fucking brilliant meal. So, like, I understand we've got a production to get off the ground.'

Oh, don't even think about running this *show*, Max thought as she and Jax rose from the table in unison. 'We have some questions for you, Lorcan. But you've got another little job to do first.' She tossed him a tea towel, and started lifting plates. 'I'll wash.'

Jax hesitated.

'Don't even think about it, Jax,' Max said. 'It's the least we can do. The Holy Father'll keep you entertained until we're done here. Sure, he can go fetch some more briquettes for the fire.'

'But does anyone want tea? Or coffee?' Jax fretted, but let Max spin her round and propel her into her sitting room.

'I'll set him straight,' Max hissed, and stepped back to let JP in with the fuel bucket.

'Where'd you get the real turf?' John Paul asked, diverting Jax from the scene of tragedy she imagined befalling her Wedgwood place settings.

'My gran's out in Mayo and my father brings it back with him after the yearly social call.'

'Yearly? Huh.' JP tossed some turf into the grate.

'Huh?' Jax prompted, stopping herself from grabbing up the fire tongs herself.

'I don't know, you strike me as someone who's into her family. In a good way.' He settled back, crosslegged, in front of the hearth, tongs in hand until the fire got going again.

'I am, yeah, but my mother and my father's mother hate each other like poison, so. And it's been determined that I take after my mother's side, which is not at all true, so it's not often that I go out there. My father's the only one who's allowed to stay overnight, anyway.' Jax laughed. 'She's an auld battleaxe, so she is.'

'I've got an auntie who's never forgiven my father for marrying a southsider,' John Paul said, and they both laughed.

'I haven't offered you any – did you want tea? Or another drink? I could—'

'I'm grand, Jax.' He looked around at the walls. 'Some

day you've had, painting walls, making Brazilian pudding, much less fish stew.'

'I like to be home. It's not very –' *Sexy*, she thought – 'em, cool, I guess.'

It was so sexy he wanted to writhe around on the floor with it. 'It's lovely.'

The sound of the turf taking flame filled the silence, only to be topped by a wave of hearty laughter rolling out of the kitchen.

Jax and JP exchanged dubious glances.

'She likes to, you know, a guy like him –'

John Paul nodded. 'Child's play, I know. She's only messing, but so is he. He's just, well, you saw – but he has access to production stuff, stuff we need, that I don't.'

Jax leaned back and sighed. 'This is getting to be important. I've been looking in the appointments section in the *Times*, and on the web, and there's nothing out there – nothing *I* want, anyway, and it's just – this could be really good, if we pull it off. If we get this right—'

As he shifted himself up, Jax noted the lovely ripple in his forearms as he did so, forearms that were nicely . . . formed, and usually hidden underneath those long-sleeved T-shirts he habitually wore, and wasn't that a new shirt he had on?

'What? Sorry.' Jax blushed, and got up to poke at the fire.

'You will get it right, the idea is sound, we just need—'

'We need to get *going!*' Max finished, hefting a tray loaded with martini glasses.

She set it down on the coffee table and brandished the cocktail shaker. 'No more limey stuff, Jax, and apparently Lorcan knows how to make a proper martini.'

He took the shaker from her, and started to shake it.

'It's all in the wrist,' he drawled. 'I've had loads of practice.'

'I wouldn't brag about that if I were you,' Max said, and took her favourite comfy chair, right next to the fire.

'So.' She accepted her glass graciously, and exchanged looks with Jax. 'JP and Jacinta are the keepers of all things technical, but I'd like to talk a bit about an idea I had.' She took a testing sip, raised her eyebrows in approval. 'It has to do with my handbag. Those women were talking freely, revealing themselves in ways that they wouldn't if they knew they were being recorded. So . . .'

'A wire,' John Paul said.

'Precisely.'

Jax closed her eyes. 'That's got to be illegal!'

'There have got to be circumstances under which we can fudge it,' Max insisted.

'What about the *When Harry Met Sally* idea?' Jax insisted in turn.

'Girls, I'm going to need more to go on than this,' Lorcan interjected, and found himself the target of two extremely vicious glares.

'Don't call us girls,' Max suggested coolly.

'I think what you both want is the same thing,' John Paul said into the breach. 'The whole point of the *When Harry Met Sally* idea is that it's kind of a blind—'

'So we execute that idea,' said Jax.

'Get them to talk about themselves, tell their courtship story,' said JP.

'Lead them into dangerous waters,' crowed Max.

'And then maybe—' said JP.

'Leave them alone—' said Jax.

'And they're under surveillance—' sang Max.

'Yeah,' said John Paul.

'Okay. Okay.' Jax worried her lip, but nodded.

'That's it. That's good.' Max sat back satisfied.

'Um. What?' asked Lorcan.

Jax sat forward, staring into the fire. Max grinned around her martini – she loved it when Jax got swept into the zone. 'We screen maybe three to five couples. We'll decide based on a preliminary session. We need a professional set-up, something almost clinical – not a conference room. Max, don't even bother, we have to keep this part offsite, out of ACJ.

'We need staff, other people around so that we lead them through activity into isolation, just the two of them. We need a room, and we need a set-up, camera and lights, but we also need the smallest cameras imaginable so that once we shut down the set-up, they think they're alone.

'What they do alone, how they really interact, that's what we want. That's reality. They don't know they're *on* – that's real reality.'

She pinned Lorcan with a look. 'And you need to tell us how to do that.'

Lorcan kicked back, and delicately tilted his martini glass around in circles. *Sounds like some dumb chick idea*, he thought, *but it might not be a total waste of time*. He glanced slumberously at Max.

He cleared his throat at Jax's raised eyebrow. 'Basically, you need a multiplexer to handle a batch of cameras – I can handle four minimum, that's minimum – and then you need a stand-alone DVR to record the input, directly to an eighty-gig hard drive, via BNC outputs or S-video adaptors. We could hook up to the SCART in a pinch, I reckon, but—'

'Ugh, I told you, Jax is the one that gets off on that kind of information.' Max cringed.

'What do you get off on?' murmured Lorcan.

'Oh, tell me you didn't just say that,' Max sneered, but Jax knew that sneer, it was the kind of sneer that actually communicated anything but sneeriness.

'Right.' Jax set her glass down with authority. 'What do we need, Lorcan?'

'I've got access to cameras as small as those buttons on your shirt,' Lorcan replied, then drained his drink. 'I've got wireless audio bugs that are smaller even than that.'

'What's their range?' asked Jax.

'Fifteen hundred feet.'

'Can we use more than one?'

'Yeah, as long as they're spaced at least ten feet apart.'

'Broadcast quality on both image and audio?'

'Yeah, yeah.'

'You don't sound too sure,' Jax cut in.

Jesus. Lorcan glared at John Paul. 'I'm sure, I'm sure.'

'We're serious about this, Lorcan,' said Jax. 'We don't have much time.'

'Yeah, fine, whatever. I can sort it.'

Jax sat back. She exchanged a look with a gleeful Max and nodded. 'We need to do a dry run. Are you willing to set something up for us, Lorcan?'

He shrugged. *As long as there were fringe benefits*, he thought. 'I'm in. We can do a dry run, maybe wire a house or something—'

'And watch from a van? *Pleeease?*' Max leaned forward, and sadly discovered that the cocktail shaker was empty.

'And if we're happy with that, are you in for the rest?' Jax demanded. 'We'll need to do an open call.'

'Open call? Since when?' *She's on fire!* thought Max, delighted.

'Tell you later. I'd like to set something up, a contract,

keep it above board,' Jax said briskly, and Lorcan squirmed. 'Let's get an idea of how much you think we'll need –'

Max took pity on the paling Lorcan. 'But first – another round of those gorgeous drinks. Your Holiness, how about something bluesy on the auld hi-fi? Lorcan, let's go shake some more martinis.'

The dulcet tones of Etta James spread throughout the house. Jax muttered over some scraps of paper she'd dug out of the sideboard drawer, in between scribbling down rapid notes and chewing on her pencil. John Paul sat back and watched.

He cast his eye around the room again. No photographs, incriminating or otherwise. No indication that this wasn't a woman in her own home – no evidence of a male, anywhere. He'd quietly gone through the cupboard in the loo, and peeked into the medicine cabinet – nothing. He'd only had the brass to stick his head into one of the bedrooms, and it had turned out to be Jax's studio space, filled with DIY bits and pieces, and an easel that held a large canvas of an oil painting in progress – a good one, at that. Nothing about the place spoke to him of anyone but Jacinta . . .

'Funny,' he said.

'Hmmm?' Jax scowled at her sketch for their prospective location.

'I took you for someone, I don't know, who had things on their walls.'

'Things?' No, they were going to need a reception space as well, and Jax began briskly erasing what she'd drawn.

'Paintings. Artwork. Pictures, like.' JP squirmed a bit when she turned to look at him. *Yeah, not too obvious, mate.*

She smiled, and he relaxed. 'I'm trying to figure out why you would reckon that,' she said lightly, wincing inside. *Sure, Jacinta, who was to notice that your walls and bookshelves were bare?*

John Paul ducked his head, embarrassed. 'You've got art, real art, in your office in work. And pictures of your family. I just reckoned that if that was the way you were in a temporary space, that's how you'd be . . . at home.'

'I do have . . . things,' she conceded. 'It's just that with the new paint, I don't know, I didn't have a chance, and I'm thinking of making a . . . change.'

Change? Change! 'Cool,' said JP. 'Cool,' he added.

Eejit.

Jacinta Vivien Bernadette Quirke, she thought, *what are you saying?*

'Where're our drinks?' Jax threw down her pencil and shoved off the couch, her momentum thrusting her through the kitchen door, momentum that would have tossed her into Lorcan's arms – if they hadn't been full of Max.

11

It seemed only right that the clutter of the Quirke kitchen should come in handy for something. Jax took a deep breath and ran cable behind the stack of newspapers that had been accumulating since 1989. Not entirely certain that she wanted her parents to come under the unblinking gaze of the lipstick cameras Lorcan had produced from his kit, and not entirely certain how she had agreed to use her family home as a location for their dry run, she was, however, sure that she didn't want them to set up in ACJ, which really was the only other option.

What were they going to do, spy on themselves?

Delicately wiggling a minuscule blob of Blu-Tack between the last bit of cord and the skirting board, Jacinta plugged male cable into female splitter, fitted the heat-resistant black box around the whole works, then shifted the tottering piles of paper as close to the protective casing as she felt safely possible.

She watched John Paul make a series of elaborate hand signals into the camera he'd just tucked over the top of the refrigerator, and then adjust it based on a reciprocal series of Morse code-like blinks from the remote in his hand.

'I've got the audio bugs wired up,' Jax said, and heard

Lorcan's voice emit out of JP's hand. 'This is base acknowledging transmission, over,' hissed Lorcan.

She and John Paul rolled their eyes – and then remembered the cameras.

Smiling, Jax washed her hands under the kitchen taps, and looked out at her father's garden. A pity that Saturday night had ended so ... clumsily. After she had made a Lorcan sandwich with Max – *Without as much tongue on my own part*, Jax thought, and shuddered – the two of them had peeled themselves away from each other and bouncily suggested they go off to a club.

Which Jax automatically shot down, to Lorcan's obvious relief, and she thought, she *thought*, John Paul's dismay. She felt a little shiver, the kind of shiver she hadn't felt in ages, the shiver of, well, of thinking that she was well thought of in certain quarters. The kind of shiver that meant, well, that she was being, em, noticed by someone else, a male someone else, and—

For fuck's sake, she thought, *she couldn't even say what she meant to herself.*

'Ready to rock and roll?' Max asked. She bopped into the kitchen with a clipboard in one hand and another remote in the other, which was currently whispering suggestively into her palm.

Jax dried her hands on a tea towel. 'Nearly there. I'll just nip out to the van and see if we've got all the angles covered.'

'This is base, over. Angles covered from perspective of base, over.'

She couldn't bear to make eye contact with Max. 'Hold your horses, Lorcan, I'll be out to you in two ticks. Over.'

Max edged out of Jax's way, and opened her mouth to make some crack to JP – and remembered the audio bugs.

Okee-dokee, she thought to herself. She knew that Jax was going to hate Lorcan's guts, she just hadn't known it was going to be instantaneous. She did a slow three-sixty from the centre of the kitchen, and nodded, satisfied. Couldn't see a thing, not a lens, not a wire.

She stifled a yawn; she'd not entirely caught up from the weekend's high jinks. If she was being honest, she was a bit put out by Jax's holier-than-thou attitude – not even a shared giggle over the silliness of it all. *I mean, seriously!* thought Max. *Just a wee snog and a boogie. And another, bigger snog, and then the inevitable tussle over the brush-off* . . . She eyed the most recent family picture tucked on the Quirkes' kitchen dresser, the one from Raymond and Angela's fortieth wedding anniversary. Forty years! Max sighed, felt – unusually – sorry for herself, and resisted the urge to turn the image to the wall.

'Okay, gang, how are we doing?' She clapped her hands as if to chase her momentary blues away.

John Paul folded up the stepladder and wedged it back between the Aga and the wall. 'Seems sound to me, just waiting on Jax.'

'JP.' JP unconsciously stroked his remote as Jax's voice sang out of his palm. 'The camera over by the wall behind the table—'

'This is base,' hissed Lorcan's voice self-importantly, 'and the eyes under discussion are in quadrant two, sector A. Over.'

'Yes, and it's also the one near to the table,' Jax said impatiently. 'Just point that a little bit more to the left, please. Cheers.'

'Over,' said Lorcan pointedly, and Max wished they had a camera surveilling the van.

John Paul shifted the camera gently, the back of his

neck itching at the thought of being seen and heard from a distance. The remote squawked Lorcan's approval, and JP hesitated as he took another, less professional look around the kitchen.

He could see Jacinta growing up here, having meals at the big table, possibly doing her schoolwork, her hair in plaits, little curls escaping around her face as she bent over her books. He could see where she'd got her talent for hominess, and wished he could take a quick nosey around the rest of the place, a nosey that might turn up more than the one he'd taken on Saturday.

That hadn't really gone according to plan. Not that he wanted to go out to Renard's or wherever with Lorcan and Max, not when they were obviously hell bent on shifting like mad, but . . . he supposed he could have stayed on afterwards, taken a taxi or something, but the whole thing had gone south so quickly, he'd thought it best to make tracks.

Should he have stayed? He just didn't know what to do, where he stood – if he stood anywhere – but surely, surely Jax had to know that he was keen on her, and he really ought to say something, oughtn't he? He'd never been this timid before in his life, and surely *that* had to mean something.

Max's hand waved in his face. She waggled her eyebrows, shook her hips, and generally took the piss out of the hand signals he and Lorcan had worked up. 'Let's go, mate,' she said. 'T-minus fifteen and counting. Over.' She grinned and led the way out the front door.

And paused when Jax, waiting on the path, used some hand signals of her own. 'John Paul, we'll meet you in the van,' she said, and grabbed Max by the elbow.

'What's up?' asked Max – as if she didn't know.

They wandered over to the plane tree that stood at the front of the lawn. Jax blew out a breath. 'It's weird in there, all that gear in my family home – I didn't want to – I don't even want to be seen from the van—'

'If it's not okay, we'll get that stuff out of there. Look.' Max scuffed a few stones with her toe. 'I know that I can get . . . enthusiastic. Um, it's kind of my thing, you know, the thing that ends up pissing people off, and –' Where was this going? Max cleared her throat, suddenly a bit choked.

'No, I know – I mean, that's part of your charm, isn't it. And the thing is . . . I really want this to work.' Jax did some foot shifting of her own. 'And, um, the thing is, well, the thing with Lorcan –'

Max squared her shoulders. 'Trust me. There is no thing with Lorcan. It's just a bit of craic. You know?' *Maybe she wouldn't know*, she thought, and then pulled herself up for the nastiness of the thought.

'I don't want him around for much longer,' said Jax, surprising herself and Max with the forcefulness of her tone. She blew out another breath. 'What if you start dating him—'

'I won't.' Max looked down the street to the van, then further off, into the distance. 'I'm not going to date him.'

'Okay.' *Not terribly convincing*, Jax thought. 'I've got a pretty good idea now of how this all works, and how we can patch it together with the gear at ACJ.'

'Fab. So . . . are we sorted?' Max shifted restlessly, and started to edge around the tree and towards the road, when they heard a frantic honking.

'What the fuck?' Max squinted at the van. 'That's not going to contribute to our low profile—'

'It's Da!' Jax hissed, and pulled Maxine behind the tree.

Luckily, Raymond was involved in walking and reading the *Irish Times* simultaneously, and failed to notice his daughter and her friend crouching behind the plane tree. He hummed to himself as well, and jogged up the steps into the house.

Jax and Max beat it towards the van, and all but fell into it as JP threw open the sliding door. 'That was close,' Max crowed, her heart beating like mad.

'How did you know to warn us?' Jax asked Lorcan, suspicious.

'It was Johnny,' Lorcan said dismissively, madly adjusting dials and knobs.

JP shrugged. 'Photographs,' he said, and Max thumped him on the back. 'Nice one,' she said, and they all gathered around the monitors.

'I don't know what he's doing here. I've never known him to take lunch at home,' Jax said, watching her father stand stock still in the middle of kitchen, apparently engrossed in an article.

They all sat in silence, and watched Raymond read in silence.

He turned the page, and they all leaned forward.

Then sat back again as Ray continued to read, in silence.

Ray's head drew back a fraction, and he scowled at the page.

They all leaned forward again, barely daring to breathe.

His face regained its previous inscrutability, and he continued to read.

'Oh my God, this is so boring.' Max started squirming.

'Wait –' said JP, and they all leaned forward.

'Well, well, look who's here,' said Angela, as she

swanned in, her voice coming into the van loud and clear, if somewhat tinnily.

'Here we go,' Max said, grinning, and Jax felt a wave of discomfort sweep over her. She didn't know what she'd expected – maybe Angela at home, alone, practising monologues, maybe she reckoned that they'd simply set things up, check out the feed, and break it all down . . . she hadn't expected to be observing her parents, watching them exchange a little peck of a kiss, live, in black and white *and* colour on the monitors, in a panel van.

'Ah, well, after all those years, can't expect much more than that, eh?' Lorcan snorted after the dry little smooch.

'Right, we've seen enough, we know it works, let's shut it down.' Jax tried for authoritative, but even to her own ears she sounded breathless and feeble.

'We kind of can't, Jax,' said John Paul, equally worried. 'If we try to shut down by remote, the equipment will start making beeping noises, and suchlike. They'll know.'

'Then we'll just turn the monitors off, and – and I'll – I'll drop in, like I was passing, and—'

'What's that white van?' Raymond folded up his newspaper and leaned against the sink.

'What white van, love?' Angela finished putting away the random goodies she'd picked up in Donnybrook Fayre, and aimlessly wandered around the table.

'There's a white van parked down near the Murray's place.' Raymond took off his jacket and draped it neatly over a chair.

'Hmmm. Maybe it's spies,' Angela replied, and Jax yelped helplessly.

'Oh, not that one again, darling,' Raymond sighed, loosening his tie.

Angela stretched seductively, and Max gaped, her

hands over her mouth. 'It's been ages, Raymond,' she breathed, as she slowly unbuttoned her tight little cardigan.

'Oh, well,' Raymond sighed, 'I suppose it has been a while. I really was hoping for the one where I'm the burglar.'

'You shouldn't have got here before me, then,' Angela retorted pertly, and tugged at his belt.

'Oh my God, oh my God, oh my God,' Jacinta gasped, and Max put a comforting arm around her shoulder.

But they didn't stop watching.

'How does this go again – no, no, I'm supposed to do that, leave it, Angela, for goodness' sake –'

'Goodness has nothing to do with it. I saw you spying on me the other night. I saw you looking at me while I was in the bath. Looking at me through your long telescope –'

'You'll never prove it, doll,' Ray snarled in an incredibly convincing fashion, much to Max's horrified surprise, 'never in a million years.'

'Oh?' Angela laughed, low, and John Paul imagined her daughter in her place, and himself in her father's, and then decided that was too weird, and then wished they could open a window or something in the van. 'Why don't I give you a little reminder about what you've been worshipping from afar –'

And she whipped off her top.

'Oh my God,' Jax bleated, covering her eyes.

'Oh, yes,' Raymond breathed, 'oh yes, I remember . . .' And, grabbing her by the hips, he lifted her on to the kitchen table and the kiss they exchanged was far from a peck.

'Oh, yes,' Angela gasped.

'No,' Jax squeaked.

'Yes, yes,' murmured Raymond.

'No, NO!' shouted Jax, and after much confused fumbling, which Lorcan did his best to circumvent, the screens went black.

Thunderstruck and silent, Max, Jax and JP slipped into the foyer of ACJ:Dublin, with John Paul hoofing it down the stairs to his office without so much as a goodbye, which was just fine with Jax, who was blushing so hard that she was sweating.

Max stroked her friend's back. 'No wonder they're still together,' she said, lamely trying to keep things light.

'He'd better not have a back-up of that disc,' Jax hissed. 'He'd better not be lying.'

'I'll snoop around the van when we go back, to, uh, get the stuff,' Max replied. Could she ever eat at that table again?

'I've betrayed them,' Jax moaned, stalled at the first landing on the way up the stairs. 'I've betrayed their trust, and their privacy.'

'They'll never know!' Max threw up her hands. Jax had been mumbling guiltily the entire way back to work.

'I'll know!' Jax shouted, and there was a hush that preceded everyone jumping up in their cubicles to see what was going on. Max strolled over to divert their attention.

Rushing up the stairs didn't help Jax's already scarlet complexion, but she had to get out of the hall, had to get away from prying eyes, and had to get behind the door of her office.

I can't believe I almost watched my parents have sex on the kitchen table, she whimpered to herself.

They needn't know, whispered a cunning little voice

that sounded an awful lot like Maxine.

She charged into her office, saw that her chair was missing and, presuming it to be in Max's cubicle, charged out again and into Max's, breathlessly rushing around to wheel her chair out again, when Max's phone rang. Automatically, she lifted the receiver.

'Maxine O'Malley's office,' she wheezed.

'Can I speak with Maxine, please?' asked a heavily accented American voice politely. *New York*, thought Jax. *Italian?*

'She's away from her desk at the minute. Who may I say is calling?'

'Michael LaMotta.'

'Right, so, let me get a – right. And you're with . . . ?'

'I'm her husband.'

12

Panicking, Jax simultaneously slammed down the phone and crunched up the Post-it note she'd written on.

Max swept in, as if on cue. 'Who was that?' she asked, kicking an empty shoebox out of the way.

'Wrong number.' And without another word, Jax left the room and, uncharacteristically, slammed the door.

She hadn't her coat, much less a cardigan, but she wasn't noticing the cool breeze coming down from the north as she blindly hurried down the street.

Husband? Max's husband?? Max had a *husband*?!?!? She began a circuit around Fitzwilliam Square, head down, arms wrapped around her ribs.

Husband?

'How could she, how could she?' Jax muttered. How could Max keep such a secret? Why should she? And what did this say about their friendship – it *was* a friendship, wasn't it? It wasn't just business, was it?

Were Max and *Michael* together or not? Certainly not, thought Jax, remembering Max and Lorcan crawling up and down each other like vines. Why did Michael LaMotta have Maxine's work number, then?

Were they separated? Were they divorced? Was he abusive? Was he lying? Was this all a mistake?

Jax shivered and headed back to ACJ. What was going on? And why, she thought bleakly, hadn't Max thought enough of her to tell her?

With the major brainstorming out of the way, and the open call all set up at the Gatehouse Pub for them to audition couples for their programme, it was just a matter of a session or two of location scouting, Maxine thought.

As far as the Barge went, it was one of Dublin's premier meat markets, and if they didn't come across at least fifty guys and gals intent on playing away, she'd eat her Marc Jacobs handbag. And if it wasn't actually a proper open call – one that they had advertised in the trade papers, for instance, or had called agents about – it was close enough. They'd be there with a camera, right? There'd be loads of people walking through the doors, correct? If the camera just so happened to entice the loads of people to them, hey, that was essentially an open call . . .

As far as the set was concerned . . . could it be a simple matter of ringing around friends to see if they knew of anything going, an office in between residents, a stately home momentarily unoccupied, maybe even a *pro bono* suite in the Four Seasons? They all sounded feasible to Max who, spinning around in her desk chair, resisted rolling over to press her ear up against her and Jax's dividing wall.

It wasn't like she couldn't hear how quiet it was in there – in fact, the silence was deafening. Sure, that thing with her folks was totally not cool even by Max's desperately curious standards, but it wasn't *still* bugging Jax after, what, two days . . . three days . . . was it?

Maybe Jax was concentrating on her share of the work. Jax was ensuring that no one (as in Niamh Bourke) started smelling rats or nixers. Jax was helping them keep the profile so low that it was on the Asian subcontinent . . . Jax wasn't *mad* at her or anything, was she?

Max jumped up and paced around the limited perimeter and reviewed the sequence of events: rigged the Quirkes' place – talked in the front garden – assurances re. Lorcan and not dating him in a million years – Ray showed up – van – watched Ray and Ange get it on (Max cringed and covered her eyes instinctively; even still, it had the power to send a shudder of embarrassed fascination through her) – er . . . got back to the office, had a little shouty thing on the stairs, no big deal – then back up here and . . . Jax had just crashed down the phone, then slammed out of the cubicle . . . and things had been weird ever since.

Maybe it was time to have that sneaky little lunch with Angela . . . She could do with a little insider information . . .

Max picked up a couple of magazines that had flopped off an overcrowded shelf and stood, absently paging through them. And every time she'd asked Jax what was going on, she'd said, 'Oh, nothing, what are you on about?' but in a snippy tone she'd never heard before. Impatient. And kind of . . . pissed off?

Max shoved the mags back on the shelf, and as she moved to fiddle with her micro-stereo, they slid noiselessly to the floor again. She knew that Jax was kind of moody – that was *her* defining fatal flaw. Once, when they were working in New York, Jax had gone silent for three and a half weeks, over some stupid miscommunication about whose idea was the source for their latest ad campaign. *Jesus*, Max thought, *that was epic*. 'Oh, yeah,' she said aloud, to keep herself company. 'World-class sulker, Jacinta Vivien Bernadette Quirke.' Oh, man, and the time she teased her about that Vivien business. That was only five working days, but still.

At least she knew what she was dealing with . . . and she started spinning again, wondering why Jax hadn't come knocking at her door—

Max leapt up at the thumping that threatened to knock her door off its hinges, and triumphantly swept it open.

She found herself face to face with Nasty Niamh.

'On your own, are you? Unusual,' Niamh sniffed. 'And where's your partner in crime?' *Oh, yes, the famous team of Max and Jax were clearly on the outs, weren't they?* she thought.

Max grabbed up her handbag and shoved past Niamh. 'Mind your own business,' she snapped, so flustered that she couldn't even snap back with her usual flair. She stormed down the stairs, not realising the rashness of her exit.

Niamh's eyes lit up with glee. With the kind of sigh that really ought to have been inspired by oral sex, Niamh slid into Max's office and set about the kind of fast, thorough, and subtle snooping that was her speciality.

She ignored the tantalising piles of papers and the myriad bags – gym, hand, shopping – and went straight to the one place she'd had her eye on for months: Maxine's filing cabinet.

Just the kind of place Maxine O'Malley would try to conceal something, as no one would ever assume that she'd keep anything in it but several pairs of shoes. Sure enough, behind last season's slingbacks and countless packets of spare tights, there hung, sadly, a few file folders. *Decoys*, thought Niamh. Delicately manoeuvring her thumbnail into the very last folder, she felt a surge of triumph. There was indeed something in it, an envelope, or – yes, it was an envelope, odd size, an American envelope, shorter than A4. Scrawled across in Maxine's barely legible hand was 'NYC – Weldon and Weinberg, Esquire.' *Esquire? Lawyers?* With a glance at the door, through to the empty hall, Niamh dared herself to open the thing, sloppily shut as it was by its half-broken clasp. Dare she? Of course she dared ... and the paperwork inside was what uranium was to Marie Curie, what relativity was to Einstein. Niamh Bourke read and knew that she had made the discovery of a lifetime. Her heart beating with malevolent exultation, she read on, and knew power.

There is *something soothing about winding cable*, thought Jax. She and JP sat on the floor of his office, winding in silence, sorting out the duds, and checking for faulty wiring. Most needed to be thoroughly dusted, relegated as they had been to the ACJ junk pile – and for no good reason, as John Paul had been ranting. JP had a sensitive trigger as far as poorly maintained tools were concerned – one that Jax wouldn't have disagreed with, had she been able to get a word in edgeways.

Jax wound. And sighed. And scowled.

'I get the feeling you're not sharing my outrage.' JP gathered up a pile of consolidated cable and, using twine, starting lashing the lengths into bigger bundles.

'Oh, no, I – I mean – well, no, I actually don't care about the state of the cables.' Jax sat and looked at him.

He looked back at her, and they both smiled.

'I'm delighted you didn't feel the need to couch that for me.'

'So that's what I do, couch?' Jax leaned back.

JP, in the spirit of this new honesty, nodded. 'Couch, dress up – dress down, for that matter, equivocate, fudge—'

'Lie?' Jax folded her arms. And her legs.

'No, you're no liar, Jacinta Quirke,' said JP as he took up another pile to consolidate.

'No, I'm not. But I am a terrible ... I don't know. Evader. Evader of my own real opinion.' She uncrossed everything, and sat forward, toying with the end of a cable. 'So that is kind of lying, in a way.'

John Paul shrugged. 'Lying to yourself, worst of all.'

The gaze that Jax lifted to meet JP's was, from his point of view, too devastated for the conversation at hand. 'Jax, I didn't mean to – you look – if I was out of line—'

'No, I like to think I know the worst about myself.' Jax smiled wanly. 'And I like to think that I might do something about it. But what if –' she worried the hem of her jumper and picked off little pilly, woolly balls of yarn – 'what if somebody, a friend, a good friend, somebody that you thought was maybe your best friend—'

'And was a woman called Maxine?' JP offered, and stopped winding wires.

Jax's shoulders slumped. 'A woman called Maxine, who fancies herself, I suppose, the mysterious foreigner, although since when Yanks are *foreigners*, I'd like to know—'

'So yees had a fight, or something?' This was dodgy territory, but he was curious, and eager to present another of his assets for Jax's consideration. The keen observer, the good listener – the man who asked questions, all the things that were relentlessly evoked in 'what women want' conversations.

'God, you don't fight with Max, you wrangle, and squabble, and fidget things to death,' said Jax, fidgeting with her split ends. 'You don't actually achieve any kind of conclusion, because once you feel like you're getting somewhere, and getting through her unique brand of logic, she slams the door on it. End of conversation. Boom.'

'You know, you kind of sounded exactly like her just there – sorry. Right.' JP cleared his throat. Jacinta could get a look on her face when she wanted to. 'Em, so for someone as confrontational as she comes across, she's actually crap at confrontation.'

'Exactly!' Jax left off shredding her hair. 'And for someone who's always digging into other people . . .'

'What's up, Jax? Exactly?' John Paul shifted forward until their knees were almost touching.

'I can't say. I can't – I can't betray – I was going to say "betray her trust", but she hasn't trusted me with this.' *I wish that JP was Fergal – no, I don't: I wish that he was who Fergal is supposed to be –* 'Sorry, it's not your problem at all.'

'Maybe Max's thing isn't your problem?'

Jax smiled ruefully. 'You mean, it's not my business.' JP winced, and grinned, and Jax had to laugh – the first laugh she'd had in days. 'It's probably not, but when women are friends . . .'

'Jesus, you needn't tell me.' JP shuddered, and Jax laughed again.

They returned to the bundling job, and JP decided that there was no point in quitting while he was ahead. 'Em, people are talking, like. About you two.'

Jax nodded. 'Oh, sure. Of course they are.'

'Are you – are we going to be able to finish this gig?'

Jax tied off the piece of twine she'd been working with. 'We'll get over this, I suppose. It's just another thing that Max has swept under the rug.' She took up the last bunch of cable. 'Things are starting to shape up, we've got the cattle call tomorrow night . . . and Max and I – we always manage to get over this stuff.'

13

'Sure she didn't get over it until she was in her early twenties.' If it occurred to Angela that she was behaving a teeny-weeny bit indiscreetly, she didn't entertain such thoughts for long. Besides, these anecdotes about her daughter were well worn, and Jacinta knew that her mum had party pieces on everyone in the family.

And if she was behaving imprudently, it was nothing against what she expected in return. Eyes gleaming, Angela leaned across the little table towards Max, and ran her freshly manicured fingers up and down the stem of her wine glass.

A fine, boozy lunch with Maxine O'Malley. She had been gasping for one for ages, and now that they'd finally fixed it up, she intended to give a little to get a lot more.

Max hid behind her own wine glass for a few seconds. *Oh, boy, Maxine,* she thought, *if ever a notion had the likelihood of blowing up in your face . . .*

'It seems so unlike her – and yet so like her, if you know what I mean.' Max decided it was too late to ungrasp the nettle; she'd gone as far as to ask Angela along to a tête-à-tête and there was no point in not getting exactly what she came for.

A cosy, squiffy lunch with Angela Quirke. She was going to milk it for all it was worth.

'I do, I know exactly what you mean.' Angela stroked her manicured hands down her sparkly, dangly earrings. 'Sulky madam, but . . .'

'But', and Max topped up their sauvignon blanc, 'you always know the *why*. The *because*.'

'. . . And ever since I found out, I haven't known what to do, how to talk to her, how not to talk to her, if you know what I mean . . .' Jax trailed off, miserable, and her father playfully tugged at one of the curls that had liberated itself from her scrunchie.

They sat at a cosy table for two at the Avoca Café a mile from Max's and Angela's luncheon venue, and a million miles away in attitude and snootiness. As Jax and her father huddled over bowls of soup, she couldn't stop brooding over the business with Max; it was like a worm in her brain, and she had to *do* something.

If anybody could tell her what to do, it was her da.

'Give us a moment with this, Jacinta,' said Raymond, as he slowly spooned up a delicious Thai chicken curry. Well, marjoram, of course, and coconut, but there was a touch of something else, a splash of – Jax's woebegone expression diverted him from his gustatory wonderings.

'Right,' he said, diverting his attention from the far less complicated thoughts about seasoning. 'So Maxine is in fact married to this lad.'

'Michael. Michael LaMotta.' It felt such a relief to Jax to say his name aloud – it made him less of a figment of her imagination, somehow.

'Maxine and Michael,' Raymond said, and caught the twinkle in Jacinta's eye.

'Maxine O'Malley LaMotta,' she snorted.

'Good Lord. That's grounds for divorce right there,' Raymond chuckled, and then both he and his daughter wore twin looks of desperate guilt. 'No, dreadful of us, dreadful,' Raymond conceded.

'You'll keep this to yourself, won't you?' Jax asked as she worried a bread roll to shreds.

Raymond sighed. 'Speaking of divorce ... if your mother knew that I knew something like this and didn't tell her ...'

'I know, I know,' Jax said, and they both stared down into their soup as if it held the wisdom of the ages.

'I understand that this may be disturbing news, but, pet,' Raymond turned towards his daughter, 'I don't understand *exactly why* this is exercising your mind so much.'

Jax looked up at her father bleakly. 'I thought we were friends. And now I feel like I don't know her at all.'

Angela's tale of Jax's rigorously ordered cot ran underneath the presentation of their huge salads, interjected with both women's exclamations at the copious amounts of greens, etc. on their plates, and the ritual exhortations by the staff of 'oil and vinegar?' and 'black pepper?'

'Just a *dash*, darling, just a *dusting*.' Angela smiled up at the server, who deftly poofed a whisper of pepper on to her chicken Caesar.

'But that's why we get on so well,' Max mused over a forkful of Nicoise. 'I'm the kind of loosey goosey one—'

'And charming with it!' Angela tapped her crystal against Max's.

'And Jax is the – well, steady, I guess, but not like plodding, or dull. Reliable.'

'Oh, my poor sweet girl,' Angela moaned. Max wished she'd take some of the bread – although it was always hard to tell with Ange what was the drink and what was her customary degree of melodrama. 'My wee diamond in the rough. My little pearl in the oyster. Maxine. Surely you've had some influence on my little dove, fashion-wise. Surely you girls have gone shopping together at some stage.'

'Nope.' Max waved for another bottle of wine, and Angela whooped her approval. *What the hell*, Max thought. *In for a penny . . .*

. . . In for a pound, thought Angela as she leaned forward again. 'Never?'

'Ever. When she was in Manhattan, I had to trick her into coming into Saks—'

'Saks Fifth Avenue!' Angela trilled, and sighed.

'And to this day, Ange, honest to God, I haven't recovered. She touched *nothing*. Admired *nothing*. Lusted for *nothing*.'

'Bloody *hell*.' Angela shook her head sadly. 'It must be all my fault. It's always the mother's fault, isn't it?'

'And it's not like she's cheap.'

Angela rapped the table with her fork. 'Not a bit of it. But what she does is plough it all into that house. Not that I'm not delighted that my little sausage has security, not at all, and at good value, she got good value for money on that place, although *why* in the world we didn't hold on to it all those years ago – ah, who knew, who knew. But she *ploughs* all her capital into that place, feathering that nest for that good-for-nothing chancer of an abandoning –' *Oh, dear*, she thought, *mustn't go too far*.

Come on, come on, come on, Angela! Max thought. 'Of an abandoning . . . ?' she coaxed.

*

'What I'd like to know are, I assume, things that you can't tell me.' Raymond took Jax's arm as they crossed the threshold into St Stephen's Green.

'Like what?' *As if this wasn't enough*, thought Jax.

'Fairly obvious facts, darling,' Raymond replied patiently. If only Jax knew how like her mother she was at this moment: the sulky scowl, the annoyance at being left out, the need to feel connected to a loved one on every level – it was all there written on her face.

They sat down on a bench and Raymond patted her on the knee. Oh, how she wanted to cuddle under his arm like she used to, and Jax did the best she could, a kind of thirty-something-year-old woman version of trying to hide in her father's armpit, and leaned against his shoulder. 'Like, if he was abusive, you mean?' she asked, rubbing her cheek against the silky sleeve of his jacket.

'Yes, and whether or not they are already divorced, or separated—'

'He called himself her husband!'

'—and whether or not she was the initiator, which, one must deduce, she was, if she's not openly recognising the relationship, and he still thinks of them as a couple – or at least, of himself as a husband. And whether or not, again, she had good reason to do so.' Ray paused and cleared his throat. 'Or, based on the little I know of Maxine, she's a game girl, and a good friend to you—'

'There's a "but" lurking in there.'

'But.' And knowing Jacinta's fierce loyalties, Raymond trod carefully. 'Maxine doesn't strike me as someone who – and don't bunch up like that, pet, let me say my piece and I hope you'll hear it. I don't know that Maxine is ready for the long haul, as it were.'

Jax sat forward again. 'I know,' she sighed. 'In New York, she started talking about moving here before she'd even worked out how, if you know what I mean. She's a great one for the ideas, and all, but whether or not she sees them through all the way . . .'

'So perhaps she's doing in her marriage what she does in her life. It's impossible to separate the two.'

'I suppose.' Jax picked up one of the waxy dogwood leaves that littered the path. 'It makes it worse, keeping it a secret.'

'Marriage is a secret, in a way,' Raymond mused. 'It's a state agreed to, generally, in a public forum, in front of family and friends, but then, of necessity, it needs to disappear. Within itself. Or else it cannot survive.' Raymond leaned forward, his lean hands clasping his knees. 'No, it cannot survive. You'll understand this yourself, Jacinta, when your time comes – the family may well be the cornerstone of society – how that family is comprised is, of course, changing, as it should, as society is changing – so, family may be this so-called cornerstone, but marriage is private. The secrecy you are talking about may just be a vital kind of privacy, and in a marriage, that privacy is absolutely sacred.'

Jax leaned back slowly, praying that that video they'd made had really been destroyed.

Given her personality, Angela was no stranger to 'moments of truth'. Knowing her daughter, Maxine most likely had next to no information about the dreaded Fergal. Angela's nostrils flared at the thought of him, at the phrase 'the dreaded Fergal'. Angela knew that her little girl had, well, strict rules governing privacy, and knew, in her heart of hearts, that any divulgence, even a little tiny trickle of an anecdote, would be tantamount to treason.

But, but, but – this was *Maxine*, Jacinta's *best friend*, best friend and *business partner*, and writer of a potential vehicle that Angela wanted in on more than she wanted to draw her next breath.

Who cared what the show was about? She wanted a *part*.

'I hesitate –' And Angela hesitated. She swept a fine-boned hand over her shining cap of hair and glanced up at Max from beneath her eyelashes. 'I do, I do hesitate. But I tell myself –' And here, Max noticed, Angela unerringly found the one spot of light in the place, the one beam of weak sunshine that was diffusing through the restaurant's cunningly designed window treatments. 'I tell myself that if there's anyone in the world, anyone, who could convince Jacinta to, to *reconsider* her choices—'

'I don't know, Ange, I can't even convince her to get some highlights.'

'You're her best friend,' Angela said, drilling a look of melancholy entreaty right between Max's eyes. 'Surely you ought to know everything . . .'

Best friends. Best friends ought to know . . . Max treated herself to a large mouthful of the sauvignon blanc. 'Sure. Sure. But oughtn't she be the one –'

Jax gave up trying to be a grown-up woman and slipped her hand into her father's. As they left the park and headed towards his office, she let herself get lost in the thoughts Raymond had triggered, while avoiding the one that made her feel sick to her stomach with guilt.

'I'm going to go out on a limb here, Jacinta,' Raymond sighed, and felt her hand tense in his. 'And just ask you how honest you've been with Maxine yourself.'

'I don't know what you mean—'

'Jacinta.' That was another tone of his that she heartily disliked, primarily because he only used it under extreme duress. It was sharp and no-nonsense, and in direct contrast to his usual mellifluous tones. 'There's been an unspoken agreement in the family that we would not belabour you about Fergal, especially since your mother does enough belabouring for the lot of us, but I will say that we are concerned about the choices you're making around Fergal, and would like to know if you'd like to talk to us about them.'

A red light at Baggot Street was a natural stopping point. Jax started biting her nails.

'I just wonder that you haven't lost sight of the whole point of being engaged to someone,' Raymond said, squeezing her hand. ' "Engage" being the operative word.'

'You really ought to have been a barrister,' Jax joked.

'I'm not that terribly interested in other people's problems – only those of my nearest and dearest.'

'Thanks, Da,' Jax said, hugging him before she set off back to work. 'For listening. It helped.'

'I don't know that you got much off me,' Raymond said, then kissed her, sighed, and trotted up the steps of his building.

'You won't tell her, will you?' she called as her father went through the door.

His casual wave did nothing to settle her mind on the matter.

'Engaged! Me arse! Engaged without a *token*, without a symbol of the *contract*? Because let me tell you, pet, marriage is a *contract*, it is love and fidelity and blah blah *blah*, but it is also a contract, a very *cut and dried* agreement by both parties. And without some token of good faith, you've got nothing. Nothing!'

Tell me about it, Max thought, and shakily poured out more wine.

Which Angela failed to notice, as she was busily doing her favourite deep-breathing technique. 'You must excuse me, Maxine,' she apologised, once she had recomposed herself. 'I do take this whole business personally, a bit too personally, perhaps, but, well. Raymond and I have not been the most conventional of parents –' Max hoped that, someday, she'd have fully erased the sight of them on the kitchen table out of her mind. 'Not that we were running about the place, *smoking drugs* or what have you, but we – Raymond and I – did our best to have a partnership, to show the children what it was like when two people entered into that contract, when two people loved and respected each other and, most especially, what it was like to have two people who weren't *strangled* by gender roles.'

'Sure, sure,' Max agreed. 'But Jax—'

'I suppose the biggest mistake a mother can make is to expect her children to do anything against their grain.' Angela sighed. 'What about *your* mum, love? Have you deeply disappointed your family?'

Actors, thought Max, *can be scarily perceptive*. 'Oh, you know, nothing out of the ordinary. Just didn't turn out to be exactly like them, is all.' *Enough of that!* Max sat back and gestured with her wine, trying to look blasé. 'Did you disappoint your own mother?'

Cagey little minx. 'I sincerely hope so,' Angela smirked. 'But I disappointed her in the conventionally unconventional way, if you take my meaning. And Jacinta seems intent on being conventionally conventional.' She pouted for a moment, and shook it off. 'Not that I don't adore her completely. But . . .'

'But Fergal . . .'

'A cipher! A blank! A sphinx! They met in seventh year – that's like the last high school year to you, I believe – and seriously began dating after college – do the *maths*, darling, it's outrageous – and down the years, he made appearances at family functions, but even then, even at *seventeen*, he was always sneaking in and sneaking out, always hovering around the edges of a party or a christening or a wedding, always slithering in and slithering out—'

'So what was his family like?' But Angela was in full flow.

'—muttering his excuses and leaving Jacinta there, *leaving* her on her own, standing about like a pillock, a sweet little lost pillock, making excuses and smiling away, but I *know* her, I *know* her, and I *knew* her heart broke every time.

'And the engagement! Hah! Wouldn't even let us give them a meal, much less a party, "Oh, no, Mum, no fuss, we're not like that." Rubbish!—'

Max cut across a burgeoning rant, 'I'm not getting any idea of why she'd support this . . . well, it's a fiction.'

'She takes her promises very seriously.'

'There's serious and then there's pathological, if you ask me.'

'She has enormous integrity,' Angela huffed defensively, and knowing Jax, reading the signs in her progenitress, Max knew to back off in a hurry.

'She does, of course she does. And she's lovely, she's a lovely woman, so it's not as if she couldn't get another boyfriend or fiancé or whatever. In fact—' *Oh, shit.*

'I knew it! I knew it!' Angela leapt up, arms raised, and

tossed her head back in delight. 'Raymond owes me fifty smackeroos!' She threw herself down into her chair, her eyes on fire, and Max saw her life flash in front of her eyes. 'Tell me everything.'

This is your own fault, Maxine O'Malley, and you deserve what you get. 'Angela, listen, I'm just intuiting, okay? This is not hard fact. Say nothing.'

Angela tilted her chin pugnaciously. 'You cannot expect me to keep this to myself.'

Shite! 'You're putting me in a difficult position here, Angela.'

'I have, of course, been utterly upfront with you,' she responded, crossing her fingers in her lap.

'For the sake of my friendship with Jax' – *yeah, right* – 'I really need you to keep that quiet.'

'Let's make each other an offer we can't refuse.' Angela topped up the wine and allowed herself, to Max's relief, a tiny bread roll. 'I share information with you – you write me into your show.'

And the whole point of being a good producer was the anticipation of the other side's agenda. *I*, Max thought, *am going to make a kick-ass producer*.

'And how I explain this to my partner . . . I don't know.' *I need a stogie, a good Cuban cigar.* Then Max ruined it all by giggling.

'Oh, I've all my faith in you.'

Max blew out a stream of metaphorical smoke. 'Deal.'

And Angela ruined it all by giggling. 'I understand, love. I do.' *And it's really just a matter of tuning in the auld radar at this stage anyway – infinitely more fun.* 'I'm sure everything will be revealed at some stage anyway.'

'Yeah.' Max came over with an uneasy feeling, and

didn't think it was her Niçoise. 'Now I've only got to figure out how to explain how you got involved.'

'As I said before, I have total faith in you.' One of Angela's favourite sights in the world was that of watching someone else produce their plastic. She sighed, contented. 'Oh! Here's an idea!'

Uh oh. 'Hmmm?' Max feigned disinterest as she briskly signed the bill.

'Why not do a think tank out at the house! You and your team! And we'll get the fire going, and hot toddies, and you can hash it all out, and I'll make myself available, I mean, I'll be *present*, and it can be as if you were *inspired* by me . . .'

Oh, boy. 'Our whole team? I don't know, well, we're not big, there's only three of us – four of us –'

'No, love, it's perfect, it *is*,' Angela insisted. 'That big old barn of a house, and the two of you, in comfortable surroundings – we'll get you back on an even keel in no time. Yes! Assemble your team and bring them round, we'll have a big bang-up meal – oh, dear, love, are you choking on that – here, have some water – something went down the wrong way, did it?'

14

I *need a full day in the garden*, thought Jax. A full day, alone, in my garden, by myself, out of doors – not perched on a bar stool or out to dinner. One whole day, alone, digging into dirt rather than other people's affairs; alone, so she wouldn't have to pretend something wasn't bothering her, when of course it was.

The Gatehouse Pub was starting to hop: the long bar had a crowd ranging four deep from the men behind the taps, and it seemed that the whole of the city centre was swarming up one staircase and down the next. Every one of its four levels was packed, packed with gussied-up girls and studiedly dressed-down guys. Max wiggled her way around the place, putting up signs and having the craic with a clutch of Welshmen who were over for the rugby.

This is going to work, she thought as she slipped away from the Cymrus and chatted up a bunch of lads lounging by the door. They were out in the field, they were doing actual work, they'd soon be talking to actual couples about their actual relationships with broadcast quality equipment. No more messing about with cameras in handbags – they were on their way.

And, Max thought, *no more worrying about what's*

worrying Jax. We'll just carry on like nothing's wrong, and then nothing will be wrong!

Although Jax's gloomy face wasn't going inspire many to darken their temporary door.

'What's wrong with ya?' Max rattled a little bag of peanuts under Jax's nose.

'All this socialising is wrecking my head,' Jax said.

'So, what, you'd rather be poking around in the dirt or something?' Max downed the rest of the nuts.

'Yes, exactly,' Jax muttered, agitating the ice in her G&T.

'This isn't socialising, this is work.' Max sent a wave to JP. 'What'll you have?' she asked as he squirmed over to them.

Jax tried to keep her eyes fixed on JP's face. Don't look at his hands, Jacinta, she told herself, blushing as she remembered that neck massage. Don't think about how lovely and strong his hands felt, coaxing the kinks out of her shoulders, don't *dare* think about his thumbs stroking up and down the nape of your neck. Had she ever even noticed the nape of her neck before, how sensitive it was, how it seemed to—

'Jacinta?' A voice called over the crowd.

Jax looked over blankly, then smiled, as best she could under the circumstances. 'Howaya, Jamie.' At least Max had backed off from poor John Paul as she assessed the new lad for camera-readiness.

'Jesus, haven't seen you in yonks.' Jamie ran a hand through his gelled but thinning hair and appeared to be sucking in his belly somewhat. A tall man, he appeared to be a jock gone to seed, his muscles – displayed beneath his tight-fitting, short-sleeved shirt – looked as if they were blurred around the edges. His wedding band, a quarter-inch of gold, glinted in the bar lights.

'Not since the wedding,' Jax agreed. *And here we go—*

'How the hell is Fergal?' Jamie ran his hand through his hair again. JP stared at him with intense dislike, and Max with a burgeoning gleam of interest.

'Grand, grand.' Jax tossed back the rest of her gin. Max signalled to the bartender and leaned towards Jamie.

'You and Jax go way back, do you?' She extended a hand, grateful that Jamie had been stroking what remained of his hair with his left hand.

'Jamie, Maxine; Maxine, Jamie. Jamie, John Paul, right, right.' Jax's introductions trailed off into a mumble. God, was she really going to be able to stick this? Wasn't this the longest of long shots? What good could possibly come from hanging out in this pub all night hoping that people would be stupid enough to want to be on a programme that barely existed?

'Jax!' Max thumped her in the ribs. 'Jamie says you've known each other for ages. Everybody in Ireland knows each other for ever!'

'Ah, sure, he was known as the Playboy of the sixth class,' Jax snorted, and Jamie had the delicacy to blush.

'Those days are over,' Jamie said good-naturedly, and displayed his hard-to-miss ring. 'I'm well married now.'

'How is Majella?' Jax asked, resigned to the small talk, and that glitter in Max's eye.

'She's super, just super; home with the wee one.' Jamie had his wallet out before anyone could blink, and photos were passed around.

'Does she not miss you of an evening?' Max asked.

'This, it's work like, gotta take the clients out, show 'em a good time, you know the way.' Jamie shrugged. 'It'll be a night of it, too – Germans.'

They all nodded knowingly. 'Are you out, em, socialising often?' Max handed him a fresh jar of Guinness.

'A fair bit,' Jamie said. 'More than my due, to be honest. I'm the chief salesman, so . . .' He tailed off, allowing them to fill in the blanks with their own imagination, one he knew they'd think was filled with posh company cars, expensive dinners, and five-star perks.

Salesman, JP sneered to himself.

Bless him, thought Jax charitably.

Hmmmm . . . Max grinned.

'You must get hit on all the time. Out on the road, lonely meals in hotels, all that travel . . .' Max let her voice tail off meaningfully.

'You wouldn't believe – and I mean it – you wouldn't believe the rate that I get hit on, now I've got one of these on my finger,' Jamie asserted, once again presenting the impossible-to-overlook band.

'Shocking,' Max gasped.

'It is, Maxine, it's shocking. I was only out in Sligo last week, showing around some Japanese we had in, and there we were, out for the evening, and didn't some of the local talent come sliding up to me at the bar – and they saw the ring, sure they did—'

'Who could miss it,' John Paul muttered, and Jax laughed. They smiled into each other's eyes, and then quickly looked away. And looked back again.

'He hasn't changed,' Jax murmured.

'Max certainly dives right in there, doesn't she?' John Paul shifted closer to Jax to avoid being pushed out of the way by a tipsy hen party, and she caught a whiff of a lemony scent off his shirt. Clean laundry. She sighed. What a lovely smell.

She smiled up at him, and he felt his heart pound like

a cat in a microwave. 'She's like a terrier. A terrier with a credit card and fondness for the high street. She's convinced that we'll make a go of this thing.'

'You can, of course, Jax,' JP said eagerly. 'You've got an excellent concept, and—'

'—*When Harry Met Sally*-type of thing, talking to couples, we'd love to meet your wife, get you both to talk about your relationship, the way you met,' Max said.

'Right, right, totally, I know Majella'd be totally into it,' Jamie enthused.

'We're sorting out the studio space, we may try to keep it casual, come out to yours, if that's all right, maybe shadow you for a day or two—'

'That's news to me,' Jax grumbled, and set her empty glass on the bar.

'You've got to hand it to her, she gets things done.' John Paul watched as Jamie and Max exchanged numbers.

Jamie ran his hand through his hair one more time, for the road. 'See you soon, right? Excellent! Well done, Jacinta!'

'Easy peasy!' Max sang. 'Didn't even have to seduce him with the camera!'

'Yes, but, we should have had some footage, all that stuff would have been great on tape,' JP said.

'Shite. You're right. Well, next time. I think I'll just—'

'Jacinta!' A bubbly-looking woman reeled over and all but fell into Jax's arms. 'Oh my God, like, it's been ages! Helllloooooo!'

'Dara, how are you?' Jax disengaged herself from Dara's boozy embrace.

'Grand, grand, you know, out with the lads from work. I'm in IT, you know,' she boasted.

'Hi, I'm Max, and this is John Paul.' JP felt grateful for

the lack of religious varient. 'We're in advertising, you know. Jax is a creative director for one of Dublin's biggest agencies.'

'Oh my God! Fab!' Dara wobbled, then giggled, but she wasn't so far gone that she didn't quickly inspect Jax's left hand. 'How's Fergal?'

'Grand, he's—'

'We were all at university together,' Dara gushed, nearly tipping over. 'All of us, all those years, and sure I haven't see either of them for ages.'

'So you said.' Max turned, whispered into JP's ear and he sloped off up the stairs.

'Have you not married him *yet*, Jacinta?' Dara boomed, and Jax felt her body sag into the defensive slouch that she was beginning to detest.

'You married yourself, Dara?' Max cut across, forcing Dara to focus on her.

'Nearly engaged,' she boasted, waggling her as yet unadorned ring finger in Max's direction.

'That's interesting,' Max said, 'because we've got a project going on the side, about modern relationships, modern marriage, all that kind of thing. We're looking for people to talk to, couples, to talk about themselves on camera, and—'

Dara pulled herself up straight as an arrow, holding her hands out for emphasis and possibly for balance. 'Conor and I are the perfect couple. Totally. We are. So totally. Perfect.'

'Wow, great,' said Max, getting out her mobile. 'We've got some lads upstairs with a camera, I wonder if you'd like to come and sign up to be filmed?'

Max pointed Dara in the right direction, and, mission accomplished, with much tottering on the part of their newest player, she turned to Jax, triumphant.

'Fish in a barrel!' she crowed, and grabbed Jax's drink for a celebratory slug.

'I'd rather everybody wasn't someone I knew,' Jax protested testily as she pushed by Max to go up to the 'set'. 'And she's terribly drunk, it's not right.'

'Hey, she's compos mentis as far as I'm concerned. And she said yes, so fair game!' Max flew up the two flights of stairs in a heartbeat, as if flying on certain success.

Jax wasn't so sure. It seemed, where Max was concerned, that no one was safe once they said yes to this project.

She'd do well to keep that in mind.

It wasn't hours and hours, but it felt like it. As the night wore on, and the crowd got tipsier, the quality of the pool they were fishing in got too close to the bottom feeders for Jacinta's taste.

'I've got an idea!' Max jumped up from behind the tripod and Jax groaned. 'Let's take the camera downstairs and see what we get!'

'What difference is that going to make?'

'We haven't got anything *good*.' Max began to pace, and Jax hovered protectively by the camera. 'People are just clamming up the instant they see the stupid thing.'

Jax worked the 'stupid thing' gently off the legs. 'We've got the gaffer tape over the light, maybe if I just carry it around like it's not working ...' She sat down on a banquette with the camera on her lap.

'Too late, am I?' A pair of trousers slid into the frame. 'Thought you girls had a TV show going on up here.'

Jax shifted to cross her legs and the frame took in the speaker, a suit with tie loosened, hands perched on casually notched hips. Max flicked a gaze at Jax, who returned a nearly indiscernible thumbs-up.

'We're women,' Max smiled sweetly at the tosser, and Jax opened up the frame gently.

'Ah, sure,' he smirked. 'Know how to run that thing?' He glanced at Jax briefly, dismissively, and turned his questionable charms back to Max.

Pig! Jax zoomed in on his smug grin.

Asshole! Max shifted herself, infinitesimally, away from him.

'Oh, we know a lot of things,' Max purred. Jax shivered at the sight of that seemingly seductive, but actually pitiless little smile.

And, if she was being honest, she shivered in anticipation of a bloodless, but nevertheless ferocious, disposal.

'Gary!'

Jax crossed her legs, which shifted the camera, which in turn opened up the frame to include the newest speaker, an almost transparently thin blonde, clutching her handbag in a death grip.

Gary shot away from Max's vicinity and into the arms of the blonde. 'There ya are, pet, I've been looking all over.'

Max beamed over at the suspicious blonde. 'I'm Maxine, and that's Jacinta. And you are?' She smiled at the blonde, and extended her hand.

'Mary,' she replied and, hesitating, shook Max's hand.

'We've just been talking to Gary about a television programme that we're working on, and we've been scouting in the bar, looking for real-life couples, talking about modern relationship—'

'Sure, we're only getting married in two months.' Gary

grinned, brushing his hand down Mary's back.

Max could see Jax's nostrils flaring dangerously. 'So you'd probably be too busy—'

'We're up to our eyes with the plans,' Mary squeaked.

'TV? Like *Big Brother*?' Gary's eyes glittered like ice.

'Oh, now, I don't know—' Mary stuttered.

'Ah, sure, love, it'll be grand, especially since you've lost all that weight.' Gary took out a business card. 'We'd love to.'

15

'Will we not have Sunday lunch in the dining room for once?' Jax worried a button right off her shirt.

'But, pet, this table was made for wheeling and dealing! Ideas! Creativity! Don't you want your project to bear fruit?' Angela gestured wildly to take in the whole room, a bottle of wine in each hand, as Raymond carefully prepared the zest of one lemon.

'It might make a nice change, Angela,' Raymond interjected smoothly – but not without, Jax noticed, a heavily lidded glance in his wife's direction.

Jax twisted her cardigan up around her breastbone and thought she heard a rip.

Angela cleared her throat seductively, and went to caress her husband's back. 'Hmmm, you may be right, Raymond, perhaps *cette chambre* needs a wee little break.'

'I'll go set the table, so!' And Jax flew out of the room, accompanied by her parents' low laughter.

How did this happen? Jax laid out the fancy fabric place mats, and precisely set the cutlery on the matching napkins. How did they end up here, again, using her family home as the locus for this project? She had her own place! Max had a flat! Why couldn't they go to JP's for a change? What in the world were they doing here? What in the world was she doing, at all? Jax sat down at her place and stared at her shadowy reflection in the glass of the dresser doors. How many times had she sat in this very spot, dreaming away while her mother performed some event or other over the Sunday roast, dreaming away into her future, her life, her life as an artist, maybe – or as an anthropologist, that year or two she wanted to be an anthropologist . . . And never once, while she sat there daydreaming, did it occur to her that she wouldn't be *something*, she wouldn't *be* whatever she wanted to be. It never occurred to Jax to *not* do anything, so it wasn't as if she spent all her time mooning over some boy, imagining her wedding dress, naming children. Certainly not. So, as to that . . . Did she want . . . did she want to . . . did she honestly, really want to marry—

'Oh, this is all so exciting!' Her mother came into the dining room and cast her arms around Jacinta's neck. 'I'm so delighted we can be of use!'

'Whose idea was this, anyway?' Jax untangled herself from Angela's signature stranglehold, and rose to finish with the knives and forks.

'Oh, surely it was mine – or was it Maxine's?' Angela waved a hand airily. 'Who knows? Who remembers? Maxine mentioned something in passing and I just assumed that the two of you had put your heads together.' And she swept out of the room again, and glided up the stairs.

In Jax's experience, early exits always signified guilt, and she couldn't bear to think what her mother was up to.

As if she didn't know. Of course she'd give Angela a part in the show – she'd already worked it out – but half the fun was watching her mother machinate.

A car door slammed loudly in the street. 'There's Max,' Jax called up the stairs, and heard a bedroom door slam. Right. The two of them were definitely cooking something up . . .

'Hello, hello, hello!' Max sang as she peeked into the dining room and grinned at Jax with raised brows as she surveyed the table. 'We eating in here? Unusual.'

'My idea, but Da was very supportive.'

They winced, and grinned, their first true feeling of accord in weeks.

'Jax—'

'No.' Jax moved quickly into the front room.

Max followed briskly behind. 'But—'

Jax shook her head and knelt by the hearth. 'Your timing is rubbish. I don't want to talk now. Okay?'

Max plopped down on the loveseat. 'Fiiiiine.'

Jax raised a brow at Max's immediate assumption of zero responsibility. 'You could give me a hand with this, you know,' she scolded lightly as she laid some briquettes and kindling into the hearth.

'Only if you want me to set your hair on fire,' Max said drily. 'So. We've only got four weeks left. We need to get ourselves sorted.'

'Shite!' Jax sat back on her heels and unfurled her hair from her scrunchie, only to twist it all up again.

'You know, a third of the population of this planet would kill to have hair like yours. If you'd just—'

'Never mind about my hair!' Jax took her whiskey, and leaned back against an ottoman. 'Four weeks to deadline!'

'I know, it's killer. Have you rung that RTÉ woman?'

'Em . . .' Jax reached forward and laid another brick on the fire. 'I will. Tomorrow.'

'Jax!' Max poked her in the thigh with the toe of her

boot. 'Do it! We can't blow this connection! We've only got four weeks!'

'Four weeks . . .' Jax murmured, and felt the energy of a challenge, of an all-but-impossible deadline, surge through her system. She grinned up at Max. 'It's insane.'

'It's brutal.'

'It's time to get down to it.'

Max turned towards the door as the bell sounded. 'Talk about timing!'

Jax rose to answer the door, and was almost knocked back by the blur of Angela rushing to greet her guests.

'Hellloooo, I'm Angela Quirke, Jacinta's mother,' she cooed, in her best Marilyn Monroe – had Ms Monroe hailed from South County Dublin.

'I'm John Paul and this is Lorcan.' Jax's mum. Meeting Jax's folks – well, in person, anyway. JP blushed.

Sweetie pie, thought Angela indulgently, as she also processed the cheekiness, if not downright rudeness, of the other.

'Lorcan,' he said, holding out a hand for a handshake that Angela ignored. She didn't like the way he was *looking* at her.

'Indeed,' she intoned frostily, and beamed at JP. 'Do come in. I'll just fetch my husband,' Angela said. 'Toddies, lads?'

As JP assented for them both, Jacinta grabbed Lorcan's arm in a death grip.

'If you so much as—'

'Mind the flesh, Jesus.' Lorcan looked to Max for back-up, and received a cool look in return.

'You mind!' Jax's voice dropped to a threatening snarl. 'If I get any indication off you that you're messing about, or if you say *anything* rude to my parents—'

'You're beautiful when you're angry,' he sneered, and he ran a finger down her face.

'Here's Raymond – oh.' Angela stopped dead at the sight of Lorcan stroking Jax's cheek. Not *him*, she wanted to scream. *Good* God, *Jacinta, have you no taste at all?*

Jax jumped back from Lorcan, and JP pulled him aside for a word.

'Let me take those, Da,' she said cheerily, and she passed around the glasses.

Angela glided further into the room, her bright eyes assessing Lorcan – *Oh, shit*, thought Max. *She thinks it's—*

'So, Loughlin—'

'Lorcan, Missus Quirke.'

What in the world was her mother doing with that look on her face? Jax gestured to the sofa, and JP sat, but Lorcan was helplessly trapped in the web of Angela Quirke. 'Mum. Mum! Will I introduce Da, or will you?'

'Sure I can speak for myself, so I can!' *Oh, God, Da, not "Jovial Ray Quirke", please!* Jax thought.

'Howaya, lads, howaya, welcome to the gaff, the family gaff, as it were.' Raymond distributed hearty handshakes, with Max cheekily putting herself forward for one as well – which no one noticed.

Raymond Quirke flustered. Max had never seen the like.

'Well. Well. Hope you're all in the mood for a good feed, hope your bellies are rubbin' against your backbones; we've got a mighty roast in the oven, a mighty roast.'

'I'm vegetarian.' Everyone stared at Lorcan.

'You? You're joking!' Max snorted.

'I'm vegetarian,' Lorcan insisted, with surprising dignity.

'How inconvenient,' Angela said, looking up at him in order to look down her nose.

'Right. Right. Vegetarian. We'll see what we've got, sure, no trouble at all, no trouble—' And Ray beat a hasty retreat into the kitchen.

Angela's retreat was far from hasty, and could effectively be described as withering.

'You're a vegetarian? I don't believe it,' Max said, to take the focus off Jax's reddening face. 'Vegetarians are nice people.'

'I'm nice,' he murmured, and made as if to nuzzle Max's neck.

'Let's get to it, shall we?' Jax thumped her binder down on the coffee table, sat down on the floor, and refused to make eye contact with Max.

Here we go again, Max sighed into her whiskey. *So much for that truce*.

'At the very least, a five-minute demo for the tender, in four weeks' time.' Jacinta looked around at the group – well, at JP, then at Max. No point in deceiving Lorcan into believing he actually had creative input.

'Professionally speaking, it's gotta be at least ten minutes, like,' Lorcan said, stroking Maxine up and down her thigh. Maxine batted his hand away, and the two engaged in a series of brisk slaps.

'Perhaps you might consider acting professionally if you're going to attempt to speak professionally,' Jax replied, not even deigning to look up from her notes.

'We'll have to get everyone in, then,' Max said, and kicked Lorcan in the ankle for good measure. 'And we won't trouble you,' she said to him, 'once we've got all the gear in place.'

Lorcan fought the urge to nurse his ankle – Max had a hell of a left foot – and shrugged. 'I'll start to think you don't fancy me, Max,' he murmured, and Jax exchanged an exasperated look with John Paul.

'Knock it off, Lorcan,' JP demanded, and Max got up and moved to sit on the ottoman next to Jax.

'More than anything, we need a location,' Jax said.

'What about my flat?' Max hazarded a poke at the fire,

and an explosion of sparks flew up from the blazing briquettes.

'No, too casual.' Jax leaned back against the sofa, inadvertently cuddling herself up against JP's leg.

His whole system went on alert, and his leg went tense.

'Sorry,' Jax blurted, looking up at him. 'Sorry.'

'No, you're all right,' JP stuttered.

Janey Mac! Maxine thought. *Just get down to it, you two!*

'Sooooo . . .' Max leaned forward and set her glass down on the table. 'We've got the couples – Mary and Gary, Dara and Conor, and Jamie and Majella. I think Jamie and Majella might be the clangers, maybe they should go first.'

'Why? Why are they going to be the clangers?' Jax demanded.

'Well, they're only just married, and they're new parents; I expect they'll have that – that *vibe* about them, that wrapped-in-cotton-wool thing about them.'

'Oh? And what would you know about that, Maxine?' Jax smiled thinly, tilting her head questioningly.

Max poked at the fire again, sending sparks flying on to the carpet. 'It's a fairly typical state of being, Jacinta. Nothing special,' she mumbled, grinding out the burning embers with her heel.

'Oh, really?' Jax shifted up to a kneeling position and cocked her head the other way. 'Oh, really, Maxine O'Malley?'

JP cleared his throat. *Something strange going on here*, he thought and, against his better judgement, decided to defuse the situation.

'So, well, we have to start with somebody, and it may as well be Jamie and his wife. I mean, Jax is mates with them, or whatever, and it might be easier on us all.'

Jax shook her head. 'Fine, but let's do Dara and Conor

at the same time, as we've very little time to waste.'

'Whatever,' said Max, scraping her shoe against the edge of the hearth. 'We need to talk location, but I have another idea that I wanted to put forward.'

'Would this be the "probably illegal following people around without their knowledge idea"?' Jax asked.

'You don't have to make it sound like that!' Max sat back with a thump, and had to fight off some sulking of her own. Okay, so bringing Lorcan tonight wasn't such a great idea, but he'd been pestering to see her, and she needed the buffer of the group, and maybe she should have just told him to fuck off, why hadn't she just told him to fuck off, but here she was now, with Jax acting all weird, and who knew why – and they had to get their shit together or else—

Or else what, Maxine?

'So what is it like, then?' Jax countered.

'It's like – it's like filling out their personalities, finding out what they do –' Maxine made it up as she went along – 'who they are when they're not just the "other half".' *Nice one, Maxie, work it.* 'What they do, how often they are in contact during the day, who their friends are, how do they talk about their significant other, and yadda yadda. We fill these people out – and they mostly know we're shadowing them—'

'Mostly?' Jax demanded.

'Mostly. We have to be invisible some of the time, Jax, it just won't work otherwise! They'll always be on their guard!'

Jax shook her head. 'I'm just concerned about the legality—'

'We'll word the release form, em, differently,' John Paul proposed, receiving a wary but relieved look from Jax.

'That's an excellent idea,' Max said, and Jax nodded reluctantly.

'I'll have to let Da have a look at it,' she said, 'I mean, I know he's not a solicitor—'

'Have a look at what, love?' Angela sashayed back into the room with Raymond in her wake. 'May we sit in? We do feel a part of it, somehow.'

'Certainly, Angela. But would you excuse us for a moment? I need to confer with my colleague.' And Max yanked a snorting Lorcan by the elbow and out of the room and to the front door.

'Come on, Max, you've got to laugh,' he sniggered, and she drilled a lethal elbow into his ribs. 'Hey, I'm getting a notion that you like it rough.'

I've made a mistake, and you're going to have to leave. You eejit. 'You're behaving rudely—' *So just get the fuck out of here and forget I ever, ever let you put your tongue in my mouth.* 'And you need to cop on to yourself.' *And don't even think you're ever going to get a leg over Maxine O'Malley.* 'Or else you're going to have to go.'

'You didn't mind it the other night—'

'Shut *up*!' Max let out a strangled shout and stomped down the path. She stopped at the gate and spun around. Lorcan strolled towards her, confident that, somehow, in some way, she was playing hard to get.

'Look.' She took a cigarette from him, and accepted a light. Exhaling, she turned away again and leaned against the wall. 'Just stop fucking around, okay?'

'I'm not fucking around. It's just – how can you not laugh?'

'You're going to have to go.' *And where the hell are we going to get all the gear we need? And when did it all get so important – important enough that I'd put up with a jerk like you?*

'Ah, come on, Maxine. I'll be a good boy, all right?'

Lorcan swivelled over to cuddle his hip against hers – and she didn't move away. 'Good enough, anyway. Right?'

'One snide remark,' Max said warningly, 'one dodgy look—'

'Fine, fine.' He tossed away his smoke, and watched while Maxine delicately crushed hers out on the wall. He leaned in, and she smoothly slipped around him and headed into the house.

She was greeted by a beaming Angela, seated cheek by jowl with a purposefully motionless JP on the sofa, and a cautiously optimistic-looking Jax.

'What'd I miss?' Max slid on to the two-seater, next to Ray. Lorcan hung about with nowhere to sit.

Angela took a moment to send him a disparaging look before she turned to Maxine. 'We've got you a location!'

Max looked to Jax, who nodded slowly and said, 'It's not a terrible idea.'

'It does make sense, Jacinta,' said Raymond, who Max was glad to see seemed returned to his usual, easygoing self. He turned to her and smiled. 'My office, of course.'

'Of course!' Max shouted. 'Why in the world didn't we think of it ourselves!'

'Perhaps we were trying not to involve my parents in this agai— at all,' Jax mooted – and sent Lorcan a warning glance. 'Are you completely sure about this, Dad?' Jax started chewing on a cuticle.

'It is simply sensible,' Angela said, desperate for Raymond not to start thinking about it in great detail. 'It is Raymond's business concern, it's a fully restored Georgian mansion, it looks official, and it's fully dressed – all you'll need to do is step in and get down to it!'

'A big place, is it?' Max locked eyes with Angela, and saw agreement within.

'Enormous,' Angela sang, patting JP on the knee and squirming forward on the sofa.

'Hmmm. Sounds like we'll need a front woman of some sort. To organise everybody, get them where they're supposed to go.'

What's she up to? Jax perched on the arm of the sofa on the other side of John Paul. *She certainly doesn't need to do my mother any favours – does she?* 'I'd agree with that,' Jax said, eyeing Max sceptically.

'Maybe you could do it,' John Paul piped up, looking at Angela. 'You're an actress, aren't you?'

'Well – em – do you really think – er –' *Damn it, that wasn't the cue!* At sea, Angela threw a desperate look in Max's direction.

'It's up to Angela, of course,' Max said, looking over to Jax.

Jax laughed. 'Great minds think alike, it seems,' she said, and smiled brilliantly at JP. 'Well, what do you say, Angela Quirke? Ready for your close up?'

And that, thought Angela peevishly, *was my line!* 'I'd be delighted,' Angela replied, rising gracefully and extending her hand to JP. 'Do let me know when you have lines for me to study.' She shook Max's hand formally, even Jax's, and pointedly ignored Lorcan's as the phone sang shrilly from the hall. Angela grimaced, but rose.

'Leave that, Angela,' Raymond suggested, wishing his wife a prolonged triumphal turn about the room. 'The machine will get it.'

She bustled out into the hall. 'No, no, you know I don't understand the machine, and what if it's an *emergency*, what if it's my *agent* – Ha-llloooo – Yes, of course it is – Come again?' There was an ominous silence from Angela's end. 'Indeed – Oh, yes, all fine, and why wouldn't we be?

– Jacinta? Yes, you're quite lucky, I say quite lucky as she happens to be in tonight, having her Sunday lunch, accompanied by several of her many friends – Oh? Of course.' They heard the sound of the receiver slamming on the phone table, and the furious clack of Angela's heels on the wooden floor which preceded her return to the dining room.

She paused in the doorway, and slowly turned her gaze on to Jax. 'It's for you,' she pronounced. 'It is Fergus.'

'Fergal,' Jax corrected automatically, as she, equally automatically, made for the door. 'Fergal,' she repeated as she made her way around her mother, and out to the phone.

'Hello?' Jax's voice lowered to an indistinct murmur. 'Hello, yes, hello . . .'

Angela sat, her face like stone, and she and Raymond gazed at one another almost unblinkingly, with Ray's expression far more conciliatory than Angela's stormy glare. Lorcan wandered around, bored, and JP proceeded to lash away at the fire until he had almost put it out. Max simply wished for fewer witnesses and a seat nearer the hall.

It wasn't the world's longest telephone conversation. It certainly wasn't anywhere near being in the running, especially when one wondered when Jacinta and Fergal had last spoken. But what it lacked in length, it more than made up for in portent, and the atmosphere was positively seething with morbid curiosity by the time Jax reappeared in the doorway.

'He's back,' said Jax, worrying the hem of her shirt. 'He's back. In Ireland. To stay.'

17

They were as ready as they were ever going to be. The shooting schedule was sorted. The couples had been contacted. The release had been tweaked. Max had finessed the shooting schedule and JP had done so many dry runs with the gear that he could have wired it all up with his eyes closed. The location was perfect, the timing was excellent, and nothing was standing in their way.

Which was why Jax was in the middle of a complete and total nervous breakdown.

'. . . if they read that thing too closely we're leaving ourselves open for a lawsuit, if anything happens to the equipment we're borrowing from shagging Lorcan, we're bollixed. And my mother! How did my mother become a key player in this, I'd like to know? What if she isn't up to it? She's not used to this kind of thing, it's not like a play with a script; she'll be making it up as she goes along –'

Max ignored her and wondered where she was going to shop for her first on-camera outfit. Let JP sort this one out. It wasn't exactly the worst thing in the world for him to be hovering over Jax concernedly. They made their way back up to the office after another busy, long lunch.

'– and what if we're crap? What if the whole thing is rubbish, and we've dragged you into this, John Paul? You could have been looking for a new job all this time, and sure, if you want to bail, of course you can, we'd totally understand –'

JP paused in the doorway, and held Jax back for a moment. 'I'm in this one hundred per cent, Jax,' he said, meaningfully.

'Good. Good. I'm glad. It's – it's important to me – us,' said Jax, meaning more than she could say.

'Speaking for myself, I would have hunted you down and killed you if you'd left us now, Your Holiness.' Max playfully nudged him into the wall.

'*Some* of us do not appreciate this level of noise in the common areas.' Niamh Bourke loomed in the doorway to her office like a gargoyle come to life.

Max held a hand to her ear, her eyes searching the hall. 'Jax? JP? Did you hear something? Nah, me neither.' She turned smartly on her heel and headed up the staircase.

'It's all right for some, carrying on like fools and taking advantage. It'll be all right for those, once they get a certain memo coming across their desks. Their *untidy, unused* desks!' Niamh came out into the hall, and Max trotted back down towards her.

'And who would be the author of said memo? Would it ever be yourself, Niamh Bourke?' Max craned her neck and tried to get a look over Niamh's shoulder, into her office. 'Whatcha got in there, Niamh?' Max winked at Jax, who merely shook her head and made for the stairs herself. 'What is all that stuff? Taking away some parting gifts?' For Niamh's office, as far as Max could see as they tussled on the threshold, was crammed with boxes and bits and bobs: computers, monitors, stacks of papers, file boxes, filled every available space.

'I'll have you know the inventory has begun – I'll have

a record of every paperclip in this place, so don't get any wise ideas, Maxine O'Malley!' And she slammed the door.

Then she turned the key.

And threw a deadbolt.

And, quite possibly, propped a chair beneath the doorknob.

'Yeah, yeah, yeah,' Max muttered, and pelted up the steps.

Niamh braced her back against her buttressed door and listened to Max clatter up the stairs. *Oh, it's all right for some, Maxine O'Malley*, she whispered to herself. It was time for a dose of comeuppance. Double-checking that her door was locked tight, she headed for her office cupboard.

No hiding sensitive documents in filing cabinets for Niamh Bourke. Sliding a false back wall down and to the side, Niamh reached an unerring hand to the lock box that she kept concealed there. Covering her tracks and covering up the hidey-hole, she placed the box on her chair and went across to her kettle, under which she had taped the key to the box's lock. Taking the extra precaution of crouching beneath her desk, she revealed its treasures.

Inside was a myriad of incriminating evidence she'd accumulated over the years, including some incredibly graphic pictures of J of ACJ with his mistress – although Niamh wasn't exactly sure that was the term one applied to a male lover. She pawed fondly through the stolen letters, purloined and printed-out emails, and various and sundry photographs of colleagues in compromising positions that exceeded even the usual Christmas-party excesses.

Underneath them all lay what was surely Niamh's best

work. So deliciously provocative that even she hesitated to use it. The letter lay innocently on her palm. Shaking with nerves and excitement, she stroked the envelope, its typed address failing to betray its authorship. Unable to resist, she slipped the company letterhead out from its sheath, and quickly scanned the missive. 'Sure, that's her flippant tone down to the ground,' Niamh murmured to herself, and that was a perfectly convincing signature.

Folding it carefully, she slipped the sheet into the envelope once more, and taking a fortifying breath, she licked the gummed edge sensuously, passionately, as if she was ministering to the body of her amour.

Heart beating wildly, she slipped the letter into a previously prepared FedEx envelope, and sealed that up as well. Rising, replacing the key and the box, she slipped into her coat and out of the office, keen to send this particular package off personally.

Mr Michael LaMotta was in for a surprise . . .

'Cow,' Max sighed as they finally reached the top floor. 'You know, I think I'll miss auld Niamh Bourke.'

'Did she say she was doing inventory?' John Paul looked at Jax. 'We'd better get that cable out of here.'

'Doesn't Lorcan have cable?' Max asked.

'The less we have to deal with him, the better,' Jax said, moving up another flight.

'Yeah, but, if Nasty Niamh has her nose to the ground –' Max said.

'Since when is that a concern?' Jax asked.

'Excuse *me*, but you're the one always quivering on about, "Oh, no, don't take that pen, Maxine, don't use the stapler!" We'll just tough it out with Lorcan.'

JP didn't know when to quit. 'But I thought that you

wanted to get rid of him. That's the deal, yeah?'

'I'm taking care of it,' Max grumbled. 'We'll lose him after the first shoot.'

'It's not like I'd expect you to hesitate, like, not like you'd be worrying about hurting his feelings – right?' He looked to Jax for reinforcement – and actually shuddered at the chilling look in her eye.

'You'll find, John Paul, that the better you think you know Maxine, the less you actually know about her,' Jax said coolly, leaning a hip against the banister.

'Additionally, JP,' Max said, easing her way up the few stairs that separated herself and Jax, and getting into her face, 'you'll find that the more indifferent the behaviour of Jacinta Quirke, the more there is to hide.'

'*I've* nothing to hide, Maxine O'Malley,' Jax replied, turning towards the top of the staircase. 'I wonder, can you say the same yourself?'

Speechless, Maxine stood still on the stair, and JP, fed up with getting in the middle of them, disappeared noiselessly all the way down to his basement office.

The very next day, a man stood at the window of his fifty-second-floor midtown office, absently hung up his cell phone, and gazed sightlessly down on to Lexington Avenue. He flipped the compact phone over and under his fingers with the dexterity of a magician, with the panache of a three-card monte hustler.

If you asked him, he'd tell you that in the morality stakes, advertising was little better than three-card monte. If you asked him, he'd say it was a living, that he was a glorified salesman, that he was a blue-collar worker in a wannabe white-collar field, only a step up from the telemarketers whom everyone was hung up on – or a door-to-door encyclopaedia huckster.

Michael LaMotta had no illusions about his job, and his title of senior vice-president in charge of accounts was, to him, just a long-winded way of saying that he'd aged well in an industry that was notorious for eating its young. He'd given as good as he'd got all his years in advertising, and even in as soft a market as the current one, he felt the security of his Midtown eyrie, and had not one, single, solitary regret.

Well. Mostly.

He flexed his fingers and reached for the letter that had been in and out of his hand for the past thirty-six hours. *Loser*, he chided himself as, yet again, he read the information that it contained.

He shook his head. He'd held off, trying to do the Dr Phil thing and give her some space, but he'd had enough of the damn space. She'd had enough time. It was time he took action. He could go to her, take away even more of that goddamn space, in less than a week, less than a day, in a heartbeat –

He rose, all six foot three inches of him, and wandered the edges of his spacious corner office like a caged lion, his beautifully tailored suit draping over his fit body, moving effortlessly with it. He ran a nervous hand through his thick, short black hair, and in the twilight, he caught himself staring East, as if he could see her, see into her mind.

As patient a man as he was, it was getting down to now or never. Especially when he was dealing with a woman like *her*. As he read and reread the document he held tight in his hand, which had winged its way, express, from Ireland, read about her latest exploits at ACJ:Dublin, read the words she'd typed that he'd hoped she'd someday write, or say, he chanted to himself: *'Now or never, LaMotta, now or never. Now or never, now or never'* – and he was not the kind of man who took *never* lying down.

18

From the exterior, the beautifully maintained Georgian edifice in Merrion Square looked no different to its beautifully maintained neighbours: while its door took a left turn at conservative and was painted a bristling yellow, its clear-glass fan light was as elegant as one would expect, its window boxes, bursting with petunias and geraniums, were as abundant as one would desire, and its brass plaque, quietly displaying the title *Quirke and Associates*, was as sober as required by a tally of accountants. However, at 6.05 p.m. on this Monday evening in early April, were one able to swing back the façade of the graceful building to reveal the cross section of its four storeys, one would be forgiven for assuming the place was not an accountancy firm, but an ant hill.

The rumblings of curiosity on the part of Raymond's employees were quelled by the gift of a half-day off work. The confusion had begun when it became apparent that someone had dropped in over the weekend and dumped a nest of wires on to the conference-room floor, while the table itself was littered with complicated-looking little boxes and locked silver suitcases that looked as though they were sturdy enough to emerge unscathed from a series of grenade launches. Around lunchtime, several strangers started moving authoritatively between floors – wasn't that little Jacinta, Ray's youngest? – consulting loudly in the stairwells, shouting into what looked like walkie-talkies, and basically behaving as if they had the run of the place.

Consequently, Raymond had sent an email round at 2.15 p.m. suggesting that the work being done in the offices – what exactly the work was he chose not to say – was interfering with everybody's ability to concentrate, and that they were free to go.

Jax jumped out of the way of the last accountant as he briskly made for the door. Double-checking that she wasn't going to be flattened by another fleeing auditor, she left the foyer, which was now under observation by a minute lens concealed by a flower arrangement, and made her way up the stairs to the third floor, and command central.

Her father hovered around, bemused, as he watched the team continue their wholesale takeover of his building, and flinched at the sound of hammering coming from below.

Jax rushed up to meet him. 'It's not what it sounds like,' she said breathlessly. 'It's not anything being hammered into the walls, it's a temporary rig that JP and Lorcan are lashing together.'

Raymond smiled wanly, and it was Jacinta's turn to wince. 'Sorry, Da,' she said. 'More than you bargained for, eh?'

Patting her cheek, he took a deep breath and managed a less pained smile. 'It's a big job – and it's very impressive, Jacinta.'

'Yeah, makes us look like we know what we're doing.'

'How's your mother?'

158

Jax immediately headed back up to the control room. 'She and Maxine are, em, discussing the script.' She grinned cheekily down at him. 'We've got it all running on camera six . . .'

'But what's my *motivation*, Maxine? Who am I, *why* am I? Why am I *here*, today, of all days?' Angela's voice came over the speakers as Jax turned up the volume, and she and her father huddled over the monitor to watch the show.

You're here to answer the shagging door, thought Maxine, cradling her throbbing head in her hands. *You're here today because we are finally immortalising something on tape, and because we feel sorry for you.*

Angela tossed her pages down on the table. 'I certainly don't *need* to put myself in a vulnerable position for *nothing.*'

'Oh, come on,' groaned Max. 'I mean, who's doing whom a favour, here?'

'Oh, dear,' murmured Raymond, watching from the safety of the third floor. 'Oh dear, oh dear.'

'Favour?' Angela's eyebrows disappeared into her hairline. 'Hmm, yes, let's see, who exactly is doing *whom* a favour here. Would it be the fledgling, inexperienced production company essaying a seat-of-the-pants, fly-by-night—'

'Fly-by-night! Fly-by-night!'

'That's not a bad name for the company, in actual fact,' JP mused as he passed by the door.

'—reality television programme, which, I must say, I *must* say, is not exactly the most original proposal to come my way.'

'Come your way! What, you're hanging up when the Abbey rings' – Max mimed talking on the phone – '*So sorry, pet, I'm simply not available* to do *Lady*

Windermere's Fan, simply not available, I'm starring in the latest RTÉ high-profile vehicle, you understand –'

Raymond shouted with laughter. 'Good Lord, that's Angela down to the ground.'

Angela had the hide of a rhino, but that little dig hit home. *Time to change tack*, she thought, and dropped down into a chair, dejected.

'Oh, here we go,' Jax shook her head and continued to keep one eye on the monitor, and the other on the recording device. Who knew? This 'making of' footage might come in handy for something . . .

Pressing her fingers to her lips, as if trying to hold back a wave of emotion, Angela held up a hand. 'I just want to do my best for my girls – I do think of you as mine, Max, I know we haven't known each other terribly long, but you're my Jacinta's *best friend*, and you're so far away, so far away from your *own* mum, and I – I –'

Max cast her eye up to the lens that she knew was there.

'Let's see you hold out against this, Maxine O'Malley,' mumbled Jax.

Dropping down across from Angela, Max stretched out a hand. Angela took it, and ducked her head down further, hiding her triumphantly shining eyes – which, of course, Max knew she was hiding. 'Angela,' she began, 'we're on the same side of the playing field—'

'We *are*,' Angela replied, sniffing rather convincingly. 'We're on the same *team*.'

'And I certainly don't want you to feel that you're not being heard,' Max continued.

Angela closed her eyes and reached out her other hand, took Max's. 'I need to be *heard*,' she breathed, her voice breaking slightly.

'Remember when she played Blanche in *Streetcar*?' Raymond asked fondly.

'I think it's *Cherry Orchard* you're remembering,' Jax replied.

Lorcan slid into the room and behind the control panel. 'It's twenty minutes to mark,' he said sharply, and Jax mimed cracking him over the head with a blunt object.

'I'm hearing you, Angela, I'm hearing you,' Max soothed. 'But what we need, tonight, is really very simple. I understand that it may not be the kind of challenge that you are often required to rise to' – she raised a hand to stem the imminent tide – 'but the couples we're interviewing tonight need you to be their guide into what we're calling the first-floor studio, to bring them tea or water—'

'Like a bloody *waitress*,' Angela howled, and jumped up again.

Max once again cradled her head in her hands. 'You're going to be attending to them. Making sure that A, they are comfortable, B, they don't get cold feet and bail and C, they don't suspect that they're being monitored from the moment they walk in the door.'

Angela paused in her route around the room. 'That's interesting.'

'Once we've done a post-mortem, we'll review the tape and *then* we can talk about changes to the script, maybe do some improv,' Max said.

'I see. I *see*.' Angela's pace around the table was now thoughtful. 'It's true *cinéma vérité*, I need to stay on my toes, keep open to the shifting moods, the *subtext* –'

Max anticipated an end to the negotiations. 'You'll have

a monitor of your own in the kitchen – you may have to respond quickly if we need you to go in and run interference. Let's get you wired.'

'Wired? How exciting!' Angela hopped up on to the table.

'Likes the auld table top, doesn't she?' Lorcan smirked, and Raymond looked at him curiously.

'Lorc, you want to check those Diatech pinholes on the edges of the front door jamb?' JP bounded into the room, and Jax could have kissed him.

'What pinhole cameras?' she queried, just to ensure that the subject stayed changed.

Lorcan prodded a few control buttons. 'It's to get the crowd coming in – and they're fine, Johnny.'

John Paul ran an agitated hand through his curls. 'Would you just go and—'

'Lads,' Jax intervened, 'it's almost time.' She turned to her father. 'Da, would you let Mum know we need to get her wired?' Casting another inquisitive glance at the officious Lorcan, Raymond went in search of his newly placated wife.

Max breathed deeply through her nose, and adjusted her smart new suit jacket. She'd left Angela in her ante-room, mumbling to herself – Max wasn't sure, but she thought it sounded like *Juno and the Paycock*. She fussed with her hair, making sure it swung with apparent carelessness over the ear that concealed her earpiece.

'Plus ten post mark, subjects still not on premises.' Lorcan's smug voice came in loud and clear in her left ear. *Eejit*, she thought. *Okay, no more procrastinating – I'll give him the boot after tonight.*

'Let's keep the line clear, shall we?' Jacinta's voice

came through patiently. 'Max, can you give us another sound check, please?'

'Testing one, two, how do I look? I got this in Richard Alan, I never go there, but—'

'Thank you, Maxine,' Jax cut her off smoothly. 'JP, let's run through the cameras once more.'

The big brass knocker on the building's bright yellow door thumped three times.

A collective yelp of excitement danced around the wires, and then there was silence.

'Camera three,' Jax murmured, as Angela leisurely strolled to the front door. As she opened it – 'Camera one,' Jax called – Dara and her boyfriend Conor were revealed on the threshold, Dara nervously clutching her handbag, Conor yawning.

'Welcome,' said Angela warmly. 'Do come in.'

'Camera three,' Jax called again, giving them a long shot from down the hall as Dara and Conor moved into the foyer.

'If you'll just follow me,' Angela suggested, and moved up the stairs as Jax called for camera four. 'I'm afraid we'll have to ask you to wait for a few moments, if you don't mind. Just finishing up with the technical business.' She gestured towards a sofa that was set in a conversation nook on the landing, and hung Dara's coat on a coat stand.

'I'm in IT,' Dara blurted.

'Camera five,' Jax said, her voice gaining confidence. 'We'll stay here for a while, lads.'

'Lovely!' Angela smiled at Conor. 'Please take your feet off the coffee table. It's an antique.' Conor grudgingly changed position. 'Now. Coffee, tea?'

Max stood in front of the monitor that she would

conceal in the cupboard once Dara and Conor came into the 'studio'. Framed as they were, mimicking the 'live' shot that would commence once they entered, it looked exactly like those clips from the Meg Ryan movie. Excellent. Max nodded, and crossed her arms – and was surprised to feel her heart beating like a bass drum.

'Quiet, please,' Jax urged.

Quiet was, in fact, the pervading theme of the next several minutes. Dara and Conor sat.

Conor put his foot back on the table.

'Honey,' Dara warned, and he made a show of shifting it off again.

'Antique, me arse,' he mumbled.

'Well, it is,' Dara managed. 'It's old-looking.'

'Not the only antique around here,' Conor snorted, and the sound of smashing crockery emanated from the kitchen.

'Mum!' Jax admonished.

The silence was deafening.

Conor yawned, and then looked at his watch.

Dara looked about nervously.

'Better get them moving, Max,' Jax advised, and with a self-conscious tug on the hair covering her earpiece, Max sailed out into the waiting area.

'Stand by for camera six, and the live unit, seven,' Jax said, and stood tall. *I love this. I love doing this.* She beamed at John Paul, who reached out to stroke her down the arm, stopped himself, and recovered by readjusting his headphones.

'Hello! Sorry for the delay!' Handshakes all around, and Max led them on to the set.

The small conference room had been rearranged to accommodate a cosy, plush sofa, facing a straight-backed chair and a professional-looking camera. Several lights were arranged around the sofa, out of frame, and John Paul's subtle use of coloured gels gave the space a depth and – most importantly – legitimacy.

'Please have a seat.' Max beamed. 'I just need to adjust these somewhat, make sure we're getting you both to your best advantage.'

Conor sat down heavily and Dara perched, eyeballing the whole set-up eagerly.

'Roll live unit,' Jax said.

'So.' Max sat down, opened a swanky leather portfolio on her lap, and nonchalantly flicked a remote at the camera.

In the control room, JP flicked a switch that started the camera's little red eye blinking. Max smiled at the fluttering Dara and the comatose Conor, and began.

Max heard a collectively drawn breath waft through her earpiece. She cheated her good side slightly to the lens she knew was observing the proceedings from beneath the ornately framed painting that hung above the subject's couch, and glanced down at her script.

'On behalf of the team, I'd like to thank you, once again, for participating in our project. Dara, I know you and Jacinta are old friends, but I'd love a little background on you both, just for the record.'

Dara glanced up at the camera and self-consciously fussed with her beaded necklace; Max was tempted to check Conor for a pulse.

'Well, I'm thirty-three, same as Jacinta, and Conor's thirty-six. I've always thought the man should be older.'

Ooookay, Max thought. She made a note of that little tidbit, and moved swiftly on.

'And you were born in . . . ?'

'I'm from the country, down the country, Tipperary, but we moved up when I was two. Conor's a Dublin man. I've always thought that one person should be from one place, and the other person from the other.' She laughed, and Conor reacted by blinking.

'Seems like a nice balance,' Max began.

'Oh, it is, it is! We're very balanced, I think, very balanced – like, I'm the one from the country and I like to go hill-walking, and Conor's the one from the city, so he knows it really well, he's got street savvy, like, and I'm the one working in business, and Conor's the artist – and he's the deep one, and I'm the bubbly one!' She fussed again – necklace, rings, skirt – and ended with a stroke of Conor's knee.

Conor moved his knee out of the way, and leaned towards his end of the couch.

Dara clutched her hands together, and smiled broadly.

'So, Conor. You're an artist?'

'Writer.'

'Ah, ha.' Max leaned towards him as if she could will him to speak in a complete sentence. 'What kind of writing?'

'Poet.' And he yawned again.

'Haiku?'

'Wha'?'

'Nothing.' *Right, Max, don't let him determine the rhythm*, she told herself, and Jax's voice whispered over the wire to counsel – 'He's useless, but it's probably the point.'

'I'd love to hear how you two met, seeing as you're both from such different walks of life,' Max said brightly, warming the wilting Dara with her kind regard.

'We were at a party, and I'd just ended, like, the worst relationship of my life,' Dara ran her fingers self-consciously over her necklace, 'and I was on the prowl, right? And it was summer, and it was a barbecue, a gorgeous day, drinking since, like, midday, and at about, oh, when was it, Conor? When did you get in to the party?'

'Late.'

'It was, it was late, and he walked in, and I thought, *Oh my God, wow*, and he walked right over to me.'

'She was standing by the drinks table.' Conor shrugged.

'And we got talking, and that was that.' Dara clapped her hands on her knees triumphantly, and Max nodded warmly, thinking of cutaways.

'Anything to add, Conor?' Max was nothing if not dogged.

'Nah.'

Max consulted her notes again, and then looked up at Dara with a sympathetic and curious expression on her face. 'Dara, you mentioned something that really struck me, you said, "I'd just ended the worst relationship of my life" – I wonder, would you mind telling me about that?'

'Yah, sure,' she said, worrying her necklace again. 'I, um, well, um, I guess – it was just . . . bad. Like, he never was the one to ring me and set up times to meet, and we'd been together for ages and he wouldn't even talk about moving in together or anything else, and it wasn't like I felt he heard me or anything, not like Conor, right, honey?'

'Wha'?'

Jax and JP exchanged a look that was mixed with sympathy and excitement. She whispered down to Max, 'Keep her going on this.'

'Uh huh.' Max reckoned that response was good

enough for both the crew and the 'cast'. 'But things are different, between you and Conor.'

'Oh, *yah*, so totally different!' Dara reached out for contact again, and Conor once again subtly shifted away from her touch.

'So you're living together?'

Dara froze. 'Uh, not as such. Like, we spend the entire weekend together, either at mine or his.'

'Nothing wrong with the old-fashioned approach to a relationship,' Max soothed, and Dara nodded in relieved agreement. 'So, speaking of old-fashioned, would you consider your relationship to be exclusive?'

'Oh, *yah*,' Dara said, nodding at Conor.

'Exclusive?' He grunted, actually making eye contact with Max.

'Yeah, exclusive, you know, not seeing other people, faithful to one another, committed, no playing away – you know.' Max winked at him.

He shrugged again. 'Yeah, whatever.' And shrugged again. 'If you're with someone, you're with them,' he said. 'If you don't want to be with them, you leave.'

Max nonchalantly flicked the remote at the camera, and JP smoothly flipped the switch that turned off the little red light.

'Mind if I leave you for a moment? I just need to run out to the control room, check in with the team. I'll be back in a few – please, just relax.' Max rose and calmly left, shutting the door behind her. She headed for the kitchen and joined Angela at the monitor.

'Poor silly sausage,' Angela murmured. 'Yer man's as thick as two short planks.'

Max grinned, and quoted, ' "If you're with someone, you're with them." Warms the cockles of my heart.'

'Quiet, please,' Jax urged. 'How long are you going to stay out, Max?'

'Until they start throwing things?' Max joked, and heard Raymond's nervous cough in the background. 'Just winding you up, Ray. Let's see what happens – we'll know what to do.'

'Well, that wasn't so terrible, was it?' Dara chirped, smiling over at Conor, who looked to be disappearing between the cushions.

He yawned.

'I think we came off very well,' Dara continued brightly. She leaned in to kiss him, and had to settle for a glancing smooch on his cheek.

'Well.' Dara switched her attention from her necklace to her rings.

Conor's eyes roamed around the room once, and then gazed listlessly at the camera.

Dara tweaked at Conor's collar, and he batted her hand away. He yawned again.

Dara fussed with her cuffs, and then moved down to her hem.

Conor closed his eyes.

'Oh my *God*,' Max moaned. 'People are so *boring*!'

'Cut,' ordered Jax, as the door knocker went, signalling the arrival of the next couple.

'*Do* give my mother your best, isn't it lovely to see you, and to meet your lovely wife!' Angela led Jamie and Majella to the first set-up on the landing, and bustled off with their coats.

'Terribly smart suit, Majella, really *sharp*,' Angela observed. They'd agreed that Angela needed to warm up the next subjects more than she had the last time.

And she was more than happy to do it.

'Thanks.' Majella ran a hand down a narrow lapel. 'We've to dress like this for work, but there's no reason not to be stylish.'

'What do you do for a living?' Angela asked politely.

'I'm a barrister.'

'*Shite!*' was the general reaction down the wires.

'Mum, you've got to keep her distracted when you hand over the release,' Jax whispered.

Max, watching from the main set, marvelled at Angela's control – you'd never know that she'd been exposed to a hurricane of expletives, much less frantic instruction, through her ear.

'Angela, I was hoping to get some additional information before we began.' Majella crossed her legs authoritatively.

'Max, will you jump in, or –' Jax asked.

'I understand perfectly, Majella,' Angela boomed, cutting off Jax, and any possible reply from Max. Careful to stay out of the camera's line of sight, she shifted over so that Majella and Jamie were cheated towards the pinhole lens. 'Fire away.'

'Just a few queries, Mrs Quirke.' Jamie gently pressed his foot over his wife's. He remembered a bollocking he'd received at Angela's hands, twenty-five years ago, like it was yesterday. 'We're just, you know – and Majella – barrister –'

'I've agreed to this, Jamie, in good faith.' Majella crushed the spike of her heel into his toe. 'But I insist on knowing what the ultimate goal of this video shoot is, what we're exposing ourselves to.'

'Oh, is *that* all.' Angela sighed, and patted her heart lightly, and cleared her throat as if to deliver a speech.

Which she proceeded to do. 'In reaction to the kind of dire and scurrilous programming that has *dis*graced our airwaves for the last several years, Night Flight Productions is pursuing the line that modern relationships are actually quite old-fashioned. We are seeking out couples, like yourselves, to *refute* such statistics, to share with us your successes – and, if you're willing, and only if you're willing –' this last was warmly directed to Majella, who began to look appeased – 'the unique challenges facing marriage in today's society. Not *too* terribly scandalous, hmmm?' And she laughed like a little bell.

Majella briskly yanked at her jacket. 'Well, I do understand the nature of such releases. I did a course in entertainment law.'

'How *exciting*,' Angela burbled.

'Yes, it was, really, that's why – well, when Jamie brought this up, this shoot, I thought, well, yes, it's exciting, to be on the other side of the, well, the cameras.'

'No one is immune,' JP whispered, and Max giggled with relief.

'In*deed*,' Angela breathed.

'But I don't – I refuse to do any nudity.' Majella crossed her arms, and Jamie blushed.

Angela shook her head in sympathy. 'This form merely gives us the full and complete rights, in perpetuity and universally, to use any and all footage in which you appear, for such programming as we deem fit and appropriate for our means. What a mouthful!' And Angela handed over the release. 'Do fill one out for the both of you,' she urged.

'Ah, it's grand.' Jamie signed his name with a flourish. 'Go on, love. It's Jacinta, after all.'

And Majella signed.

Angela smiled benevolently, snatched the clipboard

back from Majella, and retired elegantly to her post ...
where she mugged triumphantly for the camera.

Jax and John Paul's laughter filled her ear as Max
immediately called the couple on set.

'As Jamie wasn't really looking to pursue the law for the duration—'

'I couldn't stick it,' he admitted wryly, and he and Majella shared a hearty laugh, full of innuendo and private experience, 'so it seemed to me—'

'You hear all sorts of things about people getting together on the job,' Majella continued.

Curiously, Max looked both annoyed and wistful at the same time.

'Ah, but it's all attitude,' Jamie insisted.

Majella nodded. 'If you're both grown-up enough—'

'And committed,' Jamie added, shrugging to take the edge of the cumbersome and self-conscious weight of the word 'committed'.

'—then it doesn't matter if you work together.'

And Max heard JP sigh in her ear. She grinned.

'So you met on the job, Jamie chucked it in—'

Majella laid her hand protectively over Jamie's knee. 'He achieved quite a high level at the Law Library,' she said coolly. 'It was more a matter of Jamie wanting to play to his other strengths.'

'You're a salesman, is that right, Jamie? We were talking about . . . *Germans*, I think, when we met.' Max leaned towards him, beaming.

'What's she up to?' JP murmured.

'What are you up to, Max?' Jax demanded. Max flicked her earpiece dismissively, and Jax growled warningly down the line.

Majella rubbed her hand up and down Jamie's thigh as Max continued to bathe him in the warmth of her regard, and her low-cut top. 'He's chief salesman, and the company are internationally known. He's shot up the ranks.' Jamie ducked his head modestly . . . after another sweep of his hand through his coif.

'It's so sexy, isn't it, when men are good at what they do?' Max pretended towards female complicity, and was delighted by the forbidding look on Majella's face.

Sacrificing myself and my good name for the cause, thought Max, and she decided to hammer another nail in the coffin of her reputation.

'Jamie, you'd be on the road fairly regularly, wouldn't you?' Max gently eased her neckline lower.

Jamie immediately made eye contact with his wife. 'Em, yeah, well, part of the deal.'

'Interesting,' Max breathed, and she heard Angela hiss, '*Vixen!*' in her ear. 'Days at a time, then?' Max pressed on. 'With the two of you separated?'

'What exactly are you implying?' Majella demanded in her best barristerial tones.

'I won't lie to you,' said Max, lying, 'but quite a few of the couples that we've spoken to for this project admit to, er, extracurricular activities whilst apart. Given that Jamie is in fact away for a good part of the time—'

'Not a *good* part of the time,' Jamie protested.

'Well, I just got the impression, when we met, in the bar, Jamie, that part of the gig, especially when entertaining foreign colleagues ... well, things could get out of hand.'

'I'm sure you misunderstood,' Majella sneered. 'Unless, of course, Jamie told you things he hasn't bothered to tell *me*.'

Go on, Max prayed, *nasty marital spat, right here, right now, cameras rolling, go on, go on—*

'Max, let them alone, they're not going to get into anything with you in there,' Jax suggested.

'Excuse me for a moment.' Max once again pretended to shut down the camera. She hurried out, as Majella withdrew her hand from Jamie's grasp.

Max joined Angela in the kitchen, and waited with bated breath for the big fall-out.

She was as surprised as the rest of the team when Majella and Jamie burst into laughter.

'As if you've got time for a bit on the side,' Majella snorted, and they both cracked up all over again.

'Hmmph,' said Max. 'How annoying.'

'This is excellent,' retorted Jax. 'Stay out.'

'Yeah, yeah,' Max replied, disgruntled, and they carried on watching.

'You're the one who could be playing away, while I'm off slogging around Ireland,' Jamie offered.

'Yeah, right. "Mam, will you come watch the baby, I've to go out for an hour and have a blistering affair." '

'An hour? Hardly seems worth the aggro.' And they laughed uproariously.

Jax's eyes gleamed as she watched Max shuffle indignantly around the kitchen. 'How are we on back-up?' she asked JP.

'Plenty, and all systems are going,' he said, grinning over at her.

Majella sighed, 'I suppose a woman like that would never understand.'

Max's nostrils flared dangerously.

'Now, Maj,' Jamie said.

'Well, hitting on you, right in front me? *That's* intelligent,' she scoffed, and Jamie put his arm around her shoulders and they cuddled.

'Did I not tell you!' Jamie brandished his left hand in the air. 'All the time now! Ever since I got this!'

'Maybe you shouldn't wear it.' Majella pretended to pout.

'Not on your life,' Jamie said, and they met for a sweet kiss.

'Maybe we should have insisted she take her top off,' Angela yawned, and Max laughed, shortly and bitterly.

'Did you get those yokes, the wipey things?' Majella asked.

'Yes, in the middle of my high-powered, head-of-regional-sales day,' Jamie snorted. 'Laying it on a bit thick there, pet.'

'It's true!' Majella yawned prodigiously. 'Your boss has only to catch up with the programme.'

'Speaking of programme, did you set up the DVR?'

'Oh, come *on*,' Max moaned. As Majella and Jamie continued to sit there and perform their *normality*, Max became more and more annoyed. When they lapsed into a comfortable silence, a silence as different from Dara and Conor's as Penneys was from Dolce and Gabbana, Max started pounding rhythmically against the counter top with her hip.

'What's she up to? Not terribly professional, I must say. Unless she's off to trowel on more slap.'

'Ha!' Max kicked the wall.

'Maj,' Jamie sighed. 'So she's a bit desperate or something—'

'HA!' Max leapt to her feet, and Angela, stronger than she looked, threw herself across the doorway to prevent Max storming out.

'Will we head?' Jamie proposed.

'We've already signed the release, so we're screwed in that respect.' Majella snapped her compact closed, and rose. 'We can't control what they've got now, but they needn't get any more off us.' Jamie rose as well, and they walked off the set.

As Angela rushed to head them off at the pass, Max sulked. 'Miss Perfect, with her perfect marriage, and her wipey things and her stupid DVR,' she groused, hammering her boot against the fridge. 'Smarty pants lawyer cow, showing off. "Oh, who has time for an affair, la di da."'

'Max!' Jax stood in the doorway. 'Come on, it wasn't that terrible.'

'It was rubbish!' Max fully kicked at the cupboard.

'Stop knocking around my father's kitchen!' Jax demanded. 'Frankly, I'm delighted; it certainly shows more of my side.'

'We should just erase it,' Max groused.

'We need both sides, and you know it!' *And I wonder what you're* actually *angry about,* Jax thought spitefully.

'Well, that's going to set the world on fire,' Lorcan sneered, and Max and Jax left off arguing to glare up at the camera.

'Let's wrap, and sort out what we've got tomorrow,' JP suggested. Angela, coming in with the tea set, beamed up at the camera. 'I think we did a great job tonight, and it's early days, after all.'

'Lovely fellow, that,' she whispered to Max, which, of course, meant: to everyone. John Paul blushed, and Raymond lowered his lids assessingly. As JP looked away from the monitor, he missed Angela rubbing her thumb against her fingers, and Raymond's answering shake of the head.

Didn't Angela shout something about fifty quid at lunch the other day? wondered Max, as she fled down a corridor away from Lorcan.

Jax hovered in the doorway, smiling up at her father while he passed. She watched JP burn a quick dub of the night's footage, shut down the mixers, and wrap whatever cable could be wrapped in order to keep the place organised. She watched as he ran long fingers through his curly hair, sexy fingers, sexier hair, and wondered what it would take – for surely between the two of them there was a wealth of shyness – what would it take for the two of them to –

She knew what it would take for her to do something. She had to feel – to *actually be* – free. And she'd never be free if she didn't free herself, if last week's stilted, pointless chat with Fergal was any indication. She knew, deep down, that if anything was going to get done, it was she who would have to be the one to do it. *It's up to you, Jacinta Quirke*, and nipping out of the building, she pulled out her mobile and made the phone call she should have made years ago.

Late the next day, the post-mortem began in the depths of ACJ, in front of JP's computer.

'The quality is excellent, JP,' Jax said. 'I was worried that the sound was going to be like in a tin can, but it's clear as a bell – crisp.'

'But it's still like it's observing, you know, like we're listening in on it,' Max added. 'And Jax, nice use of the cameras, really good coverage; we'll barely have to cut this together.'

Jax smiled serenely. 'I'm happy enough,' she said, completely thrilled with herself.

'It's fucking fantastic!' Max bellowed. 'Let's all get a little American here! It *rocks*, we rock, look at me, I look amazing! Too bad our talent sucked.'

'Right so, we can't use them as the main event, in any case,' said Jax, as they all watched Conor begin to snore all over again.

Max clapped her hands authoritatively. 'So. What did we learn?'

Jax pulled at a thread dangling off the bottom of her shirt. 'Well, on the plus side, we know that we know what we're doing, we're getting broadcast quality footage, and we all work well together.'

'Yeah,' said John Paul. 'And that Ray's office as a location will do us fine, and we've enough gear to light it all up if we wanted to.'

'Speaking of gear . . .' Jax said darkly.

Max kicked her chair back, on to its back legs, and leaned against the wall. 'I know, I know. I heard his crack about table tops through my earpiece.'

'I'll do the honours,' JP sighed, intending to drop Lorcan an email – or maybe he could cut right to his voicemail on the mobile.

'I said I'd do it,' Max said hastily. She thudded back against the wall, and missed the rather chilly look that Jax sent her way. 'I'll put him off.' *In more ways than one . . .*

'So what else?' She crashed back down on all four legs of her chair again.

'Em –' John Paul cleared his throat.

'Go on, go on,' Max sighed, tossing a stress ball she'd picked up from hand to hand. 'Only three weeks to go!'

He looked at Jax apologetically. 'I was thinking about that idea that Max had, about stalking the couples –'

'Following! Not stalking! Involving ourselves in their lives! Jeez!' Max threw the ball down in disgust.

Covering her uneasiness, Jax picked up the thoroughly squished ball and put it on JP's bookshelf, which she started to tidy. 'I don't know –'

John Paul leaned forward and focused on Jax, on her not thinking he'd betrayed her. 'I think we need to, Jax. Get them used to us hanging around, and then really stick it to them when we get them on set.'

'Why do we have to stick it to anybody?' Jax left off with the books and sat back down again, looking at John Paul, begging him not to be an opportunistic, selfish—

Come on you two! Max thought. *Get on with it! In more ways than one . . .*

'It's not even stuff that we'll use a lot of,' John Paul guessed. 'Just for cutaways, exposition—'

'It's crap television, otherwise,' Max interjected. 'The whole point is to get to the guts of the idea, not just have a bunch of people talking about how they met.'

'What if we work on the script more, just flesh it out, and figure out a way to, I don't know, trigger them so that when we leave them alone, they give up more?' Jax tugged unconsciously at the hem of her shirt.

'The script is fine,' Max said defensively.

'I'm just saying that maybe the psychology of it needs to be pushed.'

'And maybe they need to get to know us better, too,' JP

cut in. 'If we're hanging out with them, in a casual way, then they relax their guard.'

'Hanging out, not stalking,' Jax said firmly.

'Okay, compromise, kids.' Max tilted her chair back again. 'We tweak the script and see where we could have set some triggers. I'll start testing out a mobile unit and see how it works. Then, all going well, we pick a likely pair who want to give up their privacy for the little screen.'

Jax cringed. 'This is why I hate these programmes.'

'It'll be fine,' Max said airily. 'They're all gasping to do it.'

'It's, it's manipulative.'

'Yours can be the warm, fuzzy section of the programme.'

'Just because I'm not intent on exposing people as liars and cheats doesn't mean—'

The door crashed open so suddenly that it bounced off the wall. In one smooth motion, Jax leapt to her feet, Max's chair hit the floor, and JP scrambled to quit out of their project.

Niamh stood in the doorway, her eyes immediately zeroing in on the footage that JP was trying to hide – footage that, unfortunately, prominently featured Max.

'Oh, pardon *me*,' she said frostily. 'I'm sure I didn't mean to interrupt – I naturally assume that when I enter an office on these premises, that work pertaining to ACJ:Dublin will be on the cards, not ... personal projects.'

Bully, thought Jacinta. *I am so sick of being bullied.*

John Paul smiled warmly up at Niamh – it was always worth trying to kill someone with kindness. 'How are you keeping, Niamh? Can we help you with anything?'

Niamh sniffed derisively. 'Don't try any of that so-called charm on me, John Paul O'Gorman. Surely you've more sense than to get yourself mixed up with these two.'

'Ohhhhhh my Godddddd,' Max groaned dramatically. 'Please tell me you've come to say that we're shutting up right now, this minute – anything to end the misery of having to see you on a daily basis ever again –'

'Well, Maxine O'Malley, we can only wonder who's been happy enough to get shut of you, seeing as you moved across an ocean, three thousand miles away from your proper hearth and home. From your *loved* ones.' Niamh crossed her arms triumphantly over her putty-coloured cardigan, and Max gaped at her.

'What are you talking about?' Max unfolded herself from the chair slowly. What the hell was Niamh Bourke implying?

Jax swiftly moved to stand between them. 'Was there anything you wanted from us, Niamh?' she asked softly.

'I was only passing and I heard the uproar behind this closed door –'

'Closed door?' Jax asked, still softly, as she edged slightly forwards. 'Uproar?'

'I don't know how many times I've complained about the noise that American makes –'

'Neither do we, Niamh,' Jax said softly, softly. 'But believe me when I tell you we are heartily sick of it. Sick of it, sick of you, sick to death of your eavesdropping, and your troublemaking, and your vindictiveness. We are busy here. We are working. Leave us alone.'

So subtly had Jax been creeping forward, that Niamh didn't even realise she was out in the hall until the door closed in her face.

'Jacinta Vivien Bernadette Quirke!' Max crowed. 'Still waters run deep!'

'Hush,' Jax demanded, her ear to the door – as much to hear Niamh move off as to shield her expression from Maxine. Niamh Bourke knew – she was as sure of it as she was sure of her own name: Niamh Bourke knew about Michael LaMotta.

Shite.

She turned from the door and looked at Max bleakly. 'Can you not stop baiting her? Just for this last little while. Keep off her back.'

Max kicked the chair. 'It's her fault, she's always at me – what was that? "That American"? What the hell was that about?'

'Max!' Jacinta gripped her shirt around the increasingly ragged hem. 'Back off. Unless you want everyone in ACJ to know your business.'

'*What* business?!' Max shrieked.

Jacinta's shoulders dropped in defeat. 'Your private business. Please.'

Max's eyes narrowed. 'What are *you* talking about?'

Jax stood her ground. She'd decided that the only way she could keep Max's secret was by keeping her knowledge a secret from Max, which seemed an easy enough concept in theory, but was suddenly proving extremely difficult in practice. 'Leave it. Please.'

Max didn't like the chill that was running up and down her spine. *She* had nothing to hide – well, nothing to hide that wasn't easy to hide. It was easy to hide something when no one had a clue that there was anything to hide.

'Will we go off-site, or do this tomorrow, or . . . ?' JP didn't know what was going on, and he didn't want to know. In his now officially unofficial capacity as human sacrifice, he stepped between the women and tried to get everything back on track.

'Let's start again tomorrow,' said Jax. 'Max?'

'Yeah. Sure. Tomorrow.'

'Niamh, there ya are.'

Niamh had had too many years listening at doors to jump when she got caught, and turned smoothly to face Tommy, the elderly mailroom fellow. Luckily, his cataracts prevented him from having seen what she'd been up to.

'C'mere,' he rasped. 'Sure I never know what to do with these yokes, these special delivery capers. Give us a clue here, will ya, Niamh?'

The DHL envelope he held out seemed to be limned with a glowing golden light the moment Niamh clocked the return address. *That took no time at all,* she all but sang to herself. *He must have sent out a reply before he even finished reading the letter, I'll wager.* Niamh snatched the envelope out of Tommy's hand, and sent him a rare smile.

'I'll take care of it for you, Tommy,' she said, steering him back up the stairs. 'It's for the American one; she's all the way at the top of the place, you needn't wear yourself out over one of these silly, wasteful things. And what's wrong with the proper post, I ask you? Weren't you a postman yourself, Tommy, back in the auld days . . . ?' Sending him on his way, Niamh clutched the envelope to her bony chest fervidly, and disappeared like a wraith up the next flight of stairs, to the privacy of her office, the better to enjoy the bounty of her latest scheme.

Jacinta slowed her pace to a crawl, annoying the commuters who were legging it for the LUAS. Ranelagh at 8 a.m. was less a sleepy village than a bustling commuter town, and she edged herself out of the flow of humanity that was eager to wedge itself into the trams and get on with its day.

She breathed deep as she leaned lightly against a building. This had to be done, and she was sure she should be doing it, but should she be doing it just because she thought that she might possibly have a wee crush on some fella who, she was fairly certain, had a sort of *gra* for her, maybe, perhaps, she hoped he did. Did she hope? Was she ready to leap out of one thing and fall into another?

'Jacinta!' She looked up, and there he was. Fergal. After all this time. Big as life, and she felt . . .

'Mind your coat,' Fergal cautioned, reaching to brush off a smear of brick dust, and stopping short of touching Jax's back.

'It's grand,' she said, putting up her hand to stop him just as he reached out, and she stopped short of touching him, too. They both looked down at their hands.

'Right,' said Jax, and she headed for the nearest café, went in, and led the way towards the back. She sat and, looking up, saw that Fergal had chosen a table in the window, and stood, holding out a chair for her.

He thinks I'm going to jump up and join him. And that was it – them – everything – in a nutshell, wasn't it?

'I don't want to sit there, Fergal.' She nearly smiled. 'I'm not going to make a scene, if that's what you're guarding against.'

He winced, and reluctantly joined her at the back of the café. 'Tea for two,' he ordered the waitress as he sat.

'I'd prefer a latte,' Jax told the waitress. 'So will that be tea for one?' She and the waitress looked at him questioningly.

Fergal shrugged, and Jax saw in his grown-up face the sulk of the teenager, forced into attendance at another Quirke family function, the ill-tempered pout brought on by his authority being circumvented, the flash of annoyance that promised cold detachment to follow.

'Please yourself,' he said, looking at his watch.

'I won't take up much of your time,' Jax said smoothly, feeling acid in her throat, feeling bile rise, wanting to toss something in his face to wipe off that smug condescension. 'In fact, I don't want anything from you at all, really. I'll even pay for my own latte.'

Fergal made a production out of sliding out of his suit jacket and draping it over the back of his chair – once he'd wiped the top of the chair clean. He finally met her gaze, and she sighed at his good looks, refined into affluent adulthood, at the cold grey eyes that observed her aloofly, as if – well, they were strangers, weren't they? They'd had years of friendship that had led into five years of partnership in Ireland, with an engagement to boot, and then . . . then, the early glamour of separation, the brutally expensive telephone calls, the frequent flyer miles to

Paris, Rome, meeting halfway, four holidays a year . . . and then down to emails, a holiday in the winter, one in the autumn . . . then meeting at Christmas, the odd text . . .

'What? Sorry?' Jax broke out of her reverie to see that the forbidding look had melted away, and she wanted to cry, a little, at the mischievous smile on his face – there, that was the other side of the spoiled twenty-something, the big, bright smile, that little dimple in his left cheek.

'Away with the fairies, as usual,' he said, and reached across to run his finger down her nose.

'Remember that paper you wrote, you turned it in, too, what was it, last year of college?' She smiled, and batted his hand away when he would keep on tickling her nose.

'*The Evidence for Tír Na nÓg: An Archaelogical* – I can't remember the rest of it – *Based on the Writings of JVB Quirke, Professor Emeritus, Oxford University.*' Fergal laughed, leaned back and poured his tea. 'I got a high pass on that one.'

'I know you did, you chancer.'

'Jacinta—'

'Fergal, I'm not going to make a scene,' she assured him, with less asperity. 'I haven't seen you in I don't know how long, and I – I've never been good about saying what I mean, or what I think, but I'm trying, I'm trying to be honest and direct with you, and I know you've been avoiding this, but what's the point, really, and I—' She looked up at him, and saw her feelings displayed on his face, and she relaxed, a little – they were adults, weren't they, after all? Hadn't they always been friends?

'I don't know where to start,' Jax admitted. *But I know how I want it to end.*

He nodded, looked down at his hands; Jax followed his gaze, and felt her head go light. 'I'm afraid I do.'

Something was up, thought John Paul O'Gorman. Something was definitely going on with Jacinta Quirke. Something, he hoped, that was good. Something had changed, something had come over her, in the best possible sense, and while it seemed to have happened overnight, it was a good feeling.

There was the way she had taken to touching him, for emphasis. A pat on the hand, a tickle in the ribs, And there was the way she looked at him, dead in the eyes, smiling, laughing, and something else, something just underneath the warmth, something that alluded to the source of that warmth, heat, it was heat, and fire.

He followed Max and Jax up the stairs of Ray's building as they prepared for another night's work; lost in thought, he ran full up against Jacinta's back when she stopped short to open the door. He felt her jump, involuntarily, and then rather than leaping away, as she might have done in the past, she relaxed against him, for a split second, for a split millisecond, and then, only then, moved forward.

John Paul blew out a breath, twitched his shoulders, and rubbed both hands over his face. *Okay*, he thought. *Right. Right so*.

'Off we go,' she murmured and headed up to the third floor.

Max grabbed JP by the elbow and tugged him towards the back of the ground floor, and a small, mostly empty office at the very back of the hall. 'So, have you two finally, you know?' She nudged him, and winked.

'What makes you – it's none of your – no.' JP looked out over the building's back garden.

'She hasn't said a thing about what's-his-name, even though he's been back ages.'

'Fergal.' John Paul invested that one word with the kind of loathing many would have assigned to baby seal clubbers.

'Yeah.' Max winced and cast her eye over JP's moody face. 'Maybe – but why would she – they might have made up, maybe.'

JP said nothing, but looked as if he'd folded in on himself.

'But why would they, I mean, the whole thing's like a joke, isn't it?' Max wriggled on to the window sill. 'Hey.' John Paul looked at her, and she was somewhat taken aback by the depth of his misery.

'You tell me,' he said bitterly, his buoyant mood sinking like a stone. 'You're her—'

'Yeah, yeah, yeah.' Max cut him off. 'Best friend, but hey, we're grown women, and just for your information, it's a sexist assumption, "Oh women, they tell each other *everything*" . . .'

'What are you all cheesed off about?' JP sniped.

Max banged her heel against the wainscoting. 'I don't know – I hoped that this project would *show* her what a waste of time her relentless fidelity was – and that throwing the two of you together would, you know, result in the two of you getting together.'

'I think that there's no organising Jacinta,' JP said, practically bent over in two with dejection.

'She's like her mother there,' Max agreed.

'I'd like to see you bring that up,' JP said, and they both laughed.

'She'll deny it to the grave.'

'Have you not tried getting anything out of Angela?'

Max turned towards him confidentially. 'Well. We had a boozy, girly lunch. I was trading off her role in the programme for some info—'

'And you'd better pray that Jax never finds out!' JP cried.

'But I got nothing.' Max started peeling paint off the window sash, until JP batted her hand away. 'A monologue about his offences, but no real meat. Angela had an uncharacteristic attack of conscience.'

'Now what are you two doing back there, with your little heads together?' Angela's eyes glittered like a wolf's in the low-lit hallway.

'Oh, nothing, shop talk, like,' JP stuttered.

'So, have you seen hide or hair of Fergal?' Max demanded.

Angela jammed herself between the two on what little space was left on the window sill. 'Well!' She rubbed her hands together and leaned back as Max and JP leaned in. 'I rang her today, for a little chat about the *programme* and segued into the *future*, but she mentioned nothing about him, not that that's *unusual* –'

'Surely they haven't made it up?' Max asked.

'God forbid,' Angela declared, with a mischievous glance at JP, who twitched under Angela's arch regard, but also felt the elation of an implied imprimatur.

'I do hate to interrupt, but it's' – Jax ostentatiously checked her watch – 'thirty minutes to mark.' And turning on her heel, as though she hadn't a care in the world, or a curious bone in her body, Jax made her way back up the stairs.

Nosey madams. Jax laughed to herself. *Nosey mister. Nosey, adorable mister.* She hummed to herself as her mother, her friend and her . . . colleague all leapt off the window sill and scattered like ten pins.

*

Up in the booth, the relentless conversation about 'what they had' went on relentlessly. This relentlessness was easier to sustain in the absence of Lorcan whom, Max claimed, had gone quietly.

'Seriously, JP.' Jax leaned towards him, and he imagined grabbing her face, gently, but grabbing it all the same, and *kissing* her, right there in front of God and her father. 'What have we *got*?'

'We've got a good contrast between Majella and Jamie, and Dara and Conor,' he said, and Jax started making notes. 'We might cut them up, like a running joke, the silences and whatnot . . . maybe we can use a few clips of the footage Max tried to get in the handbag, you know, the rough stuff really is okay these days. That part about, what was it – "it's not the same when women do it", or something.

'And we'll see what we get tonight. We really need some, like, solid examples of infidelity. Live admission. Because otherwise, Jax is on the upside of the argument.' JP and Jax grinned as Max squawked in their ears.

'I have not yet begun to skew the data in my favour!' she hollered good-naturedly. 'It's just a little matter of manipulation of reality.'

'And how do you propose to do that?' Jax demanded.

'Oh, leave it with me.' Max made a kissy-face at herself in the mirror and winked at Angela. 'You'll see.'

The door knocker crashed, and Jax switched on camera five's monitor just in time to watch her mother wilt like a dying lily. 'Not *Camille*, is it, Mum?' she asked, but Angela ignored her daughter as she shuffled wretchedly towards the door.

'Welcome,' Angela whispered, her voice breaking. 'Do come in, and please follow me.' She gestured weakly with her left hand, and the large white handkerchief that was clutched in it fluttered despairingly.

Gary trotted up the steps alongside Angela, leaving Mary to tag along in their wake. 'Nice gaff,' Gary commented, avariciously taking in the sumptuous surroundings.

'Yes, well, take a good look, a nice, long look.' Angela sneered to herself, her vacant eyes snapping to life with anger. 'There won't be a stick left in the place once I'm done with him.'

Raymond's attention was suddenly diverted from the *Evening Herald*. 'What was that? What did your mother say, Jacinta?'

As if realising that she had witnesses, Angela visibly brought herself back to reality. She laughed, faintly, and offered, 'Let me take your coats. Gary, is it? And Mary?'

'Oh, if you don't mind, I'll just hold on to my—' Mary stammered.

'Give over, love, let the lady do her job.' Gary rolled his eyes and snatched Mary's coat out of her arms, shoving it into Angela's.

'Tea?' Angela asked weakly. 'Coffee?'

'Coffee for me.' Gary sat down on the couch and looked around as if he were the king of all he surveyed.

'Um, water, please, if it's not too much trouble.'

'No trouble at all,' Angela sniffled, and tottered towards the kitchen, leaning on the wall for support.

Gary toyed with a small, decorative crystal box as Mary hovered, looking worriedly after Angela.

'Sit down, will you?' Gary held up the box and struck his finger against it, assessing its authenticity. 'This, is it Waterford?'

'She doesn't look at all well.' Mary worried the strap of her handbag and drifted over to the couch.

'Is this Waterford?' Gary demanded, and yanked Mary on the arm for good measure.

The anxiety on Mary's face was immediately replaced by assessment. 'Swarovski,' she replied, and then her apprehension returned. 'I'd better see if she's all right.'

'She's fine. Is Swarovski better than Waterford?'

Mary rose and headed for the kitchen.

'Angela!' Max warned.

'I *know*,' Angela snapped, and she grabbed up the tea tray and nearly bowled Mary over.

'Oh, dear, I'm so *sorry*,' Angela wailed.

'No, not at all, you're fine, you're fine,' Mary reassured her.

'I'm so clumsy!' Angela set the tray down on the table and started wiping at Mary with her handkerchief.

'You didn't spill a thing!' Mary cried, as she, in return, patted soothingly at Angela.

Gary was inspecting a gold-rimmed porcelain dish.

'I'm a clumsy ox, and I'm stupid, and ugly and *horrible*,' Angela sobbed, and Mary dared to put a hesitant arm around Angela's shaking shoulders.

'Here,' Mary soothed. 'Let me get you a nice damp cloth.' She turned towards the kitchen, and Angela threw herself into her arms to prevent her going.

Gary had moved over to a sideboard and was opening and closing its drawers.

'No, I insist, please sit, have your drink. This is all about you, and your video appearance.' Angela steered Mary back to the couch, and heard Jacinta frantically calling camera angles, trying to keep everyone in frame. 'Milk?' she asked Gary, distracting him from his scrutiny of a pair of platinum candlesticks.

'Black, sugar.'

'How many?'

'Sorry?'

'Sugar? How many?'

Gary brayed with laughter. 'Just black – sugar.'

Mary tutted.

'Oh, I can't joke? Is that it?' Gary stood in the centre of the room, hands on out-thrust hips, and Mary cringed. 'Tying on the old ball and chain and I can't have a bit of craic with another woman?'

'Gaaaaary,' Mary whined, clutching her glass of water defensively.

'Men,' Angela sneered, winking at Mary, a sneer that crumbled into one sob – another sob – then evolved into a howl. 'Mennnnnnn!' she cried, the word drifting behind her like a ribbon as she rushed into the kitchen and slammed the door.

'I should really see if she's all right,' Mary fussed.

'She's fine.' Gary selected a biscuit.

'I don't think she's fine. She was crying, for goodness' sake.'

'Oh, like I didn't notice? I don't notice things?' Gary roared.

'Gaaaaary, that's not what I meant. Of course you notice things.'

'I notice things,' he barked, mouth full of biscuit. 'I noticed when your arse got bigger than my BMW.' He laughed again, somewhat less soggily due to crumbs.

'Pig!' Jax bounced angrily up and down in her chair.

'Asshole!' JP gaped incredulously.

'Jacinta, what was your mother talking about, what did she mean about "every stick in the place"?' Raymond nervously prowled the control room.

Mary had drained her glass rather than reply to Gary's

insult. 'I really think I should go look after yer one, she seems so upset,' she agonised.

'Hey, how about looking after me! Your husband to be!' Mary tried to wriggle out of Gary's grasp, fending off his seeking lips, and what began as a silly tussle escalated into ferocity as Gary refused to back down until Mary responded to his advances.

'Jesus.' John Paul exchanged a glance with Raymond, who had stopped his pacing and was watching the monitor uneasily.

'I'm going in,' Max announced, and she strode for the door.

'. . . No reason for me to do without, to do without the good things in life. I work for a corporation but I'm an independent thinker, not like some feckin' office drone. So I *need* the good things in life, I *deserve* them – and I've got taste, let me tell you. I know what's what, I know my Waterford from my Swarovski. I know a good thing when I see it.' Gary raked his eyes up and down Max's legs.

'And I presume that includes your lovely wife to be.' Max smiled at Mary, who sat, frozen, a look of wretched self-consciousness on her face.

'Boss's daughter,' Gary smirked, and Mary's usual air of misery ratcheted up several notches.

'And do you work in . . .' Max consulted her notes – 'retail, as well?'

'Oh, I've been working in our corner shop since I was fourteen,' Mary said, and Gary glowered.

'It's a chain, like,' he bluffed, elbowing Mary rather harshly in the ribs. 'I've built it up from that corner shop into a series of newsagents all over the city. Ryan's, you've seen 'em, right? Ryan's?'

'I'm sure I must have – although it's a fairly common surname.' Max turned fully to Mary, leaving Gary to glower at the wall. 'Mary, have you taken up a profession yourself?'

'Well, I did the leaving, and I came top of my class,' she boasted hesitantly. 'But my father—'

'What's she need uni for?' Gary spat. 'Little newspaper heiress, after all.'

'I like to read,' Mary went on, her voice becoming increasingly wispy. 'I read a lot.'

'Makes me sound like some class of eunuch, eh!' Gary swept her into a half-embrace that looked like it might dislocate her shoulder.

'Speaking of sex,' Maxine interjected – ignoring Gary's '*Phwoar!*' – 'apart from being deeply interested in how you two got together, we're very curious as to how couples like you stay together—'

'Old man Ryan's a crack shot!' Gary yelped, and fell about the place laughing his glutinous laugh. Mary smiled, and looked as if she might cry.

'What we're talking about here is faithfulness.' Max leaned in and did her best Oprah. 'We're talking about the long haul; down the years, year after year, years of the two of you, joined in holy matrimony, "till death us do part" –'

'It's my death if we don't get down the aisle!' Gary gasped, in hysterics.

'Mary, what are your thoughts?'

'I think that a promise is a promise, and that the commitment is really very important,' she replied, heavily weighting every noun. 'I think that if you say you're going to do something, and be with a person, then you should honour that very, very important agreement—'

'Thinks it's important, so she does,' Gary cracked, once

again reaching out and violently hugging his fiancé. He shook her until her head bobbled on her neck. 'Important, is it, love? Darling? Dear?'

'He's bad news,' said Jax.

'But he's excellent footage,' JP countered.

'Forgive me if I sound, well, pedantic,' Max said.

'What, that crowd that goes after kids?' Gary asked, outraged.

'Not paedophile.' Mary laughed a mean little laugh that had everyone sitting up and taking notice. 'Pedantic. Overly attentive to correctness.' She shook back her hair, and Jax was sure she was going to pay for that bit of audacity later.

'Thank you, Mary. I don't mean to split hairs, but I wonder what sort of agreement you've struck as regards fidelity.'

The flush of Mary's success drained from her face, and she stiffened, dropping her gaze to the floor. Gary looked from Max to Mary expectantly, waiting for the next translation.

'You know what I mean by fidelity, don't you, Gary?'

He nudged Mary, who obediently answered. 'Loyalty. To your husband or wife. Especially sexually.'

It was Gary's turn to freeze, and JP zoomed in on his unusually immobile face, on his suddenly shuttered gaze. 'Like, not shagging around?'

'Precisely.' Max sat forward.

'Once we're married, you mean?'

'Sure.'

'Well, that's what happens, isn't it? You get married and that's it.' Gary leaned forward, elbows on knees, and glared up at Max.

'Mary? Mary?' Max sent a worried glance up at the

camera that was covering her – Mary had gone deathly pale, and it wasn't immediately apparent that she was still breathing.

'Yes, it's important, when you're married. It is the most important thing,' Mary insisted dully.

Max made a show of reacting to her earpiece. 'Oh – I – right. I've just got word from the control room that I'm needed for a few minutes. I'll send Angela in with some refreshments, and then we'll wrap things up.'

Angela passed Max on her way out. Still clutching the handkerchief – now soggy and limp – she lurched towards Gary and Mary, clasping a supporting hand on the presenter's chair, leaning her body into it weakly.

'Coffee? Tea?' she asked, then proceeded to turn her back on them and wander aimlessly around the room, stroking the furniture, the paintings on the walls, the walls themselves, poignantly, forlornly.

She made a circuit of the room, and then let herself down gently into the chair that Max had vacated. 'Going well?' she asked, putting on a brave face, and, again, failing to wait for a response. 'It must be so nice to talk about your relationship, your love for each other, your wedding plans . . .' Angela took in a shuddering breath and hid her face in her handkerchief. 'Your *hopes*, your *dreams* . . .'

'Are you married yourself?' Mary enquired, and it was all Angela needed. The howl she let out was a combination of wounded-animal-meets-banshee, an earthquake of shaking limbs, of shrieks and moans that were not only convincing, but also heartbreaking and chilling at the same time.

'Look what you've done,' Gary gibbered, incensed. 'Stupid cow!'

Little prick, thought Angela as she swooped towards

him. 'It's not her fault!' she shrieked, and reached out a hand to Mary who gratefully grabbed it, happy to focus on someone else's pain. 'How could she know that I've only just discovered my husband is having an affair with my best friend, who just happens to be twenty years younger!'

'What is she *talking* about!' Raymond bellowed uncharacteristically.

'It's a set-up, Raymond, just a set-up!' John Paul jumped in front of Raymond and wrestled him away from the door.

'My best friend! Oh, Mary – the betrayal, can you comprehend the betrayal—'

'It's not like it was your sister!' Gary joked.

'My sister is *dead*!' Angela screeched, and Mary, beside herself with compassion, got up to take the weeping woman in her arms.

'I never had a sister,' Mary choked, and sniffled.

'At least you've got your Gary, your faithful, loyal, committed fi-fi-fiancé.' Angela looked up into Mary's face and wailed.

'This is too much.' Jax covered her eyes.

'Wait,' Max ordered.

'I'm not happy about this,' Raymond mumbled.

'You have your whole lives ahead of you,' Angela warbled. 'Your faithful fellow by your side, loving only you, promising to be faithful to you and only you, for ever and for always—'

The scream of pain that erupted from Mary rivalled even Angela's, and was perhaps the more powerful for its veracity. Gary leapt to his feet, and made for her, but Angela had already risen to lead Mary swiftly from the room.

Max passed the weeping woman as she crossed the threshold, and shut the door behind her.

'No, I don't like this at all.' Jacinta turned to John Paul, whose scowl now matched Raymond's.

'I'm going to go down there and stand by,' he said, watching as Max led Gary back to the couch, and sat down beside him.

'I'll join you.' Raymond prepared himself by tightening the knot on his tie.

'You'll be all right?' JP asked, but Jax had already slid into the driver's seat and started running the cameras. She nodded up at him, and he reached out boldly to stroke her hair. 'I won't let it get out of hand. Tell Angela to sit with her on the secondary couch, and we'll go down the backstairs and slip into the kitchen.'

'Mum, did you get that?'

'Darling, poor dear. Let's sit here on the couch and you tell me all about it,' Angela sniffled, while nodding into the hidden camera in the landing.

With a last caress, John Paul led the way to the first floor.

'Then that lady started screaming that her husband went off with a young one, and then, em, Mary took her outside.' Gary leaned back against the arm of the sofa, straining to look bothered.

'Looked like Mary was in bits,' Max replied.

'She's all sensitive, like, cries at movies, always moaning to her girlfriends about one thing or the other.' Gary scoffed, eyeing Max's legs again.

'. . . and he said what difference did it make, if he was fooling around, I was lucky anyone was going to marry me, and he'd do what he liked until we got married, anyway,' Mary gurgled into Angela's shoulder.

'Prick!' Angela averred.

'But I love him!' Mary wailed, pulling away and covering her face with her hands. 'I loooooove him!'

'Sorry if I triggered anything. You know, set something off.' Max edged as far away from Gary as was possible.

'Bladder's up around her eyes.' Gary leaned across, and went for a woebegone look. 'The things I have to put up with . . .'

'All in the name of love,' Max chirped, wanting to gag.

'Not like I'm hitched up yet,' he murmured, reaching out to toy with Max's sleeve. 'And if it wasn't for the old man . . .'

'If it wasn't for my father that wanker would be digging ditches, and happy to do it!' Mary spat venomously. 'Didn't even do his leaving, and always slagging me. I'm not stupid, I'll do a course if I damn well please. I'll get a job, I can work, stupid bastard –'

'Bastard,' Angela echoed.

'And of all people, the one he went off with!' Mary's previously waxen face was on fire with anger, her previously stilted posture loose with rage. 'Stupid slag, barely out of her teens – oh, I could do him, my father's got great friends in the guards, I could do him up right and tight.' And she ripped Angela's handkerchief in two.

'Let me get you another, pet.' Angela jammed into the kitchen with the lads, and peered up into the lens. 'Jacinta! What'll we do?'

Maxine shook Gary off, and tried to keep it light. 'She might not put up with it, at the end of the day.'

'What, she's going to dump me, like? Me, putting the

roof over her head, paying the bills, paying for the bloody wedding, while she sits on her big fat arse, reading her *books* all day long?' Gary snorted, and the disgust on his face was stunning. 'Look at you,' he said, leering. 'You're not sitting on yer duff the whole day, acting the princess.'

'Well –'

'Doing your little video job, moving and shaking. You're up for it, so you are.'

'You think so?' Max sneered.

'I caught the vibe, that night in the pub.' Gary leaned in and Max arched her back. ' "She's up for it, that one," I said to myself.'

'Max, this has got to stop. It's enough,' Jax ordered.

'Right.' Max stood and extended her hand to Gary. 'That's that, really. I wouldn't want to interfere with the private doings of an engaged couple—'

Gary grabbed her hand, catching her off guard, and yanked Max into his lap. 'What she don't know won't hurt her.'

Max had barely taken a breath when the men rushed in, JP in the lead. Jax watched as Mary pushed them all aside with a bloodcurdling cry and proceeded to bash Gary about the head with the tea tray. Angela leapt around in the background, waving a fresh hankie, and Jax mercifully shut everything down.

'Well, how's that for dramatic,' Max said lightly. She grinned gamely around. 'My heroes.'

'What a session!' Angela breathed deeply of the balmy night air and danced down several steps, and spun round to look up at the rest of the crew. 'I thought the part about my dead sister was particularly inspired.'

'You were superb, Angela; you've got a future in improv,' Max jogged down to link arms with the jubilant actress, hoping against hope to divert the gathering storm.

'Do you know, Keith Johnstone said *exactly that* to me in the late seventies.'

'Stop,' said Raymond as he, Jax and JP, a wall of censure, stood at the top of the stoop.

'Oh, now,' Angela brazened it out. 'Yes, it all could have gone terribly wrong, but it *didn't*, and think of all that *lovely* footage.'

'It's the best stuff we've got so far,' Max chimed in.

'And it wasn't as if we were alone in there, we knew that we were all wired up into each other, and that you were merely a *whisper* away,' Angela added.

'Angela,' Raymond snapped, and Maxine felt Angela shiver. 'Maxine,' he added, in the same tone, and Angela felt Max tense. 'It is not my place to chastise you, two grown women – it is not my project, and I will leave it to Jacinta to express the sheer *disbelief* I expect we all feel as regards your behaviour.'

'Raymond Quirke, do not take that tone with me,' Angela ordered.

'But *that* is my place,' he continued, gesturing towards the building. 'Donated in good faith to my daughter and her colleagues. Whether or not that makes me part of this *team*, it involves me to a significant degree.'

'Oh, how I *loathe* this sort of "man of the house" proselytising.' Angela made a production out of rolling her eyes and flapping her arms about.

'The *arrogance* of it, the *arrogance* of the two of you, Angela and Maxine, is deplorable. Deplorable, disrespectful, and unacceptable.'

Even Angela couldn't counter that. She looked up at an uncharacteristically cowed Max.

'Well.' Angela shook back her hair. 'Hmmph.'

'Da.' Jax moved to stand in front of him. 'This is my responsibility.'

'Oh, pardon me, as if I don't have any say!' *Best defence is a good offence*, Max thought.

'Did I have any say? Had we had any discussion at all about this idea, about this little "manipulation of reality"?'

'Yeah, well, it was spur of the moment – kind of.' Max hated being rebuked, especially when it was justified. She grimaced and looked to John Paul for back-up, but got none.

'Okay, okay,' she mumbled. 'Sorry.'

'I'm sure you'd prefer it if I went through you for a shortcut,' Jax replied coolly. 'I'm sure a nice, big barney would suit you, take the focus off the real problem to hand. The problem being, perhaps, that this isn't working, that we're not driving towards the same goal, that the whole thing is a waste of time—'

'It's not, it's not a waste of time!' *It can't be, it can't be*, Max chanted to herself. 'Look, okay, that got scary. It was totally out of control, and thank you.' She turned to the men. 'Thanks for being there, for, you know, pitching in, although I do feel that I could have handled it myself.'

'We are, as you say, grown women,' Angela pronounced. 'We didn't necessarily need the *cavalry*.'

'Angela, I am not in the mood.' Raymond made his way down the steps. 'Out of nowhere, I hear you maligning me and our marriage, I see that odious specimen of a man pawing over my things—'

'I think yer man nicked that little glass box,' John Paul interjected unhelpfully.

'*Stealing* my things—'

'And it was Baccarat,' sniffed Angela. 'Swarovski? In *fairness*.'

'And on top of all this, on top of all this, we all watch Maxine struggle to fend off this *person*, and I use the term generously, for the sake of what? Her safety, for the sake of what?'

Silence greeted this query, and Jax sat down on the steps, dejected. 'Let's just leave it for the night, will we? We'll take the weekend, and . . .' Her shoulders slumped, and JP sat down next to her, desperate to put his arm around her.

'I suppose that's the sensible thing to do,' Angela conceded, although she'd imagined a lovely evening over a few glasses of wine reliving her stellar performance. She exchanged a charged glance with Max, and made her exit before Raymond said another word.

Raymond and Jax did their own share of meaningful

glancing, and he turned, with a last troubled, frustrated look at Max, and headed after his wife.

'Okay, look—' Max began.

'No, Max,' said John Paul. 'We'll take the weekend. I've got the footage, I'll log it all, maybe lash together a rough cut of what we've got, and we'll talk on Monday.'

'It wasn't that big a deal!' Max insisted.

'I don't want to get into this now,' Jax bit out.

'I know how to handle myself.'

'Oh, I don't doubt *that*.'

'Oh, what, is this going to get personal?'

'Would you both let it rest?' JP cut in.

'Hey, buddy, just back off,' Max shouted.

'Creative differences?' They all turned to look at Lorcan, who'd been lounging, unnoticed, on a parked Merc. 'No wonder you can't get this thing off the ground.'

Jax opened her mouth to retort, and then rose. *Does Maxine tell the truth about anything? How did he know we were working tonight?* 'I suppose you're here for your equipment.'

Lorcan shrugged. 'Or whatever. A few scoops. A night on the tear.' He strolled over, smirked up at Maxine.

'Yeah, come on, let's go out for a jar,' Max agreed.

'Oh, yes, let's,' Jax replied, to JP's disbelief. 'After you.'

The two couples made their way towards Grafton Street and the usual pre-weekend party. Smokers dotted the pavement in little clutches of addiction, and large groups of young ones routinely spilled out of one pub and surged towards another.

Max, in the lead, called over her shoulder. 'Baileys, or Grogans, or Kehoes?'

'Kehoes,' Jax suggested and, grabbing JP by the hand, nipped down Clarendon Street.

'Jax—'

Jax grinned, and pulling on his hand, legged it past Neary's, and away.

'What's got into you?' John Paul huffed and puffed as they leaned against the wall at Powerscourt.

Jax shook her head and let out a rollicking laugh. Composed, she stood and looked at him, brushed the long floppy curls out of his eyes, and smiled. 'Quite a lot,' she said. 'Quite a lot has got into me, and no' – she touched a finger to his lips – 'Don't ask. It's not important. Not tonight. Tonight, none of it really matters. All right?'

'Can I ask where we're going – or is that out of bounds?' He shifted his body to shield her from a marauding stag party.

'Hmmm, you know what? You can ask all the questions you want,' she teased, 'but I'm only going to answer the right ones.'

'So will we go to Nearys, or Fallons, or Gallaghers?'

'No, let's go across. You live in Smithfield, don't you? Let's go there.'

Max stopped dead near Kehoes. 'Where've they got to?' She looked around wildly, trying to spot Jax's explosion of curls, or John Paul's lanky frame.

'They know where we're going,' said Lorcan, moving in for a cuddle.

'Bugger.' Max dug out her mobile and speed-dialled Jax. She paced back and forth across the road, and Lorcan lit up a fag.

'Her voicemail's on.' Max threw her phone back in her bag, and looked fruitlessly up and down Grafton Street.

'Do you want a drink or not?' Lorcan asked impatiently.

Max shrugged and headed up the road. *Leave me flat – no problem.* Shaking off Lorcan's groping hand, she pushed her way into the jammed pub.

Jax and John Paul crossed the Millennium Bridge in companionable silence. The nights were getting longer, and the sky, full of scudding clouds that obscured and revealed the waxing moon, was a deep cobalt-blue at the horizon. Couples wandered up and down the boardwalk, hand in hand, arm in arm, and Jacinta felt at one with them for the first time in years.

What would happen, she wondered, *if I did the simplest thing and slid my arm through his?*

She felt his arm twitch, then relax, then squeeze her to his side in accord.

'So, I'm thinking up a question,' he said, attempting a blasé air.

'Yes, thought you'd gone quiet,' Jax replied, and led them over to a bench.

They sat, watched the lights dance on the Liffey. JP stretched his legs out in front of him and casually, smoothly, reached his arm across the back of the seat, behind Jax. 'Emmm . . .' *Do you fancy me? What's going on here? Is what I want to be going on here, er, going on? Have you dumped that long-distance plonker or haven't you?*

'Are you cold?' he asked.

'It took you all that time to come up with that?' Jax laughed.

'That wasn't a question! You know what I mean.' He playfully batted the back of her head. 'Is there a limit?'

'There might be,' Jax considered. 'I haven't decided.'

John Paul nodded, and watched the passing show for a few moments. 'Why did you go into advertising?'

Jax groaned. 'Going for the jugular, aren't you? I was counting on "What's your favourite colour?" or "What are your favourite films of all time?"'

'Those kinds of answers are more revealing than you think,' John Paul said wisely. 'I'm saving them up, and then I'll blindside you, when your defences are down. So – advertising.'

'It's not interesting,' Jax complained. 'I studied fine art photography, and film. And towards the end of my degree I reckoned I'd better have a – like a trade, and I took some design courses, desktop stuff, and got a gig at an agency . . .' Jax looked over at JP, who nodded in agreement. 'And then I started getting better gigs on the job, including commercials, and it all seemed to fall into place.'

'Why did you stay in?'

'My cautious friends at Bank of Ireland would have frowned on me playing fast and loose with my mortgage. They're rather risk-averse. And you?'

'Ah, pretty much the same,' John Paul said. 'Did everything in university, film-wise, and then got roped into the technical stuff. I like to know how things work, how to fix them. Too much knowledge is a dangerous thing.'

'Oh, yeah. That's for sure,' Jax replied fervently, thinking again of Max and Michael LaMotta.

Max slapped her mobile against her thigh as Lorcan droned on and on. She was forced to pay him mind, however, when he abruptly stuck his tongue in her ear.

'Thought that'd get your attention,' he smirked, tickling her ribs.

'Eejit.' Max, jammed in between him and the stranger to her right, grabbed up her pint and drained it.

'I love it when you talk—'

'Don't,' Max ordered. 'Please. I mean, really.'

'Let's go back to mine,' Lorcan said. 'Get out of this lunacy.'

In your dreams, pal.

'. . . *To Kill a Mockingbird*. *The Philadelphia Story*. *Les Quatre Cent Coupes* – sorry, my French is dreadful. Em . . . *Steamboat Bill, Junior*. I know they say that *The General* is Buster Keaton's best work, but I disagree. So, analyse me.'

'Hmmmm.' John Paul stroked his non-existent beard. 'They're all in black and white.'

Jax opened her mouth then snapped it shut. 'Wha— they're not – oh, bollocks.'

'So that says a lot right there.'

'Black and white.' Jax squirmed on the bench in discomfort. 'That's me, all right.'

'I'm not done. In fact, they only reinforce what I already know about you, Jacinta Quirke.'

Jax tried for a mysterious mien. 'I don't think you know all that much about me, John Paul O'Gorman.'

'You like to laugh – and to cry, only maybe not so much in front of anybody, which I suppose is like most. But the sort of crying – that's different. The kind of crying when you empathise, the kind of tears that come when you watch somebody living their life, and something happens, and they do their best to get through it, and you know that they're struggling – and also in there are the kind of tears that happen when the character succeeds, after all that time, after all that struggle.'

'When Scout finally meets Boo, and she takes his hand, and they swing on the porch swing –' Jacinta covered her face with her hands.

Jacinta Quirke, I love you.

*

'Come on, Lorcan, a little snog, a little night out on the town – let it go. I'm outta here.' Max shoved her way out of Kehoes and headed for the taxi rank on Dawson Street.

'Just looking for a laugh, right?' Lorcan looked around, hoping no one he knew was around.

'It's not funny any more.' Max let a half-naked – or so it seemed – hen party flow past her and between herself and Lorcan. 'It's not anything, any more. It *was* a laugh. Past tense.'

'I want my gear back.' Lorcan tried for a manly sneer, but the best he could produce was a petulant sulk. 'And yees owe me.'

'For what?'

'For the gear. For the use.'

'I have to work out a rate with Jax.'

'Surely we could work it out between ourselves, Maxine.'

Max shook him off, and joined the mercifully short queue at the rank. 'Don't tell me that actually works on anyone.'

'Worked on you.'

Finish it, Maxine. Now.

'Lorcan. I'll risk leaving you thinking I'm a tease – funny how it's just messing when it's a guy, but when it's a woman, it's teasing – but I digress.' She moved up to the top of the rank. 'We'll compensate you, and that's that. I'm not . . . available.'

I'm not. I'm not available. Oh, God.

'You've a powerful gift for observation, JP,' Jax said.

'Oh, I'm only getting started. Uh . . . you root for the underdog, you like your, em, idiosyncratic family, but you also want to be your own person, you have a strong sense of justice – and a romantic heart.'

He wasn't sure he could take it, the way she was looking at him, the way her face had gone all soft and sweet, and it was worse when she added a brilliant smile. 'That's just lovely. Aren't you lovely?'

'Will we go for a drink?'

Jax shook her head. 'I'm sick of drinking, sick of pubs, sick of other people. I don't want to be out with other people. I don't want to be out.'

He rose, and held out his hand. 'Then let's go in.'

It had been ages since John Paul had bargained desperately with God, and he certainly couldn't remember it ever working out – he'd never got that go-kart, or got to meet Ray Houghton, or been chosen for one of the American space shuttle missions – but these were all pointless whims compared to the miracle he now begged his Maker to perform.

Honestly, God, I promise – well, you decide what you want me to do. I'll do it – except for the priesthood, like – just please, please, please let the lads not be home – they can have my seat on the space shuttle, anything, please—

'Your flatmates are away.' Jax waved a note under JP's nose.

Thank you, thank you, thank you – em, I'll go to Mass on Sunday . . . if I'm not otherwise occupied . . .

'Want a cup of tea? And that's not a question, either.'

'I'll think about that,' Jax said, and wandered off to the loo. She shut the door behind her and leaned against it. She hurriedly jerked up her skirt – well, they weren't the sexiest pants on the planet, but they'd do. She unbuttoned her blouse – ugh, how old was this bra? She shook her hair back nervously, and moved so close to the mirror that it was as as though she'd like to go through it. Rebuttoning her blouse – God, it was awful, it was quite simply the ugliest top she'd ever seen in her life – she breathed so heavily that she misted up the glass. She sat down on the toilet, and turned the water on and off in the sink for effect.

It had been a long time since she'd been in this place – had she ever been in this place? She and Fergal, they'd just fallen into it, without much fanfare, the result of a protracted courtship and, perhaps, of a feeling of inevitability. Not exactly fodder for a romance novel.

My God, Fergal Delaney is the only man I've ever been with in my entire life and I'm in my goddamn thirties! She gaped at herself in the mirror, and flushed the toilet. *Well, there were those random snogs while backpacking in France and Spain, but otherwise . . .* 'I don't believe it,' she whispered to herself as she turned on the taps again. 'What is wrong with me?'

Nothing that couldn't be rectified in this place, at this time, right now. She yanked open the door and made straight for the living room where John Paul sat, as nonchalantly as he could manage, on the couch. God only knew what was going through his mind, as Jax headed straight for him without a hitch in her step, what raced across his grey matter when she straddled his lap, what sort of synaptic carnival lit up his head when she grabbed him on both sides of his head and started what had all the earmarks of an heroic snog. God only knew, because at the first touch of her lips on his, hesitant, soft, then confident, and hot, thinking became the last thing on his mind.

22

When your eyes are closed, and the woman that you've craved for who knew how long, was cuddled up on your lap exactly as you'd imagined she could be, in those highly detailed fantasies – well, not *fantasies*, not like porn or anything, but like thinking about her on the long walk home, with the iPod going and some unwinding to do from the stress of the work day, the kinds of – of, scenarios – scenarios, a better word than *fantasies* – that generally ended with them exactly where they were now, maybe not on his couch (maybe in a posh bar somewhere in town, maybe on a beach in Portugal) but here, snogging . . .

Snogging: a coarse word, a random word, a word assigned to women who didn't matter, who were just one-offs, *not that I'm a slag – if blokes can be called slags – but it's not a word to use in relation to Jacinta Quirke: there's got to be another word I could use to describe—*

'What?' John Paul blinked, and her mouth was gone.

'You weren't exactly all there.' *I'm a terrible kisser, aren't I?*

'I was thinking about you, actually.' He smiled, and sighed, and ran his hands up and down the sides of her body.

His strong hands, lovely hands. Surely they couldn't touch her that way unless they – he – well, this was just a snog, wasn't it? *Don't get your knickers in a twist, Jacinta – your not-terribly-sexy knickers—*

'Jacinta,' John Paul murmured, moving those hands up to cup her face – her face, her lovely face, the eyes gone all distant and unsure, 'we don't have to – I know that you – listen, I got to ask you—'

'No more questions. Later, maybe . . . now, no.'

Later, later – and JP picked up the train of thought he'd lost: that when your eyes are closed and you've got the only woman you've ever fancied quite like this, teasing your tongue with hers, running her hands up and down your chest, leaning into you, leaning full up against you – that when life was like this, time went away; it didn't matter any more, what time it was, what day it was, what year, what country, what planet. *Later, later* – Jacinta's whispered words beat in time with his heart – there was more time, later, later, she wasn't going anywhere, there was no rush – time was theirs, theirs alone.

He shifted her down and to the side, raising himself above her on his elbows, brushing those astonishing curls out of her face, stroking the softness of her face, the delicacy of her neck, her sweet-smelling neck. He didn't want to rush her, rush this, there was no rush, surely, they had all night, all weekend, all—

Hurry, she thought. *Hurry before I change my mind, before I start thinking too much.* She reached up and pulled his face down to hers, turned hers into his neck, lifted her body to meet his, reached down to toy with the buttons on his shirt—

He caressed her hip, reached around, felt her stomach quiver, as he slipped his hand underneath her top to stroke her belly, her back ... He propped himself up again. 'Jax—'

'Don't stop – I don't want you to.'

'I – I think—'

'We think too much, you and I.' She smiled as she tucked her hands cosily in the back pockets of his trousers. 'Let's not think too much right now – all right?' She laughed. 'Remember when "cup of tea" was code for a shag? It still may be, for all I know, I've been – I haven't been—'

Her eyes had come over uncertain again, and John Paul shifted himself so that he was wedged between her and the back of the couch. 'We can drink cups of tea till we float away,' he said, tickling her nose with a lock of her own hair. 'We'll do whatever you want, Jacinta. I just want to be here with you.' *But I don't want to just* shag, *like – shag was as bad as snog. I want to make love to you, Jacinta Quirke—*

It's only a shag, it's only a shag, Jacinta repeated to herself, not wanting to understand what she saw in his eyes. 'I want to be here, too,' she sighed. 'And I'm not thirsty.' As they dissolved into another searing kiss, she slowly unbuttoned his shirt, playfully, tantalisingly, and was delighted by the groan of longing that he gave once she'd begun to run her hands over and over his skin. 'You're very fit,' she breathed, as her fingers ran over his pecs and, surprise, surprise, his highly impressive six-pack. 'Just the right amount, not like you're stuffing yourself full of steroids or anything. Do you go to a gym, or—'

'I'm not exactly in the mood for questions, myself,' JP murmured, as he ran his fingers over the buttons of her top. He teased her in turn, with light, dipping kisses as he undid them, one by one, one from the bottom, skipping up to the top, back and forth, all the while dropping delicious, tortuous little kisses on her lips, her neck, her cheeks, her earlobes. He eased the edges of her shirt apart, teasing there too, running his fingertips over her ribs, almost daring himself to see how long he could hold back – he didn't want her to think – if he went too fast, she'd think – but surely she was hoping that he'd – *I do think too much*, John Paul thought—

Jacinta, pressing on his chest, rose up and shrugged off her blouse. *Good riddance to you*, she thought, and she stood, drawing JP up with her; he reached behind and undid the clasp of her bra, and both shook with the thrill of flesh meeting flesh, thrilled with the anticipation of more. Jax impatiently drew JP's shirt off his shoulders, he in turn trying to step out of his shoes while coaxing the zipper of Jax's skirt down, all of this while making their way down the hall to John Paul's bedroom.

Room – mess? Bed – made? Sheets – clean? John Paul struggled to think, and then stopped struggling and abandoned all thought processes. They added more kissing to their repertoire, thumped against the walls of the hall, laughed when a picture crashed to the floor, gave up on the clothes in exchange for speed; they achieved the bedroom, shut the door, pressed up against the door, fell on to the bed, clothes dispensed with, duvet shoved aside, until there was nothing but Jacinta, nothing but John Paul.

Hesitation was gone, uncertainty left in the front lounge, doubt scattered down the hallway like the broken glass of that cracked picture frame, and Jacinta let herself feel, feel everything from the heat of John Paul's mouth on hers, from the gentle strength of his hands on her breasts, his fingers teasing her nipples, the warmth of his thighs between her legs as she wrapped herself around his body. John Paul let himself forget to think, again, at all, as he cradled Jacinta's head in a hand, the other roaming her body freely, sensuously, allowed himself to enjoy her lush curves, her gorgeously soft skin, as he'd wanted to, perhaps ever since the first time he'd seen her.

Thoughts and feelings became a blur as they pulled each other closer, closer, and Jacinta reached down and stroked JP until he thought he would die with it, and her own fraught breathing almost pushed him over the edge; he retaliated by slipping fully in between her legs and, using his hand, touched her, and relished the response he felt there, knowing it was her response to him, to them, and he brought her to her first climax, feeling her shudder against his hand. She watched him as she came, her eyes hot with passion and release, and gripping him by the hips guided him into her even as she trembled.

Even as she trembled she wrapped herself around him, body and soul, sighing luxuriously into his ear as she rose to meet him, as he plunged into her, again and again, heedlessly, wildly, as she urged him on, again and again, revelling in the feel of him against her, inside her, this man, only this man, only for now, here and now. Feeling him reach his own peak filled her with power, a sensual, magnificent power, and, stroking his back, caressing his arms, running her hands wherever they could reach, Jacinta achieved another release of her own, as sexual as an orgasm, the release of years of concealment, of years of diminishment, and felt, as surely as she felt John Paul's heart beat furiously against hers when he fell against her, spent, that she had finally left those lost years behind.

*

Cocooned in John Paul's fresh sheets – *Thanks, God, again, wow, really coming through tonight*, he thought – they spooned and looked out at the moon as it shone over Smithfield.

'Nice view,' Jacinta murmured, and then giggled as John Paul pulled back the sheet to get a look at her.

'Oh, yeah,' he sighed as he buried his face in her hair.

'You'll get lost in there, and I haven't the energy to organise a search party,' she warned, and he pulled her tight against him.

'It's beautiful – amazing. You get a notion of it, some days, but most of the time you're camouflaging it. Which is for the best, I suppose.'

'Oh?' Jax wiggled around until she was half on her back and looked up into his face.

'Ummm hmmm, or else you'd get no peace at all, Jacinta Quirke, fending off the hordes, tripping over the men falling at your feet.' He nuzzled her earlobe, and she turned back again to cuddle into his body.

'Ah, sure.' She shrugged, tingling with delight. 'I think if I don't do something about it, Maxine O'Malley will take a pair of shears to it herself.'

'Should we have left them? I mean – well, I'm not saying, like – I don't mean—' Jacinta had discovered an extremely ticklish square inch of John Paul's torso, and zeroed in on it at this stage. 'Don't! Don't! Please! I surrender! Jesus!' Laughing, she rolled back and pretended to threaten him with wiggling fingers. 'Seriously,' he continued, jerking back protectively, 'I told you, I've seen Lorcan's worst – he can be pretty persistent.'

'How persistent? Like scary persistent?' Jax worried her lower lip – a lip, she was happy to discover, that was nearly destroyed with kissing.

'No,' JP explained cautiously, because it *was* actually scary persistent. 'Irritating, annoying persistent, and I think it'd be like a match to dry tinder with Max. I didn't want to hang out with them – now that I've seen the alternative, in any case . . . I'm glad we legged it . . .' And here he interrupted himself to settle his lips back on Jax's for a moment . . . or two . . . or three . . . 'It was only after what went down on the set, it seemed . . . harsh.'

'Maxine knows how to handle herself, I expect,' Jax said acerbically. 'As regards flirting like a maniac, anyhow.'

'What's the thing – the thing that you know?'

Jax started pulling nervously at the hem of JP's top sheet, having no garments within easy reach to worry. She was halfway to rending the hem entirely before John Paul pulled it gently from her grasp. 'You needn't,' he began.

'I don't know. If I was to tell anyone, it would be you.' This was said somewhat absently, but it lifted JP's heart stratospherically. 'I can't, though. I certainly don't know why I'm bothering with loyalty, but there you go – can't change me spots.'

'I'm dying of curiosity,' JP admitted.

'That was where you were supposed to say, "Don't change a thing",' Jax pointed out.

'I mean, I know she's got more on the go than meets the eye,' John Paul continued, leaping like a fish on a griddle to avoid Jax's finger probing his ribs again, 'and what was that, with Niamh, the other day? That thing about—'

Jax turned on her side again, to brood at the moon. 'She knows. She's an evil, scary, persistent nutter, and she knows. Oh, I'd dearly love to get something on her.'

'We'll fix her up with Lorcan,' JP suggested, and rolled Jax back towards him.

'You know, I don't think I despise Lorcan enough to do that,' Jax mused. 'Imagine that.'

'And here I reckoned he was your own personal anti-Christ,' JP laughed. They kissed, again, softly, gently, searchingly. 'Will you stay? Will you stay with me?'

'I should – it's late – or early—'

'Stay. Please.'

'I'll stay.'

Another kiss, deeper, sweeter, hot, hotter, the kind of kiss that leads to only one thing – until John Paul shot up from the mattress.

'What? What?' Were his flatmates back? Wasn't her bra draped over the sofa? Where were her awful knickers?

'I haven't even put on any music!' Dragging the top sheet around his hips while simultaneously covering Jax with the duvet, he ran around the room, chucking random items of clothing and other detritus into the wardrobe. 'Water!' he yelped, Jacinta leaping in response. 'Water? Do you want water? Candles!' he shouted and pelted out of the room and down the hall, taking a moment to yap in pain as he trod on the broken glass from the fallen picture in his bare feet.

'Don't go to –' *Don't go to any bother – it's only a shag – isn't it?*

Why did she feel as if she'd ended – or was about to end – one mess only to get mixed up in another? Not that there was anything messy about what had transpired tonight. Jacinta snuggled under the duvet, and permitted herself a very, very smug smile. *Not bad, Quirke – considering*. Oh, that had felt good – better than good: extraordinarily, hugely fantastic. She propped herself up against the headboard and meditatively ran her fingers through her hair. What had been the trigger? What had prompted her to take this decision – for take it she did, from the moment she'd tugged JP off down Clarendon Street.

Was it out of anger at the way things had disintegrated? *No, there was nothing angry about any of what had transpired – after running off on Max, anyway.* Was it the need to ally herself with someone other than Maxine? *Oh, that sounds cold.* Was it because the Gary/Mary session cut too close to home? *Well, it's not as if Fergal would ever talk to me like that – or would ever have the chance.* Was it, plain and simple, that she was attracted to John Paul and had had the guts to do something about it? *Maybe –*

'I can see you thinking from here.' John Paul interrupted her ruminations, and she watched him set candles about the room, the kind of candles laid aside in a kitchen drawer against a power outage, stuck haphazardly in beer bottles, and watching him lighting them with utter attention, she felt her heart skip a beat, and sink, all at once. He grinned over at her. 'There're the best we've got – three lads, what can you do.'

He handed her the glass of water and dropped the sheet to the floor, and Jacinta forgot her apprehension at the obvious romance of his actions, and made room for him in the bed.

'Thanks,' she said, sipping.

'Just for the water?' *O'Gorman. You. Feckin'. Eejit.*

Jacinta set the glass aside. 'No, not just for the water.' She pulled the duvet down, and raised herself up on her knees as she edged John Paul down on his back, straddled him, settled herself down on to his hips, watched his eyes begin to flutter shut as he responded to the feel of her against him. 'Umm, yeah, thanks for that,' Jacinta whispered. She caressed his nipples and licked them, ran her tongue lightly up and down his torso, all the while gently rocking against him. He reached up, fondling her breasts, her nipples, and she sighed, 'Oh, thank you, yes', and he grabbed her hips, her ass, and she thanked him for that, too.

And when she took him inside her fully, she laughed, wickedly, clenching herself around him, his resonant moan giving her as much pleasure as the feeling of him. 'Oh, yes, John Paul, thank you, thank you', and she rode him, rode until she had no breath left for gratitude, had no words left for language, and was left with her body and her own cries as expression.

As they lay, basking in the afterglow, John Paul whispered, 'You're very welcome', and their laughter forged an intimacy as breathtaking and potent as their physical connection. John Paul sighed, confident that it – they – everything was finally sorted, and before drifting off to sleep, wondered whether he should take her out to breakfast or have a homemade fry . . .

When he woke, late the next morning, she was gone.

23

Even when an agency was in its death throes, there was still protocol to be observed. Every Monday morning, the group meeting still had to take place, despite the fact that it was increasingly lightly attended. With little to keep her own personal attention engaged, Max fixed on the striking silence that Jax and John Paul were actively cultivating between themselves.

Max leaned back in her chair and observed them through slitted eyes. It wasn't as if they were always nattering their heads off, or anything. Not like they were in a constant state of discourse, talking shite about nothing. If nothing else, she'd noticed, there often existed a comfortable silence between them, a blissful accord, a happy calm – which was exactly *why* Max thought they ought to get together in the first place.

Today, though, the silence was rich, deep and portentous, underscored by the fact that neither met the other's glance, which they would have had they noticed that each was sneaking little looks at the other when the other wasn't looking.

Jax had found a spot on the spotless conference room table to stare at – when she wasn't flicking her eyes at JP.

John Paul, on the other hand, squirmed around in his seat, leaning forward, leaning back, crossing his ankles, uncrossing them, slouching down, sitting up straight – when he wasn't peeking over at Jacinta.

Maybe it was worth getting dumped with Lorcan, Max thought, and lacking anything better to do – she decided to find out what was going on. Even though it was desperately obvious.

'Hey, Jax, nice scarf,' Max said.

Jax jerked up in her seat and tugged the flowing fabric tighter against her throat. Her throat, she'd been horrified (thrilled) to notice, was covered in love bites, absolutely covered in them – an archipelago of hickies. She blushed a virulent puce, and didn't respond.

Mind your own business, Maxine O'Malley, she thought as she tried to adjust the scarf without revealing what it hid, while continuing to avoid looking at JP. She couldn't bear to look at him, acknowledge him . . . talk to him.

Not that she didn't want to talk to him, but she didn't want to *talk* to him. She didn't want to say the stupid things you always say after . . . the explanations about why she'd left like that, no note, no text, nothing. She didn't want to have to look at him and remember what it felt like to be with him, to smell his skin, to feel his hands on her body, to lie there, next to him, head on the same pillow, face to face, seeing in his eyes what she hadn't seen, maybe had never, ever seen, in Fergal's—

She snapped out of her reverie as Max lashed a wadded-up ball of paper at her head.

'What?' Jacinta asked. 'Yes?'

'Away with the fairies,' John Paul murmured, and Jacinta felt breathless all over again.

Nope, didn't bite, thought Max – and that phrase was guaranteed to get a rise out of Jacinta Quirke. *Time for Plan B.* 'What'd you get up to this weekend, Your Holiness?' She spun to face JP.

'Went to Mass,' he mumbled, and Jax jerked up and looked at him, full in the face, for the first time. Max watched them look at each other, and inexplicably, as cynical as she was, she felt her heart leap when a little smile touched Jax's lips, and JP's eyes went all slumberous and twinkly.

Hee hee! Max hid her smile in her coffee cup. 'Not that surprising, considering.'

What was the point, again, in telling Maxine to leave the Pope jokes alone? John Paul twitched superstitiously. Have some respect. And talking about respect . . . how about a note, Jacinta? A text, a phone call, maybe? And how about returning a phone call, or a text, not that he sent loads, or anything, not like some desperate eejit, but . . . But.

He felt desperate, the way he sped into the office this morning, hoping to catch her before they had to go in to the meeting, hoping to see her, to touch her again – not *touch* her touch her, but have contact, like; the contact he'd wanted over breakfast, through the day, the light, absent touches that people take for granted, the ones that are so important in the beginning, if this was a beginning, at all – a beginning for them, the two of them, as a – pair. A pair. 'Couple' seemed too big a word, somehow. A pair. Jax and JP. Maybe.

Maybe. Surely. Surely! After a night like that! And not just, you know. Not just because the sex was like gangbusters. JP shivered a little and slid another provocative glance in Jacinta's direction, remembering the third time they'd made love, the way she'd run her hands and her tongue all over him, the way she'd moaned and thrashed when he'd reciprocated, the smug little smile on her face as they cuddled afterwards, the way they'd lain there, facing each other, heads on the same pillow, the way her eyes, those clear blue eyes, smiled into his, the satisfied kind of smile that surely, surely must mean something.

Maxine, go off to the loo, please, just get out. I need to – what if I just said, 'I need to talk to Jacinta about something', what if I—

'Yeah, so, what'd you two get up to, after you abandoned me with Donkey Boy?' Max grinned at Jax, and, picking her battles, let her gaze bore into JP.

Jax had never been so happy to see Niamh Bourke in all her life.

'Well,' Niamh said, her voice dripping with the kind of deep fulfilment that insider information always gave her, 'I wonder what you three are doing in here, seeing that your creative director has gone over to Shannon and Malone.'

'Decco's into S&M!' Max hooted. 'We had no idea.'

John Paul saw a flicker in Niamh's eyes that he construed to mean she hadn't a clue as to what Max was on about. 'Google it, Niamh,' he suggested, unable to resist the dig. 'You'll figure it out – or not, as the case may be.'

Max laughed again, and Jax rose to do the necessary. *I am sick of protecting everyone from this horrible creature—*

'Oh, and Jacinta,' Niamh purred, 'you've a very showy bouquet down at reception, larger than taste might decree, but I suppose that's an errant fiancé for you, hmm?'

Max darted a quick look to John Paul and Jacinta and

saw two stricken faces. *I'll try peacemaking for a change*, she thought, and got to her feet.

'Mind your own business! Do you hear me!' Everyone heard Jacinta's startling roar. 'It is not your duty to spread news around this place, private news about private property, you loathsome busybody, you nosey, horrible cow—'

Jacinta felt herself propelled mid-tirade out of the room, with Niamh gasping with both pleasure and distress – which might have caused John Paul to revise his opinion about her ignorance as regarded sadomasochism, but he was too busy pushing past her to get down to his office. 'JP!' Jax called, but he sped down the stairs and into the basement.

'Goddammit!' Jax fumed as she pounded up the stairs, a nonplussed but jubilant Max hot on her heels. She followed behind as Jax stormed into her office and barely escaped being sliced in half by the slamming door.

'I have had it up to here with that interfering bint, that dried-up, pathetic, evil, rotten, plotting—'

'Get it off your chest, Jaxie,' Max joked, only to find herself on the receiving end of a threateningly pointed finger.

'Don't start with me, Maxine O'Malley,' Jax fumed, spinning and pacing around her tiny office like a caged animal. 'I would suggest that you leave me alone and don't go sticking your nose where it doesn't belong.'

'My nose hasn't been anywhere it shouldn't be. It's quite obvious that there's something or other, em, in the air, let's say—'

'You! You mind your own business!' Jax had grabbed up her stapler and madly started stapling away at nothing, spitting the little pieces of metal, like shrapnel, at the floor.

'You think you're so – so – *suave*, smirking at me, smirking at John Paul, throwing out your little comments like hooks. Do we look that stupid? Do we look that thick? Do we—'

'You look like two people who –' *are falling in love? Maxine, cop on to yourself –* 'who had a nice weekend.' She smiled and leaned casually against the door.

Jax threw the stapler across the room, where it slammed against their separating wall, and fell to the floor, empty.

'We need to talk.' Jax dropped down into her desk chair and glared up at Max. 'That session with Gary. It was insane, Maxine, putting yourself on the line for some stupid footage.'

Max rolled her eyes. 'Line, schmine – I wasn't "on the line",' she replied scathingly. 'We were all wired to kingdom come; it's not like I was alone—'

'How could you do it?' Jax stared up at her, bleak and angry. 'How could you put yourself out there like that, with him? We knew he was a pig, we knew he was, at best, a flirt, at worst, a serial adulterer.'

'Serial adultery – serialised adultery – this could spin off, you know,' Max mused, and jumped when Jacinta slammed her fist on her desk.

'This is not a joke! I am serious, Maxine, and I want an answer. How could you throw yourself at him like that?'

'*Throw* myself at him? *Throw* myself at him?' Max gaped at Jacinta. '*He* threw himself on to *me*. What do you take me for?'

The silence stretched on and on, with Max's disbelief increasing alongside Jax's belligerence. 'What do you take me for? Come on, Jacinta,' Max goaded, taking up where Jax had left off and pacing back and forth in front of her desk. 'Deliver your judgement from on high, from that high horse, Miss Morality, Miss Fidelity – ice princess, more like, engaged to the invisible man, hanging on to some ridiculous agreement with someone who isn't even there—'

'That's none of your *business*,' Jax insisted.

'Hanging on to her family, oh, Mummy, oh, Daddy, come be in my TV show—'

'*You're* the one that, God only knows why, wanted my mother in this thing – and don't even bother, I know an Angela Quirke scheme when I see one, I've had much more experience than you.'

'If you had any *experience*, you wouldn't get so spooked over a little bit of a grab, a silly little nothing that came to nothing.'

'Oh, don't give me that hard-boiled New York bullshit, Maxine O'Malley – you took a chance and it fucked up. Do you hear me? You fucked up.'

'Oooh, the great Jacinta has spoken!' Max felt it all going out of control, but could do nothing to stop it. 'Another strict and moral judgement from the honorable Jacinta Quirke, who, herself, is involved in the most dishonest fiction I've ever seen in my life.'

'You wouldn't know an honest emotional promise if it bit you on the arse!' Jax surged to her feet and they got in each other's faces. In her heart she knew this was hurtling out of their reach, but could do nothing to halt it.

'Honest promise!' Max hooted humourlessly. 'What crap! It's hilarious, given that, if your neck is anything to go by, you were at the very least snogging the face off John Paul O'Gorman, if not shagging the life out of him. Where's your fidelity now?'

'Where's yours? Mrs LaMotta,' Jax spat. 'Mrs Michael LaMotta.'

There was a moment of ringing silence, as if the very air itself had taken a shocked, stricken breath. Jax felt a hot twist of guilt, but it was too late to back down now. Later, she'd curl herself up into a ball at the remembrance of the look that passed over Max's face before it hardened, froze; a look of nauseous sorrow. For now, she leaned in as Max got further into her face.

'You bitch,' Max whispered. 'Running off and telling Niamh.'

Jax gasped. 'What? I never did—'

'That's what she's been hinting around, isn't it?' Max's voice began to rise. 'That's what she's been insinuating, isn't it? Isn't that what you were trying to tell me, when you were telling me to leave her alone? That you'd already betrayed me?'

It was Jax's turn to look sick and sad. 'I would never, Maxine. Surely you know that, I would nev—'

'It's exactly what you would do,' Max spat, pushing away from the desk to kick at the wall. 'Just the thing you'd do, Miss Prim and Proper, and what could be better than to find yourself a partner in crime, in narrow-mindedness—'

'How dare you. After all this time, don't you know me at all—'

'Don't you know *me*? As if I would make a play for Gary—'

'What about Lorcan?' Jax threw up her arms, her voice rising to mow over Maxine's. 'Flirting with him, snogging him, just to get his gear – and then lying to him, and me, me and John Paul, saying you took care of it—'

'That wasn't anything,' Max scoffed. 'It was for the project, it was for both of us. Don't you know me, after all?'

'Don't do me any favours, Mrs LaMotta.'

'Stop calling me that! You don't know what you're talking about.'

'I won't deny that, I certainly don't know what I'm talking about, because you didn't tell me.'

'There's nothing to tell – nothing that you'd understand, in your little world, your little cut-and-dried world where everybody lives happily ever after.'

'Sounds like you're trying to convince yourself, more than me.'

John Paul hesitated on the landing. He'd known something was up when the sound of rushing footsteps on the floor overhead made him fear for his ceiling; heard the rumblings as he made his way up to the accounts floor, passed avid yet cowardly co-workers as they thronged the stairs; and was further convinced of it as he got closer to Max and Jax's offices, passing through a bullpen full of whispering, gossiping creatives hanging over their walls. The shouting was unlike anything he'd ever heard between Max and Jax, and he wondered at the wisdom of intervening – but somebody had to.

'Friendship, me arse!' Jax shrieked as JP opened the door.

'Yeah, you ain't kidding, sister!' bellowed Max as she pushed past him in the doorway.

'Hey, I've got a—' he began, only to be cut off by Jacinta.

'We've got nothing to say to each other until you're ready to tell me the truth,' Jax threatened as she pushed past JP as well.

'Don't hold your breath,' Max spat as she legged it down the stairs.

'I've got a—' JP tried again.

232

'Fine!' Jax shouted, and shoved past JP again to regain her office, slamming the door in his face.

'Rough cut,' he said. Staring at the closed door, he chose his skin over the DVD in his hand, and made his way down to his own office past his goggling colleagues.

24

If Max didn't start screaming, she was terrified that she'd start crying, of all things – crying over what? A fight with some silly, uptight goody-goody? One who really needed a total makeover? Ha! Max charged through the mid-morning crowd to St Stephen's Green and jumped on the LUAS.

If she couldn't start screaming, and she refused to start crying, then she damn well was going to go shopping.

House of Fraser or bust, she thought as the happy little bing-bong of the tram signalled their departure. Feeling lucky to have gotten a seat – surely all these people hadn't just had screaming fights with their best friends in the middle of the morning and were also in need of some retail therapy – she wedged herself against the window and dully watched the passing traffic as they headed out to Dundrum.

How had Jax found out? If she knew one thing about Jax, it was that she was rigorously scrupulous, and would never have gone through any of her stuff. And what stuff did she have to go through, anyway? So there was the question now of how Niamh – had she hacked into some files, or something, computer files, or – *Oh, shit*. Max banged her head lightly against the side of the tram. The shoe drawer. *I should have burned those stupid documents . . .*

The documents that Mike refused to sign. The divorce papers that he wouldn't acknowledge. How many times had she tried to goad herself into forging his signature? Maybe that's why she'd had them around – right? *Stubborn dopes – the both of us.*

Max closed her eyes as she thought back to a scene she never willingly thought about. It had been some clash, all right.

'Sign them.' Max stood, defiant, shaking inside, sick inside, her head light enough to make her fear fainting. 'There's no point in –'

Mike turned away from their living-room picture window, the one that gave out on to Central Park – well, on the general direction of Central Park. He'd moved out weeks ago, after yet another championship argument, after Max had holed up in her office for weeks. 'I agree,' he began, equitably enough. 'There is no point. There is no point in me signing those papers because I refuse to recognise these proceedings. And I refuse to recognise these proceedings because I refuse to believe that is what you want to do – even though you are, in fact, doing it.'

'Sorry, you wanna stop talking like this is a David Mamet play?' Maxine threw the papers down on their coffee table, the one they'd commissioned from that hippie dude up in Woodstock, the table that, the hippie dude had said, was carved all over with their energetic images, or some such hippie crap.

She loved that table.

'There is no point in me signing these papers because I'm not divorcing you, Maxine!'

'Sign the damn papers, Michael, and let's end this farce.'

'Farce? This is not a farce. Not to me. So, okay, you fucked up, let's move on—'

It had devolved into a random cycle of shouting, all variations on the same theme went on and on, it seemed, until Max locked herself – like a dope, like a *girl* – in the bathroom. 'Sign the papers,' she screamed through the door, only to be greeted by silence.

She finally heard Mike sigh, heard his hand run down the door as if he could reach through and touch her, gently, consolingly, and she fought desperately against the tears.

'You know what you can do with those papers,' he said, as gently as his hand had stroked the door. 'I'm not leaving you. I'm not divorcing you. I forgive you. I forgive you, Maxine. So fucking deal with it.'

But I can't forgive myself. Max jumped up from her seat just in time to get out of the tram and head for the Dundrum Shopping Centre, where she fully intended to vaporise her Visa.

Jax was fairly certain that she'd never sat more still in her life. Watching her computer clock tick away the day – it was getting on to 4 p.m. and she hadn't moved since ten-thirty – she giddily wondered if she could market this as some kind of transcendental meditation tool. *Found out the awful truth behind your so-called fiancé's silence? Fallen out with one of your dearest friends-slash-business partners? Then you need Quirke's Quirky Clock-Watching Meditation . . . Thingie.*

'Oh, God,' she moaned aloud as she dropped her head in her hands – again. 'This has been the worst – well, it's been a pretty bad day,' she said, aloud, again, to keep herself company. The thing with Max had been pretty rotten, but the worst, the very worst, was the look on JP's face when Niamh – evil, horrible, hateful, despicable Niamh – when Niamh ... and Fergal! Flowers, now? Typical. Now he was home free, he could afford to make gestures. Jax wrapped her arms around her head and wished she could erase it all.

Erase her stupid behaviour, running off like that on Saturday morning, shutting off her mobile, unplugging her phone, hiding like the coward she was, and then purposely getting in to the office bang on ten for the meeting, not wanting to risk running into JP, not wanting to risk – *not wanting to risk, plain and simple, you wimp.*

The phone went again. She'd been dumping her calls to voicemail all day. Her mother had already rung seven times, asking about the weekend and where was she and what time was their call on Wednesday. *Shite.* She grabbed the receiver, willing herself to handle whatever it was, be it Max, or her mum, or whoever, as straightforwardly as she could.

'This is Jacinta.'

'It's me. JP.'

'Oh. Hi.'

'All right?'

'Yeah.'

'You sure?'

'I'm fine.'

Fibre optic silence ensued – far too reminiscent, for Jacinta, of the last year of Fergal's phone calls.

John Paul jumped into the breach. 'Listen, I want to – I need to – talk to you, Jax.'

'I can't talk now,' Jax replied, slightly frantic. *So much for that honesty notion.* 'I – I have to do this paperwork, the accounts have to – I – JP—'

'We're going to have to talk sometime.'

'Not today!' Jacinta put a hand to her throat. She wasn't sure she'd ever hollered this much in her life – and a teeny, tiny part of her brain was whispering encouragingly. 'Please,' she continued, less hysterically. 'I want to talk to you too, JP, but not *talk* talk, if you take my meaning. Please.'

'Can we not go for a coffee, away from the—'

'From the gossiping hordes? No thanks. I really have to go.'

'Yeah, right, fine.' Down in his office, John Paul paced, wrapping the phone cord into knots. 'If you don't want anything from me, maybe you want to think about how the hell we're going to do the shoot on Wednesday.'

Jax furiously massaged her forehead. 'I can't think about that now, JP!'

'Listen, this isn't even my project!' Jacinta pulled the phone away from her ear as JP shouted down the line. 'It's not my responsibility to take charge of this shoot, it's up to you, and Maxine, so let's hope you two get over your little hair-pulling session and get on with things. I'm in this too, you know.'

Jax let the hair-pulling remark pass. 'I know you are, and we'll work it out, but at the moment, I couldn't care less, to be honest with you. I've had a shitty day—'

'Yeah, well, I had a shitty weekend, if you're wondering, leaving texts and messages like an eejit—'

'I said, I do *not* want to get into this now!' Jacinta dropped her head on to her desk again, and roared into the receiver, hoping that no one in the bullpen would hear this latest round of hue and cry. 'I've already been very clear about that, and—'

'There's a thing or two you need to be clearer about,

Jacinta Quirke, and I'll be waiting for an explanation.' And he slammed down the phone.

I've got to get out of here, Jacinta thought – but she sat, motionless, and went back to watching her clock.

Yeah, JP, okay, you said what you needed to say, wasn't exactly the way you wanted to say it, but you did . . . John Paul mechanically removed a DVD from the burner and set up another one. It was monkey work, probably not the best thing for him at the moment – the mindlessness made it that much easier for him to visit and revisit the look on Jax's face when Niamh came in with her little announcement.

She'd – Jax – looked . . . not happy, was JP's best guess. Surprised, but not in a good way. Like, shocked, maybe? It was just another confusing detail in a big bloody mess of mixed signals and obliquity.

What's yer problem, man? You've had girlfriends before – plenty of them, well, not like you're an operator, but you've, you know, been in love before and whatnot – so what's the problem?

But she did say that she wanted to *talk*. At some stage. Soon. He hoped.

Right. Something was up with Jacinta and what's-his-name, something that instigated a really, really big bunch of flowers. It could be either of two things: they'd got back together, and Jacinta's look was pure guilt after what had passed between herself and himself (John Paul), or they'd broken up, she'd dumped him (Fergal) because of himself (John Paul) and . . . and she was, em, reacting to Niamh's broadcast . . . because she – okay, okay – she hadn't had a chance to tell him (John Paul) about dumping him (Fergal) . . .

Or something.

One thing was for sure, they definitely needed the next shoot to flesh out their pilot. The chances of Jax and Max sorting out their differences by Wednesday were slim to nonexistent. Picking up his phone, he decided he'd have to call in the reserves.

'Hello,' he said, friendly but businesslike, 'I'd like to speak to Raymond Quirke, please.'

At six-thirty, Jax made her way down the stairs as stealthily as possible. She didn't want to look like she was creeping, but that's what it felt like – it felt like skulking, like sneaking. As she made her way towards the front door – one more staircase to go – she allowed herself to feel relief, to lift up her head, to descend the way she would on any other day—

Niamh materialised, as she often did, as if out of nowhere. 'How the mighty have fallen.'

'You know, Max reckons you're a virgin,' Jax mused. 'A withered auld maid – and I used to defend you, thinking that you had no friends and were secretly sad and lonely.' Jax looked her up and down. 'What a waste of my time.'

'Yes, you're a world-class time-waster, aren't you, Jacinta Quirke?' Niamh was, by all appearances, unmoved by Jax's little speech. 'You came in, eager and capable, fit for your duties – now look at you, corrupted by the company you keep, lazy, malingering, stealing from the agency . . .'

'Stealing?' Jacinta felt her stomach pitch.

Niamh laughed lightly. 'Oh, we'll see what we see. Took you for an honest, moral young woman, but then you did have to go keeping company with that American one.'

'Don't even think about going down that road.'

'Quick to defend her, aren't you, despite events of this morning? And don't think I can't put two and two together. Oh, I can just imagine what all that effing and blinding was about.' Niamh's nostrils flared with excitement. 'She's a right hoor, isn't she, Jacinta Quirke, messing about with the men – messing about and her still married to Mr Michael LaMotta—'

'I won't say it again,' Jax cut across, wearily. 'You've no right sticking your nose—'

'I know you agree with me.' Niamh moved closer to Jax, too close, enough so Jacinta felt the need to brace herself against the banister as she strained away. 'You've no time for those who don't keep their promises. You're faultless, Jacinta, and there's still time, you can still clear your name, clear your association with that Jezebel!'

'You nutter!' Jacinta pulled away from the fervent, heavy-breathing woman and pelted down the stairs.

You'll see, Niamh ranted to herself as she locked her office door behind her. *I'll show you – I'll show you all.* Running a loving finger over the collection of little cameras that she'd rented, Niamh opened up the instruction manual at page one.

She was nothing if not patient.

And no one – *no one* – felt sorry for Niamh Bourke.

Slamming the heavy door behind her, Jacinta fought the urge to lean against it, to slide down it until she lay on the stoop. *Freak!* she thought, gooseflesh popping up all over her arms. *Mentaller!* She gave a strangled little screech that she swallowed before it could fully flow when she realised that she wasn't alone.

A tall, dark, handsome man, in an impeccably cut suit, stood on the pavement, looking up at her. He was holding a suitcase – although 'suitcase' didn't even begin to do justice to the quality of the leather luggage that was casually gripped in his hand. His voice, deep and resonant, with a heavy New York accent, boomed up at her. 'Pardon me, I'm sorry to trouble you, but I was hoping you could tell me whether or not this is, in fact, ACJ:Dub—'

'Oh, *no*,' Jax wailed. 'Oh my God! It's you, isn't it? That's all we need! I don't *believe* this!'

And grabbing Michael LaMotta by the arm, Jacinta dragged him up the road and away from the building.

25

Angela swept into John Paul's apartment in the way
that Wellington must have swept into his tent at
Waterloo. 'John Paul,' she declared, unexpectedly
embracing him, 'tell us everything.'

'I can only tell you what I know,' he said, shaking
hands with an uncharacteristically dour Raymond.

'Subtext, darling, subtext. I shall spot it in a heartbeat.
I've made a *career* out of it. In fact, that's the only reason
I was able to stick *that soap opera* in the early nineties.'

Angela dove into an anecdote, and John Paul
murmured appropriately as he moved to the breakfast bar
and the bottle of white wine he'd had chilling.
Surreptitiously rubbing stray marks off the wine glasses
he'd bought on the way home from work, he gathered up
the lot and set it down on the coffee table.

'If it's as bad as I think it is, we might like to break out
the whiskey,' Angela predicted.

Raymond patted her back soothingly. 'Let's hear what
John Paul has to say.'

It was far less than it had seemed when he'd rung
Raymond in a panic. He took them through the events of
the morning – blushing as he realised that they were
sitting on his couch, the very couch on which Jacinta had

cuddled on his lap, the couch on which he had first laid his body over hers, the couch which had been festooned with her bra and panties—

'Em. Sorry.' He shrugged, looking down at his shoes, and missed the fire-bright look in Angela's eyes, and the less subtle dig of her elbow into her husband's side. 'Anyway, they were screaming at each other, I mean, howling, and Jax said something like, "Friendship, me arse", and Max stormed off, and then I rang Jacinta later and she didn't want to talk about anything—'

'Typical! Typical!' Angela downed her wine.

'—and I said something about the shoot, and she didn't want to talk about that, either – and I mean, we need that footage, I've done a rough cut, it's really rough, but it's kind of . . . thin, I guess you could say. Not much human interest.'

'Good *God*, we've only just begun!' Angela fought down the alarm that ran rampant throughout her nervous system. 'We've barely scratched the surface! And we're running out of time!'

'I agree,' said J.P. 'I think that we've got a good foundation, but we need to start building on it. We've got a little over a fortnight left, and we can cut together enough footage to buy some time to finish, but we can't finish if I can't get them to look at what we've got because they're not talking to each other.'

'Jacinta is far too stubborn to drop something halfway – particularly something like this, something with so much . . . potential.' Angela blinked at John Paul and smiled.

'I was hoping that you two could, em, throw some light on the subject, somehow,' John Paul said, looking between them somewhat anxiously.

'I don't, as a rule, interfere in my children's lives this

way,' Raymond began, to an accompaniment of scornful grunts from his wife, 'but I think this is very important to Jacinta, on many levels. Not simply the project – and you all seem very good at what you're doing, highly accomplished, indeed – but as regards her friendship with Maxine.'

'We are missing a key element,' Angela mused. 'There is something else here, something brewing below the surface, something else – Maxine is rather secretive about her private life, I wonder if there's something there.'

John Paul never saw it: whether Raymond twitched, infinitesimally, whether he stopped breathing for a heartbeat – JP had no notion of what tipped Angela off, but tipped she was.

'Raymond Quirke! You know something!'

'Angela—'

'Do *not* even attempt to deny it! I know that look in your eye.' John Paul couldn't see it, but that was marriage for you, he guessed. 'How long have you been *hiding* something from me?'

Raymond sighed into his wine, and wondered about that whiskey. 'I am hiding nothing from you, darling.'

'Rubbish!' Angela leapt off the couch in an attempt to loom over him, which failed miserably as he was nearly as tall as she, though still seated. 'You *know* something.'

'I know something,' he replied, ignoring Angela's fierce '*Ha!*'. 'Something that was told to me in confidence, by Jacinta, who came into possession of this information in an indirect fashion.'

'The mother is *always* the last to know! *O! Come, pick up the sword, wretched hand of mine. Pick up the sword, move to where your life of misery begins—*'

'That's enough, Angela.' Raymond cut her off. 'None of

that Medea business, if you don't mind.' Angela clammed up, but regarded him dangerously as she gracefully sank back on to the couch.

Raymond leaned forward and studied his folded hands. *I've got no choice, Jacinta,* he thought glumly. *And it's all for the greater good – I hope.*

'Let me begin by saying that Jacinta took me into her confidence with the proviso that I would, in fact, respect that confidence. As you know, I do not take such assurances lightly.'

'Well, *we* won't tell her who told us, if that's what you're worried about,' Angela cut in impatiently.

'Which is rather a meaningless vow, my dear, as there is no one else who could have provided you with this information, unless it was Maxine herself—'

'Raymond Quirke, spill the goddamn *beans*!' Angela thundered.

Raymond cleared his throat, and began to fuss with his cuffs – and it made JP smile to see so much of Jacinta in her father – or vice versa. He topped up their wine, and received a grateful glance from Raymond, who once again cleared his throat.

He sighed, and commenced.

When he finished, Angela all but levitated off the couch.

'This is positively *Shakespearean*,' she said, her voice vibrating with exhilaration. She placed a firm hand on Raymond's shoulder as she gazed off into the middle distance. 'I shall consider forgiving you for neglecting to inform me about this extraordinary plot line – my *partner*, my *husband*, my *boon companion* – because it is, indeed, utterly remarkable. Oh, yes. Oh, yes,' she murmured to herself, as she wandered across to consider the view over

Smithfield. 'Two young lovers, pledged for life, for better, for worse, torn apart across an ocean, by – by what?' She spun to face the room, not seeing the woebegone Raymond, the astounded John Paul. Throwing her arms wide, she glided across the room as though she were moving downstage. 'By misunderstanding? Betrayal? Infidelity? Of *course*!' she projected, as if she were on the Abbey stage, her voice filling the room, building until it threatened to shatter the wine glasses. 'That explains everything! Infidelity! The rotter! The bastard!' She took a moment to glare at the men. 'What could she do but flee, *flee* from hearth and home when faced with such callous disloyalty, *flee* across the great expanse of water, to wash away the past and begin anew! A stranger in a strange land, the past another country, and she – *she*! A new woman, a *tabula rasa*, one to whom nothing terrible had ever happened, or ever would again . . .'

And she exited majestically for the loo.

Raymond and John Paul sat in the throbbing beat of silence Angela left behind.

'She's very good,' JP said weakly, overwhelmed by it all.

Raymond drained his glass. 'Oh, she is. She is, indeed.'

'Is she . . . right? Is that what happened?'

'John Paul, between a man and a woman, anything could happen, and what has just been enacted for us is, of course, a viable scenario – but whatever the circumstance, I expect it all comes down to betrayal of . . . of expectations.

'I don't know the exact circumstances, as Jacinta doesn't know them herself,' Raymond went on. 'But I suppose that something to do with this secret had to have come out today to cause them to fall out so drastically.

Jacinta was far too hurt by what she perceived to be Maxine's betrayal – by not sharing this personal information – and I expect Maxine would in turn feel betrayed if she found out that Jacinta had known, for any length of time – Oh, God.' Raymond dropped heavily against the back of the couch and covered his eyes.

'Wish we had this on tape,' JP joked, and then poured out the last of the wine.

'I wish we hadn't ever got involved, even as little as we are,' Raymond replied. 'The more we examine what we know, the more I realise how little we know – and by interfering even a little, we may be creating something far worse, far worse. I would suggest cancelling the shoot and—'

'Don't be ridiculous.' As ever, Angela's timing was above reproach. 'This is what we're going to do,' she began.

Furious, Max slammed the taxi door behind her and pounded up the steps of Raymond's Victorian – Elizabethan? – townhouse. How dare they proceed? How *dare* they ring her as if she were an *employee*? How dare Jacinta and John Paul collude behind her back – stealing the project, putting *Angela* up to phoning her to confirm her call time?

Incensed, Jacinta paced the control room. How could Max have gone behind her back, to her own mother, her own father, and tried to take over the production? Maxine, who'd been *hiding* the last two days, skiving off from work, and plotting and scheming? If she thought she was going to get away with this, she had another think coming.

Unprofessional, back-stabbing, gutless – she'd show Jacinta and all the Quirkes what she was made of. Max banged the knocker vehemently, smirking as she ran over in her mind the little script she'd devised last night, a little script she hadn't been sure she'd trot out – but she was sure now.

Backstabbing, pushy, unprofessional – she'd show Maxine O'Malley that she wasn't about to be rolled over and disregarded. Jax briskly buttoned up her new camera-ready suit and reached for her mobile. She hadn't been sure she was going to send that text – but now she was positive.

Angela opened the door and graciously gestured Maxine in. 'Hello, pet, you're right on time.' She turned a wicked giggle into a delicate cough as she watched Maxine's eyes flare with anger. 'Can I get you a cuppa before the hordes descend?'

'Hordes?' Maxine asked casually as they made their way up to studio one. 'I wouldn't call ten or fifteen couples hordes.'

'Oh, of course, you weren't at the meeting yesterday.' Angela smiled indulgently. 'Well, we had a little brainstorm and thought it might be a good idea to cast our nets further, as it were.'

'Oh, really?' *Going behind my back, as if this didn't matter to me, as if I didn't matter—*

'We did try ringing you, but your lines were, apparently, *down*.'

Max shrugged and saw that the couch on the landing had been removed. 'What's going on here?' she demanded.

'We've set up a secondary studio, do come this way.' Angela led her into another, smaller conference room, opposite the kitchen, in which a replica of their master shot had been set up, with another camera, the little couch, and another presenter's chair. 'We're going to have you and Jacinta running concurrently, with' – and here Angela motioned, with practised airiness – 'a live feed on the monitor so you can see what the other is up to.'

Shit, that's a really good idea. 'Seems unnecessarily complicated, but since I had no say—'

'Nothing's set in stone, of course. Everything's negotiable,' Angela purred. 'We'll go talk it over with Jacinta – shall we?'

'It's fine.' And Max headed into the kitchen to brood.

Angela winked at the camera planted over the Paul Henry painting, and JP whispered, 'Well done' in her ear.

And if he was recording it all, he decided, why not? At this rate, who knew what might come in handy? That footage of Angela and Max arguing on the first day was pretty entertaining . . .

'Any other major decisions taken that I wasn't involved in?' Jacinta demanded.

'No, none that I can think of.' John Paul tried for nonchalant, but wobbled a little at the mix of resentment and hurt in Jax's eyes.

'I'll remind you of your own words – this isn't your project,' she said sarcastically.

'Will we get into this now?' Who knew he could be so detached and cool-headed? 'We're only twenty minutes from mark.'

'I'm not *getting* into anything, I'm just reminding you—'

'Because I'd love to sort things out between us, Jacinta. I'm not keen on keeping secrets from you.'

'Secrets? What are you talking about, secrets?' Jax demanded. Angela, watching on an ancillary deck down in the new studio, covered her eyes, and Raymond covered his mouth. The little red light on the machine glowed innocently, alerting anyone who bothered to look that the recording was being successfully made.

'Deceptions? Is that a better word?' JP hoped that Raymond and Angela were otherwise occupied. 'Delusions? Dishonesty?'

'You're only a walking thesaurus, yourself.'

'I won't lie to you, Jacinta.' John Paul rose and reached out to her. She avoided him, and he pursued, and gently nudged her back towards the far wall of the control room. Angela uncovered her eyes and covered her mouth.

Raymond covered his eyes.

'I won't lie, and pretend that Friday night and Saturday morning didn't happen. I won't lie to you and tell you that it doesn't matter that you're engaged to someone else—'

'John Paul—'

He touched a finger to her lips, and began to trace them, lovingly, with his fingertip. Angela sighed rapturously, and Raymond peeked out from behind his hand. 'I won't pretend that it's no big deal that you're not really available, because I don't want to lie to you. I can't pretend that we weren't together, that we didn't make love –'

Raymond dove for the 'off' switch, and Angela fought him off like a lioness.

'That I didn't want to make love to you all weekend long –'

Angela stopped short of raking her husband's eyes out with her nails, and leapt up on to his torso to throw off his momentum.

'That I've never felt like this before, in my life, and—'

The door knocker went, and Raymond grabbed Angela, who was in danger of spilling over backwards and dragging them crashing to the floor.

'Not now, JP,' Jacinta whispered. 'Not today. There's too much going on – please. If you care, then please give me some time.'

He kissed her lightly – on either cheek, on the mouth – and Angela clapped her hands, then rubbed her fingers at Ray. He handed her a hundred euro – the wager had increased to double or nothing – and headed for the control room.

Angela tucked the money into her cleavage and skipped off to answer the door.

Angela's use of the word 'hordes' was, unsurprisingly, something of an exaggeration, but there was a seemingly endless flow of couples of all shapes and sizes making their way into Studios One and Two. Max and Jax had passed each other, coldly, on their way into their respective places, to interview their respective couples, without comment – while both noting each other's new outfits – and Angela was efficiently and entertainingly greeting, corralling, and warming up the participants.

Max shook hands with her pair, Deb and Rob, who looked astonishingly alike, and Jax fiddled with her earpiece as she introduced herself to Amanda and Peter, who had just been snogging like maniacs on the love seat.

'Sorry, Deb, Rob, I've got to – I've got to go off-script here for a second.' Max leaned conspiratorially towards her latest subjects. 'Look, while your romance is undoubtedly heart-warming, it's not really what people want to know about.'

Jax cast an eye at the monitor that was set up outside the subjects' sightline, and directly in hers. She had Max's voice humming into her earpiece – as hers was in Max's she supposed – and stopped paying attention to Amanda,

who was droning on and on about how well she got on
with her future mother-in-law.

'Let's face it,' Max went on, and Jax held her hand up
to silence her mystified subjects. 'You're both extremely
attractive people, and I'd find it hard to believe that
temptation hasn't come calling, that neither of you has
been pursued by someone who, despite your level of
commitment, hasn't thought they might have a chance.'

Jax turned her attention back to her couple. 'Your level
of commitment is simply breathtaking, Amanda, Peter,'
said Jax, nodding warmly to them both. 'It's something,
I'm sure, that extends into the rest of your lives – to your
job, or, say, your friendships, as well.'

Max continued her line of attack. 'And so what if
they did think they had a chance, those dirty, rotten
cheaters!' Max beamed at the increasingly wary Deb and
Rob. 'They could try all they like and you'd never give in.
Right?'

Jax glared at the monitor, and by extension, Max. 'It's
crucial, don't you think, to be as transparent as possible in
all your dealings with those close to you?' asked Jax, as
Amanda and Peter exchanged confused glances. 'To share
ideas, small and large, especially when such ideas have a
serious impact on the other person – let me explain. Say
you had an impulse to do something, let's say, maybe you
had arranged to go on a trip with a friend, and you show
up at the airport, kitted out for the Canaries, only to find
out that your friend had booked you on a skiing trip. Now,
honestly, how would you feel about that? Wouldn't you
feel as if you'd been lied to?'

Max leaned forward and pinned Deb with a look that
had her shifting uncomfortably in her seat. 'Or would you
give in to the pressure? I mean, Deb, in fairness, say

George Clooney pitches up to you in the Octagon Bar, Rob is away on business in Siberia, and you're a little tipsy, and you figure – what the heck! George Clooney, Deb! It's a one-off! So what!' Max threw up her hands.

'Em,' John Paul managed.

'Er,' Raymond replied.

Angela scowled at the monitors. *Interesting, but surely irrelevant.*

'*I'd* say you had reason to be put out, at the very least!' Jacinta looked eagerly from Amanda to Peter, who stared back, confused.

'So say you do, Deb; say you have a one-nighter with a Hollywood movie star – it doesn't have to be George Clooney, it could be Brad Pitt – and you come over all guilty, and you break up with Rob, and then you make a new girlfriend.' Max leaned in towards Deb. 'Do you *really* have to get into all that old business with that new friend? Do you?'

Jax stared aghast at the monitor. 'Maxine O'Malley, what in the name of God are you going on about?'

'Excuse me.' Angela waved a dismissive hand in the general direction of the voice that had spoken from the hall, and remained glued to the screen.

'Um, who's Maxine?' Amanda ventured, and Jax shushed her abruptly.

Deb exchanged a tense look with Rob. 'I – I don't know – I would never—'

'Hypothetical, Deb! So you fool around, make a mistake, get on with your life. Do you have to be dragging it around with you for ever?'

'Only if you haven't got over it, which I seriously don't think that you have, Maxine!' Jax stood, and didn't notice Amanda and Peter slip out of the room.

'What I'm saying is,' Max shouted, 'what I'm asking you, Deb, Deb and Rob, is it anybody's business?'

'Excuse me, but what the hell is this? Jacinta told me something about a video shoot, but—'

Every molecule in Angela's body stilled. That voice. That voice – a dead-ringer for Robert DeNiro (whom she might consider meeting in the Octagon Bar), in timbre and accent. De Niro – American – New York . . .

Surely it couldn't be?

'Is this who I think it is?' she trumpeted, spinning around like a dervish and circling Michael like a tiny, well-groomed tiger. 'Is it you? Betrayer of hearts! Thief of promises! Despoiler of innocents!'

'Angela, what's going on down there?' Raymond rose, and after a nod from JP, headed down to the kitchen.

John Paul didn't know where to look, where to watch, and he hoped that the server didn't crash.

'Mum?' Jax couldn't clearly hear what was happening on the other channel, as Maxine was still going at it relentlessly with an increasingly unnerved Deb and Rob.

'– she would never,' said Rob, less and less assuredly. 'And anyway, women don't do that, once they get married. It's all they're after, like – getting married.'

'Oh, really?' Deb sneered. 'A lot you know.'

'What the hell is Maxine doing in there?'

That came through loud and clear – for both Jax and Max.

'What the fuck?' Max rose, and jiggled her earpiece in disbelief.

Deb and Rob started a bitter argument *sotto voce*.

'Uh oh,' Jax muttered.

'Jax?' asked John Paul, half out of his chair.

'Angela?' Raymond queried, and came face to face with Mike.

Deb laughed nastily and Rob rose and stormed out of the room.

'Could somebody answer a simple question—'

'Ha!' Angela threw back her head and glared up at Michael. 'Defiler of dreams, how dare you come in here and demand answers! You have far too much to answer for, you who poisoned the sacred waters of the loving cup, you who tainted the fruits of your bounty, you who—'

'I'm sorry, lady, I don't mean to cause you offence, but are you for real?'

'Oh, my God,' Max gasped.

'How dare you question my integrity, you womanising, lecherous, philandering—'

Michael appealed to Raymond. 'What the fuck is she talking about? Is this lady out of her mind, is she crazy, or what?'

'That crazy lady is my wife!' Raymond roared, grabbing Michael by the lapels. 'Do not speak of my wife—'

'I'm here to speak to *my* wife!'

'Holy shit,' said JP, and throwing down his headphones, hurried downstairs.

No one noticed Deb burst into tears and run out of the room.

Everyone stood, staring at Mike. Jax slipped out into the hallway, biting her thumbnail. *Not such a bright idea, after all, Jacinta Quirke.*

'I apologise for barging in on your production, but I'm here to see Maxine, and I wonder if I could—'

Max stood in her doorway. Angela brought her clasped hands up to her heart once she'd got a look at Michael's face. *I was wrong!* She reached back for support and found Raymond's hand. *I was utterly and completely wrong! Good God!*

'Mike.'

Without saying another word, he went into the room, and she shut the door behind them.

And immediately opened it again. 'Shut it down,' she ordered. 'Shut it all off.' And she closed the door once more.

'I'll do it,' said Jax, and she ran up the stairs.

I should have minded my own business – like I told Niamh, like Maxine told me, Jax lamented to herself as she flipped switches and turned off recorders. *No more of this high-tech eavesdropping,* she thought as she made her way back down – only to find her mother, father and JP engaging in some old-fashioned snooping.

'Here!' Angela hissed, holding out a glass.

Jacinta shook her head, and took a seat as far from the door as possible, but it soon became apparent that extraneous listening devices weren't necessary.

Max and Mike's voices rose, and if it hadn't been obvious that they were having a blistering row, the texture of their voices could almost be called beautiful. Their intonations were a muffled ribbon of vowels and soft consonants, a graceful but turbulent spiral of whaddya *hadda*shoulda*you*godda*you*godda*youhadta* with the occasional percussive fuck*dat* FUCK*dat,* spun breathlessly in bass and alto counterpoint. Jax sighed; she couldn't imagine ever having gone at it with Fergal like that, and felt that that was something of a shame; she couldn't imagine having that kind of energy to work things out.

Surely that's what Max and Michael were doing – working things out? Maybe she'd been wrong about Max, wrong to think the worst of her, maybe it was time for Jax to mind her own business and accept her friend the way she was, and hope that she and Michael were achieving some kind of resolution, and that things could go back to the way they were, between Max and Michael, between herself and Max, and—

'You! This is all your doing, isn't it? You're dead to me, do you hear me? I *quit!*' Max, coming out of the room suddenly, roared at Jax, and without a backward glance, stormed out of the location.

They all turned to Michael as he stepped out of the studio. He shrugged. 'It's a start.'

Angela threw herself against his chest and looked up at him beseechingly. 'Michael. Darling. I was so wrong about so many things!'

'This your mom?' Mike asked Jax, who nodded. 'Mrs Quirke, you're a real character, you know that?'

'Call me Angela, poor Michael, oh, Michael.' She appeared to swoon, and Raymond peeled her off Mike and led her away.

'We need to talk,' said Jax.

Mike grimaced. 'I don't know, you're already in deep shit with her, you know . . .'

'I know.' Jax looked up at him grimly. 'We need to talk. Let's go.'

She turned to go, stopped, and looked back at John Paul. 'I can't—'

'I'm not going anywhere.' He grinned, sounding brasher than he felt. He and Michael exchanged a manly nod, the backwards sort that led with the chin. JP watched them go, then went up to dismantle the whole works.

26

Two could play this game.

Oh yes they could, thought Max. Especially when one of the two – namely herself – was infinitely more devious and cunning than the other.

Wiring herself up expertly, and with a few personalised touches she had added based on past experience, Max cosied the camera lens between her breasts, anchoring it with toupee tape. *Just the right angle to get up in somebody's face*, she thought, fiercely focused on the job to hand and not on what had gone down earlier that week.

Oh, sure, it was tough knowing that everybody in the shop was gossiping about her and Jax, that they were watching her every move, that Niamh Bourke was in her own special kind of heaven, and that Jacinta was sitting there next to her, all day, every day, saying nothing, staying out of her way –

Which was exactly what she, Max, wanted. And if Jacinta thought that a turn like Wednesday, good or otherwise, didn't deserve another – well, she was in for a surprise.

Max had been shadowing Fergal for three days now. She'd Googled his details, found his office – conveniently located near to ACJ – and recognised him from all those photos that Jax used to have scattered about her home. He was nothing if not dependable – *Ha!* thought Max as she slipped the mixer into her handbag – and following him around had been boring, but fruitful. She knew now that she had a lot to learn about this spying lark, and that she couldn't get clean audio to save her life, not from a distance, anyway.

Hence the boob cam. Anyway, it was past time she and Fergal got up close and personal.

She boldly crossed Baggot Street, and inwardly bemoaned the fact that his offices were so close to ACJ, and that he regularly patronised the smart Italian deli that she and that traitor Jacinta Quirke habitually—

There! 'Hey! Fergal! Fergal Delaney!' Max barrelled up to him, chest aloft, and jigged around in his face until it occurred to her that it wasn't good for the footage.

'May I help you?' Fergal retreated behind his blandest expression, and reddened slightly at the sight of the bounty thrust in his general direction.

'Not me, pal, but you can certainly help out a friend of mine.' As Fergal continued vapid, she threw her shoulders back further and went on, 'Jacinta Quirke? You know her, don't ya? Your *fiancée*?'

He didn't even blush! He didn't even twitch! He simply raised his hand, his left hand, to smooth down his tie, and—

'You bastard!' Max shrieked, grabbing his hand and forcing it closer to her cleavage. 'That's a wedding hand! You scumbag! She *waited* for you! She put her entire life on hold! How dare you—'

And in quick succession, Fergal's hand was wrenched from hers, a murmured apology was made, Max's arm was grabbed, and she was propelled up the road.

It was, of course, Jax, leading them up Pembroke Street.

'Jax!' All acrimony forgotten, Max turned her friend and grabbed her into a hug. 'That wanker! And for you to find out like that, in the middle of the street!'

Jax pulled away, and kept them moving up the road. 'I knew.'

Max led them over to a wall. 'Since?'

Jax shrugged and leaned against it. 'A couple days ago.'

'How?' Max pulled herself up and started banging her heels against the stone.

Jax gently laid a hand on Max's calf. 'I met him for a coffee. I instigated it. I was going to break up with him.'

'Hallelujah!' Max shimmied a bit in celebration, and stopped, as it hurt her bum.

'Yes, well, somewhat surplus to requirements,' Jax muttered. 'I had my speech all set, and then I saw the bloody ring.'

'Omi*god*.'

'Umm hmm, and then it all went on from there.' Jax began the ritual shredding of her split ends; Max gently drew her hand away. 'He's been married for six months, so it could be worse, and her father, funnily enough, is in oil.'

'Asshole,' Max blurted.

'Yeah,' Jax sighed, and an amicable silence ensued . . .

'Hey. Sorry.' Max grumbled.

'Yeah. Okay.' Jax sighed. 'Er, about . . .'

'About all of it. For not telling you about Mike. You and I met in the middle of it all, the whole break-up, and I liked you because you didn't *know* any of it, the whole me-and-Mike thing . . . and then I guess when you get to know somebody, they have to know stuff.'

Jax flexed her fingers, wanting to pull at something,

yank at something else. 'I couldn't stand the thought of more deception in my life – I suppose I picked on you when I really wanted to get at Fergal.'

'Sorry I said all those things.'

'Me too.'

'Good.'

'Grand.'

Jax squinted over at Max. 'I can't go on, though, if we're not going to be straight with one another.'

'Yeah, okay, I know. Sorted.' Max heaved a big, cleansing breath. 'That was kind of a big deal for nothing.'

Jax shook her head. 'No it was *not*. It was about the state of our friendship. It's all about trust and honesty – the kinds of things that don't matter when you're younger, when your best friend is the girl behind you in the classroom queue—'

Max jumped off the wall and clapped her hands. 'I've got it! We'll start over!'

'What are you like?' Jax glared at her in confusion.

'It's a great idea! Let's go!' She held out her hand expectantly. 'Hey! I'm Maxine O'Malley. You're new here.'

'Maxine, you are mad as a brush.' Jax looked up and down the street, mortified.

'Come on, come on!' Max begged, jumping up and down.

'Hello. My name is—' Jax cringed. 'I hate this play-acting business, you know that.'

Max jumped up and down again, hand still extended.

'For *fuck's* sake,' Jax breathed, and shook Max's hand. 'Hello. I'm Jacinta Quirke and I'm here in ACJ:New York for a work-exchange kind of thing, em, for a while.'

'Let's be friends!' Max chirped, and hopped back up on the wall.

'You're a bloody lunatic.' Jax laughed; a pure, clear, booming, belly laugh. 'And this is almost exactly the way this transpired, anyway—'

'Well, Jacinta – I'll call you Jax – since we're going to be friends, let's pledge to tell each other everything, no matter how embarrassing or how ashamed we feel about stuff in our lives.'

'You felt ashamed?' Jax turned to her sympathetically.

'No, no, come on, we're starting fresh, you can do that sympathy thing later. So. Got a boyfriend?'

Jax stuck out her chin. *Fine, I'll play.* 'Yes. In fact, I have a fiancé, who moved to Saudi Arabia without much consultation with me, without even asking me along – not that I was going to go along and get myself fitted for a bloody burqa – where he proceeded to stay for years and without bothering to tell me that he'd met someone else, a Saudi princess, thank you very much, whom he married without telling anyone, not even his bloody weapon of a mother, so I suppose I shouldn't feel too bad, seeing as I was hiding behind the whole situation as a way of not bothering about stupid relationships, which I am crap at anyway.'

'Oh, I'm crap at relationships, too!' Max said excitedly, jolting Jax out of her self-pitying moment. 'I married this big, sexy, loud account exec, and then when we were actually married I basically sabotaged the whole thing and went off and had an affair! Oops.' Max grimaced, and looked away.

'Oh, Max,' Jax sighed, throwing her arm around her friend.

Max went on, her voice only just audible. 'Yeah, stupid, so scared of everything, of Mike and me, the for ever part, or whatever, and I fucked it up, and it was pretty awful and I couldn't live with the lie so I told him, and it was . . . bad. It was bad. We were so mean to each other.

'And then the jackass starts forgiving me! All the time, "I forgive you, Maxine", and I couldn't stand it so I tried to divorce him and he wouldn't sign the damn papers and – and I left.'

'And then he rang one day at work, I picked up the phone, and I asked who it was and he said he was your husband.'

'Ah.'

'And I did *not* tell Niamh Bourke, Max, as if I would.'

'I know, I know. I know what she found, and how she found it, but not what she did with it.'

'And then,' Jacinta continued, 'the day we had that big barney, I came out of the office after having been cornered by the increasingly unhinged Niamh and walked right into Michael.'

'Did he bring a pen?' Max joked.

'Surely you know he's crazy about you.' Jax shook her head – how thick could they both be?

'I don't know anything any more,' Max whispered.

'Why not take a look at this, then.' Jax reached into her shoulder bag and handed Max a disc.

'What is this?' Max turned it over in her hands – it was unlabelled.

Jax grinned cheekily and took yet another leaf from Max's book. 'See you Monday,' she called as she impulsively flagged down a taxi and slammed the door behind her.

Even if she only took it to the end of the road, and then hopped on a bus, it was well worth the look of disbelief on Maxine O'Malley's face.

27

'And when I say "iced water", I mean ice – ice cold, tons of ice, I don't even care about the water, gimme a glass of ice. I know, it's like an American thing, ice, right? But I gotta have ice-cold water.' Mike smiled up at the waiter, who wasn't deceived by the apparent geniality. It was ice-cold water, or it was his tip, and if he had to run out to the Spar to get the ice, he'd get the ice.

Max rolled her eyes. 'Jesus, LaMotta. You and the fucking ice.' She sat, on her couch, in front of her television, watching the DVD Jax had given her. She curled up beneath an Avoca throw, was swathed in its comforting scratchy plaidness, as if it could, in its woollen perfection, collude with her in pretending that what she was watching didn't really matter.

'Thanks for coming out with me,' Jax said, and Max had to marvel at the aural balance Jax had achieved, as opposed to her own efforts: Jax had got a nice, consistent level to all the voices, even the waiter's.

'I don't – I know it's not really my business – Max and I, I suppose we haven't known each other all that long, but – I hope I wasn't rude to you—'

'Jax!' Max shouted at the TV.

'Jacinta,' Mike said, less impatiently. 'If it wasn't for

you, how would I have gotten to Maxine in the first place? Getting to actually see her would have taken me much longer without you. Also, I appreciate that you have been straight with me, so in return I can only be straight with you.'

The waiter arrived with a pint glass full of ice, a pitcher, and an additional water glass.

'Would you look at that!' Mike thumped the waiter on the back. 'This is what I call service! Nice going. Nice going.'

'Oh, you've just made life hell for all future waiters of the Universe,' Max mumbled, but her eyes shone with glee. She watched Mike measure out ice to glass to water in the kind of ratio he could usually only control at home.

'So what can I do for you, Jacinta? Ask me anything you want – within reason,' he said.

'I don't even know how you two met,' Jax began.

He nodded. This part was easy. 'We met on the job, which is not my policy by any means. But in advertising, working the insane hours you do, as you well know, how do you meet anybody? I ask you. So. Maxine was on a rampage, I could see, hopping between the best agencies in town, so I figured, hey, what the hell, she's not gonna be here more than nine months, a year, tops.' He took a deep drink of his iced water.

'That should have been my first clue, right there, huh? Maxine O'Malley was not one to let the grass grow under her feet. In the business, it's fairly common, moving around, so I didn't think too much of it, except that at the time it worked to my advantage. I wanted to – to take a chance on Max, you know what I'm saying?

'The thing was, also, that out of necessity the event was kept kind of secret, especially in the beginning, although who we thought we were fooling is beyond me. We're – I guess you would say tempestuous, if you were being romantical about it, and just plain fucking noisy, if you were being a little more truthful.'

Max laughed along with Jax, and they said in unison, 'That's true.'

'How long did you date?' Jax asked as the waiter, Mike's new best friend, set down their starters – and more ice.

'Look at this guy!' Mike thumped him on the back again, and the waiter hoped his tip was big enough to cover chiropractic. 'He's a genius! We dated for about a year, year and a half—'

'Two years!' Max corrected.

'Although Max would tell you it was two, as she considered the six months we were both hovering around each other to be part of the courtship.'

'Wiseass,' Max muttered.

'How did you propose?' Jax forked up a bit of calamari.

'Ah, God, what a fiasco—'

'It was "romantical" – *romantical*, LaMotta!' Max slid off the couch, the better to get into Mike's face.

'So we're on the Circle Line, it's this cruise that goes around Manhattan, and I had this big speech, about the circle we were making on the boat, and how I wanted to close the circle of one phase of our lives, and open another circle—'

'Oh,' Jax sighed.

'Oh, *brother*,' Max groaned.

'And what happened was, we got into this, uh, discussion about the relative merits of being out by the railing, where I had envisioned my speech transpiring, and of staying inside because the weather – there was a bit of drizzle going on—'

'It was pouring rain!' Max threw her arms into the air for emphasis.

'And I convinced her to come outside.'

'Dragged! Dragged!'

'And she got kinda pissed off about it, and then we ended up, uh, you know how it is with her, negotiating everything to death, she just negotiates everything to death.'

'Yes,' said Jax. 'I know.'

'And I ended up, well, to be honest, Jacinta, I ended up shouting at her. "I was gonna ask you to marry me, all right? All right?" and everybody out on the deck applauded and Max kicked the side of the boat, and I gave her the ring, and it all worked out okay, but it was kind of wet out there.' Mike started on his grilled Portobello mushrooms.

'We were totally soaked,' Max whispered. 'Soaked to the bone.'

'And then, planning weddings is generally stressful, and she had changed jobs at this point, and we weren't really talking about what we were gonna do, and all Max cared about was the dress, so I thought we'd get a wedding planner, and either I hated one, or Max hated the other . . .' He made an event out of shaking more ice into his water. 'She bought three wedding dresses,' he said, and Jax gasped.

'I don't know why I'm surprised,' she said, once she'd recovered.

'Exactly. I mean, she's an Olympic shopper, but three wedding dresses? It all worked out okay, though, since we used one when we eloped.'

'Eloped?' Jax moved her plate out of the way, and leaned forward eagerly.

'She couldn't make up her mind – did she want trendy, did she want lacey, did she want stylish? So she got this forties suit, like *His Girl Friday*, with a little hat and veil, and a long skirt, classic – classy. But since we hadn't exactly reached a firm agreement as to our overall wedding theme, I thought the purchase was a bit rash.'

'Hmm, I seem to recall the words "waste of fucking money" being bandied about.' Max snuggled into the blanket and leaned back against the couch.

'I felt that you dressed that way only if you were going down to City Hall to do the do.' Mike grinned, and Max grinned, and both leaned in as he continued. 'So one day, I'm leaving for work, and she says, "Oh, I'm sick, I'm not going in." She says, "I'm taking the day – wear the pinstripe." I'm not making a connection between these two thoughts, but I put on the pinstripe, leave for work.

'I'm going out for lunch, I get a call from a client about a lunch meeting, I put it in the book, leave the building. And a town car comes tearing up to the kerb, and the door flies open, and it's Max, all dressed up, with a bouquet of roses and a buttoneer for me – she'd set up the bogus client lunch – and the driver takes us down to City Hall and we get married.'

Jax's eyes filled with tears, and both Mike and Max leaned back and looked away.

'That's fantastic,' Jax breathed.

'It was fast,' Mike said, fiddling with his cufflinks. 'Five minutes, tops. I don't think we felt married, not until we did the family thing. That was the second dress. Jesus, she spent a fortune on this big poofy thing, Vera Wang – it was beautiful, she was beautiful, but that dress, it looked like it could swallow small children whole.

'So we did the whole deal: church, family, drunken uncles and screaming nieces and nephews, dancing till dawn, big honeymoon, the whole nine yards.' The main course arrived and Mike declined further ice. He toyed with his pasta, and shrugged. 'I liked City Hall better.'

'What about the third one?'

'Never saw it. I'd put money down that it's got a Grace Kelly vibe – big hat, white gloves. She used to watch *Rear Window* for all the wrong reasons.'

'Depends on your point of view. No pun intended,' Jax said lightly.

Mike laughed, but it was bleak, and Max felt a pain in her chest and her throat, a pain that she thought she'd put away, for ever, that she thought she'd run far away enough from to never feel again. *Damn it, Jax*, she thought. *It's all your fault.*

'And then, I don't know, you know how she is, always making it somebody else's fault – I couldn't do anything – forget right, forget wrong, it was like, somebody took out this microscope, and she became a – a – a vigilante for like every little thing that wasn't textbook marital bliss. You ever meet her folks? Never heard them raise their voices, ever, and I guess Max didn't think that was the way things outghta be . . .

'So, reality set in, and it all went crazy. We had to find an apartment, we had to move, Maxine had changed jobs *again*, and New York City on top of all of it is just plain insane – and it was like, it was like we forgot who we were, why we loved each other in the first place, all this pressure to "be married", you know.

'Okay, example: we like to discuss things, right? In a

sometimes heightened fashion. We like to hash things out between us—'

'It's called *arguing*, LaMotta. It's called *fighting*,' Max snorted.

'—and maybe sometimes voices are raised or items that are sitting around might be thrown in the heat of the moment – by me, by the way, I'm a thrower; Max is a kicker – but, you know, no harm, no foul. That's how we express ourselves, we're vocal people.'

'We're *loud*, LaMotta,' Max laughed, her voice breaking.

Mike briskly shovelled pasta into his mouth, washed it down with more ice water. Jax waited patiently, and Max had to give her credit for figuring out Mike's rhythm, and flowing with it.

Mike wiped his mouth with his napkin. 'My grandmother could make a fortune in this country – that sauce was not sauce, if you know what I mean.' He looked at Jax, and Max saw the anguish he'd never allowed himself to show her, and it broke her heart.

'Two vocal people, who discuss things with passion, and then all of a sudden that's not okay, that's not what married people "do"; they don't raise their voices, they gotta be Mr and Mrs Perfect. So here we are, two champion talkers . . . and now we're maybe not always saying the things that mattered. Maybe starting to mistake tone for meaning. Maybe too full of pride, the two of us, to say what we mean.

'I wanted – I didn't want to have a bad marriage, and frankly, we didn't start having a bad marriage until we had to start behaving like we weren't mostly idiosyncratic people, the majority of the time. And that was kind of our theme – vocal and kind of idiosyncratic—'

'Loud and crazy, honey. We're loud and crazy.' Max shoved the coffee table out of the way, and touched Mike's face on the screen.

And Jax chose that moment to zoom in. While most of Max was hanging on every word out of Mike's mouth, she took a moment to wonder how Jax pulled off a zoom with one of the buttonhole cameras.

'Every relationship has a theme, right? And ours was like, Eleven. That was our theme – eleven on the amp, like in *Spinal Tap*? Nigel's got an amp that goes to eleven, and that was us, eleven, and suddenly it's a big fucking problem that we're eleven, and the *idea* that, all of a sudden, that was a problem, was a *joke* to me. It was a joke, Jacinta. And I wasn't laughing.'

Mike raised his hand to call for the bill. 'No, no, no,' Max whispered, and reached up and touched his face again.

Jax's voice came up softly, and Max saw her hand enter the frame, and reach out for Mike's. 'If you could tell her anything . . .'

'Ha, I know how you women operate,' Mike laughed, roughly.

'Oh, no, you don't,' said Max, kneeling forward.

'You'll tell her everything,' he added.

'I won't tell her a thing, Michael,' Jax urged, in her gentle way.

'Which isn't precisely a lie,' Max noted.

'I would say . . .' Max let the blanket drop as she framed her face with her hands, hardly daring to breathe. 'When I met Max, I was ready. You spend your life thinking there's always somebody else out there, somebody better, but it turns out that that somebody actually isn't better – they're only somebody else. So I'm at the point where – and do not think I'm saying that I settled for Maxine, that is not what I'm saying. I was there, at the point where I was ready to go, okay. You. You're the one that I want to spend my life with. My *life*, Jacinta. All of it. The good and the bad – for better, for worse. These words were not a joke to me.

'Were they a joke to Maxine? No, because she behaved so . . . *dumbly* – I know that's not a word, but it is exactly right. It was dumbness, not stupidity, that made Maxine do what she did. The affair, and the part afterwards. It was dumb fear, or something. And she's no coward, but I think that she didn't take the words we exchanged – twice – lightly, either. I don't know exactly what went on in her head, but I can guess. "Oh, shit, fucked up, worst thing I could do" – and I wouldn't disagree with that – "Gotta get out of this, gotta divorce LaMotta."

'Which, just between you and me, is the easy way out. Marriage is work, and if anybody tells you different, they're lying. How much of it is hard work, that's a choice. I choose to work hard until the work gets easy again – but I ain't doing this work by myself.'

Mike sighed, signed the tab, and added on a tip guaranteed to make the waiter weep with gratitude. 'Jacinta, maybe I could have handled it better. I went cold on her, I went distant, and as I said, that's not our style. I was so floored, I couldn't be the "me" that I usually was with her, and . . .'

'It wasn't your fault,' Max gasped.

'It wasn't my fault, but I was *at* fault, if you get me. I was *at fault*, and I knew that she was wrecked, and I gotta respect her for telling the truth, but at the time, as you can imagine, I wanted to make it worse. And I made it worse, and I wouldn't get into it with her – I was punishing her, and . . . I just want to stop. I want us to stop punishing each other. Excuse me. I can't – excuse me.'

Mike rose abruptly and exited the frame, and Jax let it run, the empty frame, his jacket on the back of the chair, that ridiculously expensive pen of his sitting next to his platinum Amex, and Max sat, washed in the blue light of the television, and wept.

28

'Hello!' Max called merrily down to Jax as she watched her make her way up to the top of ACJ. 'Recovered from Saturday?'

'Oh, just about,' Jax sang in return. 'That was the hoolie to end all hoolies. I got you a latte, thought you might need the boost.'

Arm in arm, they chatted their way through the bullpen, a bullpen oddly free of any sound, even that of the most cursory click of a mouse.

Shutting her office door closed behind them, Max gave Jax a thumbs-up. 'That ought to do it. Although I still say we should have stretched it out for another day at least.'

'You know there's no way I could have sustained it,' Jax replied. 'I am not my mother's daughter.'

'I wouldn't say that – especially when you get that imperious look on your face, like now – it's pure Angela-Quirke-as-Cleopatra.'

'Did she ever tell you about that one?' Jax let out one of her big laughs. 'We were unearthing snakes out of the cupboards for months. I'm convinced there are one or two still lurking in the kitchen.'

She sighed, then frowned in confusion as she watched Max's movements around the cubicle. 'What are you doing?'

Max shook out a series of shopping bags and set them around strategic points in the tiny room. 'What's it look like I'm doing?' She began shoving old newspapers, and more shopping bags, into a Harvey Nicks bag that looked like it had been designed to carry a six-year-old child.

'I'm not sure, as I've never seen you go through motions remotely resembling these, the ones that require you to bend down, pick something up, and put it in a bag with the view to discarding it.'

'Ha, ha.' Max filled the child-sized bag in no time, and proceeded to pack a few Debenhams bags full of magazines and broken CD cases.

'Look, will we start sorting for recycling? I could—' And Jax stopped at Maxine's quelling glare.

'She came in here, and I know what she found, and where she found it,' Max hissed softly. 'And there's no way that I'm going to leave myself open to anything else.'

'There's more?' Jax gasped, dismayed.

'*No!*' Max tossed the filled bags into the bullpen, waved cheekily at her curious colleagues, who blushed as one, and shut the door again.

'Is that – is that clothing?' Jacinta cringed as Maxine opened a large freestanding filing cabinet and started emptying it.

'I don't know why they give us these things in the first place – weren't we supposed to be paperless by now?' She heaved out a variety of items. 'You never know when you might need a spare jumper, or pair of trousers.'

'Or a backless sequinned evening gown.'

'It's diamanté.'

'Oh, that's different.' Unable to sit still, Jax started harvesting stray pieces of paper from off the floor, from off the shelves of Maxine's bookcase, from between the books themselves, from underneath the desk.

'Okay, I gotta ask you, in the spirit of our new transparency.' Max shoved the several bags of clothes out the door and closed it again. 'Weren't you pissed off? Hurt? Didn't you want to kill Fergal? Didn't you think you were going to pass out with the shock?'

'I'm not made of stone, you know,' Jax huffed, stuffing a Pia Bang bag full of paper, which she in turn leaned neatly against Max's desk. 'I went all dizzy when I saw the ring—'

'You had no other notice, no warning?' Max threw up her hands, stirring up a small tsunami of dust.

'No, and can I say I was surprised that I wasn't more surprised without sounding like a complete saddo?'

Max grimaced. 'I don't know. I don't think so.'

'Me, neither.' Jax sat back down for a quick sulk. 'I can't tell you how I hated the questions. *Jacinta Quirke, whenever are you going to make an honest man of himself?* Or, *Will you never set the wedding date? Or is it Doomsday?* And it wasn't as if I was going to tell the—' She stopped short. 'Why would I tell the truth?'

Max said nothing, simply tapped herself on the nose and started breaking down shoeboxes.

'All right, all right. But! As if I was going to tell Orla or Sorcha or the dog in the street, *"Oh, I suspect he's lost interest"*, or *"We're barely in communication"*, or *"I'm fairly certain he's met someone else"* – don't throw those books away, sell them to Chapters, they take second-hand—'

'Not worth the trouble.'

'Don't! I'll take them!' Jax wrestled them from Max and started packing them up in a Tesco bag. 'I may need the dosh,' she muttered.

'Ah, now,' Max cajoled. 'Let's wait for the daily injection of pessimism until we've seen whatever JP's been trying to show us. So ... talked to JP?' she asked silkily.

'No.' Jacinta started packing up another bag of books. 'Watched any good DVDs lately?'

Max made a noise that successfully combined agreement and dismissal, and started flinging old videotapes into a box.

Jax waited patiently and watched as Maxine sat down at her desk and opened the smaller filing cabinet's top drawer, and began to extract what appeared to be a year's worth of tights and stockings from it. Several pairs of slingbacks followed, but the manila folder that Max had unearthed from the back didn't follow suit, and remained in her hands.

She spun in her chair and looked out of her half of the window. 'Remember that day? When we got the memo?'

'Of course.'

Max blew out a breath. 'It was like – it was like the time before – the time when I – the guy. The affair. *Affair*,' she jeered. 'Makes it sound way more important than it was.' She kicked over the bag of shoes and tights, and Jax had to grip the arms of her chair to stop herself rushing to pick it up.

'I moved around a lot, as you heard, as you know – and I want to know how you got that really superior audio – okay, okay.' She grinned at Jax's reprise of the Angela Quirke signature glower, but her eyes were terribly sad. 'The last agency, before ACJ:NYC, it started going bust, and I wanted out, out of advertising, and I had this script. Unfinished, as all my scripts are ...' She trailed off and

Jacinta let her have her silence. 'Yeah, script, TV series, found a producer, started taking meetings – dinners, drinks, whatever.'

Jax grimaced. 'Sounds a bit familiar.'

'Huh? Oh, Lorcan.' It was Max's turn to wince. 'I didn't shag him, like.'

'Small mercies,' Jacinta muttered. 'Not that I'm getting all judgemental or anything—'

'Not much.'

'—but when you compare him to *Michael* . . .'

If it were possible, Max looked even more forlorn. 'It's like a – it's like you biting your nails, or something, a bad habit. A bad habit for me to do dumb shit when it comes to guys. I don't know why I – it's like, dopes like Lorcan just *do* something to me – can I plead insanity? Can I not talk about the Lorcan thing? Ever again?'

'Yes, but go on.'

'So, meetings, dinners, and Mike was like, "Yeah, yeah, do it", he – he thinks I'm a good writer. He put in some money . . . God, I hate myself.'

'Max –' Jax shifted forward until she was leaning on Maxine's desk.

Max leaned back and closed her eyes. 'Got scared, of all of it, and the marriage business was the worst, I – I don't know, I can't describe it, it was kind of like LaMotta said, the whole "death us do part" thing, and me, I couldn't stay in a job for a year without getting bored.'

'I can't imagine the two of you ever getting bored,' Jax said lightly.

'I fucked the producer guy, for no – I was going to say "good reason", but what's a good reason?'

'It sounds like you panicked,' Jax said briskly but kindly. 'Panicked, and you being you, you automatically did the one thing designed to create the maximum amount of chaos and heartache—'

'Whose side are you on?'

'—for yourself,' Jax finished softly.

'Yeah, I – I fucked it up.'

'Stop saying that.'

'I fucked up – you said it yourself, the other night.'

'I will not let you use words that I said in anger as a hammer to beat yourself with. Nor will I sit here and watch you use it as an excuse to do nothing, fix nothing, just run off to the next thing.'

'Trying to start another row?' Max's voice started to rise.

'I find I quite enjoy it!' Jacinta managed to bark this quite primly, and Max started to laugh.

'I've created a monster.' She grinned.

'I refuse to let you take all the credit.'

'Look, in the spirit of our new transparency, I've got to say I've had enough transparency and maybe we could put it off for a while. I can't fix it all in one go, Jacinta.'

'I'm not – it's just – I like Michael,' she finished faintly.

'Yeah, who doesn't. And I like John Paul.' As Max leaned forward across her desk, Jax leaned back. 'Your turn, pal. Tell. Everything. Now.'

The barely audible knock was little more than a warning scratch. 'Speak of the devil.' Max smiled and started swinging back and forth in her chair.

'Sorry, I – where is everything?' John Paul looked everywhere but at Jax.

'Doing a bit of clearing out – in advance of any announcements.'

'Oh, God . . .' Jax started rending the cuff of her blouse.

'Don't do that,' JP said, laying a hand on her shoulder, and Jax went still as a stone. 'Was there a memo?'

'Nope, but the voice of experience is sounding in my head. Nothing to worry about today.' Max closed her eyes, massaged her temples, as though channelling that voice. 'But soon, I reckon. So. Will we watch your rough cut, JP?'

'You two . . . sorted?' he asked.

Jax smiled thinly at Max. 'Maxine, JP termed our furious and potentially disastrous falling out as, hmm, let's see if I remember – as "hair-pulling".'

'Oh, really?' As she rose and pinned JP with a look, Max allowed herself to fully savour the relief she felt. *I am – we are – going to finish this thing and it's going to be great!*

Down in JP's cave, the three sat in front of the last freeze-frame as it held on JP's monitor.

'It's not so great,' Jacinta ventured. 'Not your fault, JP, I'm not saying that—'

'It's lacking a bit in human interest,' he said, finally meeting her eyes. She immediately dropped hers.

'What'd we get from Wednesday?' Maxine asked.

'Em, the most interesting stuff was you two,' JP joked. And nobody laughed.

'We got nothing out of the whole shoot?' Jacinta started back on the cuff, and JP laid his hand over hers.

'Bracketing kind of stuff, if you know what I mean. Cutaways. Nothing – substantially thematic.' JP hit the play button again, and they watched the five-minute montage of footage go by once more.

'I think – I'm not sure – maybe – but the thing is—'

'Jax!' Maxine tried not to shout, and it was a close thing. 'Please. What do you want to say?'

'I can't write it, you need to, but I can set it out – if we did some voice-over? Shot some jazzy cutaways in bars, on the street, of couples snogging, fighting, the usual sort of Saturday-night scene. Picked some music, dolled it up, and then at least we'd have the trailer that we can send in. We don't need the whole thing done.' This was something, at least, that Jacinta could fix. She might not be able to get Max and Mike back together, or her head round what was going on with John Paul, but this – this she could put right.

'Okay. I can see it. Okay!' Max stood and grabbed up her bag, coat and scarf. 'I've got some stuff at home, from following, uh, people around, when I was working out the spy cam. We've got to use that stuff, Jax,' she went on as she saw Jax formulating a refusal. 'It's worth a shot.'

And she scampered off, delighted to leave them alone in a semi-dark room.

'Yes, exactly, and then move that section back to there.' *I can do this*, thought Jax as she watched John Paul shift around a couple of scenes. *I can sit here and work with this man, and not worry what he's thinking—*

I can't take this, thought JP, her body so close to his as they both leaned towards the monitor, as if willing the piece to improve. *How can she sit there like that, after – after everything?*

'We could use some of Max's spy stuff here, if it's strong.' As long as he kept his eyes on the computer, he'd be able to stand it.

Jax worried her cuff, and he lightly touched her on the back of the hand, a touch that sent them both into immobility. 'It seems a waste, if we're not sure if we can use it – and I thoroughly doubt that we can. God help us, Max'll come back with a lawsuit.'

'Do they sell those at BTs?' *Oh, Jaysus, O'Gorman. You. Are. Pathetic.*

Jax giggled, but still couldn't look at him. 'So, what's the point? Because it is going to be better than the other stuff – and if you tell Maxine I said that, I'll have to hurt you—'

Hurt me? You're killing me.

'—and we'll just end up torturing ourselves over it.'

Torture? I'll tell you about torture – torture is sitting here beside you, practically in the dark, behind a closed door that could be easily locked, locked for as long as need be, which, if last Friday night-slash-Saturday morning was anything to go by, could be a very, very long time . . .

'Would you mind—'

'Mind?' *Mind kissing you, touching you, holding you, telling you everything? Everything I want to say, how much I feel, right now, with you—*

'If I cut. A bit? I know how to do it – and it's not that you didn't do an excellent job—'

'I'm no editor,' JP said, rising to switch seats with Jax. 'My least favourite part.'

'Oh, I think I love it,' Jacinta breathed, just as they stood facing each other before changing chairs. They stood, frozen, and their bodies seemed to vibrate from the near contact. John Paul couldn't help himself, he leaned in and rubbed his cheek against hers, and, thrilled, felt her shudder and sigh.

'I can't—'

JP smiled. *I think I know how to do this now* – and he ran a hand down her side, around to her back, as he shifted himself away and then dropped down into the chair, never breaking the eye contact they'd finally made. 'No hurry. First things first.' And he leaned back, delighted by the slightly miffed look in her eyes.

Seemed like a waste of time to him, but he was willing to wrongfoot her for a while.

Jax briskly created a new project in Final Cut Pro and started importing video clips. JP watched her – she was good, really confident, making cuts and moving things around like lightning, much better than he, and he decided that she would be able to talk while she was working.

'So . . . Max slept with George Clooney?'

'Of course not!' Jax scoffed, and waited a beat. 'She slept with Brad Pitt.'

'Fuck *off*! Before yer one, the one with the blood?' John Paul gaped.

Jax held on as long as she could – which wasn't very long, and exploded with laughter. 'She gets around, but she doesn't get *around*.'

'What was she going on about, then?'

Jax grimly kept her eyes on her work. 'Ask her. You want to know anything, ask her.'

'Her husband – Mike – he's cool, right?'

'Sure, why wouldn't he be?' Jax rendered a section on which she'd applied a special effect and watched the clock tick by.

'We didn't know if – you know, if he'd like, been the one to – well, what if he was knocking her around, or something?'

Jacinta's frown melted away. 'He wasn't.' *You are a sweet, sweet man, aren't you?* Then the frown returned. 'We? Who's we?'

JP squirmed in the ensuing silence, then frowned himself. 'Did you hear that?'

Jax immediately went to the door.

'No.' John Paul rose as well, and looked around the

room. 'That noise. Like one of ours. One of our, em, remotes. It sounded like that.'

Jax shook her head, and sat again. 'How could it be? We've got them all, haven't we?'

'Yeah . . .' John Paul decided he would strip the office down after they were done.

They went back to watching the footage rather than each other. John Paul started to nod. 'I see. I see what you're doing. It's good.'

Jax sat back and scrolled back to the beginning. 'It's not great. We'll need those pick-ups.' She grabbed a pen and started making a list. 'Can you nudge us through it, scene by scene, and I'll start writing up an outline?'

I'd be delighted – especially as it required that he budge up against her, very nearly into her lap.

Oh, not such a great idea, Jacinta – and she tried to lean away without making him think that she was trying to get away from him.

'There's this shot, of Max looking at Michael when she opened the door, before you shut everything down. It was – you couldn't get that, fictionally, if you tried.' John Paul leaned over a little more than necessary, and felt Jacinta quiver.

'I know,' she said, every nerve ending tingling. 'He's a lovely man. All brash and brusque, but really very – he loves her. He does. And I just know she loves him. And I should have learned my lesson by now.'

'Ah, you can't help being interested, can you? Wondering what's going on with them, how they got to this stage, where they're going . . .'

Much safer to wonder about them than about us, Jax thought as she scribbled a note she couldn't read herself. She erased it and tried again. And made an even more illegible scrawl as JP leaned over and nuzzled her ear.

'JP –' she breathed, not letting herself fully respond, not able to pull away.

'Just checking.' And he sat back and continued to click through the cut.

'Checking what?' Jacinta demanded, peeved.

John Paul merely smiled, and clicked away.

'Checking what?' She threw down her pad and pen.

'Ah, you know how it is, when you're interested in someone –' *Interested! Doesn't even begin to describe it!* – 'sometimes you feel like you're imagining things, making things up, just to please yourself.'

Tell me about it, thought Jax, and with nothing better to do, she tried to grab the mouse from JP.

He kept her hand in his hand as he continued. 'So I was just checking to make sure I wasn't making it all up. The softness of your skin. How your body feels against mine – no, don't bother, I'm not trying to *talk* talk, I'm just . . . talking.'

Jacinta haughtily raised her chin, and it was all JP could do not to laugh. *If Angela could see you now, she'd be looking in a mirror.* 'That's perfectly all right with me, as I'm under far too much pressure at the moment trying to deliver this project.'

'We'll have to have a dinner some time, you and I,' JP mused.

'Oh, will we?' And Jacinta turned back to the monitor . . . disappointed that he didn't try to push any further.

'Yeah, whenever.' JP shrugged and turned to do some paperwork on his desk.

Ha! Jacinta wished that the editing process wasn't digitised – she'd have loved to start chopping some film up with a guillotine. *I'm not going to be subject to someone else's whims, not right on the heels of the last one! Ha!*

'We may as well go out tonight,' she suggested loftily. 'We've got work to do that can't be finished here.'

'Oh, I agree,' he replied, without looking up from his papers.

'Fine.' Jax saved the latest changes and quit out of the programme. 'Grand. I'll let you know when I'm free to go. I've got my own things to take care of as well.'

'Cool.' John Paul picked up his phone and, smiling absently at her, began dialling.

'Fine,' she spat, and wondered if Maxine still had that bag of clothes around.

John Paul hung up the phone – Met Eireann was forecasting a fresh and changeable evening.

M ax was escorted to the main doors of Brown
Thomas, and stood on the threshold, snarling to
herself.

*All they'd had to do was say 'no' – had they really
needed to make such a big deal out of it?* Maxine freshened
her powder before heading out on to Grafton Street. She
certainly wasn't going to tell Jacinta that she'd been held at
Security – and over what? A few attempts to talk to
customers on camera? An effort to get some people to talk
to her for a hot new TV programme?

At least she wasn't barred from the shop for life.

Six months wouldn't kill her.

Shaking back her hair, straightening her jacket, Max
made her temporary exit from the hallowed halls of BT
with her head held high – and almost stumbled when
she looked up and saw Michael. He was standing there,
in the middle of the street, with no thought to the
host of shoppers and gawkers and buskers that were
swirling around him as he stood, patient, unyielding,
gorgeous.

She thought of the video, of his hasty retreat from the
table, and she fought down the lump in her throat. Hitching up her shoulder bag, she casually strolled towards him,

magically negotiating her way through the swarm without looking.

'What, you staking me out?' She glared up at him.

'What, you think I don't know you? I bet they got a brass plaque in the fitting room with your name on it.'

Max shrugged, and turned towards the bottom of the road. Mike followed.

'Whadda you want?' she asked churlishly, still smarting from her encounter with BT's powers that be.

'You know, for an intelligent woman, you ask some stupid questions.'

'I'm not getting into it here, with you, in the middle of the city centre,' Max declared, leading him through a crowd gathered at the crosswalk.

'I got all the time in the world,' Mike said loftily. 'I got no rush.'

Max snorted. 'As if you could stay out of the office for more than two days running.'

'People change.' He ran his hand down her back, making her jump, and stopped. 'People change,' he went on, 'and sometimes they change, and then change back. People – they're funny. You know and I know, as we are both in the business that we are in, that humans are changeable, unpredictable, funny beings. Give me a tour,' he said, abruptly changing the subject.

'Go buy a guidebook,' Max replied ill-naturedly.

'Come on, give me a tour. Your new hometown.'

Max scowled up at him. He beamed down at her innocently.

'Come on,' he said, wrapping a lock of her hair around his finger. 'I'm a fish out of water here.'

'Shark, more like,' she muttered, batting his hand away as she turned and started walking – fast. 'That's Trinity

College. Jax went there.' Mike made as if to go through the gates, but Max kept going.

She hustled him down Westmoreland Street, across the bridge. 'The River Liffey.'

Racing against the red man, she pointed up the wide avenue. 'O'Connell Street. Bunch of statues. Spire.'

'Who's that guy?' Mike pointed up at the ornate sculpture above them.

'Daniel O'Connell. Luckily, they put him here, on a street that had his same name.'

'Yeah, ha, ha. So, what'd he do?'

Max shrugged. 'They call him the Liberator – so, he liberated . . . something.'

'Maxine, you been here, what, six months—'

'A year!'

'Oh, okay, so that must be eight months, eight months you been here and you don't know who that guy is?'

'I *live* here,' Max groused. 'Working in an ad agency, not as a tour guide.'

'Don't quit your day job.'

'I may not have a choice.' Max did something she'd never imagined herself doing in all her time in Dublin: she sat on the bench at Daniel's feet.

Michael joined her, hitching up his trousers, patting down his tie, draping a long arm across the back of the bench – and Maxine felt her belly tremble with longing.

'This is some town,' Mike said, as they watched the pedestrian traffic ebb and flow. 'I mean, it's not New York –' he paused as if to fully eradicate that blasphemous thought from his mind – 'but it's good; a good town, busy, but not so big that you get too much attitude.'

'Dublin's great when it's not crap,' Max said, and Mike laughed.

'I heard that all day long, in a variety of ways, from just about every Irish person I met.'

'So that's what you're here for, making friends, influencing people?' Max couldn't bear to look him in the eye, not when he was so close, not when they'd sat this way, exactly this way, countless times – their first date, that long walk downtown along the Hudson, it was summer – was it the fourth of July? Labour Day? – and they had sat on a bench and then, for some reason, no reason – except if it had been the fourth of July or Labour Day – inexplicably, fireworks shot up over Jersey. She'd joked about it, all those chemicals from the factories along the Turnpike finally exploding . . . only because her heart had leapt along with the radiant pyrotechnics. *It's him*, she remembered thinking. *This is him. He's the one*.

She couldn't bear it any longer. 'What do you want, LaMotta?'

'O'Malley, I want to take you to dinner.'

'You came three thousand miles to buy me a meal?'

'See, I love that, you'd never say "meal" like that, back home.' He grinned at her, delighted with her grasp of the Irish lexicon. 'So, we'll have a meal.' He rose and held out a hand which Maxine ignored. 'Let's go.'

'Where?' *I'm doing this, even if I'm acting like I'm not doing this. I'm going out to dinner with LaMotta and pretending that I don't want to—*

'I met a guy today, at the news-stand – sorry, *in* the news*agent's* – and I said, "Hey, where do you take a woman when you want to impress her, I mean really knock her socks off?" And he told me.' Michael moved to the kerb to flag down a taxi.

'You gotta go to the taxi rank, and queue,' Maxine said. He looked over at her in disbelief. 'What, are you kidding me?' And thrusting out an arm, a taxi responded almost against its will.

Holding up traffic, Michael held the door open for Maxine, who unbent enough to laugh up at him before she slipped into the cab.

Michael smoothed down his tie as he got in behind her, and planned on giving the taxi driver the tip of his life.

'Ready?'

Jacinta stood, hoping she gave off an aura of innate self-confidence. Having plundered Maxine's cast-offs, she'd found a stretchy, shiny, silvery-blue top that perked up the short, black, fitted gabardine jacket she'd worn. She and Maxine were nowhere near a size in the trouser department, however, so Jax had hoped she'd compensated up top by using some of the make-up she'd found in Max's in-tray.

Not my colours there, either, Jax worried behind a cool and detached façade. *I really must get some new slap*.

'Ready, steady, go,' JP chanted, smiling down at her, trying hard not to indulge in a once-over that he thought would be both crass and too telling under the circumstances, if he really was going to play it cool. 'I've just got to move my bike.'

'I didn't know that you cycled to work – I thought you walked.'

JP held up his helmet. 'Motorbike. I had it in the shop, had to replace the cams, couldn't do it myself.'

A motorcycle. Jacinta's inner sixteen-year-old swooned at his feet. A motorcycle. *My God, remember that crush you had on the dark one from CHiPs?*

'Oh.' Jax pretended disinterest and sailed out the door of the agency.

'Will we go for a spin? Before the meal?'

Jax watched JP masterfully unlock what he had to unlock, and manfully haul the machine upright. Jax felt a breeze, a tease of summer drift across her face, and noticed the envious looks of a couple of girls passing them on the pavement.

'I've got a spare helmet.' He held it out to her.

Jacinta shrugged, her heart fluttering madly in her chest. 'I don't mind.'

'Cool.' JP casually slung himself on to the back of the bike – a 2001 Triumph reissue of the classic 1959 model, if Jacinta wasn't mistaken – and revved the engine. Jax slipped the helmet on to her head and all but leapt on the back, sliding her arms around John Paul. She let out a whoop of pure joy as he edged into the traffic, opened up the engine, and headed south.

'And then, because, obviously, Erik Estrada was a fruitless dream, I diverted all that energy into motorcycles. One of my older brothers had a rackety old Harley – don't get excited, it was basically an engine, a seat, and the two wheels –' Jax told him.

'What more do you need?' JP, reclining on his side on the Aer Lingus blanket he'd unearthed from his rucksack, smiled up her. They were at the beach at Greystones, a light breeze was drifting off the ocean, and Jax was alight with happy memories.

'He never let me ride it – that he knew of. I know, hard to believe, I'm convinced I used up my lifetime allowance of rebellion by sneaking around on that bike.' The wind was crisp, but not unpleasant, and Jax wrapped her arms around her knees and considered the darkening sky.

'You're a dark horse, Jacinta Quirke.'

If I lie back he'll kiss me.

'Yes,' she hummed, stretching her arms above her head . . . and not lying back. 'God, I love the ocean. It's such a relief to be out here. Not a bad idea.'

John Paul knelt up, and said, 'I've got another not-bad idea – unless you're keen on going out some place posh for a meal.'

'I had no expectations around the event.'

'Right.' As curious as she was, she refused to turn around and see what he was doing. Instead, she closed her eyes and breathed deeply, as calmly as if she were curled up in front of her hearth, or digging in her garden.

'Good, keep them closed.' And of course all she wanted to do *now* was open her eyes, see what he was up to, even though she had a pretty good idea he had brought—

'A picnic.' She sighed.

'And this lovely bottle of white to yourself, as I'm driving. Not that I'm trying to get you drunk or anything – and I'm not mad about not drinking, but it seemed like it would be a crap picnic without wine – not that I'm a big drinker, at all, but—'

Jax couldn't help it. She had to. This was basically a date, even if she didn't really want it to be – didn't she? – but it wasn't as if they hadn't already been intimate anyway, so what was the harm of one little kiss?

'It's perfect,' she said. 'And as I've to hang on to you all the way back to Dublin, best make it one glass.' *We can always finish it off at mine . . .*

As if to drown out that wayward thought, Jacinta began to loudly admire the spread JP had laid out.

'Oh, yeah, that guy in the newsagent's wasn't kidding, huh?'

Leave it to Michael to get a recommendation for l'Ecrivain from a newsagent's in George's Street. Max raised her champagne, and Mike ran his glass up and down hers.

'I got a million toasts I could make – maybe you'd better say something.'

Max shook her head and started to drink, only to have Mike grab her hand and stop her. 'Come on, say something. It's gotta be bad luck to toast and not say something.'

'*Sláinte*,' she said and downed half the glass.

'You think I don't know what that means, but I do.' Mike sat back and enjoyed his first sip of the Dom Perignon Grand Vintage 2003 that bubbled away happily in his crystal flute. 'I've picked up a lot in the short time I've been here, what, five, six days. People are pretty friendly, but not in a sick way, not like getting in your business, you know?' Without waiting for a reply, he poured out more champers and went right on talking. 'No, people here, they're like New Yorkers, just enough conversation to make everybody feel good, feel like you're living in the world, and then it's over, nobody's following you home, or nothing.'

'I don't know.' Maxine took a less comprehensive sip of her champagne. 'I once sat next to this lady on the bus, and she told me all about her husband with the heart attack and her son with the bad car accident – who sounded clinically depressed, if you ask me – and the daughter-in-law who lost her job, and the dog who was afraid of the cat . . .'

'Yeah, but it's all in that accent, I love that accent. Oh my God, check this out.' Mike smacked his forehead in disbelief. 'Everybody's telling me, "You've got a lovely accent" and I'm like, what the fuck?'

The waiter intervened at this point with Maxine's moules mariniere starter, and Michael's crab cakes with anisette relish.

'Hey,' he whispered, leaning forward. 'These are *starters*. You ask for an appetiser, nobody knows what you're talking about.'

This is insane, Max thought, busily spearing mussels out of their shells. *How can I stand this? How can he? Like nothing ever happened? This is – this is breaking my heart—*

'Listen, I had lunch with Jacinta the other day.'

Max looked up at him, and he misread her bewilderment. 'I got her in the shit with you, I know – did you fix it up with her? Good – and I felt like I owed her an explanation, but then I started thinking, maybe I talked out of turn, I don't know, but I didn't want you to hear from her what I said, I don't want to – I want us to be—'

'Truthful? Faithful? Up front? Loyal?' *All the things I wasn't.*

'I know you're thinking, "unlike me", or whatever, but let me tell you, Maxine, I'm getting pretty sick of this routine.'

'What routine?'

Mike sat back and threw out his arms and then slapped them back down again. 'This routine, this campaign to Keep Maxine O'Malley Feeling Like Shit.'

'Put a lid on it, you're too loud.'

Jesus, enough with the loud! Here we go again! He took a calming breath. 'Okay, you're right, we're in public, we'll wait on this. How're the mussels? This crab cake is outta this world.'

Maxine stabbed a few hapless mussels and sopped up some garlic butter with a piece of bread. *He doesn't know*

– of course not, how could he know that Jax had been recording him?

'It's not a routine. It's not a campaign.'

'That's what it looks like from where I'm sitting, you know, keeping on beating yourself up for something that, okay, admittedly, wasn't great, and in fact was the worst thing that I think you could have done to me—'

'And it's shit like that that tells me, no, you are not over it, and maybe you're just looking for another way to punish me, so maybe I'm just making myself feel like shit so you can't get in there first!'

The waiter, with great but restrained assurance, removed their plates and scraped away stray crumbs. Another waiter set down another ice bucket, minus a bottle, a carafe of water, and presented Michael with a large empty glass.

'I gotta have my iced water,' Mike said, filling his glass to the brim. He drank, and Max sat back, suddenly drained.

'I can't go over and over this any more.'

'Me, neither,' said Mike, and after a short struggle, held her hand.

'What do you want?' Max demanded – afraid that she knew, afraid that she wanted to know.

'That, in short, is the purpose of my trip.' And Mike sat back and drank more water, his eyes smiling at Max as he said nothing.

Jax gave up. So, she'd had two glasses of wine, small ones, tiny ones, and the night was coming in, and it was a bit chilly, and they'd had some lovely food – olives and hummus and flat bread and sundried tomatoes – and it was too terribly easy, and perfect, to curl up on the blanket, spooned with John Paul.

'It's getting cold,' JP said, cuddling closer.

'Ummm . . . but the sound of the ocean is gorgeous, isn't it? I must get one of those CDs, the nature-sound yokies, one of the ocean. But just the ocean, no pan pipe accompaniment, or anything.' She closed her eyes and listened, and breathed in the heady mixture of the salt air and the scent of JP's skin.

'I can make it for you, come out here with some gear, make you a CD,' he murmured in her ear.

'Maybe. Wouldn't want to put you out.'

I'd do just about anything for you, Jacinta. 'It's cool,' he said. 'No problem.'

'Thanks,' she sighed, and pulled his arms closer around her. 'This was a brilliant idea.'

'Thought it might be nice to get out of town. Help us in the return to form.'

Jax stroked a hand down one of JP's, down those long, lovely fingers. 'Everything's getting back to normal. Except none of us has been looking for jobs, our footage needs serious help, and I'm too scared to think how little time we have left.'

John Paul closed his eyes and breathed in, breathed in Jacinta and thought, *And I'm mad about you, and you seem to be about me, but you're getting flowers from what's-his-name, and I should ask you about that. I should, but I don't want to know.*

He disentangled himself from her and stood. 'It's getting cold, too cold for you out here, in that little top.'

Jax rolled over to look up at him. 'Too little?'

'Oh, no,' John Paul replied, feeling his entire body yearn in response. 'Just right.'

Jacinta smiled and held out her hands. He pulled her up, and kept pulling until she was in his arms. As their lips met, they might have been surprised to know that they both were having the same, desperate thoughts – *More, more, whatever I can have, let me have more, more.*

'I can't take much more,' Max said calmly as the staff cleared away the remains of what had been a sinful dessert on top of an exceptional dinner.

'So we'll skip the cheese. It's cheese last in Europe, right?' Michael barely lifted a finger and the waiter hurried off to get them the bill.

'This is what I'm talking about.' Maxine delicately blotted her mouth with the heavy linen napkin, and arched a brow at her husband. *Husband.* She shook her head and continued. 'I always hated this, this bomb-dropping manoeuvre, there's this big set-up, and you dance pretty close to the abyss, to the fire, to the fiery abyss, and then you just back off, but the bomb never goes off, it just sits there, and all I can do is hang tough and wait for the explosion.'

'No more explosions.' Mike shrugged and handed over his credit card. 'Well, okay, let me rephrase that, maybe it's time I got to the point – as if you don't know what the point is, Maxine, as if you can't comprehend what the possible point of me flying four thousand miles—'

'Three thousand!'

'Three thousand, four thousand!' Their voices began to rise again, they couldn't help it, didn't really know how to; it was a work of art in itself, their volume, and to ask them to keep it down was like asking Maria Callas to hum. 'Let's say three thousand, five hundred, okay?'

'Okay!'

'See! Progress!' Michael roared and signed the bill, and slapped the elegant leather billfold against the waiter's chest. 'We just had a compromise! Whether or not it's precisely correct! Three thousand, five hundred miles!'

Max wanted desperately to wrench the tablecloth, still crowded with dessert plates and wine glasses and Mike's goddamn iced water, off the table, like some demented magician, to release her frustration. She closed her eyes instead. 'Michael, please, I'm begging you, enough already.'

'So, we'll go.' And rising, he extended his arm – which she took, even though she knew he knew she didn't want to, and that it burned her butt to take it to avoid another *discussion*, and that she'd get him back for it – but what he didn't know was that she felt like she was about to break into three thousand, five hundred pieces at his feet, and that if he had, finally, worn her down, worn through her intransigence, it was because she was maybe close to being tired of fighting him.

Maybe.

Maybe very close.

Too bad about the helmets – Jax wanted nothing more than to nuzzle John Paul's ear, something that, she knew for a fact, drove him wild. As they slowed down to accommodate the traffic on the Canal Road, she made up for it by running her hands up and down his chest, and felt his heart start beating double-time in response.

Her delighted giggle was lost in the wind.

He just about made it to her place in one piece.

It's got to be cheeky of me to bring up that last bit of wine, JP thought as he shut down the engine. *I mean, it would be worse if I drove off with it, like, without even offering—*

He felt Jax slip off the back of the bike. She took off her

helmet, and rather than give it to him, gave him her hand.

'Come in,' she said simply, and he did.

'You're not coming in.'

Mike shrugged. It was enough, more than he'd expected, to hold her hand all the way to her apartment. Out of the restaurant, in the taxi, down the street. *Holding my own wife's hand* – he stopped himself. If he was pissed off, at this point, it was because the things he wanted to do, to show, to give, were still up in the air. *Grateful to hold my own wife's hand* – and, philosophically, he decided that right now, there wasn't anything else he'd rather be grateful for.

'I've got to work tomorrow. Early.'

Mike grunted. 'Yeah, right, no need to lay it on that thick.'

'We gotta finish our pilot.'

'Hey, I wanna hear all about that. Is Angela, like, the star? She's a pip, that one, she's a pistol.'

Max laughed a little. 'She's in it, but it's not about her.'

'Too bad. She's fucking hilarious – in a good way. Jeez, you shoulda seen her when she saw it was me.' Mike rolled his eyes theatrically.

'Whadda you mean, saw it was you?' Max frowned.

'She saw it was me, she started doing some friggin' Shakespeare thing on me, calling me names, despoiler, torturer, I don't even know what. She went nuts.'

'She doesn't know you – didn't know you,' she said, and Michael looked at her and shrugged.

'Coulda fooled me.'

'There's no way she could have known—' and she stopped short, stormy eyed.

'I don't think Jacinta said anything.' Mike shrugged

again. 'Hey, don't give me that look; I walked in halfway into this thing, I'm just saying. I asked her about her mom – her mum – and she talked like, I don't know, she didn't talk like she thought that her mom – mum – would know me.'

'What? That makes no sense.'

'Yeah, it does, she talked about her mum – mom – mother – Angela – like she was sorry that we hadn't met under different circumstances, that maybe I could meet her parents another time. Something. But not guilty.'

'Hmm.' Maxine started to fish her keys out of her bag, and didn't even notice that Mike automatically held out his hands to hold the bag while she searched with both hands – and that she, just as automatically, let him.

Keys found, she realised what she'd done, what they'd done, and looked up at him, and saw, again, the longing and pain that Michael was very good at hiding.

'I've got to go in,' she said, turning away. 'Thanks for the meal.'

'Hey.'

'You're not kissing me!' she burst out, closing her eyes, like a child, a frightened child.

'I'm not trying to,' he replied lightly, heavy in his heart. 'But I am calling. Tomorrow.'

'Fine.' Max let herself in the building, and Mike walked away, deciding to stroll down the quays to his hotel.

And in the shadows, someone watched it all, and recorded it all.

'I would have told you if I'd told them, because we're not *not* telling each other things any more, right?' Jax plonked down on to Maxine's sofa, annoyed. 'It's true. So don't bite my head off.'

'Well, then, who told them? How did Angela know Mike was Mike?'

'Shite.' Jax closed her eyes. 'I, em, well . . . I did tell my father. But he promised me he wouldn't tell my mother! Sort of.' She slid further down the couch. 'Does it really matter, at all? At this stage?'

'Lots of loose ends,' Max muttered as she haphazardly set out some snacks. 'Time to tie up the loose ends. Oh, and Mike mentioned that you two had lunch, or dinner, or whatever, and I in turn *didn't* mention that you had taped the whole thing.'

'This has gone completely bonkers,' Jax began to complain, but was cut off by the buzz of Maxine's intercom. 'Is that Michael?' she piped.

'Nope.' Max released the downstairs door and put her flat door on the latch. 'It's JP.'

'Oh.' Jax bustled into the kitchen to get some bowls for the nuts and crisps, and some napkins. A little bit of cut lemon might not go amiss, and she started washing

Maxine's dishes in search of a paring knife.

'You have thirty seconds or less to tell me everything.' Max hung over the breakfast bar.

'Maxine—'

'Twenty-nine, twenty-eight, twenty-seven—'

'We've shagged – made love – a bunch of times over two meetings.' Jax dropped a bowl and it smashed on the floor.

'How many times!' Max kicked up her feet and balanced on the edge of the counter.

'Eight.'

'Four per?'

'Fuck's sake, Max!' Jax couldn't fight the small, self-satisfied smile. 'Three . . . and five.'

As Max whooped and bounced and came dangerously close to landing face down on the broken bowl, John Paul entered, and knew.

He knew that Jax had told Max about them.

He wasn't sure how he felt about that. But he knew he wasn't going to show them that he knew they had just been talking about him. No way.

Jacinta swept up the shattered pottery and cringed. *He knows I was just telling Maxine – well, not everything, but enough, more than I should have . . .*

'Nice place,' JP said, looking out the big picture window at the view. 'It's tidy.'

'Don't sound so surprised. Coffee? Tea? Still or sparkling water? Thought we'd lay off the booze for the night.'

'Sure. Em, water. Bubbly.'

'Jax?' Max called over her shoulder as she headed down the hall. 'Get the man a nice tall drink of water.' And she shut the bedroom door behind her.

John Paul went into the little kitchen and Jax turned, glass of water in her hand. He framed her face with his hands and kissed her, and she dropped the glass.

'Oh, I don't believe it,' Jax fussed, and he pulled her in for another snog.

'I thought about you all day, down in the cave – the office – Jacinta.'

'We need to talk,' Jacinta blurted, and started sweeping up the broken glass which was now mixed with the broken ceramic. 'After. We'll talk. All right?'

'Sure,' said JP, his stomach churning. 'We'll talk. After.'

'Ready to go?' Max strolled back into the lounge. 'I'll just read the voice-over into the gaps we set.'

'It's better,' John Paul said.

'It's still not great,' Max countered, throwing down her pages.

'It's not, no,' Jax agreed. 'It's not great.'

Maxine's buzzer went, and they all turned towards its general direction.

'Pizza?' JP asked hopefully. He'd been too wired to eat all day.

Max said nothing. Michael . . . well, he'd said he was going to call, but he hadn't done, so had he meant call as in American telephone call, or had he got so deep into the indigenous vocabulary that he'd meant *call* call. She lifted the receiver and, annoyed (delighted), buzzed him up.

'Fucking stalker,' she griped, for form's sake.

John Paul drooped in disbelief. 'You've got a stalker? On top of everything else?'

'No, I don't have a stalker. On top of what else?' And he was saved from having to reply by the brisk knocking on the door.

'Michael, howaya,' Jax said, and sighed at the sight of him and Maxine, side by side. *They were just gorgeous, weren't they?*

'Hey, howaya. I met this guy today, on the tour bus; he was hilarious, taught me all the slang.'

'You said you were going to call.' Max could have cut out her own tongue.

'Yeah, and here I am – *calling*. As in, calling to your house. If I was going to *call* call, I would have given you a *bell*.' He stood, grinning proudly, and Jacinta beamed at him.

'Aren't you great?' she crooned. 'And in no time at all. Can I get you something, coffee, tea, water?'

He pretended to think about it seriously. 'Yeah, hmm, I'll have a sparkling Ballygowan.' And he grinned again, then turned to JP.

'Howaya, you must be John Paul. We saw each other, the other day, but we didn't have time for proper introductions, if you know what I mean.' And Mike went over and shook hands. 'Jeez, you gotta get a lotta grief over that, huh? Holy Father?'

'We're working.' Max hated the way he came into a room and got right in there.

Loved it. She loved it.

'Ah, yeah, the project. How's it going?'

'It might not be a bad thing to show Michael,' said Jax, handing him his glass – one that she'd filled to the brim with ice. 'A cold eye, it's only been us who've seen it.'

'It's a not bad idea,' JP said, and he and Jax exchanged an electric look.

Michael caught it, and waggled his eyebrows at Maxine. He joined her on the sofa, closer than she might have liked, but she wasn't going to make a scene in front of her friends, she told herself.

'Yeah, fine,' Max said, and hit *play*.

They sat and watched Mike as he watched it, and when it ended, with Maxine getting up and enacting the soundtrack, they continued to watch him.

'You're not selling me,' he began. 'You got excellent production values, you got two lovely presenters – presenters! Are you hearing this? I am all *over* this – and you got some good stuff, but you're not selling me. Which is it? Is it fidelity or –' and here even he had to pause, even he had to acknowledge how close this cut to home – 'or the other?'

Jax moved away and went to look out Max's window. The sun was setting, out of frame, but the dying rays gilded the peaks of the distant Dublin mountains. 'I've been thinking and, as much as it pains me – not the thinking, ha, ha, but the thought—'

'Go on, Jax, please,' Max moaned.

'She's thinking on her feet, leave her alone,' Mike chided.

'She does this all the time! I know she'll get there, I'm just cutting to the chase.'

Jax went on as if she hadn't heard. 'But the thing is, Max was right. Nobody cares about the success stories, nobody's interested in "happily ever after". And obviously, I was not exactly a valid authority on the whole fidelity thing, either, given recent events.'

Her back to the room, she failed to notice the shock waves that were rocketing around behind her. John Paul looked as if he were shrivelling with confusion while slowly building up a head of anger; Max was looking between Jax and JP worriedly, appalled and stunned by

Jacinta's reversal; Michael didn't trust himself to look at anybody, and stared into his glass of melting ice.

'No, I was wrong – I mean, Jamie and Majella prove the point I was trying to make, but it's just not sexy – and if it is sexy, it's not scandalous, which is not good television. Maybe Gary and Mary would let us get into their lives, I know things got a bit sloppy there, but I'm convinced they'd be up for it. Like filming their wedding, knowing it's all surface, all pretence. It just seems like we have to take a stance, a firm stance, and the pro-fidelity one is pretty crap.'

'How can you say that?' John Paul's voice was pitched low, but forceful, and he stood, exuding furious distress.

Jax turned around, surprised. 'What do you mean?'

'How can you say that? So, people who treat each other like shite are more interesting than people like us?'

'Unfortunately.' Jax cocked her head. 'Is something wrong?'

'Is something wrong?' JP bleated incredulously. 'Is something *wrong*? Yes, Jacinta, something *is* wrong, something is wrong when you are into somebody and they seem to be into you, and you make love to them – did you tell Maxine how many times, did you mention that we couldn't keep our hands off each other for hours last night, and last weekend—'

'John Paul!' Jax made to move towards him and he moved away, putting the sofa and Max and Mike between them.

'Hey, maybe you and I should star in our TV show, you and me; we're the perfect couple, the perfect couple according to your remit – I'm the chancer who's pursuing an engaged woman, a practically married woman, and you're the one that's stepping out on her fiancé.'

Max gaped at Jacinta, who turned her back on them all. Mike nudged Maxine, who shook her head.

'There's no need to make this personal,' Jax said coldly, wrapping her arms around herself as if to keep herself together.

'Too bloody late, Jacinta Quirke. If it wouldn't make me sound like a total spa, I'd demand to know what your intentions are.' JP ran shaking hands through his curly hair, and took a step towards the door.

'This is neither the time nor the place—'

'What difference does it make! We've been stalking people, taping people, recording each other. There're no rules any more, nothing's secret any more, nothing's private – I want to know, are you going to marry that guy, or are you going to go out with me?'

Max reached for Michael's hand.

Jax stayed at the window.

'I don't really think it's – well, all right, I suppose it's your business, but we've only been – it's only been a few . . . times!' Jacinta shouted. 'For fuck's sake, JP, it's not like we're – we're having a laugh, what do you want from me?'

'Apparently something that you don't want to give.' JP turned away again, and turned back. 'I – Jesus, can we talk about this alone?'

'You started this holy show, you finish it!' Jacinta didn't even see Max and Mike sitting there any more, so focused was she on John Paul, her heart pounding, her heart breaking.

'I want to be with you, Jacinta,' he said, slowly, clearly – finally. 'Officially. Publicly. I won't have an affair with you – even though I guess that's what we're having. So. I need to know – I need to know what you want.'

Jacinta stood still, not fussing with any of her clothing,

not tugging at her hair, strong, and yet deflated. 'I do like you, JP – that's sounds terribly lame – and I'm not marrying Fergal—'

'Oh, now you tell me,' he shot sarcastically, yet rejoicing at the ray of hope.

'But I'm not interested in monogamy, as a concept, at the moment,' she said. 'Either as regards this project, or as regards my life.'

'Right.' JP stood, powerless to move.

'If I was, I would definitely – I mean, you're, well, you're lovely, JP, but –' *I mean this, I know I do, I mean this—*

'I have to – I'll see you – I'm gone.' And John Paul grabbed up his jacket and slammed the door.

Mike rose. 'I think I'll go chase him down, see he's okay, you know?'

'Wait.' Max dug something out of her bag and handed it to Mike. 'He forgot this, I meant to give it to him earlier today.'

'I'll give you a bell,' he said, and catching her off guard, kissed her, and left.

Jax stood at the window, her forehead pressed against the glass.

Max stood at the door, her fingers on her lips.

'I made a mess of that . . . but I know I'm right,' Jax whispered. 'About the programme, about . . .' She trailed off, dejected.

Max turned to look at her. 'Maybe, maybe not. Maybe we were both kind of right in the beginning, and now we're both kind of wrong.'

'I can't dive into something else, I can't.'

'Sounds like you're trying to convince yourself more than me.'

'Maxine O'Malley, you've got a terrible gift for throwing people's words back at them.'

'You're not kidding.' They both sat down on the couch, and Max shut off the TV. 'That was all pretty dramatic,' she sighed. 'Now that's good television.'

'Were you taping us?' Jax demanded, and Max hunched her shoulders.

'I couldn't help it!' she cried. 'I was so pissed off, your sound was so good, and I haven't been able to figure it out, so I was messing around here, and—'

'We've more on ourselves than we have on anybody else.' Jax picked up the bowl of crisps, set it on her lap, and dug in listlessly. 'That's probably the problem, you know.'

Max scooped herself a handful of crisps and ate them one by one, her eyes faraway, her posture gradually reflecting an increase of energy; the energy of a thought process building towards a potentially brilliant solution, the energy of pure inspiration that surged through her musculature until she was rising from the couch, all but floating around her living room.

'Oh my God, it's so obvious – but that's always the way – I think we could have it. It might just work – it might just—' Max laughed. 'I sound like you!'

'What?' Jax broke out of a dismal reverie. *I've made a huge mistake, haven't I?*

'Jacinta. Don't worry about JP now. I've got it. I've got an idea.'

Jax sighed down at the empty bowl. 'Uh oh.'

'Gimme two pints of the black stuff. Good man yourself.' Michael beamed at the less-than-enthralled barman, and turned back to John Paul.

'You don't know me from Adam,' he said, 'and right at

this moment, I'm thinking, that's not such a bad thing. I got no preconceptions, or whatever – I feel loyalty, I do, to Jacinta, even though I just met her, but I just met you, too, and I can see you've got it bad for her.'

'I got it terrible,' JP agreed, and they stood and watched the barman pull their pints. After a brief tussle over payment, Michael slapped a twenty on the bar and John Paul carried their jars to a table in the back.

'Wait, wait, you gotta let them settle,' Mike warned.

'Yeah, I know,' JP said, cracking a small smile. Michael LaMotta was nothing if not keen.

'Of course you do! Hey, what am I like!' He thumped JP on the shoulder, and they sat again in silence, watching their Guinness transform itself from light brown to pitch black.

'So' – they toasted – 'you and me, we come from different countries, I'm maybe a little bit older than you – but, hey, we're not so very different, and I think we got a lot in common.'

JP looked dubious. 'I don't know. I mean, I'm just a bloke,' he said. 'You're a man, like.'

Mike shook his head and leaned back. 'Nah, I'm a guy. My father's a man. We're guys, you and me.'

'Is that the same as being lads?'

'No. Absolutely not. We are not lads – lads are mooks.' Mike shrugged expansively. 'We're *guys*. Guys who both share an attraction to completely and totally pigheaded women.'

'Jesus, you're dead right there. But I hadn't a clue as to just how stubborn. It comes out in little flashes with Jacinta, not like Maxine – no offence,' he stuttered, because, for all his affability, Mike looked like the kind of guy you wouldn't want to offend in any way.

'Maxine, she's very . . . how can I say this? She's vocal. You always know – well, mostly' – and here Mike partook of a long draught of the black stuff – 'You pretty much know when and why she's digging her heels in. But Jacinta . . . she seems like she could be a mystery woman.'

'Not about everything,' John Paul defended her.

'But about a thing like this . . .' Michael tailed off meaningfully, and they both drank.

'This thing . . . I don't know, I mean, I'm going to sound like an eejit—'

'Like I said before, I got no judgements, nothing. You say what you like.'

And JP did, cataloguing every impulse, every signal he'd picked up, or thought he had, from the very first day he'd seen Jacinta Quirke. He took Mike through the events of recent times and didn't miss a beat, even when going up to fetch another round. Michael sat, listening patiently, nodding, urging, accepting.

'So, if I may?' John Paul, parched, exhausted, nodded permission. 'You are, without a doubt, crazy about this woman and, frankly, I haven't spent enough time in your presence to know for sure, but I'd say she's into you too – but!' and Michael held up a hand lest JP interrupt – 'I think she's coming out of some pretty nutty personal business, and that your timing is the problem.'

'Timing?' This, to John Paul, was a streak of blazingly glorious possibility in his desolate landscape.

'All in the timing.' Michael drained his pint. 'You want to be the rebound? Keep doing what you're doing. You want to be the one and only in her life? Take a break, go easy on it, give her space. They say all this on *Oprah* all the time, and it makes sense. Dr Phil? Genius.' He rolled his empty glass between his hands. 'Although why you would take the advice of a guy like me, a guy whose wife cheated on him and then refused to allow him to forgive her and then in turn filed for divorce and ran off to Ireland, is, of course, up to you.'

'Look,' JP began. 'I haven't spent much time with you and Max, either, but I reckon she would have found a way to get rid of you, whether or not you wanted to, if she really wanted to. If you take my meaning.'

'I wouldn't have put it past her to forge my signature on those papers.' Mike went on, hopefully. 'So, I think I got a chance. I know she wants to get back with me. I know this in my heart. I think. And my mission is exactly the opposite of yours. Come on, I gotta eat; if I drink any more of that stuff, I'm gonna fall down.'

They made their way out to the street, and Mike put on his shades, despite the fact that there was no sun, and that it was 6 p.m. in April in Ireland. 'My mission, as I say, is at the other end of the spectrum to you.'

'Meaning?'

'Meaning I give that woman the slightest breathing room, I'm history. No space for Maxine. I'm gonna be all over her like a rash.'

They used Max's office, and had been holed up in there since – and Maxine wouldn't stop complaining about it, remarking on it, and applauding herself for it – 7 a.m. Frantically running through the clips that JP had so neatly produced, they made notes, and made further cuts to the clips, and when they got stuck went back to old-fashioned tools as Max wrote on a legal pad, and Jax sketched out storyboards.

Max's phone rang. 'O'Malley. What? Obviously, I'm here. I got in early . . . *Yes*, it has been known to happen. Whadda you want? I'm *fine*' – she rolled her eyes at Jax, who wasn't having any of it – 'What? Okay, okay, how are you?' And she rolled her eyes again as she listened. 'So you bonded. Nice . . . No, it was; it was nice, I'm glad, you're a good listener for a guy. Yeah, yeah – listen, honey—' Max froze, Jax looked up, and silence vibrated out of the receiver.

Max hung up.

Jax continued to sketch. *None of my business*, she sang to herself as she tried to think how to cut from the crappy but arty footage at Cocoon, to one of the set-ups in Raymond's office.

'Yes, it was Michael, okay?' Max randomly scribbled down the page.

'Oh? I'd never have guessed—'

'Fucking LaMotta, calling me morning, noon and night – he hasn't been this ardent since we – since we got married.'

Jacinta pretended to continue to draw. 'That's interesting,' she murmured. 'So maybe he wasn't Mr Perfect who hadn't exactly got his Mrs Perfect? So, possibly, all the flaws weren't only on your side?'

'Well, I don't know what he's after,' Max said.

'Maxine O'Malley, what a ridiculous remark. Everyone and their cat knows what he's after, for pity's sake.'

'Yeah, so. But why now?' Max tilted her head back and went for a short spin in her chair.

'What do you mean?' Jax doodled a little drawing of herself, but with shorter hair – not too, too short, but more shaped and, picking up a couple of coloured markers, drew in some sunny streaks.

'Why now? We've been apart for two years, two and a half –'

Jax laid on some more streaks. 'So in O'Malley-time that's fifteen, sixteen months?'

'And I mean, he rang and rang – and then he didn't.' Max stopped spinning. 'He stopped. And then I moved here.'

'Did you move here because he stopped?' Jax left off streaking her cartoon hair, and looked up. *It's so obvious you're made for each other*, Jax thought impatiently. *Both of you in this pointless agony –*

'And he found me, somehow,' she went on, leaning her elbows on her desk. 'I had covered my tracks – I thought, not reckoning on Niamh Bourke – but even still, he found me.' She felt her spirits lift at that. 'He did, he found me.'

'Yes, it's the loveliest thing.' Jax drew a little picture of

Max and Mike, sitting on a sofa, and wondered – what if they – was it too much? – but what if –? 'What if we—' she began, but stopped when Max stood up abruptly, frowning.

'What's that noise?' she asked, prowling the edges of her office.

'I didn't hear anything.'

'Wait.' Max stood still, and Jax sat still, and nothing happened for what seemed like ages.

'It sounds like one of ours,' Jax said. 'And JP said that the other day; we heard the same sound down in his cave. It sounds like it does when a camera goes into stand-by mode, after we've been recording for a while.'

Shit, Maxine mouthed. She grabbed her pen and pad. 'Do you reckon we're being watched?' she scrawled.

Jax opened and closed her mouth several times. 'Will we get back to our work, our agency-related work, now, Maxine?' she said, making faces.

'I think we'd better get out of here,' Maxine wrote.

'Yes, exactly, the work we're doing for the company, our poor company, but here we are, still working hard –' and she made another series of faces that she thought belied her words.

'Write it out!' Max wrote, then waved her legal pad in Jax's face.

'It's down.' Jax blew out a breath. 'That last noise. It's a timer. It goes on and off. Whoever – and hmm, I wonder who's got us under surveillance, although how she figured out how to use this stuff is beyond me, she can barely operate a doorknob – whoever has set us up has set the camera up to go on and off. It saves memory.'

'She's finished!' Max dragged her chair around frantically, ready to start pulling down lenses and wires and bugs.

'Wait.' Jax tapped her pencil against her chin. 'Leave it.'

'Are you outta your mind?'

'God, you've gone all New York since your husband pitched up.' Jax smiled as she watched Max try to focus her outrage. 'Let's leave it. We're not ready to let her know we know, and besides—'

John Paul came in without knocking. 'Howaya,' he said. 'Got your email, Max.' *Take it slow, O'Gorman, niice and sllllooooooooow.* 'Jax. How's it going – are you well?'

Jacinta really didn't know how to reply to that.

'I had an idea,' Max said.

'Uh oh,' said JP.

'Jax, you want to run through it?' Max leaned back on her desk, and nudged her chair forward for John Paul.

'I'd be delighted, if I don't get thrown off my train of thought – I had an idea before, I've forgotten it, and – well, fine.' *I can do this, it's just a pitch, despite the fact that this has all gone –* 'Personal. I believe, when we were all at Max's, that I brought up the word "personal", and I also said, after Max and I were left alone, that the problem with this pilot was that we have as much interesting footage of ourselves as we do of our subjects. So.'

She took John Paul and Max through her storyboards, with Max interjecting sections of script as necessary. JP listened, a neutral look on his face, and sat quietly when she'd finished.

'Right. So, using the bits that we shot on set, we're making a show about ourselves making the show, and the, em, personal things that have happened to us in the process; that is, you and Max falling out, Mike showing up, and you and I and our . . . situation.'

'It's fab!' Max exulted. 'We've got the whole process,

from my handbag to the good stuff we got at Ray's, from the pub, from Wednesday, when we had that fight, Jax.'

'And the stuff you got when you were stalking Fergal.' JP tossed the DVD on Max's desk. 'Cheers, Max.'

Jax gritted her teeth and managed a strained smile. 'Well, in the spirit of our new transparency, Max, may I say that that would have been somewhat out of bounds – had I not done the lunch with Mike.' She sulked.

'You taped Michael? Does he know?' JP winced. 'I don't think he's the kind of guy you want to be on the wrong side of, Jacinta.'

'He's not Tony Soprano – even though he does kinda sound like him sometimes,' Max said. 'So we've got all that stuff, plus . . . whatever has been illegally, without our prior consent, recorded in our cubicles.'

JP looked around. 'I found some eyes in my office. We twigged them the other day. I left them, though.'

'Good. I said the same.' Jax reached out to squeeze JP's arm and stopped herself. She thought how rotten the world would be if she couldn't just reach out when she felt like it, to touch John Paul, even with light affection, how sad it would be if she—

'What?' She looked over at JP's neutral face. 'What?'

'I said, it sounds okay – and I'd like to see the release form – but is it enough? We still need to get into the theme—'

'Yes!' Jax paged through her storyboards. 'I had an idea.'

A brisk knock on the door sounded, and in walked Michael.

'You weren't kidding, you're really working!' He looked over Jax's shoulder, gave JP a light manly punch on the shoulder and, before she'd even begun to cultivate annoyance at his preemptory entrance, Michael kissed

Max and sat down on her desk. 'So how's it going?'

'It's going good.' Max got up to go and sit somewhere else, and then sat back down again because there wasn't anywhere else to sit.

'We're rejigging the whole thing,' Jax said, and then realised what JP had meant when he'd said that you wouldn't want to get on the wrong side of Mike. As easy-going as he appeared, sitting on Max's desk, his sheer height, and bulk, and Italian-Americaness combined to make Jax think of cement shoes and bridges in Brooklyn. 'Em . . .'

'Here, let me.' And as Maxine went through the whole thing again, Jacinta made a few more sketches and took the time to actually write down the idea she had.

'That's better. Almost there.' Michael thumbed through Jax's sketches, and nodded. 'Yeah. Almost. It's got a pulse, but I don't think the heart's beating yet.'

'Pulse? Heart? This from an ad exec? What about the demographics? The spin? The skew?'

'We've got this thing, Maxine and me—' Michael explained to Jax and John Paul.

'Don't mix them up in this,' Max interjected.

'—this thing whereby I say anything that sounds remotely creative, and Maxine accuses me of being a soul-less number cruncher whose only focus is on the bottom line.'

'Don't even play that, LaMotta—' Max began, but he kissed her again, quickly, a silly little peck, and she clammed up.

'So, yeah, it's almost there.' Mike pondered a moment. 'Hey, what about yer one – hey, did you hear that – I'm a native, I haven't even been here a week, huh? How about that?'

320

'What one?'

'Your mom – mum. Nah, that's weird – to me, that's weird, I can't say it. Your mom. Angela. She's gonna be in this, right? You could make a whole show about her. And Raymond. They've been together what, how many years? They gotta know something about fidelity. Come on! Am I right?'

Max, Jax and JP all breathed as one.

'Intercut with all this stuff,' Max said.

'I wish –' and Jax covered her mouth with her hands then howled when she saw John Paul's face.

'You said!' Jax wailed.

'I got it off Lorcan. I knew he wouldn't erase that footage – feckin' chancer.'

'Oh, shit!' Max started jumping around the room like a lunatic. 'You have it?'

'Have what?' Michael was catching up, but he hated being even a fraction out of step. 'You got what?'

'They'll never, ever go for it.' Jax slid down in her chair.

'Well, Raymond won't,' said Max, wheezing from her romp around the cubicle.

'Em . . .' They all looked at John Paul. 'He might be convinced. He feels really guilty about telling us what Jax told him.'

Max nodded. 'Yeah, we could use that, stuff like betrayal really kills a guy like Ray.'

'I haven't spent much time around him, I admit, but you could tell that he'd rather dig his own eyes out with a teaspoon than betray the trust of a loved one,' added Michael.

They all looked at Jax.

'I can't – I have to think about this. I'm not running off, or hiding things, or anything, but I have to – oh, God, it'll kill him, it will – I have to – leave it with me. I have to think.'

She gathered up her supplies, and clutching them to her chest, turned to leave the cube, but was stopped by JP's hand on her arm.

'I've got something else for you to think about.' He didn't have the guts to lean over and steal a kiss the way Michael kept stealing them from Max, but he could, and did, caress her arm as he spoke. 'I could push the issue, and pursue you, but I'm not going to. I could keep at ya, and keep at ya, but I won't. I know you, Jacinta Quirke, and I want you to know that I want to be with you – but it's up to you. Whenever, whenever, just let me know.'

Unbeknownst to him, he fell into a mimic of Mike's speech patterns. 'You want to go rebound on somebody else, that's up to you, but it ain't gonna be me. I care about you too much, and you've been through too much, and I want to start fresh with you, square one. I'll wait for you.'

'You're assuming quite a lot,' Jax said imperiously – and ruined it by leaping away as JP took a chance and leaned in to kiss her.

He smiled, his brown eyes twinkling as he traced a finger over her mouth. 'Up to you,' he said lightly, resisting the urge to add *babe*. 'Let me know.'

'Well – I – don't do *me* any favours, John Paul O'Gorman!' And she stormed out of the office and into her own, and then out of it again and down the stairs.

'Here we go again,' Max sighed. 'Only you're in the hot seat this time, pal.'

'He can take it,' said Michael, and he and JP nodded at each other.

'I think—' John Paul shut up when they heard the camera engage again.

'What? What?' Mike demanded, as JP and Max started communicating via hand signals.

'We're outta here,' said Max as she steered Mike towards the door.

Once on the stairs, Max and John Paul filled Michael in on the general malevolence that was Niamh Bourke.

'It can't be anyone else but her – but how are we gonna figure that out?' They stood outside her locked door, glaring at it.

'She never leaves,' John Paul said. 'Gets in at dawn, I reckon, and locks the place up behind her.'

'Howaya, lads.' Tommy the elderly mailroom fella huffed up the stairs. 'She's not in today, if yer lookin' for Niamh.'

Maxine actually shivered in anticipation. 'That's unusual, Tommy.'

'It is, it is,' he agreed, and paused to catch his breath. 'Funeral.'

'How . . . tragic.' Max beamed.

'It is, it is,' Tommy breathed, and prepared to go up the rest of the way.

'It's just – you know how she is, Tommy, such a stickler for the forms, and the invoices—'

'She is, she is,' Tommy said. 'You need them, now. You need them forms. When I was in the GPO—'

'You do, you need them,' and Max covered cutting across him with a brilliant smile. 'It's just that she keeps them all to herself, and I've got to get in my forms before end of business, or she'll – she'll just be so angry with me, Tommy.'

There was nothing like the threat of tears to get an auld fella discombobulated. 'Ah, well, let me hunt up the key, sure I'm the only one with it, now, and she's fierce about me keeping it to myself.'

'I'll never tell,' Max swore, sniffling.

'All right, now, mind them waterworks,' Tommy grumbled as he, Max, JP and Mike looked first one way down the hall, and then the other. Tommy produced the key and unlocked what sounded like a dead bolt and, considering his usual lack of fitness, leapt spryly away from the door as if in fear of a booby trap.

'You'll say nothing,' he hissed.

'Nothing!' whispered Max, and she led the way into the heretofore unbreached sanctum.

'You got that letter, did ya?' Tommy asked, from a reasonable distance.

'Letter?'

'That one from America, that special delivery one, from New York City, I gave it over to Niamh to bring to ya, them stairs is desperate for a man my age—'

'The letter from . . .'

'Janey, you got it, did ya? It's a federal offence to interfere with the delivery of the post.' And Maxine went over and soothed the increasingly hysterical chap, assuring him of the receipt of the envelope, all the way out the door and halfway up the stairs.

She shut the door behind her and looked at Michael. 'I received a letter,' he said, 'signed by you, via overnight express, telling me that you'd been having second thoughts and that you wanted to talk things over, hash things out.' They looked at each other, both banking a kind of fury that had JP busily combing the office for electronics rather than watch them go through this. 'I replied by DHL.'

'She had no right to deceive you.' Max crossed to him, and hesitating, reached out. 'She's dead meat.'

Mike put his arms around her, burying his face in her

hair, rocked her. 'She is dead meat,' Max whispered. 'You hear me? You think I'm gonna let her do this to you?'

'Found the switch box,' JP said, and Max moved to go over to see, but Mike held on a little longer.

'I got no history with this woman, but if you want her brought down, we'll bring her down. Otherwise,' he said, capturing her face in his hand, brushing his mouth over hers, 'I ain't complaining.'

Jax's inner monologue was a series of half-thoughts, broken phrases, and guttural snarls. She couldn't even focus on what she was most angry about: the fact that the kitchen table footage existed, the fact that she immediately thought to *use* it, the fact that her colleagues were discussing her father's integrity as though it were something to *manipulate*, the fact that Mr John Paul O'Gorman, *so* magnanimously, had offered to wait for her, as if she was a table at Café Bar Deli, as if she was a bag of chips!

She tore a swathe up and down Grafton Street, blindly snatching tops of every description, trousers of every cut, pants, bras and sundry accessories from racks in shops on both sides of the road. She went up, went back down again, nipped into Powerscourt, unthinking, uncaring, signing her name to credit slips willy nilly while grumbling to herself, blurting out arbitrary words, and essentially making retail history.

'Stupid – Well, thank *you* – Eejit – And what about those cameras – As if I would – Lorcan! Dammit—'

'Tony will see you now.' Jax looked up, mid-tirade, and composed herself as she rose to follow Foundation's receptionist over to the appointed stylist's station.

Tony ran his hands through her hair, marvelling at its

texture while gently bemoaning its length. 'Oh, pet, not a moment too soon.'

'You ain't kidding.' Jax handed over a scrap of paper. Tony considered it, looked at her in the mirror, looked at the drawing, then back again. 'You sure, angel?' he asked.

'I'm sure,' Jax replied. She met her own eyes in the mirror and saw them light up with rebellion. 'Do it.'

'No. Absolutely not. I refuse.'

Gobsmacked, everyone watched Angela storm out of the room and flee up the stairs.

It had all begun so cheerfully: Jacinta had arrived well ahead of her friends and had a few moments with Raymond and Angela, who both made the proper and gratifying amount of delighted commotion about her haircut, her outfit, and her manicure, without making her feel as if she had ever been lacking in any way.

Angela opened a bottle of champagne.

Happily, Maxine, Michael and John Paul all arrived together, and their response was equally satisfying. Michael gallantly kissed her hand, and Maxine babbled almost incoherently, demanding a blow-by-blow account of each and every purchase.

Angela opened more champagne, and John Paul lurked on the edges of the group, quietly sipping his bubbly, *looking* at her.

And who could blame him? Jacinta had thought. She'd chosen well from her unbelievably flattering and diverse new wardrobe and kitted herself out in a pencil-slim, raspberry-coloured skirt and a white fitted blouse, from under which peeked a sherbety-orangey little lacey camisole thingie. Additionally, several strings of brightly coloured beads draped around her terrifically presented frontage, thanks to a WonderBra. Her feet were positively caressed by kitten-heeled leather slides, her legs silkily encased in nude Wolford stockings.

As if that wasn't enough, there was her hair. All that hair. All that hair that had been the bane of her existence, curling out of control, dragging down her face. She wasn't hiding behind it any more. She gave a passing thought to how different her adolescence might have been had there been such products at her disposal – smoothers, scrunchers, moulding goops – but it was, in fact, very, very well worth the wait.

The artfully designed tangle brushed her shoulders in front, and curved in a delightful bell a few inches down her back. Sunny highlights in several shades of light blond tumbled around her face, and enhanced her natural colour.

'How much did you *spend*?' Maxine asked.

'I don't know,' Jacinta replied, and Max ran around the house screaming with exhilaration.

Once everybody had calmed down, Jax took a preparatory breath and turned to her parents, smiling. 'Listen, we've had an idea about the programme, and we'd like to talk to you about it.' Max, Mike and JP stood behind her, and kept their beaming smiles in place, but Angela smelled a subtext.

She shot Raymond one of their imperceptible signals, and they followed their daughter and her friends into the front room.

Despite the tailoring, Jax was still Jax, and while all her cuticles had been trimmed, and her split ends disposed of, and her clothes were so new as to fail to provide any stray threads, she managed to find a cushion to fiddle with. She'd given this loads of thought, and felt she'd come up with an angle that didn't feel too much like an *angle*, like she was trying to hoodwink her folks but—

Get on with it, Jacinta!

'First, on behalf of all of us, I'd like to thank you – as inadequately as I can – for all the help you've given us so far. We couldn't have done it without you, Mum, and Da, the use of your office saved our necks.' Jax laughed lightly, and her colleagues echoed her, with a second or two delay.

Raymond smiled slightly, and Angela arched a brow.

'Well, we've done a rough cut, then we did another one' – here they all laughed self-deprecatingly; Raymond rubbed his chin, and Angela nodded sagely – 'And we realised that the most interesting material was the stuff about ourselves. Which sounds dreadful, I know! But we've cut some of it together – like during the shoot on Wednesday, JP had all the cameras recording the whole time, so we've got Maxine coming in and meeting you, Mum, and being all stroppy—'

'Hey,' Max interjected, prompting another laugh from her colleagues. Angela laughed along – she could see where this was going.

'And since you're already in it, Mum, we thought we could, uh, feature you and Da. The point is, it's about relationship, and fidelity, and, well, Michael said himself the other day—'

'I said, "Who knows more about staying together than Ray and Ange?" Huh?'

Angela peeped up at him from beneath her lashes, and she gripped her husband's hand in hers. *This was what she'd hoped for, in her wildest imaginings . . .*

'Well, *I* think that sounds fine, don't you, Raymond?' Angela perched on the edge of the couch and beamed around at everyone.

Night Flight Productions, however, knew that they were far from the home stretch.

JP risked an encouraging squeeze on Jax's shoulder.

Raymond nodded, not taking his eyes off his youngest daughter – whom he was reading so well. 'I suppose we'll need to sign a release.' He smiled.

'Em. Yes. Er.' Jax stalled. *I don't think I can do this –*

'What happened was, we rigged your kitchen one day, to test out some equipment.' Max kept it brisk, and short. 'And what happened after that, just before we finished running checks and were about to break everything down, was that Ray came in at lunchtime, and then Angela came in from the shops, and, em, uh, we kind of captured an, er, intimate moment.'

'Intimate? Moment?' queried Raymond, in the Undertaker Voice, and Jax tensed in anticipation. The Undertaker Voice was, to all intents and purposes, the means to a slow death by calm, cool, unruffled and hushed logic.

'Maxine, darling, what are you saying?' Angela wondered.

Jacinta held up a hand. These were her parents, she'd allowed the whole thing to happen, and it was up to her to break it to them. 'We have footage of you and Da doing, uh, having, em, making, er – sex. Sex on the kitchen table.'

A dog barked in the street. Children laughed giddily across the road, and car doors slammed. They even heard an aeroplane fly overhead. Birds sang, the wind gently blew down the chimney, and the six people in the living room sat.

'Is that so, Jacinta?' Raymond asked, his pitch subterranean. 'Is that it, exactly?'

'Yes.' She thrust out her chin, ready to take the worst.

'I'd certainly like to get a look at that,' he murmured, and smiled suggestively down at his wife.

'Do you mean you have a video *tape* of your father and I engaged in a private act on the kitchen table?' Angela's voice rose in direct opposition to Raymond's Quiet Voice. This, in the Quirke household, was known as the West End Voice, which generally promised, and delivered, a pasting of monumental proportions. 'And what do you propose to do with it?'

Brazening it out, Jax rose to face her mother, and said, as quickly as she could manage, 'We wanted to use it – not all of it, we didn't get the entire, em, activity, but just a bit to cut to quickly.'

'No. Absolutely not. I refuse.' And with that she left the room.

After she had gone, Raymond looked around at the others. 'Angela, as a rule, doesn't do nudity, but I confess I am rather – well, I don't imagine you thought you'd get this reaction ...' he trailed off, his face the picture of distress. 'I must go to her –'

'Let me.' Jax smoothed down the silky wonderfulness of her skirt and left the room.

She found her mother sitting on the edge of her bed, her back to the door, and when she went to her, she was dismayed to find that Angela had tears running down her face, real tears, unaccompanied by histrionics and well-rehearsed movements, tears tracing tracks down her mother's face without an applicable monologue, without drama.

'Oh, God, Mum, I'm so sorry, we all are, we didn't

think – I made them stop, I did, we don't have all of it, I swear. And then that wanker Lorcan said he'd erased it all, but he hadn't, he'd saved a bit; we had several cameras going, and—'

'Several cameras!' Angela continued to gently weep, and stare at herself in the vanity mirror. 'There was surely a day when I would have sold my soul to be the focus of several cameras. But not like this, Jacinta.'

Jax sat down gently next to her. 'Mum, we really want you to be in the show. I'll understand if you don't want to have anything to do with this, but I – we need you, and Da, and there would be quite a lot of time spent, on you, and—'

Angela sighed, and dabbed at her cheeks with a lacey handkerchief. 'You're all so good, you are, even you, now – none of you ever patronise me, poor old me, Angela Quirke, Ageing Actress – no, now, come on, I *know* what I'm like, and it's delightful that you all tolerate me to the degree that you don't pull me up on the amateur dramatics—'

'If you're going to sit here and start moaning I'll go,' Jax warned sternly, and ruined it when her voice broke.

Angela sighed, her voice carrying the remnants of tears, and she patted her daughter on the leg. 'I can't describe what it's like for me, to be thought of as too old. I do not feel a day over twenty, most of the time,' she sighed. 'To be thought of as *past it*, when I feel, in my bones, that I am in my *prime*, my *God*, if only there were parts, if only there were writers capable of delivering something for someone like me . . .' She blew her nose.

'But, darling, the thought of this little old body exposed to outside eyes – your father's seen the years go by, if you take my meaning. I am, of course, safe with him – but the *notion* that I was caught, literally, with my pants down! – oh, pet, I can't stand it, I can't stand it . . .' and she sobbed into her hands.

'We'll drop the whole idea,' Jax promised desperately. 'We'll erase everything, everything that we have on you—'

'There's no need to go that far.' Angela drew in a shuddering breath.

'I swear to you, we saw almost nothing, just a bit where Da lifted you up on to the table, and I think he went for your cardigan, and then you kind of whipped off your top, and then, em – uh – and the angle that we have is from behind you, anyway, so we mostly just see Da kind of, em, lifting you, and your back, and—'

'The camera's behind me?' Angela sniffled.

'It is, right behind you, and we stopped before – before we would have seen your – your bum.'

'Well, why didn't you *say* so!' Angela threw down the hankie and shook Jax by the shoulders. 'Well, *that's* all right!' She exited gracefully, and ruined it by pelting down the stairs.

Jax sat, wondering if one could recover from such a series of reversals in so short a space of time. She heard Angela explaining to Raymond about the camera angles, and, not quite up to another round of celebratory congratulations, crept down the stairs and out to the back garden.

Max, Mike and JP retired to the kitchen and left the senior Quirkes to peruse the footage in private.

'Is this, uh . . .' Michael gestured towards the table.

'Here, hold this.' Max handed Mike a little box from which dangled some wires.

'I don't believe you!' John Paul covered his eyes in shock.

'You were recording that?' Mike gaped at her.

'I couldn't help it!' Max wiggled a wire from around her torso. 'I just got good at this, okay? I only did a little. I'm running out of memory—'

'No more of this, okay? This was really hard on her.' JP went over to the window and watched Jacinta start to weed.

'What is she *doing*?' Max shrieked. 'In her new clothes!'

'How's my timing, Mike?' JP asked.

Mike pretended to look at his watch. 'If a woman looks that good, maybe you don't want to give her too much time . . .'

As John Paul went out the back door, Angela stuck her head in the kitchen door. 'Don't mind us,' she purred. 'We've, em, got something to do upstairs, we'll be with you . . . eventually.' She winked, and shut the door softly behind her.

It was impossible to weed with a manicure and, frustrated, Jax gave up and thought about getting the clippers to do a bit of dead-heading.

It was also impossible to negotiate a garden in kitten heels, and since those stockings had cost the earth, she wasn't about to take the shoes off, and so gave up entirely and sat on the stone bench her father had tucked at the bottom of the garden.

She idly stroked the petals of an early blooming foxglove that was growing a good five feet high. Her father wouldn't give up his secret composting recipe . . . even to her, his youngest, beloved daughter. It looked like everyone had their secrets.

'You handled that well.' She jumped at the sound of JP's voice.

'I feel terrible,' Jax said, and hid her face in her hands.

'Me, too.' He sat down beside her and leaned back against the stone wall at the bench's back.

'She was crying, JP, really crying, not pantomime tears, and I thought, we've completely lost the run of ourselves, and now we want this all to be about us, well, not just you and I, but all of us – me and my stupid, pointless engagement, and what exactly am *I* setting myself up for, exposing myself for.' She clenched her fists, fighting the urge to start tugging at her hem. 'I'll have to talk about it, how awful it was to feel like everyone was watching me all the time, laughing behind their hands – and I supported the thing, I kept the lie going on and on and on . . .'

John Paul ached to hold her. 'You don't have to be in it, you know.'

'What are you saying?' Where had that little part of her ego been hiding all her life? 'I'm not *good* enough to be on camera? This is broadcast-quality hair, thank you very much.'

'I have to say, Jacinta Quirke, I'm really liking this short-fused, firebrand side of your personality.' JP leaned towards her, only to receive a sharp elbow jab to his breadbasket.

'Ah, sure, if only I'd looked this smart, maybe I wouldn't have been abandoned! Maybe I wouldn't have been tossed over! Perhaps, possibly, if I hadn't let myself *go* I'd be married today, I'd still be with Fergal!'

'Do you want to be with him?' John Paul massaged the ache in his belly.

Jacinta plucked up a sunny Marguerite from the nearby border. 'I don't want to be with anyone who doesn't want to be with me.'

'I want to be with you, Jacinta.'

She twirled the flower around between her fingers. 'After he'd told me he'd married, I thought I might like to be by myself for a while, which is, of course, a bloody joke, as I have been nothing if not by myself.'

She looked at him out of the corner of her eye. 'Then I thought, maybe I'll just tear up the town a bit. Maybe I'll just be like Maxine and flirt like the divil and snog and be light and breezy, like it doesn't matter. The whole fidelity thing – what a cod. It certainly hadn't added up to much for me.

'Then, well . . .' she cradled the petals of the daisy in her palm. 'Oh, rubbish, I'm not built that way. And the whole problem was that I was being faithful all by myself.' She laughed, but her eyes were vulnerable, wide open with all her fears rushing to the surface. John Paul started to speak, but she shook her head. 'I'm not willing to rebound with you, John Paul.' She handed him the flower. 'I want to be in a real relationship with you.'

'Grand.' He took the flower and kissed her on the cheek.

'Grand? Grand? That's it, grand?'

'I told you I'd wait for you.'

'I am not a bag of chips!'

John Paul cracked up. 'Jesus, no, Jacinta Quirke, you're the full menu.' He stuck the flower behind his ear, made her laugh, then took her in his arms.

'Where'd you get all this stuff?' Michael was no technology hound, but he knew quality when he saw it.

'Oh, here and there,' Max said airily as she sandbagged the tripod, and then slid the camera into its lock.

'From ACJ? Not such a good idea, what with your nemesis and all.'

'We need to meet about that. I've got an idea.' Max
lifted a light out of its kit.

'Uh oh,' said Mike, as he went over to give her a hand.

A muffled thumping sounded from above.

'Oh, brother!' Max covered her ears. 'I know way too
much about the mating habits of the Quirkes. You gotta
hand it to them, though, after all these years.'

Michael put down the light and went over to take Max
in his arms.

She evaded him by jumping over the open lighting box
and hopping behind the camera.

'No! Not now!' She dragged the sound equipment in
front of her as well.

'Not now, not now! When? When, Maxine! When are
we gonna talk about this?'

'Not *now*! I don't know! Quit bugging me, would you
lay off me.'

'I came here, to Dublin, to have this conversation,
right, because what would be the point of me ringing you,
when we both know you'd just hang up, resulting in a non-
talking experience, so here I am, having flown four thou—
three thousand, five hundred miles—'

'Mike, Mike, Michael!' She moved to him, and batted
his hands away. 'No touching. I touch you, you don't touch
me.'

Mike stood, his arms away from his body, palms face
up.

She ran her hands over his shoulders, up to his face,
back down again, before resting on his waist. 'I need more
time – shut up! A little more.'

'How much?' Mike shifted, the need to touch her
almost unbearable.

'I don't know—'

'So, what, you need a day? A week?'

'What, you want a schedule?' Max backed off and went back to uncoiling cable. 'I don't know how much—'

'An hour? A minute?' Mike went back to setting up the light. 'You know what, Maxine? It doesn't matter. It better not take the rest of our lives, I gotta draw the line at that, but you go on, you take all the time you need, 'cause I got all the time in the world. All the time in the world, Maxine!'

'You? Ha!' Their voices drowned out every other sound in the house, which, had they been able to hear, would have alerted them that the kitchen door had opened, and that footsteps had sounded on the stairs. 'You, who calls the office from the taxi that's taking you home? What, this is like the first vacation of your life, you letting it go to your head? Like it so much you wanna make it permanent?'

'Bingo!' Michael boomed. 'Give the lady a kewpie doll! This vacation is, in fact, permanent!'

'What?' Max clutched the sound mixer.

'Permanent vacation, baby. I quit!'

'You did not.' Maxine didn't notice that the Quirkes and JP had clustered on the threshold.

'I sure did. Early retirement – so, okay, it's not exactly quitting, but they had some packages going around, I had some stock, I've made some investments, I'm a free agent, baby! Free as a bird!'

Max stared up at him. 'What are you going to do?'

Michael threw his hands into the air. 'Looks like I'm gonna be spending the rest of my life trying to convince my wife to spend the rest of her life with me!'

He turned and the crowd at the door shuffled into each other in an effort get out of the doorway. 'Hey, come on in!

It's your house! It's your project! You want to know about fidelity, I'll tell you all about it!' Cowed, Raymond, Jax and JP crept over to the couch, while Angela stood dead in front of Michael, hands draped across her bosom, as enthralled as if Mike were Olivier giving his *Lear*. 'Max and me, we could tell you all about it, maybe we didn't get it perfect the first time around, but I'm willing to – to start again.' He turned to her, took the mixer out of her hands, handed it to JP without taking his eyes off her, and took her cold hands into his. 'So, in case you didn't get it, that's why I'm here. Now we all know. Right? So you think about that – you take your time, 'cause if I got nothing else, I got time. Are we shooting, or what?'

O n the monitor in a darkened room, a scene played out, a familiar scene taken from a famous film: a couple, sitting on a sofa, talking about how they'd met, how they'd fallen in love, how they'd lost each other, how they'd found each other again. The image froze on the couple looking adoringly at each other, and as the camera seemed to zoom closer and closer to them, Max spoke in voice-over: 'Twenty years ago, the blockbuster Hollywood movie *When Harry Met Sally* was a huge success, and showed us that a lifetime of memories could be launched at the very first meeting.'

A sharp cut to Max, turning away from her monitor, on which the image showed. She was dressed devastingly well – sharp, stylish, knowing. She continued: 'Scenes of couples reminiscing about their early courtship provided a delightful and lovey-dovey perspective on the main relationship in the film, but in fairness, there's got to be more to it than that.'

The camera cut closer, with Max's face in full frame. 'So, you meet cute and fall in love – so what? Left, as we are so often by Tinseltown, with a happy ending, we wanted to know what fidelity was like in real life.'

There followed a quick montage of the couples they

had filmed: the nervous Dara, the sleeping Conor, snippets of the Gary and Mary mêlée. Reverb added an extra level of insanity to that last shot, and it cut to black.

Jax stepped into the frame, looking as well presented as her colleague, but softer, less edgy. She smiled calmly as she strode towards the camera, and delivered her line. 'That's Maxine's point of view, anyway. But what about those who have actually made it?'

The next montage started with a good chunk of Jamie and Majella laughing and cuddling, followed by quick cuts of happier couples they'd got from the open call, some live footage from the pubs and clubs of Dublin, shots of people holding hands walking along the boardwalk in the city centre, that slowly ground down to slow motion.

Which cut immediately to a close-up of Jax. 'Not very sexy, is it?'

The film cut to Angela's entrance into her kitchen.

'Well, well, look who's here.' And the scene ran through until Jax cut in on Angela tugging at Raymond's belt.

There was a cutaway to Jax, pretending to look confused. 'Sorry – did I say that fidelity wasn't sexy?'

'I saw you spying on me the other night. I saw you looking at me while I was in the bath. Looking at me through your long telescope,' breathed Angela.

'You'll never prove it, doll,' growled Ray.

And the image cross-faded to reveal a two-shot of Ray and Angela on the sofa in their home that mimicked the one in *When Harry Met Sally*, with the supertitle *Raymond and Angela Quirke, married forty years*, in the lower third of the screen.

Angela: *'I can tell you, I was not happy about that, being spied upon –'*

Raymond: *'But we're thinking of getting one of those wee cameras for ourselves.'*

They exchanged a warm look and laughed sexily.

'Huh?' Max snapped out of a reverie, a deep and troubled one.

'I said, are we actually going to be able to get the rights to that footage?' Jax asked, again, for the third time. She rolled her eyes at John Paul, who couldn't keep his hands off her.

Not that she was complaining.

If she were going to complain about anything, it would be the utter lack of attention Max was giving the latest rough cut, which was really shaping up into something *good*; it had been her idea after all, so what was her problem?

Of course, everyone and their cat *and* their dog knew what Max's problem was.

Michael had quit. Michael quit his job. In the industry he'd worked in since he was a mailboy. What was he going to do with himself? Max didn't, for one second, disbelieve that he would make a career out of the mending of their marriage.

Did she mind? She gazed blankly as the rough cut played out once more on the computer. Was she about ready to cave? Did it have to be about caving, about giving up? Did she choose to end it, once and for all, or ... or what?

That *speech* he made, at the Quirkes' last night, it was the last thing he said for the rest of the evening – to her, anyway. They shot for an hour and a half, getting the history of Angela and Raymond down on tape, the better and the worse, and Mike's reserve, his calm after the storm – well, it got on her nerves. Like it always did. That irritating tranquillity, especially in one normally so voluble, was like water torture to Max. *What was he thinking?* Which was a really stupid question, because she knew what he was thinking, and the stinkin' ball was in her court, and—

'What?' Max sat up. Jacinta was looking at her with a world of sympathy in her eyes. 'Sorry, I . . . I'm a little out of it.'

A little! 'We wanted your input here – what do you think about maybe lightening this up so we can fade to white?'

'Sure, yeah, great.' And Max sank back down in her seat.

'Max?' Jax asked gently. 'Why don't we do this, and we'll burn you a copy, and you can look at it later?'

'Yeah, okay, you guys don't need me, anyway,' Max said as she headed for the door. 'I got no patience for this tweaky stuff – big picture, that's me.' And without another word, she left.

Jax beamed and clapped her hands lightly, and JP shook his head. 'You'll never learn, will you? Even with all this live footage demonstrating the perils of nosing around in other people's affairs . . .'

'Don't be such a wet blanket. Roll that last bit again, please.'

Max liked the Clarence, and wasn't surprised that Michael had chosen to stay there – the U2 cachet would have definitely appealed. She approached the front desk and braced herself for a hassle – staff in posh hotels were notorious about preventing uninvited guests dropping in on their patrons.

'I'm here to see Michael LaMotta,' she said firmly.

The clerk smiled pleasantly. 'You must be Mrs LaMotta. Welcome.'

'Uh – yeah – I'm – close enough.' *What, they have a picture of me in the guestbook?*

'Please go right on up to the penthouse suite; the lift is directly behind you. Enjoy your stay.'

Max had always wanted to see the inside of that suite.

There were two doors at either end of a short hallway, one of which opened as soon as Max exited the elevator. Saying nothing, she passed Michael in the doorway and headed straight for the balcony – while also noticing that the place was stuffed to the rafters with flowers.

She stood, even though at that height the breeze blowing down the Liffey was more of a gale-force wind. 'You're pretty sure of yourself,' she said, when she felt him standing behind her.

'Not really.' He wrapped his arms around her, and she let herself lean into him. 'Not very sure of you, either, but I thought I'd chance my arm.'

Max laughed. 'You are something else. "Chance my arm." Did you buy a book, or what?'

Mike rubbed his cheek against her hair. 'Just talking to people. Talking to everybody but the person I came here to talk to.'

Max turned in his arms and slowly ran her hands up his chest to cradle his face. 'I'm not feeling very talkative at the moment.'

When they kissed, it was a heady sensation of reunion and homecoming mixed with newness, with unfamiliarity, a jittery sense of déjà vu. The force of the wind had nothing on the force of emotion that swept through Max as she crushed her mouth to her husband's, ran her fingers through his hair, tugged to pull him closer, as she let him lift her off her feet and sweep her back into the room, as his hands cradled her and stroked her and carried her to the bedroom.

He stopped, dragging a deep breath into his lungs. 'Too fast, Maxie, too fast, like always.'

'I want it to be like always,' she whispered, her voice already heavy with passion. 'I've missed it, like always—'

And his mouth found hers again, but it was light and slow and it teased her, teased her with connection and then disconnection, teased her with tongue and then without. His kisses strayed down over her cheek to her neck, and he bent her back in his arms as he feasted on her, pushed her up against the wall, fumbling with the buttons on her coat.

She pushed his hands away, divested herself of coat and cardigan, stepped out of her shoes, and tugged at his shirt, eschewing the buttons to pull it over his head, making him laugh.

'Stop, I got it, I got it,' he said in a low voice, fraught with ardour. 'Maxie,' he breathed, as he caressed her ear with his tongue. 'Max, I got so much to say –'

'What, you wanna take a coffee break?' Max laughed seductively as she eased down his fly and started to slide her hand inside.

'Yeah, so, okay, it'll keep,' he groaned as she touched him, held him, coaxed him.

And she gasped as he, in turn, undid the zipper on her trousers and ran his hands down her ass, cupping her as she writhed against him, as he reached around to sink his fingers into her. She cried out, and wound her arms around him as he led them both to the bed.

Naked, they touched each other, slower now, savouring the sight of one another, after all those months, remembering, re-learning. Max ran her fingers over his face as if she finally saw him, and he slid between her thighs, and they never took their eyes off each other, even as he entered her, even as she arched to meet him; they watched each other, felt each other, and while their hands brought them pleasure, while their bodies brought them ecstasy, it was their gaze, their unbroken gaze that rocked them down to their souls as they came together, as if for the first time.

'Remember that stupid fight we had, about hyphenation?' Max leaned up against the headboard as Michael went into the suite's mini-kitchen.

'We gonna have it again?' he called as he rustled around.

'No ... I don't think so. It just struck me that we should have maybe had that conversation before we got married.'

He came back with a platter of nibbles that ranged from crudités to chicken fingers – all properly hot or cold as necessary – and set it between them on the bed. 'They do a good suite in this place. So, you're saying you were getting back at me for being pissed off 'cause you wouldn't hyphenate?'

'I will say it one last time: Maxine O'Malley LaMotta.'

'It's like a poem.'

'It's like a nursery rhyme!' And they both laughed. 'Sure, it's funny now, but then – that was pretty bad, Mike.'

'I knew you wouldn't drop your name, and I didn't ask you to, but when I asked you to hyphenate ...' He scooped up some tapenade with a triangle of pita bread.

Max poked a piece of celery into the onion dip. 'I'm not reopening that discussion,' she said. 'I am merely illustrating the fact that there were one or two things we didn't lay out before we got hitched.'

'What, like, "Hey, Maxine, let's try not to have affairs?" '

'You want to talk, or not?' Max shifted herself away from him. 'Or you just want to say what you want to say, and then have me say what you want me to say?'

Michael opened his mouth, paused. Max was pretty sure she'd never seen him do that. 'You're right.' He leaned back against the headboard beside her. 'You are, you're right. Okay. What else?'

'Okay. A, I don't think the affair – and that word is wrong, because it wasn't like it went on for ever – was about you – let me finish! – and B, you had your own ideas about what marriage was supposed to be like. I know you were saying it was me that was trying to make us do things a certain way, but you were doing it, too.'

'Like how?'

'Okay, back to the hyphenation thing – you went and ordered all this stuff with our names on it, as in your name, as in Mr and Mrs LaMotta, even though I told you I was gonna keep my name!'

'The return address labels? With the little American Flag? This was the problem?'

Max took a breath, a deep breath, to let it all loose, and then stopped. Mike was positive he'd never seen her do that. 'It was like . . . it was like we disappeared. It was like, after all the hoopla and the drama, it all stopped, all the things that made us "us". Just like you said on the video. And I know I had a hand in that, I had preconceptions, I guess, about the way we were supposed to behave, like my folks, maybe, which I know is stupid, because I've never done anything their way my whole life . . .' She stopped again – *let's not go there*, she thought. 'And then you – it was like you stopped making an effort, like, "Oh, got Max, that's done." I never saw you, you were working six days a week—'

'I know.' He shifted over on to his side and reached out to touch her, let her know that he was there. 'I think . . . I think I got this idea like I had a wife and I had to make more money, or work harder – it was like my father had moved into my brain. I turned into my father. Jeez.'

They ate for a while in the quiet.

'Could we go back to A, if that's okay?' Michael propped himself up on his elbow.

Max fiddled with a cracker until it crumbled in her hand. 'It really was more about me than it was about you – or at least as much about me as it was about you. I was scared, the whole thing scared me, but I didn't have the words to say what I was afraid of, and then you were never there, and we were fighting all the time about that, so . . . I just did the one thing I knew that I could do that would stop it all. And then it hurt so much, all of it, I just wanted to finish it for good.' She picked up a slice of apple, then put it down.

'I forgive you, Max.'

'I *know*!' She picked up the slice of apple and threw it across the room. 'I know you do, and maybe I can forgive myself, but we gotta have the conversations we didn't have before, so we can be sure we're not gonna fuck this up again!'

Michael blew out a breath. 'I don't know if we can be

sure of anything, but I did throw out those goddamn labels.'

'Don't make me laugh! It's not all about laughs!' She flopped back on to the bed and pulled the sheet over her face.

Michael crawled under the covers, and the platter of food fell to the floor with a crash. Max laughed again, and he pulled her into his arms. 'We gotta have laughs, Maxie, I mean, that's "us". You want us to be "us", we gotta laugh. And we gotta, you know, discuss things with enthusiasm, like we always do, right? So what's the problem?'

'I don't know,' she whispered. She rubbed her face against his chest. 'Just hold me for a second, okay?'

'Okay.' And in their one-hundred-per-cent-Egyptian cotton cocoon, they held each other. And as they held each other, they relaxed, and as they relaxed, they remembered, remembered when this closeness was a daily thing, and Maxine's body remembered and accepted Michael's even if her mind was lagging, and her body responded, and she shifted herself to lie full on top of him, took his mouth with hers, took his body with hers, took his body into hers. They stayed under the covers, in a world of their own, their cries blending as they brought each other to climax, stayed there when, sated, they held each other as though they'd never let go.

'So?' Michael, wrapped in a complimentary robe, put down the phone after ordering room service.

'So?' Max shrugged. 'So what?'

'So, are you staying?'

'I ordered steak au poivre, you know I'm not going anywhere.'

Michael sat down in the suite's conversation pit, across

from Maxine, who was also bundled up in a robe. He said nothing.

'Stop *asking* me all the time! Talk about too fast, LaMotta – come on, we talked, we did some "not talking" in a highly satisfactory way, what do you want from me?'

He said nothing.

'Fuck it,' Max snarled, jumping up, gathering her clothes. 'Fuck you and your steak and your flowers and your jokes – what do you want me to say? Tell me what you want me to say!'

'I don't see why I gotta, how can you not know what needs to be said –'

'You are setting me up!' Max threw all her clothes in the air. 'What if I say the wrong thing? Huh?'

'There is only the right thing to say, Maxine!'

She ran around collecting her clothing again. 'You are setting me up, you are setting me up—'

'I am not.'

'Okay. Okay. Mr Statement. Mr Say-Something. You say.' She gestured with her bra. '*You* say. Go on. Go on. Not so easy, huh?' she goaded him as he sat in silence.

'I don't think I have to say anything – since I've been doing everything!' His voice rose to a shout as Maxine wended her way through the suite and slammed the door of the bathroom behind her.

He sat and waited for her to come out. 'You and the goddamn bathroom, O'Malley,' he sighed as he went to the bathroom door. Stood there. Waited.

He finally broke the silence. 'Okay, so maybe I am kinda – I can see why you think I'm setting you up. I guess. Okay, so, look, I love you, I want to stay married to you, I forgive you and I want you to forgive me – are you hearing this, O'Malley?' He banged on the door and tried the knob, which twisted in his hand.

The bathroom was empty. Another door led to another room, which led to the door that gave out on the hall.

She was gone.

34

'Right, so, where are we – oh, God, I hate the sound of my own voice.' Jax grimaced, but hit play.

After the fade-out from Angela and Ray's couch scene, the film cut right to Jax. 'Luckily, they didn't disown me. I'm Jacinta Quirke.'

She was quickly joined by Max. 'And I'm Maxine O'Malley.'

Jacinta: *Jax and Max.*

Maxine: *Max and Jax.*

Jacinta: *What are you like?*

John Paul stopped the segment. 'I would very much like to cut to that barney you two had in Max's office . . .' John Paul said.

'We don't have that.'

'We know who might . . .'

Niamh Bourke. Just the thought of the woman had Jax nervously pulling at a lock of her hair. JP lightly tugged it away from her worrying fingers, and took her mind off the whole thing by pulling her in for a kiss.

'Right, end of snog break.' Jax sat back and spun side to side in her chair. 'We have to wait on Max as regards Niamh – she's acting like she's got something up her sleeve, and I'd just as soon let her lead the way there.'

John Paul shrugged, concentrating once more on the file up on his monitor. 'Here, I took that montage you cut – very nice, by the way – and I thought this music—'

'Where are we coming from? Could you run it back?'

Jax: *We had no idea how real it was going to get.*

Jax's line cut straight to a montage of clips from all the surveillance they had taken on each other, both during the shoots and beyond: Max doing a boogie in the Quirkes' kitchen, her argument with Angela before the first shoot, the scary Gary and Mary footage when all hell broke loose, Jax's lunch with Mike –

A quick cut to Mike sitting on the couch alone. 'I still can't believe she was taping that. Jacinta, you wagon! So, I'm Michael LaMotta, I'm Maxine's husband, and nobody knew about me.'

John Paul's voice came from off-camera. 'It's true, nobody knew. I didn't know until Raymond told me, after Jacinta told him, after she took a call from you.'

Mike reacted in close-up. 'That was you! You hung up on me!'

Jax responded, off-camera. 'I didn't know it was you! I mean, you said you were you, but I didn't know about you, and I was so shocked.'

Cut to Max, watching this from a different location, in video assist. 'Everybody went nuts over this.'

Cut to Jacinta, in a medium shot. 'You kept going on about marriage being crap, and I never knew why.'

Cut back to Max, in close-up. 'I guess I meant I was crap at marriage . . .'

'Hey.' Michael stood in the doorway. JP stopped the footage, but the last line hung in the air.

Neither John Paul nor Jax questioned Mike's ability to run tame throughout ACJ:Dublin.

'Max here?' he asked, straightening down his tie, adjusting his cufflinks and smoothing down his hair – motions usually associated with nervousness, a state that would never have seemed applicable to Michael LaMotta.

'No.' Jax looked at her watch. 'Em, well, as it's four, I expect she's not coming in. She, em, left early yesterday . . .'

'She was with me,' Mike supplied curtly. 'And then she did a runner.'

'Oh.' Jax looked down at her shot list, and JP rolled the mouse around.

'So, how's this going? It's going good?'

'Em, uh huh.' *Oh, please, don't ask to see it*, prayed Jax.

'Let's see.' Mike moved across to loom over them at the console, and John Paul sent the cursor back to the beginning and hit play.

Where was Max? Jax flicked her ballpoint pen open and closed, open and closed, until John Paul took it from her. *What happened yesterday? I can't believe Michael is standing here, watching this, it must be awful for him –*

'It's good. Nice job. It's fun, it asks some good questions, I don't know about the answers, I don't know how they're shaping up, if I like their conclusion . . .' he trailed off and fiddled with his cufflinks again. 'So we were gonna do this Niamh Bourke thing. I don't think we can do this without Max.'

'Do you know what she had planned?' Jax asked.

'She told me all about some blackmail Niamh was doing, a couple injunctions she's got against her, we were gonna hit her with it,' Mike replied.

'We do need to see what she's got, see if we can use it –' JP began.

The door opened. It wasn't Max.

'Niamh,' Jax squeaked, too taken aback to shut down the computer programme.

'Well.' She took a deep breath, about to launch into the latest round of doom and gloom, when she saw Michael.

Her breath caught in her throat, and what little colour she had in her face faded completely away.

Michael rose to standing, and in so doing, made an intimidating enough picture to cause Niamh to clutch the door jamb for support.

'Niamh Bourke,' he said, his voice plummeting to new levels.

'M-M-M-Mr Corcoran? Sir!' she gasped, and Jax blinked, and JP twitched.

'I've been looking all over for you,' Mike replied smoothly, and gestured towards the door. 'Your office, please.'

He gently shut the door behind him.

The camera that JP and Max had rigged during Niamh's absence was tucked up on the top of a bookcase, with a wide-angle lens that took in much of the room. Niamh fluttered in, and was babbling to herself in an excited, incoherent whisper.

'Wh-what can I do for you, Mr Corcoran?' Niamh perched on the front of her desk, first on her left hip, then on her right, in a bid, it appeared, to present a seductive and casual picture.

'I think you know why I'm here, Ms Bourke.' Their view of Michael wasn't as comprehensive as was the one of Niamh, but it wasn't necessary to see his full expression to get the impact of his quietly menacing presence.

'Oh, well, would it be that injunction you're after taking out on me?' Niamh attempted an airy and confident tone; it may have sounded so in her head, but in reality it was quite shrill. 'The gardai were surely mistaken – it wouldn't be the first time, sure it wouldn't – and if I had been seen, em, several evenings in succession in the – in the vicinity of your, em, family home, it was, in fact for purely – for purely – I was only looking out for you! *I* knew what your wife was up to, I knew that she was betraying her vows, coming and going at all hours, all the while you were working your fingers to the bone to make this agency what it is today!'

She waved a hand in front of her face. 'Oh, it's very close in here, very close, I never leave the windows open, who knows who might be lurking in the side drive, trying to get at the secrets I keep safe, the secrets that you and Mr Adams and Mr Jameson count on me to secure –' And she peeled off her pallid rose cardigan.

Michael sat and said nothing.

'I'm keeping everything safe for you, Mr Corcoran,' she breathed in a way one would imagine she considered sensuous, but in her raspy, unpractised tones, the effect was distinctly repulsive, as were the accompanying gyrations.

She slung one leg sideways on to the desk.

'I could show you so many things, Mr Corcoran,' she gasped, throwing her head back. 'Oh, so many things.' She levelled a sloe-eyed glance at Michael who continued to watch her impassively.

She swung her leg back down and levered herself forward as if to present him with her cleavage, which was not only completely covered up but was also non-existent. 'I will, I'll show you all the things I've collected for you –

you'll see how loyal I am, how faithful, how constant, Mr Corcoran, nothing is more important to me than my devotion to – to your – company.'

Niamh revealed her hidden safe, fiddled expertly with the combination, and held out a thick file and even thicker book to 'Mr Corcoran', presenting these objects to him with a wild look in her eye.

'I think you'll find these documents to be extremely interesting, sir,' she said, gesturing for him to take them, and releasing an orgasmic gasp when he did so. 'She deserved an entire dossier all on her own.'

'She?' asked Michael, giving a cursory look through the logbook.

'Maxine O'Malley. Maxine O'Malley LaMotta.' She sneered triumphantly when Mike looked up at her sharply. 'Oh, yes, married she is, married to some poor, abandoned soul – although if her behaviour is any indication, I can't imagine that he himself is a fine, upstanding citizen – yes, it's desperate, isn't it?' Niamh asked, misinterpreting Michael's thunderous glare. 'People like them, their very corruption and dishonesty interfering in the lives of good, hard-working folk like you – and – and myself –'

Michael threw aside the documents where they fluttered to the floor in an avalanche. His tossed the book over his shoulder, where it heavily slammed against the door. He rose and smoothed down his tie, and Niamh wet her lips and leaned back against the front of her desk once more.

'Niamh Bourke,' he growled, 'you have been with this company for nine years, before which you had been at Adams Touhy and MacDonnell, during which time you blackmailed Mr Adams and in turn covered up his, shall we say, weakness for photographs of young men in various states of undress—'

'Disgusting,' Niamh shuddered, 'and downloaded on company time—'

'In turn, when you discovered the news of the pending merger of Adams with Corcoran and Jameson, you dug up further information about Mr Adams through channels which one cannot even imagine you navigating—'

'Oh, Mr Corcoran, I am terribly resourceful.' Niamh fiddled open the top buttons of her blouse.

Michael took a step forward, and loomed over Niamh, edging her back against the desk. 'You have accumulated damaging evidence against nearly everyone you've worked with, in an unrelenting campaign to further yourself at everyone else's expense.'

'Yes, yes,' she crooned as he leaned further over her, and she heaved herself on to the desk, her eyes heavy-lidded with anticipation.

'You have ruined reputations, careers, and lives,' he continued, and Niamh fell back on the top of her desk, pushing aside papers, her keyboard, her mouse, letting everything fall dramatically to the floor.

'You are meddlesome—'

'Oh, yes,' and she ran her own hands up and down her body.

'You are interfering—'

'Yes, yes!' And she ripped open her blouse.

'And you are fired.'

'Yes! Yes! Wha'?' And she lay there, and looked up at him in horror.

Michael got down in her face. 'What you didn't know is this: Maxine O'Malley and Jacinta Quirke are very, very important to me. By illegally surveilling them during company time, you have not only broken countless laws, but meddled with something far beyond your scope. You are finished, Niamh Bourke, and I suggest you ring your lawyers.'

Rising, he smoothed down his tie again, and left.

'She should have copped on there, that he wasn't Irish. "Lawyers".' JP shook his head as he and Jax reviewed the footage at her place.

'We don't know that Corcoran's Irish – I've certainly never met him.'

Jax's front door popped open, and in bounced Max. 'Hey, hey! How we doing?'

'Grand,' Jax said. 'Just looking at the Niamh footage.'

'Niamh footage? Excellent.'

'Didn't Michael tell you?' Jax frowned.

'Haven't seen him,' Max replied, trying for an offhand air, and failing badly.

'He said you two had, em, been together . . . the other day.'

Max shrugged. 'Yeah, whatever – so, roll it! We've only got six days to go!'

Jax looked at JP, who succeeded in producing a look of LaMotta-like inscrutability, and she scrolled back to the beginning and hit play.

Max applauded at the end of the clip. 'Oh, man, that rocked! She totally fell for it! We'll have to give her a hand when she starts packing up her boxes! Wasn't he amazing! He can be so scary, when he gets that impenetrable look; you just start babbling and saying whatever just to get him to react, oh yeah, it's pretty terrifying—'

And Max burst into tears.

John Paul jumped up and then sat back down, and jumped up again as Jax led Maxine to the sofa. He made for the front door, then the kitchen door, then sat back down again.

'Do you want to talk?' Jax asked, patting Max on the back. 'JP, there are tissues in the loo.'

And he was down the hall like a shot.

'He's a dote, Jax, he really is, and I'm so happy for you.' And, stunningly, unexpectedly, Max bawled like a baby.

'Oh, janey,' JP said, his voice breaking with panic, and he thrust a handful of tissues at Max.

'They're only tears, for pity's sake, sit down over there, or go cut some footage.' Jax tempered her brusqueness with a smile, and John Paul went back to the computer.

'I don't know what to do, Jax,' Max whispered when she'd calmed down. 'I knew what to do, all the time, until now. And then here he is, making all these grand gestures, chasing me to Ireland, firing that evil cow, and I know what he wants but I'm – what if he only thinks it's what he wants and then he . . .' She sat up and took a deep breath. 'I'm afraid he'll wake up one day and go, "what the fuck", and that would be way worse than it is now –'

Jax's front door flew open again. 'I don't know, lads, I looked at this, and to me, this does not look like pizza –'

Max fought down a sob.

'Hey, hey, come on, whatsa matter, did that crazy bitch get to you? What?' Mike threw the pizzas down on Jax's coffee table and knelt down in front of Max.

'Cut it out, LaMotta, I can't – I can't—' and Maxine jumped up to avoid him.

'O'Malley, you are wrecking my head!'

'I *know* that!' she wailed.

Michael stood. 'That's actually progress.'

'I need more time. Mike, Michael, I need more time.'

There was a pause, in which JP and Jax kept their eyes respectfully lowered.

'You want it, you got it.' Mike nodded, then shook his head. 'Yeah. Okay. So. I said some stuff to you, only you weren't there to hear it 'cause you ran away again, and I don't think I'm gonna say it here, so when you're ready to say some stuff to me, then maybe I'll say that stuff back to you, right? But now – forget it.'

'Michael—'

'If you need to think about being with me, even after the way we were together, then okay. I don't get it, Maxie, but okay – except I can't be here right now if you're not gonna tell me something right now. No? Okay.'

He shut the door quietly behind him. Max moved towards the door, laid her hand on the knob, twisted it – and stopped. 'I do, I need more time.' She turned to her friends. 'Let's get to work. I gotta get my mind off this.'

'This project isn't exactly designed to help you do that,' muttered JP, but there was no way round it, the footage had to be in Jax's RTÉ schoolfriend's hands in less than six days. He went back to the computer, pulled up a chair for Max, and brought her up to speed.

35

It hardly seemed possible, but four days later, with the guts of one day to spare, they were . . . done.

Jax gestured towards the screen. 'This was the part – I like it, and it tails with you saying how you were crap at marriage – I'm not sure – but if you think – we could always—'

'Roll it, Jacinta!' Max rolled her eyes, and Jax rolled the film.

Jax grimaced in medium close-up. 'Yeah, well, I was certainly crap at being engaged!'

The scene shifted to Angela, prowling around the Quirke living room. 'My *God*, chickens, get off the pity pot! I remember saying the very same thing to Maxine over lunch—'

Cut to a medium shot of Angela. 'I did tell you, pet, we had a little lunch, Maxine and I?'

Jax's voice comes from off-camera. 'No . . .'

The action cut to a close-up of Angela. 'At that lunch, darling, I said to Maxine, marriage is a *contract*, it is love and fidelity, of course it is, but it is also a contract, a *cut-and-dried* agreement by both parties. And that, my dears, is where you both fell down. You didn't get the balance between the *romance* and the—'

Cut to an extreme close-up of Angela: *The business of it all*.

The scene changed to an exterior, of Raymond working in the garden. 'And I remember, Jacinta, talking to you about the very sacred nature of the privacy of a marriage. Which in our case was compromised somewhat.'

Cut to Jax, wincing.

And back to Raymond. 'Albeit, em, interestingly. The sacredness is in the secretness of it, really, and perhaps Maxine had a right to her secret.'

'Yeah, okay, keep it in.' Max frowned at the screen. 'No, it's good, it'll play well with the lunch stuff you got with Mike.'

'Okay, then.' Jax looked at Max. 'Will we watch the whole thing through, again, just in case?'

Max shook her head. 'Burn it, baby. We're just about going to make it.'

'My RTÉ friend said we could put it directly into her hands, so we will make it.' Jax clicked *burn*. They watched the little watch tick.

'Should we have made only a trailer, instead of finishing the whole thing?' Jax wondered.

'Nah, we had it, why give them an inch? I'm sure we'll get all kinds of notes once they take it up, why give them any more leeway to mess with it?' Max blew on the edge of a piece of paper that she had between her thumbs and produced a shrill whistle.

'Fuck's sake, Max!' Jax scolded.

'Hey, did you see this? It's another memo.'

Jacinta blanched. 'This is it, isn't it, it's all over, we're out of business – Oh, my God, all that money, I spent all that money, that I don't have, on slap and clobber and—'

'Just read it.' Max tipped back in her chair and regarded the ceiling.

'Dear Team Players – God, not again – blah, blah, in light of recent – blah, happy to announce – what?' Jax looked up at Max in astonishment. 'We are happy to announce consolidation with – oh – MDMGB.' She sighed. 'Blah.'

'Hello, alphabet soup,' Max joked. 'Goodbye, Night Flight Productions.'

Jacinta stared down at the paper. 'I can't believe—'

'I know!' Max laughed bitterly. 'Talk about a reprieve! So you won't have to stick your neck out, worry about your mortgage, you and JP can snuggle up at the new place, which, it has to be said, is miles better than this old Restoration pile—'

'Georgian!' Jacinta snapped. 'So, you've got it all figured out, have you?'

'You've only been giving out yards about being unemployed since this whole deal went down,' Max insisted.

'Bollocks, Maxine O'Malley! You're the one who wants out! You're the one who wants to leave this thing half done, who always leaves things half—'

'Don't say it – don't say it!' Max cried, appalled at herself, 'Sorry, I – I'm sorry – for everything.'

Jax removed the DVD from the tray and inserted it into the case that bore their production company name, put the whole works with the covering letter into a padded envelope, and closed it up.

'Let's go,' she said, handing Maxine her coat. 'Now.'

'Jax—'

'Now.'

*

They jumped into a taxi and headed for the television station. Jax looked out the window of the car. 'I will apologise for what I had started to say, it was out of order.'

'It wasn't untrue,' Max grumbled. 'Which sucks.'

'I won't allow this moment to be ruined because you're jittery.' Jax clutched the envelope, her heart beating a mile a minute. 'This is too exciting, we've worked too hard, and the programme is just too bloody good to spoil it all.'

'Sorry.'

Jacinta turned to her. 'Do you think that everyone's going to leave you, Max?'

'Nobody leaves me,' Max scoffed.

'Because you leave first,' Jax replied, a statement greeted with a kick on the back of the seat. The taximan jolted.

'Sorry.' Max sank down and stared out the window. 'Maybe. Okay. So what if I do? Then I don't have to deal with it, it's just . . . over, and nobody's feelings get hurt.'

Least of all yours, thought Jax, but she held her peace.

Silence reigned as they sped down the N11 towards RTÉ. Jax fought the urge to chew on her manicure, which was more trouble than it was worth, to be honest, but then again, it was nice having nice hands, and even nicer to have a lovely, lovely fellow over which to trail said hands and perfect nails –

'So? No comment?' Max broke the silence as the taxi pulled into the station's complex. Jax paid the fare, made a dignified exit out of the cab, and then ruined the effect by dancing around on the pavement.

'We did it!' Jax whooped with joy, and hugged Max. 'We bloody well did it, and it's good, and we're seconds away from handing it in, putting ourselves on the top of the pile, thanks to me! We're going to be famous and make piles of money and we won't ever have to sit in somebody else's stupid office ever again! We'll have our own stupid office! Woo hooo!!!'

'Where's JP?'

Jax didn't seem to want to give much attention to Max's funk. 'Oh, he said it was our moment.' Jax shook back her hair – gorgeous hair that she could actually manage – and removed her wildly expensive Chanel sunglasses from her darling little clutch bag. 'He said we deserved to do it ourselves.'

'Isn't he just a paragon of modern maleness,' Max grumbled, as she followed Jax up the steps to the main building.

'He is, and as you said yourself the other day, he is a dote, and he is a massive ride, all in one,' sighed Jax smugly, and she paused at the glass doors.

'I suppose you're both "exclusive".' Max was very keen on dumping her foul mood somewhere.

'Let's not go there again, will we? I think we've worked that theme for about all it's worth. I was thinking, maybe next we need to do a whole show on friendship, especially between women, it's so interesting, and in view of the fact of what happened between us—'

'You don't want to stay? At ACJMDMGBLMNOP, or whatever the hell they're going to call it?' Max had tried for breezy and was appalled at the shakiness of her voice.

'I have an excellent feeling about this,' Jax murmured. 'We need to cut together a reel, put ourselves forward for agency work, charge them the earth, and get going on the next project, write up a few proposals.' She frowned as she stared at Max's conflicted face. 'I'm assuming that *you* aren't going to stay on there . . . are you?'

'I don't know – I can't think – all these life-changing

decisions, it's like I'm frozen, I can't figure out what to do – about this, about Mike, about anything.'

A message alert on her mobile beeped. 'I hate that!' Max rang her voicemail. 'I hate it when people go straight to your mailbox without ringing.'

Jax watched her face slide from annoyance to emptiness to devastation as Max listened to her message.

'He's going,' Max said as she shoved her mobile back into her pocket. 'He's leaving. Today. That's it. It's over.' Jax reached out, but Max was already turning, moving, running from the building, and away.

Epilogue

The speed with which RTÉ picked up their piece and scheduled it for broadcast made even Max's New-York-minute head spin. In less than two months, the crew gathered together for the premiere, and the atmosphere was one of stretches of intense focus during the run of the show, followed by explosive moments of commentary and self-congratulation during the ad breaks.

Max couldn't keep her seat, and paced around behind the couch as the next segment played, in glorious colour and sound, in the Quirke living room and all across the country.

The current scene was very near the end, and Max wondered if the network would do the right thing and cut immediately after it. Raymond and Angela had just related their (disparate) memories of Raymond's proposal and were about to get into what had become Max's favourite part of the show –

The couple were framed in a wide shot, on the signature sofa. Max's voice came from off-camera. 'I think, at this stage, our viewers are going to be gasping for your secret – the secret to the long life of your marriage –'

Angela: *'The secret is, we have no secrets.'*

Raymond: *'No, that is not precisely true, darling; we have secrets from one another –'*

Angela: *'Well, fine, then – we have a completely congruent world-view.'*

Raymond: *'Nor is that the case, Angela.'*

Angela: *'Don't be ridiculous, Raymond.'*

Raymond: *'We certainly didn't vote the same in the last referendum.'*

Angela: *'Voting! I'm talking about* values, *I'm talking about* dreams.*'*

Raymond: *'Well, yes, that's right. We have the same . . . expectations.'*

The camera cut to a close two-shot of the couple looking at each other, in agreement.

Angela: *'Expectations! How well you put it, darling.'*

Raymond: *'I seem to remember – I said this very thing to John Paul – when we were embroiled in Maxine and Michael's private business –'*

Angela: *'Not so private, now.'*

Raymond: *'Which was their free choice, love. But I surmised that whatever happened between them, and what is likely to be the stumbling block in any relationship is the betrayal of expectations. I suppose we have aligned our expectations to such a degree, that . . . that we can be easy with one another. There's love, and respect, of course, but we have aligned our expectations.'*

Angela: *'Which leaves us all that leeway to be . . . inventive.'*

As the scene faded to black, Angela waved her little feet in the air. *'Darlings,* this is superb! Really! And I'm not saying that because of all the lovely coverage!' She stood, arms outspread, and began delivering kisses around the room. 'John Paul, may I say that you are most definitely superior to the Dreaded Fergal, and delightfully photogenic as well.'

'*Mum*.'

' "*Mum*",' Angela mimicked happily as she embraced her daughter. 'Thank you, pet,' she whispered in Jax's ear. 'Thank you so much.' And she swept around to Max before the tears could fall. 'And *you*, darling Maxine – you surely have a future as a chat-show hostess! Warm, yet incisive, vivacious yet resolute! Oh, yes indeed! And *you* –' She purred as she swung around to face Raymond. 'How very *persuasive* you are, Raymond Quirke, in your arguments . . .' And while it wouldn't be the first time that Night Flight Productions had been treated to a senior Quirke snog, they were rescued by the phone, which, during the commercials, had been ringing off the hook.

Angela pounced on it. 'Hell*looo*,' she answered nonchalantly. 'It is, of course . . . Oh, yes, how do you do . . . Oh? We are, of course, looking at it ourselves . . . hmm . . . I have been with Centrestage Artistes for the last few years . . . Not *terribly* happy, no . . . Monday? I'm afraid I've a meeting scheduled at RTÉ. Would Wednesday suit – I have a commercial on Tuesday, you see . . . Fabulous, darling, I do look forward to it. *Ciao!*' Angela cradled the handset to her breast, and sank back on to the couch. 'That was Aisling McMullen, of the agency of the same name – we are lunching on Wednesday.' She closed her eyes, the better to relive the preceding moment.

'She's the biggest agent in Ireland,' Jax whispered to her father. 'Really big; she casts all the blockbuster Hollywood pictures that come through here, and into continental Europe as well. Exclusive doesn't even begin to describe Aisling McMullen.'

'Well done, Angela,' said John Paul.

'Ssssh,' she urged, and everyone respected the gravity of the moment.

Max looked wistfully around the room, at Jax and JP, at Raymond and Angela, happy for them in their happiness, envying them, a little, their certainty, and realising how close, how close she herself had come to—

Angela sprang up. 'Darling!' she called back to the kitchen. 'You're *missing* everything! What are you doing in there?'

Michael stuck his head in the doorway. 'I am making sauce. You do not mess with sauce.' He winked at Max, and withdrew.

– how close she herself had come to losing everything.

'Look, what's the big deal? I've got my passport, I've got all this ID – this is my birth certificate, for crying out loud! I'll buy a ticket! I've got to get to that flight before it goes!'

Max swore silently and adjusted the big picture hat that had gone slightly askew during her impassioned plea. She'd never met an Irishman who'd rather stare at you coldly than engage in some conversation, and the two security guards at Dublin Airport were as mute as Newgrange.

'Max.'

'. . . And here's, well, okay, it's the divorce papers I had drawn up, but look, there's my husband's name, Michael LaMotta, so you could page him, maybe—'

'Maxie.'

'I really don't see what harm it could be, to let me go after him. I mean, seriously, I let you go through my bag, I let you look in my shoes, you can do a cavity search, only please, come on, please, it's so important that I stop that plane – not *stop* it, like try to blow it up or anything, but—'

'Maxine!'

'What!' she shouted, and spun around in her chair.

Michael stood in the doorway, flanked by two dour sentries. 'Fancy meeting you here.'

'I came to get you,' Max whispered. 'I came to tell you—' And she blanked.

'Hey, take your time. Something tells me we're not getting outta here any time soon.'

'How did you know I was here?' She stood, nervously smoothing down the enormous ankle-length bell-shaped skirt of her dress, with her white-gloved hands.

'I didn't know – I decided that I was gonna come back and, let me tell you, they don't like it when you try to get out of a terminal except on a plane.' Michael smiled slightly. 'Lads, you wanna take these offa me?'

'Oh, Jesus, Mike!' Max gasped, as the burlier of his guards removed the handcuffs.

'Brings back memories,' he quipped, and Max snorted.

'You were saying?' he prompted, when it looked as if they were embroiled in another O'Malley-style stalemate.

'I'd prefer some privacy,' Max said, looking witheringly at the guards.

Who failed to react.

'I knew that was the one,' said Mike, fingering a sleeve.

'What – oh, the dress. No, this is a fourth one,' and even Maxine O'Malley, the High Priestess of the High Street, was moved to blush. 'The other one is in storage in the Bronx. It was a twenties, Mata Hari-type thing.'

'You look – you look good.'

'You won't get around me with praise like that, LaMotta.' She twisted her gloved hands, and said what she'd come to say. 'I don't want you to go. If you want to do this thing again, try this marriage again, then, so, okay. Me too.'

'You sure?' Michael asked gruffly, not really trusting himself to speak.

'I – I guess, I'm not so great at sticking to things, but I want to stick with this, with you. I can't imagine life without you, Mike – I was living it, and not really thinking about it, and then you showed up and made me start thinking about it, so if it screws up again, it's all your fault.'

'Well, that's optimistic.' The guards continued taciturn.

'So, you said something to me, that I never heard. That time. In the Clarence.' Max bowed her head, the hat obscuring her face.

'I love you, Maxie,' he said softly, as he tipped her face up to his. 'I want to stay married to you. I forgive you and I want you to forgive me. All right?'

'Yeah. All right.' And she tilted her face up for a kiss, but stopped when she felt him tugging at the glove on her left hand. 'What—' And she felt her whole self lighten with joy.

'Pretty sure of yourself, LaMotta,' she whispered when he slipped her wedding band back on her hand.

'I like to plan ahead,' he said, and pulled her into his arms.

And the police who had swarmed into the room waited politely until they were done.

'What's wrong with ya?' Mike came out with a spoonful of the sauce.

'What?' Max tasted it and closed her eyes in ecstasy, as she came out of her reverie.

'You look bummed, what's up? Frankly, I think it's terrific, the human interest is through the roof.'

'No, I love it.' Max cuddled into his side. 'I was just thinking, it would have been so sad if we hadn't worked things out. I was watching them all sitting there, being couple-y, and I would have – it would have sucked.'

'Darlings, sit, *sit*!' Angela turned to look at them, and beamed at the sight of them. 'It's about to begin!'

'It is,' said Max, and she turned to smile up at her husband. 'It's going to begin – all over again.'

little
black
dress

brings you fantastic new books like these
every month - find out more at
www.littleblackdressbooks.com

Why not link up with other devoted Little Black
Dress fans on our Facebook group? Simply type
Little Black Dress Books into Facebook to join up.

And if you want to be the first
to hear the latest news on all things
Little Black Dress, just send the details below to
littleblackdressmarketing@headline.co.uk
and we'll sign you up to our lovely email
newsletter (and we promise that we won't share
your information with anybody else!).*

Name: ——————————————————————
Email Address: ———————————————————
Date of Birth: ————————————————————
Region/Country: ————————————————————
What's your favourite Little Black Dress book?
————————————————————————————
How many Little Black Dress books have you read?————

*You can be removed from the mailing list at any time

Pick up a *little black dress* – it's a girl thing.

IT MUST BE LOVE
Rachel Gibson
PB £4.99

Gabrielle Breedlove is the sexiest suspect that undercover cop Joe Shanahan has ever had the pleasure of tailing. But when he's assigned to pose as her boyfriend things start to get complicated.

She thinks he's stalking her. He thinks she's a crook. Surely, it must be love?

978 0 7553 3746 0

ONE NIGHT STAND
Julie Cohen
PB £4.99

When popular novelist Estelle Connor finds herself pregnant after an uncharacteristic one-night stand, she enlists the help of sexy neighbour Hugh to help look for the father. But will she find what she really needs?

One of the freshest and funniest voices in romantic fiction

978 0 7553 3483 4

You can buy any of these other
Little Black Dress titles from your
bookshop or *direct from the publisher*.

FREE P&P AND UK DELIVERY
(Overseas and Ireland £3.50 per book)

Leopard Rock	Tarras Wilding	£5.99
Smart Casual	Niamh Shaw	£5.99
See Jane Score	Rachel Gibson	£5.99
Animal Instincts	Nell Dixon	£5.99
It Should Have Been Me	Phillipa Ashley	£5.99
Dogs and Goddesses	Jennifer Crusie, Anne Stuart, Lani Diane Rich	£5.99
Sugar and Spice	Jules Stanbridge	£5.99
Italian for Beginners	Kristin Harmel	£5.99
The Girl Most Likely To . . .	Susan Donovan	£5.99
The Farmer Needs a Wife	Janet Gover	£5.99
Hide Your Eyes	Alison Gaylin	£5.99
Living Next Door to Alice	Marisa Mackle	£4.99
Today's Special	A.M. Goldsher	£4.99
Risky Business	Suzanne Macpherson	£4.99
Truly Madly Yours	Rachel Gibson	£4.99
Right Before Your Eyes	Ellen Shanman	£4.99
The Trophy Girl	Kate Lace	£4.99
Handbags and Homicide	Dorothy Howell	£4.99
The Rules of Gentility	Janet Mullany	£4.99
The Girlfriend Curse	Valerie Frankel	£4.99

TO ORDER SIMPLY CALL THIS NUMBER

01235 400 414

or visit our website: www.headline.co.uk

Prices and availability subject to change without notice.